The Grilling Season

*Also by Diane Mott Davidson
in Large Print:*

Killer Pancake

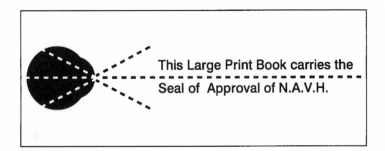

This Large Print Book carries the
Seal of Approval of N.A.V.H.

The Grilling Season

Diane Mott Davidson

Thorndike Press • Thorndike, Maine

Published in 1998 by arrangement with Bantam Books, a division of Bantam Doubleday Dell Publishing Group, Inc.

Thorndike Large Print ® Americana Series.

The tree indicium is a trademark of Thorndike Press.

The text of this Large Print edition is unabridged.
Other aspects of the book may vary from the original edition.

Set in 16 pt. Plantin.

Printed in the United States on permanent paper.

Library of Congress Cataloging in Publication Data

Davidson, Diane Mott.
    The grilling season / Diane Mott Davidson.
    p.   cm.
    Includes index.
    ISBN 0-7862-1315-9 (lg. print : hc : alk. paper)
    1. Bear, Goldy (Fictitious character) — Fiction.
2. Caterers and catering — Colorado — Fiction.
3. Colorado — Fiction. 4. Large type books. I. Title.
[PS3554.A925G7   1998]
    813′.54—dc21
                                           97-39288

To Sergeant Richard Millsapps
Investigator, teacher, friend

The author wishes to acknowledge the assistance of the following people: Jim, Jeff, J.Z., and Joe Davidson; Kate Burke Miciak, a superb, brilliant editor; Sandra Dijkstra, a wonderfully encouraging agent; Susan Corcoran, an unflagging publicist; Lee Karr and the group that assembles at her home; Connie Leonard, an extraordinary pastry chef, and John William Schenk, an inspired and inspiring chef and caterer; J. William's Café, Bergen Park, Colorado; Katherine Goodwin Saideman, for multiple careful readings of the manuscript; Mark D. Wittry, M.D., Assistant Professor of Internal Medicine, St. Louis University Health Sciences Center; Richard L. Staller, D.O., Elk Ridge Family Physicians; Meg Kendal and Alan Rapaport, M.D., Denver-Evergreen Ob-Gyn; Dana Held, Cigna Healthcare of Colorado; Mary Frazee, an unparalleled herbalist of Health-Wealth, Pine, Colorado; the Reverend Constance Delzell; Julie Wallin Kaewert; Dorsey Moore; Carol Devine Rusley; Triena Harper, assistant deputy coroner, Jefferson County; Thorenia West; Sergeant Jerry Warren, and as ever, for patience and insights, Sergeant Richard Millsapps of the Jefferson County Sheriff's Department, Golden, Colorado.

Revenge is a dish best eaten cold.

— PROVERB

STANLEY CUP
VICTORY CELEBRATION
Saturday, August 2
Featuring

SOUTH OF THE BORDER
APPETIZERS

*Layered Dip of guacamole, refried bean purée,
sour cream, cubed fresh tomatoes,
and Cheddar cheese
Tortilla Chips
Crudités: cauliflower, carrot, celery,
cucumber, cherry tomatoes
Mexican Eggrolls*

ENTRÉE
*Goalies' Grilled Tuna
Grilled Slapshot Salad
Mediterranean Orzo Salad
Vietnamese Slaw
Hockey Puck Biscuits, Potato Rolls*

DESSERT
*Stanley Cupcakes surrounding Rink Cake
Mexican Beers, Chablis, Coffee*

Chapter 1

Getting revenge can kill you. If you want real revenge, you have to be willing to pay. Life is not like the movies.

Unfortunately.

With these happy thoughts, I measured out fudge cake batter into cupcake liners and slid the pan into the oven. I set the timer and reminded myself for the thousandth time that I'd let go of the need for revenge. I wasn't a hot-blooded teenager. I was a thirty-three-year-old caterer with a business to run and work to do. Half-past six on a cool August morning? What *I* needed was *coffee.*

You never let go of the thirst for revenge.

Yeah, well. Maybe hearing other people's sad stories sparked thoughts of my own. Or in this case I'd heard one unhappy story, one story needing justice. But what could I do for a client in emotional pain? I'd agreed to cater her hockey party. A nurse had told my client Patricia McCracken that hosting this sports celebration would distract her from her problems. But whenever we discussed the menu, Patricia didn't want to talk about *vittles;* she wanted to talk about *vindication.* And I was as unenthusiastic about jumping into her revenge fantasy as I was about washing dishes after a banquet.

For five years, I'd run the only food-service business in the small mountain town of Aspen Meadow, Colorado. My son, Arch, was fourteen years old. Just over a year ago, I'd married for the second time. Add to this the fact that I'd already sought punishment for the scoundrel who'd recently wronged Patricia McCracken. I'd barely escaped with my life.

I retrieved unsalted butter and extrathick whipping cream from my walk-in refrigerator, then reached up to my cabinet shelves for aromatic Mexican vanilla and confectioner's sugar. *Stay busy,* I had advised Patricia. *It'll help. Make your guest list. Plan your decorations.* Some people despise slates of tasks and errands. But I revel in work. Work keeps my mind off weighty matters. Usually.

Take this morning, for example. After finishing the cupcakes I needed to check my other bookings, make sure our sick boarder was sleeping peacefully, then rush to pick up Arch from an overnight party. Before zipping back to my commercial-size kitchen in our small home, I was going to deliver Arch to the country-club residence of his can't-be-

12

bothered father. My ex-husband, ob-gyn Dr. John Richard Korman, was the father — and scoundrel — in question. He was the man my client Patricia McCracken obsessively hated; he was the man I had escaped from. He was known to his other ex-wife and me as the Jerk. Small example of Jerk behavior: Dr. John Richard Korman would no more pick up his son from an overnight than he would beat some eggs for breakfast. And careful of that word *beat.*

I stared at the menu on my computer screen and struggled to refocus on the task at hand. After much hesitation, Patricia had finally decided that her party would be a two-month-late celebration of the Colorado Avalanche winning the Stanley Cup. But making the plans with her hadn't been easy. One week she didn't care about the menu; the next she obsessed about details, such as how long to grill fish. After many discussions, Patricia had finally ordered Mexican appetizers, grilled fish from Florida (the Avs had beaten the Florida Panthers in the Cup finals and I'd dubbed the entrée Goalies' Grilled Tuna), three kinds of salads, puck-shaped biscuits, and homemade potato rolls. Plus a dessert Patricia's husband had christened Stanley Cupcakes. I sighed. After dropping off Arch this morning, I still faced a truckload of food prep. Not only that, but this evening's event promised to be raucous, perhaps even dangerous. I mean, hockey fans? Now *there* are folks who take revenge *seriously*.

I turned away from the computer. Our security system was off, so I opened the kitchen window and took a deep breath of summery mountain air. The postdawn Colorado sky glowed as it lightened from indigo to periwinkle. From the back of my brain came the echo of Patricia's furious voice.

"I'm telling you, Goldy. I need to see someone *punished*."

I slapped open the other window and tried to block out the memory of her anger by inhaling more crisp air skimming down from the snow-dusted mountains. August in the high country brings warm, breezy days and nights cool enough for a log fire. Heaven.

Unless you have to deal with John Richard Korman, my own inner voice reminded me. *Then it can be hell.*

Perhaps I should have told Patricia, an old friend who until now had loved cooking, to prepare herself for a descent into the underworld. I took a bag of coffee beans from the freezer, then sliced a thick piece of homemade oatmeal bread and dropped it into the toaster. The interior wires glowed red; the delicious scent of hot toast filled the kitchen.

Poor Patricia. After years of infertility and after adopting a son just before her first marriage had gone sour, she had remarried, endured a year of fertility drugs, and become pregnant. But she lost the baby. Unexpectedly, horribly, and *avoidably,* according to her. John Richard was her obstetrician. And she blamed him for the baby's death.

Now she wanted my help. I had been married to Dr. John Richard Korman, she reminded me; I'd suffered through an acrimonious divorce. How could she deal with her rage against him? she wanted to know. How could she get through this?

I'd told her I'd cooked with much imagination when I was furious with the Jerk. But no matter what I'd said two weeks ago while booking the event, it hadn't been enough. Patricia, short and pear-shaped, with bitten-down nails and eyeliner applied with a shaky hand, had fumed like a pressure cooker. She'd shaken her mahogany-with-platinum hair and complained that I wasn't helping. She wanted revenge on the Jerk, and she wanted it *now.*

I took a bite of the crunchy toast and looked out my window at a dozen elk plod-

15

ding through our neighbors' property. We live just off Main Street in Aspen Meadow, but the elk pay no attention to houses, fences, or any other sort of human presence, as long as the humans don't carry guns. In July and August the herds move down from the highest elevations in anticipation of hunting season, when hunters march into the hills in search of the huge dusty-brown creatures. When darkness engulfs the mountains, the elk's bugling, along with their hooves cracking through underbrush, are the only heralds of their arrival. Other times, you don't know the elk have been through until every last one of the leaves on your Montmorency cherry trees has been stripped. Deep, telltale hoof-prints in nearby mud usually betray the culprits.

A dog barked at the elk and the herd trundled off, leaping over a three-foot-high fence as if it were nothing. I glanced back at my computer screen, but again couldn't rid myself of the image of Patricia McCracken tapping the fleshy nub of her index finger on her bone-white Corian counter.

"Everyone hates him, Goldy," she'd declared. "John Richard Korman *and* that damn HMO that you have to belong to if you want him for your doctor. I can't believe we signed up. I can't believe I ever wanted

John Richard as my doctor. But I'm telling you. He's going down."

And so then I'd heard the whole story. Patricia had been diagnosed with placenta previa, a precarious condition that jeopardizes the stability of the unborn child. Total bed rest is usually recommended; Patricia had begged John Richard to prescribe a hospital stay. She'd been denied it.

Seven months into the pregnancy, Patricia had hemorrhaged and the baby was asphyxiated. Devastated, she'd sued John Richard for malpractice and AstuteCare, her HMO — otherwise known as ACHMO — for negligence. She said her lawyers were certain she would win. But Patricia, understandably, was depressed. She wanted more, and she didn't like the idea of waiting for vindication. She wanted . . . Well, what? Money? To drive John Richard out of his practice? To force him into a public confession?

"Will he admit he made a mistake?" she'd demanded of me two weeks ago. "Will he apologize? Will he confess he ruined my life?"

Next question. Naturally, I'd felt too sick to tell her the truth.

I spread a thick layer of tart chokecherry jelly on what remained of the toast. As the menu was set, the contract signed, and the first installment check written, I'd tried to warn Patricia gently. John Richard Korman was the most powerful, best-known ob-gyn doctor in town. The Jerk would not go down lightly. He *never* acknowledged making a mistake. And he'd certainly die before doing so publicly. But Patricia, whose fine-boned facial features and small, quivering nose above her plump body always put me in mind of a rabbit, had stiffened. She was having none of it. She had filed her suits. And she was out for blood.

I brushed crumbs off my hands. I hadn't wanted to argue with her. I'd told her to sue away, we needed to talk about setting up her party. Sheesh. A headache loomed. I really needed coffee.

I greedily inhaled the luscious scent of Italian-roast beans as they spilled between my fingers into the grinder. Tap water gushed into the well of my espresso machine. I had thought I wouldn't talk to Patricia again until tonight, but she had called yesterday. The woman was so obsessed that she'd been frantic to share news. She'd informed me that John Richard wouldn't be engaging in a prolonged legal battle with her. It seemed the Jerk was having severe financial problems.

18

Now I must confess, *that* news made my ears perk up. Being desperate for justice is a psychologically dangerous place to be. You hope that some lie, some transgression, some publicly witnessed crime will trip up your personal enemy. Nothing happens. Meanwhile, the desire for revenge can eat you up, give you insomnia, and — horrors — take away your appetite. You have to let go or die. So you need at least to *say* you're starting over and getting on with your life. All of this I had done. But now: Was this really happening? Could I watch the sun rise, sip some espresso, and rejoice in my ex-husband finally facing the music?

The coffee grinder pulverized the beans with a satisfying growl. I didn't want to be premature. I couldn't imagine that there would finally be punishment for the man who had broken my left thumb in three places with a hammer. I reached for the coffee doser and touched my hand. The thumb still wouldn't bend properly even now, seven years after the orthopedic surgeon who'd set it insisted I'd be throwing pizza dough in no time.

"He's got to pay," Patricia had insisted shrilly when she'd called yesterday. "I don't understand why you could never get him to pay, Goldy."

It hadn't worked like that. I tamped the grounds into the doser and remembered how stupefied I'd been when John Richard had gone unscathed. This in spite of the fact that he'd repeatedly beaten me. Time after time I'd had to escape from the house clutching Arch tightly, trying to get to a safe house. But after he'd smashed up my body and our marriage, John Richard had gone on with his life, his practice, his girlfriends, and his lifestyle. He'd remarried, divorced again, and taken up right where he'd left off. Until now, it seemed as if the man had been able to get away with anything. The odds looked good that he'd survive Patricia's legal threats, too.

I ran scalding water into a Limoges demitasse to heat it, then fitted the doser into place. I dumped the water out of the warmed cup, delicately placed it under the doser, and pressed the button. In the face of unrelenting curiosity from the town about the progress of her lawsuits, Patricia had spent most of the last two months at her condo in Keystone, a ski resort just over an hour away from Aspen Meadow. After booking the hockey party, she'd gone back to Keystone for two final weeks of peace, punctuated only by calls to me about her party. She'd discovered what I knew well: that it was nearly

20

impossible to avoid the nosiness and gossip of Aspen Meadow.

Steaming twin strands of espresso spurted into my cup and I frowned. When John Richard and I were married and stories had come to *me*, of his flings with patients, nurses, and anyone else who fell under his gorgeous-guy spell, I'd confronted him, cried, yelled, threatened. And I'd paid for my protests with the usual pattern of black-and-blue marks: bruises on my upper arms from being grabbed and shaken, a black right eye. Sometimes worse.

"You must have tried to do something," Patricia had protested. "Why couldn't you do anything?"

I pushed the doser to stop the flow of coffee. Excuse me, Patricia, but I *had* done something. I'd stopped listening to the gossip. I'd planned a divorce as I taught myself to make golden-brown loaves of brioche, delicate poached Dover sole, creamy dark chocolate truffles. I'd fantasized about opening a restaurant or becoming a caterer. I'd dutifully kept close to a hundred of my newly developed recipes on our family computer. In one of the Jerk's last acts before I kicked him out, he'd reformatted the computer's hard drive. I'd lost every recipe.

I sipped the rich, dark espresso, blinked

with caffeine-induced delight, and scowled at the next cupcake pan. Maybe Patricia couldn't understand why I hadn't done *more*. Let's see: I'd sought help from the church. Our priest hadn't wanted to hear about John Richard beating me up. Donations from the rich doctor might fall off. And then I'd tried to file criminal charges. But when divorce proceedings began, John Richard's high-powered lawyer had assured me that pressing criminal charges against his client would threaten his ability to pay child support. Worse — it might even bring on a custody battle.

Faced with such consequences and the fear of losing Arch, I'd given up seeking punishment for John Richard Korman. But the law had changed, and now a bruise-covered spouse didn't have to press charges. Back then, however, the legal system had failed me. Still, at age twenty-seven, I'd been glad enough to get out of the marriage with my life and my child.

"I can't believe you couldn't convince people how bad he was," Patricia had contended. "I mean, between you and Marla? Come on."

During the eight years of our marriage, and even in the six years since the divorce, the Jerk's behavior was unknown to many,

22

dismissed or disbelieved by others. And yes, he'd dished out disdain and disloyalty to his second ex-wife, Marla Korman, who'd since become my best friend. I grinned, thinking of good old Marla. She'd kill the Jerk if she had the chance, but she'd had a heart attack last year and was trying to be careful.

I should have told Patricia I *had* tried to have the Jerk penalized in some way, any way. But I'd been determined *not* to go crazy. Patricia, though, was on the edge. A very dangerous edge. I set down my coffee and stirred another bowl of cake batter. The scent of chocolate cake perfumed the kitchen. Her malpractice suit would put him out of business, Patricia insisted. She apologized that this could mean a loss of child support for Arch. I told her not to worry about us. I'd manage, I always had. Patricia claimed that no matter what, she was going to make John Richard pay, and she was going to bring down ACHMO at the same time. *Good for you,* I thought now, with an involuntary shiver.

I began to scoop silky dollops of cake batter into the next pan. I put down the spatula, sipped more coffee, and smiled. There was another reason why I'd given up the need for revenge. Just over a year ago, happiness had come into my life like an unexpected houseguest determined to stay. I'd married a homicide investigator who worked for the sheriff's department. Tom Schulz's bearlike, handsome presence, his kindness and intelligence, his affection for Arch and me, still felt like a miracle. I glanced up at one of his recent presents to me: a blond doll dressed the way you might imagine a Tyrolean caterer would be, with a snowy lace apron over a royal blue vest and skirt. Actually, the doll's official name was Icelandic Babsie, and Tom had bought it for me to celebrate an upcoming booking to cater a doll show. He'd told me I could sell the doll in a year and retire on the profits. In addition to his other virtues, the man has a sense of humor.

Tom was like a slice of capital-*G* Grace, a concept I sometimes discussed with my Sunday school class. Plus, being married to a cop finally made me feel safe. And through all this — divorce, building a business, raising a child, remarrying — I'd held my own. I'd kept my friendships, made new ones, even stayed the course in our local church, where we now had a new priest and I still took my turn teaching Sunday school and making muffins for the after-service coffee. Which brought us to the present moment.

Rejoicing in the suffering of others is a sin. Well, then. Call me a big-time sinner.

The timer beeped and I remembered the hockey fans. I checked the cupcakes — not quite done — reset the timer, and again studied the menu for the party. I took a deep breath and ordered myself to let go of all the negative thoughts that Patricia's vengeful tale had provoked.

"He's going to run out of money," Patricia's voice echoed.

I still did not know how, in addition to the legal mess, the Jerk had gotten himself into a deep financial pickle. I'd promised Patricia I'd listen to the details of *that* news when I catered her party.

I grimaced at the list of dishes to be prepared and tried to picture the setup at the McCrackens' Aspen Meadow Country Club home. The McCrackens were adding *playing* hockey to *celebrating* hockey. So I would start with beer and a vegetable-and-chip tray with layered Mexican dip served at the end of the driveway during the in-line skating, provide more drinks and Mexican eggrolls upstairs in the living room, do the grilling and barbecue buffet on the large deck, then finish in the living room with cupcakes and coffee. Actually,the McCrackens did not live too far from the Jerk's year-old million-dollar house. The million-dollar house he might have to sell. *Oh, too bad.*

Think about hockey, I scolded myself. Fix the frosting for the Stanley Cupcakes. I'd told Patricia the NHL wouldn't approve of her husband's name for the dessert. She'd retorted that she didn't care. I fitted the electric mixer with a flat beater and recalled how breathless Patricia had been with her news yesterday about John Richard's impending financial demise.

"We were *right there* when they auctioned off his Keystone condo," she'd squealed. "It went for sixty thousand below market. This must be the juiciest revenge you've *ever* envisioned," she'd added with glee.

Not quite. John Richard still had the Aspen Meadow house, a condo in Hawaii, white and silver Jeeps with personalized license plates — the white one said OB and the silver said GYN, just in case anyone wondered what kind of doctor he was — and a wealthy, beautiful, smart, new girlfriend whom I grudgingly admired.

The beater began its slow circuit through the pale, unsalted butter. John Richard's girlfriend, Suz Craig, was the executive vice-president of the AstuteCare Health Maintenance Organization. I didn't know if Suz's feelings for John Richard were being affected by Patricia's suit against ACHMO. I *did* know that as of four weeks ago, John Richard and Suz were nuts about each other. To celebrate going together for six whole months, he had given her a full-length mink coat, bought on sale at the beginning of the summer, Arch had informed me. Suz had even modeled the coat when I'd catered a corporate lunch at her home in July. And why shouldn't I have catered for her? Suz had unabashedly informed me that she was a great businesswoman. Well, so was I.

Suz was young, thin, blond, a whiz at her job — by her own accounting — and eager, I thought, to show me that she wasn't going to make the same relationship mistakes that I had. What that meant, I didn't know, and didn't want to ask. Suz had confided that she'd given John Richard a solid gold ID bracelet as a way of showing her six-month-old affection. I'd tried not to roll my eyes. The only stage of relationship John Richard did well was infatuation. But if John Richard and his girlfriend wanted to act like high school sweethearts, I wasn't going to stop them. His relationships never lasted very long.

No, Patricia McCracken hadn't been quite on the money when she'd said John Richard's financial crash was the juiciest revenge I'd ever envisioned. John Richard had not yet lost the malpractice suit. His girlfriend hadn't renounced him. He wasn't in jail; he hadn't even been publicly humiliated. A declaration of personal bankruptcy, which was what I was assuming was about to happen, was not the kind of revenge I'd always hoped for.

But it was close.

Chapter 2

When I opened the oven to take out the cupcakes, the scent of chocolate drenched the kitchen. I drank it in and immediately felt better. Thinking dark thoughts was unappealing; thinking dark *chocolate* thoughts was vastly better. That was the conclusion I'd come to yesterday as I whipped up a batch of fudge. Stirring the sinfully rich pot of candy, I'd decided I really *didn't* want to get a blow-by-blow description from Patricia of John Richard's condo being auctioned off, after all. Listening to sizzling gossip while grilling tuna during the party tonight could lead to frayed nerves, scorched fish, or worse.

Nor could I quite picture hearing about the woes of John Richard Korman while catering to a large group of hockey aficionados. The fans would be hollering with blood-mania at slow-motion videos of battered hockey players slamming other bruised and injured players into the glass — while I celebrated a vengeance I'd tried to put behind me years ago? Something about that didn't quite work.

29

I straightened and rotated my shoulders. My right shoulder was scarred from the time John Richard had shoved me into a dishwasher and I'd landed on a knife. I'd fallen on my left shoulder when he pushed me down the stairs in a drunken rage. Both shoulders seized up with pain from time to time. Yesterday, when I was making the fudge, the ache in my upper back had been unbearable. Of course I'd suspected it was because my body didn't want to be reminded of John Richard. *Let go of it,* I'd admonished myself. I'd called Patricia in and said I didn't want to hear any more about the Jerk.

"You don't want to hear before our hockey game about your ex-husband's ruin? Don't you want to hear what he said to my lawyer about the money the suit is costing him?" Patricia had shrieked. When I'd said no, she seemed stunned by my lack of interest. "You're crazy. This whole thing is a *huge* comedown for him." Then she said — I swear she said this — "You must be out of your pucking mind."

Maybe so. But my shoulders felt better today. I swirled thick whipping cream into a mountain of snowy confectioner's sugar for the cupcake frosting. Yes, I could wait to hear the news. *Now* I could wait, that is. Tom Schulz, even if he was my husband, had always felt that justice would eventually triumph. I guess that's why he's in the business he is.

It is going to happen, Tom had frequently assured me. *John Richard Korman will go too far, get caught, and be nailed.* In fact, I had been vaguely aware that John Richard was having financial problems. After all, I hadn't received a child support payment in three months. He was usually late, but not this late. Despite Patricia's dire news about the Keystone condo, I'd actually been hoping that John Richard could talk to me this morning about his money situation, without lawyers, without lying, and without loudness. Fat chance.

But, as they say, I was going to be in that neck of the woods, so I might as well try to chat with him. With Arch as a buffer, and before John Richard had had a drink or two, we could occasionally communicate. Besides, if I thought we could get something settled, it would make the chauffeuring job this morning less irksome. The house where Arch was staying was only two miles from John Richard's neo-Tudor monstrosity, while it was close to ten miles from our place.

I was doing the pickup because Arch had been desperate to attend the party. The poor kid had not made many friends at the private school he'd started attending two years ago. Now that he was going into ninth grade, he relished the idea of someone inviting him over, even if it was because he was one of the few kids not currently away on an exotic summer vacation. *An invite is an invite,* Arch had reminded me seriously as he nudged his tortoiseshell glasses up his nose and donned a too-large pair of denim shorts to go with a raggedy nut-brown shirt that matched his hair. *And I'm going.*

I slid the bowl of frosting into the walk-in, set the cupcakes on racks to cool, and scribbled a note to Tom to have one for breakfast if he craved an early-morning chocolate fix. I would be back soon, I wrote. Tom had been out past midnight working on a case. In the hours before dawn he had crept in and tried not to wake me. But whenever he pulled the Velcro straps off his bulletproof vest, I woke in a sudden sweat. For over a year, he'd been telling me I'd get used to it. I never had.

I tiptoed upstairs to check on our boarder. Recovering from mononucleosis, nineteen-year-old Macguire Perkins was spending the summer with us until his father came home from teaching a course in Vermont. A tousle of red hair, a patch of pale skin, and loud snores indicated that Macguire was sleeping, as usual. Arch's bloodhound, Jake, dozed at Macguire's side, while our cat, an adopted stray named Scout, kept a watchful emerald eye from his perch on the dresser.

I finished getting ready and quietly crept out our front door. Another fresh morning breeze whispered through the aspens. After a nastily wet spring, we were enjoying what the locals call a one-in-ten year for wildflowers. This was probably going to be a one-in-ten year for the elk population, too, but I didn't mind. I revved up Tom's dark blue Chrysler sedan that he'd left in the driveway behind my van. Backing out, I tried to avoid blue flax, blush-pink wild roses, and brilliant white daisies, all nodding in the warm wind.

Actually, one of the reasons I'd come to admire John Richard's current girlfriend, Suz Craig, was that she had learned the names of nearly a hundred different kinds of flowers that were being put in as part of an elaborate landscaping project at her country-club home. While I was setting up for the business lunch in July, Suz had taken the time to point out the varieties of campanula and columbines that her landscapers were planting between the quartz boulders and striped chunks of riprap rock. Even businesswomen who were vice-presidents needed a hobby, I supposed. The lunch had been a going-away gig for some AstuteCare people visiting from out of town. As ACHMO's regional veep, it was Suz's job to provide their "day in the mountains," a de rigueur excursion for visiting out-of-staters. The buffet as well as the day had been Colorado picture-post-card perfect: sapphire-blue sky, sweet mountain air redolent of pine, platters of chilled steamed Rocky Mountain trout, and luscious chocolate truffles.

The only mishap of the catered lunch had occurred when Chris Corey, the overweight head of ACHMO's Provider Relations, had taken a spill down an incomplete set of stone steps. Chris had sprained his ankle and Suz had vowed to fire the landscapers. One of the guests had taken a bite of trout, winked at me, and commented that *firing people* was what Suz did best. I'd made a mental note. Maybe she'd dump the Jerk before too long. I wondered how he would react.

The sedan's engine purred as I passed Aspen Meadow Lake, where the early-morning sun and whiff of breeze had whipped the placid water into jagged sparkles. At the Lakeview Shopping Center across the road from the lake, a tattered banner, ruffling slightly, announced that Aspen Meadow

34

Health Foods was under new management. Beneath the banner a beautifully painted sign advertised the upcoming doll show at the LakeCenter. BABSIE BASH! the curlicued script screamed. GO BERSERK!

I pressed the accelerator and hummed along with the engine. When I thought about Babsie dolls these days, I didn't think *berserk*, I thought *bread and butter*. Starting Tuesday, I'd be catering to the doll folks for two days. The bash organizers had warned me that they didn't want any food to get on the display tables, the Babsie costume boxes, the eensy-weensy furniture, the tiny high heels, the fanciful costumes, or, God forbid, the dolls. I'd assured them I could do all their meals, including a final barbecue, outside — complete with finger bowls, if they wanted. They'd said I should find a Chef Babsie outfit to wear. I'd been afraid to ask them if they were kidding.

Once I'd rounded the lake, the sedan started uphill toward the country-club area. Actually, Suz Craig had always reminded me of Babsie. Beyond her looks, though, I had to admit that Suz had a phenomenal mind and a charismatic personality to go with her statuesque, size-six body. I never had been able to understand how the Jerk could attract women like her.

I glanced in the rearview mirror at my slightly chubby face, brown eyes, and Shirley Temple–blond-brown curls. "He got you, didn't he?" I said to my puzzled reflection, then laughed.

The stone entryway into the country-club area had been graffiti-sprayed by vandals. The vandals' defacement of property was one of this summer's ongoing problems in our little town. Still, I knew my way to Arch's friend's house without having to decipher the spray-painted street signs. The developer for the old part of the club had been an indiscriminate Anglophile. He'd given the streets names like Beowulf, Chaucer, Elizabethan, Cromwell, Tudor, and Brinsley. As long as you knew a bit about English history, you were in good shape. I approached the turn to Jacobean Drive, where Suz Craig lived, and hesitated. I pulled over and the sedan tires crunched on the gravel. Despite my best intentions, I was suffering a typical Jerk-inspired dilemma. Would he be home yet?

Tom's cellular was close at hand. I could call John Richard first to make sure he was awake and ready for Arch's arrival. On the other hand, I didn't want to wake him up and risk one of his infamous tantrums. If I drove past Suz's and saw one of his cars in the driveway, I would know to stall on picking up Arch. But stall how? I tapped the dashboard in frustration.

Okay — I remembered that the woebegone landscapers had been planning three patios, along with a series of steps, on Suz's sloping property. The vandalism had been so bad in the country club that Suz had confessed to being afraid to have the flagstones delivered and left outside, where they ran the risk of being spray-painted with cuss words. So Suz's garage was full of flagstones, and if John Richard had spent the night with his girlfriend, one of his Jeeps would be sitting in her driveway. This, in spite of the fact that his house was close by. But John Richard never walked for exercise; he played tennis.

I revved the engine, turned up Jacobean, and immediately knew something was wrong. I rolled down the window and tried to figure out what didn't fit. The rhythmic, slushy beat of automated sprinklers buzzed across manicured green lawns. On both sides of the road bunches of trim aspens, conical blue spruces, and buttercup-flowered potentilla bushes were all picture-perfect. Picture-perfect except for one thing. In the ditch running beside Suz's driveway, one of the landscape people had inconsiderately dumped one of the quartz boulders.

One of the quartz boulders? No.

I slowed the sedan, carefully set the parking brake, and got out of the car. Then, feeling faintly dizzy, I walked toward the ditch. Suz's cheerily painted mailbox had been knocked or driven over and lay in the middle of the street. The block letters of the name *Craig* gleamed in white paint on the shiny black metal. I looked back at the ditch.

It was not a quartz boulder that lay in the dirt.

It was Suz.

Oh God, I prayed, *no.*

I moved haltingly toward the ditch. Loosely clad in a terry-cloth bathrobe, the exposed parts of Suz's slender body were blue and white. Her shapely legs were improbably skewed, as if she were running a race. Her blond hair, normally tied back in a pert ponytail, was soaked with mud. It clung to her face like seaweed. Her bruised arms hugged her torso, while her blue lips were set in a silent scream. She did not appear to be breathing.

What to do? Call somebody? Tom? No, no, no, there might be hope, if an ambulance could get here quickly. Plus, some logical voice whispered, I needed to call for help as if I didn't have any idea as to what had happened. Which I didn't. *Which I did.*

Get into the car. Dial 911. A whirring noise in my ears made thinking difficult as I ran to the sedan. Too late, too late. Emergency Medical Services wouldn't be able to do anything. I knew it even as my shaking fingers punched 911 and Send on the cell phone. The connection was not immediate, as frequently happens in the mountains. One second, two endless, endless seconds. There was no movement from the ditch. Very faintly, from a distant part of my brain, I could hear Tom's voice.

He will go too far. Get caught. Be nailed.

Chapter 3

I told the 911 operator who I was, where I was, and why I was calling. "She doesn't seem to be alive," I added. Did I know CPR? the operator wanted to know. No, no, I replied, sorry.

"Just stay where you are," the operator commanded.

For some reason I looked at my watch. Five to seven. I had to call Tom. Although I knew it would irritate the 911 operator, I disconnected and punched the digits for the personal line into our house.

"Schulz," Tom barked into the phone.

"Listen, something's happened . . ." This was a mistake. Even with the worst-case scenario, which I did not want to contemplate, I surely knew they would never assign this — what would he call it? — this *matter,* this *incident,* this *case,* to my husband.

"It seems . . . I didn't . . ."

"Goldy," Tom commanded, "tell me what's going on. Slowly."

"I . . . I was driving up Jacobean in the country-club area," I began, and then told him bluntly exactly what I was looking at through the windshield — a young woman. Looked like Suz Craig, John Richard's girlfriend. Lying half-dressed in a ditch. Not moving. Not breathing.

"Sit tight," he ordered. "If you see John Richard, or anyone, say nothing. If someone comes, get out of the car. Don't let anybody near that ditch. I'll be there before the ambulance. Fifteen minutes, maybe twenty. Goldy? I'll be there."

I closed the phone and felt relief. I scanned the quiet landscape and had a sudden memory of the time a live power line had snapped during a blizzard and landed on our street. Touching the wire meant sure electrocution. The most important job, the fire department had warned, was to keep people, especially children, away from the dark wire that had curved onto the street like a monstrous snake. And how similar was this situation? I couldn't think. I only knew I had to keep prying eyes and intrusive, questioning people away from what lay in that ditch.

And speaking of children, I had to call Arch. Of course I couldn't remember the number of the house where he was. People named Rodine. I called Information, got the number, and phoned. Gail Rodine didn't sound too happy, but I told her tersely that there would be a delay before I arrived.

"I'm leaving to start setting up the doll show at ten," Gail petulantly announced.

"I'll be there long before that," I said, and disconnected before she could whine any more.

I peered out through the windshield of Tom's car and wondered how long it would be before someone came along. Tom was right: *Sit tight,* he'd said. If someone saw me, a stranger, standing in the road looking out of place, that would excite curiosity. My heart quickened as the front door to one of the houses swung open. A chunky man in a dark bathrobe came out, bent to retrieve his newspaper without looking up the street, then waddled back through his columned entryway. I let out a breath of relief that I quickly gasped right back in as John Richard's white Jeep roared into view from the opposite side of Jacobean.

What should I do?

Don't let anybody near that ditch.

John Richard catapulted the Jeep up into Suz's driveway. Apparently he'd taken no notice of Tom's car or of me sitting in it. Springing from his own vehicle, John Richard turned and scanned the road. Did he hesitate and narrow his eyes when he saw the toppled mailbox, then my sedan? I

42

couldn't be sure. The soil between the house and the ditch had been churned up and heaped into a small hillock by the landscapers. The body in the ditch could not be seen from the house. At least I hoped it couldn't. John Richard turned back to his Jeep, reached into the passenger-side seat, and pulled out a bunch of roses.

I'm going to be sick.

I knew without knowing what had happened. They'd fought.

You left, angry, thinking she was going to be just fine. You wanted her to recover; take aspirin; cry a little. You'd call later. But she stumbled out the door, looking for help. She fell into the ditch and died. And yet here you are with roses. You bought them at the grocery store this morning. The store is open all night and always helps you with your morning-after remorse. So here you are, figuring you can just patch everything up.

Not this time.

I forced my leaden hand to open the sedan door. Fear pulsed through every nerve. But I'd told Tom I would keep people away from the ditch, and I had to do that. Even if that meant undergoing this most dreaded of confrontations.

John Richard had already bounded up to Suz's door and was impatiently ringing the bell. He didn't take any notice of me until I was almost by his side. Then he turned and faced me, and I prayed for strength: mental, spiritual, and physical. Especially physical.

By any panel of judges, John Richard would be declared one of the handsomest men to walk the earth. His wide, dark blue eyes regarded me as his angular face instantly assumed its familiar what-the-hell-do-you-want expression. The bunch of roses wobbled in his large, strong hand.

"Why are *you* here?" he demanded. "What's your *problem?*" Of course, I couldn't find my voice. When I didn't respond immediately, he smirked. "Suz said you seemed real interested in her place. Smells a little bit like *obsession* to me."

Don't get into an argument.

"Well . . . I . . . uh," I faltered. I looked at him warily. Was he going to lose his temper? Turn all that rage on me? In front of this upscale neighborhood with its watching windows? "I . . . was actually driving by . . . looking for you. I . . . didn't want Arch to arrive at your place and have it be empty." My voice sounded absurdly high.

He surveyed the street for my van. "Really."

I held my breath. *Please let the body not be visible from the house.*

"Where is Arch?" asked John Richard, the man I had once loved. The man I now loathed beyond measure, the man I did my best to ignore, despite his constant bad behavior, which always demanded attention. "Where is your *van?* Look at me, dammit." His blue eyes drilled into mine. His icy, threatening tone was all too familiar. "Why won't you *tell* me why you're *here?* No Arch? No van? This certainly smacks of the ex-wife *spying* on the ex-husband's girlfriend."

"I just —"

At that moment the familiar wheeze of my van sounded its way up Jacobean. Tom parked behind his own sedan and within three seconds was striding across Suz's lawn from the acute angle of the neighbor's yard. Smart man. Any visual diversion from the ditch would buy time. With one of his large, pawlike hands, Tom motioned for me to move away from John Richard. I inched backward until my feet bumped the edge of the porch. Tom's green eyes never wavered from John Richard as he approached the porch where we stood.

"What the — ?" John Richard was furious. "Is this some kind of family incident? You'd better tell me what's going on, Goldy," he commanded.

Take a wild guess. But I was going to say

nothing to that arrogant voice.

Bordering the expansive front step was a fat clay pot brimming with vivid red geraniums and dusty-blue ageratum. I had backed up beside it and now stared down at the tall red flowers, unable to meet John Richard's enraged gaze. "I don't really know very much," I murmured.

"Hey there," said Tom, as if we were all meeting on the golf course.

John Richard wasn't fooled for a moment. "You want to tell me what the *hell* you're doing here at seven o'clock in the morning, cop? Or why Goldy just happened to be passing by?"

Tom's wide face stayed flat, passive, totally unreadable. He blinked and took a deep, measuring breath that pulled up his expansive chest. He regarded John Richard's handsome face and athletic frame.

Finally Tom said, "We seem to have a situation here."

"What?" cried John Richard, incredulous. *Or acting incredulous,* my skeptical inner voice immediately supplied. John Richard's face tightened with fury — and something else. "What kind of situation?" His voice was stone-hard, but there was a crack in that stone, something rarely heard when he spoke: *fear.* "What's the matter with you

46

two?" He turned his wrath on me. "What, did Suz call you early this morning, Goldy? Trying to get a little girlie sympathy? Strength in numbers, right? Just like you and Marla, a whimpering duo going for the gold medal in pettiness." He swept his scathing glance over Tom and me. "So you just rushed right out early in the morning, then called your personal police squad to back you up, right? What did Suz tell you, that we mixed it up last night?"

"You mixed it up last night," Tom quietly repeated.

John Richard flung the roses down. The paper made a crinkly sound as the bouquet landed on the grass, and a bloodred petal shook free. "Well, let me tell you, both of you, this is none of your damn business, do you understand me? Suz has lots of problems you don't even know about. It really wasn't as bad as —"

He was silenced by the wail of a siren. The ambulance screamed from the club entry-way. I knew from all Tom had told me that unless a victim's body has mold on it, the paramedics feel duty-bound to try to revive that victim. Still, as the ambulance shrieked to a halt, I wanted them to do their damnedest. I prayed they would be able to bring Suz back while knowing in my heart that it was

47

no longer within the realm of possibility.

Tom strode off the porch in the direction of the ambulance. When the paramedics were out of their vehicle, Tom pointed. The medics vaulted toward the ditch.

"Jesus Christ," muttered John Richard as he shoved past me. Caught off balance by the power of his push, I fell backward onto the flowerpot. I tripped off the edge of the porch and landed facedown in the dirt. When I scraped the soil off my elbows, I thought I heard a forlorn meow. I looked around but only saw John Richard. He was a preppy vision in khaki pants and burgundy shirt as he swiftly approached the area where the emergency medical folks were establishing their territory. "Hey! I'm a doctor!" he called. "What's going on?"

The medics were already working and paid him no heed. From beside the ditch Tom issued instructions. When John Richard arrived at the side of the ditch and yelped at the sight there, Tom shook his head grimly.

I pulled myself up, brushed the dirt off my clothes, and walked down the driveway. Neighbors were clustering on their porches. Three men walked purposefully toward the activity, as if they'd been appointed by the homeowners' association to find out what was going on and therefore were above nosiness. Tom pointed to me, then swept his arm toward the approaching men. *Keep those guys away.* I picked up the pace.

"Okay, folks," I said to the men, "just stay back. Please . . . That man's my husband and this is a medical emergency."

One of them, a bald, pinch-faced fellow whom I recognized as a minor dignitary from the Bank of Aspen Meadow, narrowed his eyes at the ditch. "That's not your husband, that's your ex —"

"The ex and the current," I replied sharply. "The current's a cop and he has *asked* me to keep you all —"

"What happened?" rasped another man. He was short and pudgy and sported a goatee that matched his gray sweatsuit. "Aren't you . . . haven't I seen you . . . aren't you the town caterer?" He inhaled angrily. "I demand to know why that ambulance is here. Was there a break-in? I have children. Tell me what's going on." The third man, tan, white-mustached, wearing gardening clothes and a billed cap, nodded mutely.

"You'll find out soon enough," I said, just a decibel higher than necessary.

From the ditch John Richard squawked. I couldn't help it: I turned around. I couldn't see Suz, but I saw the medics working to hook her up to some equipment. I knew the

49

drill: Check for vital signs. In those horrible few moments they'd already sought her pulse. They'd looked into her eyes to see if the irises were fixed and dilated. The only problem I was having was in accepting the next step. A dull thump reverberated through the air. *Dammit.* They were trying to get her heart to beat. Once more the thump echoed through the morning stillness.

Even though my view was partially blocked, I knew the next stage was for the paramedics to send telemetry down to a Denver hospital. An emergency-room doctor would make the declaration to stop trying to resuscitate.

John Richard shrieked: "What the hell is that thing doing there?" He torqued his head around and stared at Suz's house.

One of the paramedics was holding something. The medic held it out to Tom, affording me a sideways view of it. He held a piece of jewelry, a thick, heavy gold bracelet.

I stared, uncomprehending, at the bracelet, then felt my eyes being drawn to the naked spot on John Richard's left wrist. My worries about personal bankruptcy seemed a century old. The street felt as if it were moving under my feet. *Steady, girl.*

"I don't believe this!" John Richard yelled.

"This is entrapment! This is a setup! Why won't you talk to me?"

The three bystanders I was trying to keep away from the ditch nudged urgently past me.

"Hey!" I yelped. "You can't go —"

But by the time I caught up with them, they stood beside the ditch. Damn them. Tom could not stop the men from gaping at the medics and poor, wretched Suz; he was talking into his mobile phone. And what was I now hearing? No. Yes. Tom was reciting the Miranda rights to John Richard Korman.

"Stop this," John Richard protested loudly as Tom's caution continued. "You have no idea what you're doing! Suz had . . . She . . . AstuteCare had more . . . enemies . . . than I have patients. She was into more —"

I could not believe my ears. This was so fast . . . too fast. What had John Richard said or done? He and Suz had "mixed it up." And the ID bracelet — where had the medics found it? Were John Richard's admission of a fight and a piece of his jewelry enough to warrant an arrest? Apparently so. But John Richard had brought flowers, he must have *thought* Suz was alive, or must have wanted to *believe* she was alive, or wanted to *appear* to believe she was alive.

51

Tom said quietly, "You're under arrest. I've just arranged for transport." He reached in his back pocket for his handcuffs. He must have brought them, I thought, stupefied. Tom must have brought the cuffs and his badge and his weapon, when I told him where I was and what I'd seen.

John Richard leaped forward and swung at Tom; the three neighborhood ambassadors jumped back. John Richard's fist shot upward again. But Tom was ready for him. He grabbed John Richard's right arm and swung it forcefully around. Cursing, John Richard fell to his knees. Tom put his other hand into John Richard's back and brought him easily to the ground. John Richard yelled, threatened, cursed, and reminded Tom of what he would do to him the minute he got free.

Tom leaned over and said, *"Shut. Up."*

Chapter 4

With practiced quickness, the paramedics transferred their energy from trying to revive Suz to pulling back. They authoritatively called out orders and pushed aside the bystanders. No matter: The group of people, which had now grown to five, had turned their attention from Suz and could not stop staring, fascinated, at John Richard. Handcuffed, he knelt in the street. Tom kept him there. Tom's muscular body leaned toward John Richard. My husband spoke into my ex-husband's ear. I could not make out what he was saying over the voices of the medics. But if the twisted look of fury on John Richard's face was any indication, it wasn't good news.

Tom turned and made an announcement to the mesmerized bystanders. "Okay, you five, here's the deal. Go stand in different driveways until we've stabilized this situation. Police officers will come talk to you when they arrive. Do *not* discuss this among yourselves." He paused to make sure they understood. Two nodded; the others just stared. "All right, thank you. Go ahead, please, move away. Now."

As the men promptly defied Tom's orders by departing in a whispering cluster, John Richard raised his angry voice, demanding to be let out of the handcuffs. The medics ignored him, as did Tom, who once again pulled the mobile unit off his belt and made a call. I heard him say the words "captain," "video," and "team."

Tom spoke again to John Richard, then helped him to his feet. The Jerk, cuffed, shook loose of Tom's arm, then stalked angrily to the base of Suz Craig's tar-streaked driveway. Tall and elegant even with his arms bound at an improbable angle behind him, Dr. John Richard Korman stood shifting his weight from one khaki-clad leg to the other. I thought absurdly that he looked as if he were considering poses for an art class. Above his gorgeous, chiseled face, which occasionally spasmed with rage, his blond hair was only slightly tousled from his exchange with Tom.

I turned away, disbelieving. Was this really happening? There was a buzzing in my ears. My eyes burned. I sat down on the curb and focused on Tom.

Tom knew what he was doing. He could switch into his take-charge mode without a hitch. He nimbly moved his beefy body around the periphery of the ditch. He gave a few more instructions to the paramedics, who plopped down listlessly on the dirt-strewn incline. He had probably told them to do nothing until the coroner arrived. Then, his face set in that intimidating expression I knew so well, Tom walked in the direction of the driveway and John Richard. I tried to remember a time when I had seen these significant men from my life standing next to each other. I failed. And this certainly wasn't the circumstance where I wanted to make the comparison of how the two appeared and how they acted. I looked away, up the street.

If I was right about what Tom had told the paramedics, the coroner would be arriving soon in his van. As my eyes skimmed the row of big, beautifully maintained houses, I wondered helplessly about Arch. I still had to go get him. I needed to stand up and put one foot in front of the other and tell Tom I was leaving. But exactly how would I say that? *I've got to go tell my son that his father has been arrested for murder?* I stayed put.

Tom, meanwhile, gently took a stiff John Richard by the elbow and guided him up the driveway toward the house. Reluctantly, I stood and followed. The buzzing in my ears was not from the sprinklers. *Get Arch, get out of the club, and get back home.* But who would take care of my son at home, comfort him and talk to him? I had a party tonight. Could Macguire help, even though he was bedridden with mono? Not likely. I would think of something. For now, I had to get away from here. The bystanders, perched like friendly watchdogs on this street full of posh houses and lush green lawns, watched my journey up the driveway with undisguised interest.

"I need to leave," I announced to Tom. I darted a sideways glance at John Richard. Tom had directed him to the far end of Suz's porch, where he perched stiffly on the edge of a white wicker couch. I flinched at the sight of his scathing stare and his silent, enraged face. I cleared my throat. "I need to get Arch."

"You do that!" John Richard exploded, but not, I noticed, loudly enough for the nosy neighbors to hear. I looked at him curiously. His outburst contained no sadness. No grief. "Go get Arch!" he yelled, his face shaking. "Tell him *why* we can't go hiking! And be sure to let him know what you and your buddy have cooked up here! Arch is bound to just love it!"

My temper snapped. "Listen!" I yelled back, "I was just driving up —"

56

"Save it!" John Richard hissed. The cords in his neck strained. "No more child support if I'm in jail! Think about it!"

"Look, you." I tried to stop the angry shaking of my voice but could not. "I haven't gotten any child support since —"

"Goldy." Tom's passionless tone mercifully stilled the exchange. He waited until he had my complete attention. "Don't get Arch yet. You need to stay here, make a statement." His face was calm. "And you should see a victim advocate."

"Victim advocate?" John Richard bellowed. "What does she need an advocate for? *I'm* the damn victim here!"

I gaped at Tom, dumbfounded. Of course. I had discovered the body. The police had to question me. And the psychologists' recommendation for a person discovering a body was that that person was traumatized and needed comfort. But this wasn't the first murder victim I'd found. I'd managed before without an advocate. Still, what was the psychologists' recommendation if your *ex-husband* was charged with the murder you'd stumbled upon? I couldn't think. I swayed as I stood between the overturned geranium pot and the wicker furniture. What had I been doing just a moment ago? Oh, yes. I'd been having an argument with my ex-husband about money. Now I was having a conversation with my current husband about an advocate.

You must get Arch, my inner voice urged. *You must tell him what's happened before someone else does.* Trauma? You bet. Undreamed-of trauma. But like most women, I couldn't take time out from the other crises of my life to be taken care of. "I don't want an advocate," I told Tom. "I'm okay."

Even as I spoke Tom was pulling the phone off his belt. "What's Marla's number?"

"Oh, right!" John Richard raged. "Let's get old *Marla* over here. One big happy family. Hey! I have an idea! Ask that fat dumb broad how she planted my ID bracelet in that ditch."

Tom ignored him as I recited Marla's number. Should Marla really come, though? I didn't want this situation to aggravate her cardiac condition. She should not come here, I muttered. When Tom asked, I gave him the address of Arch's friend, Sam Rodine. It was near enough to Marla's house that she could meet me there. While Tom murmured into the phone, the coroner's black van pulled up beside the curb. A warm breeze swished through the aspens. The babble of voices on the street increased in volume.

"I don't believe this," muttered John Richard.

"No, Marla . . . Goldy's fine, just upset," Tom was saying. "But I need you to take care of her for a while. Meet her over at the Rodines' house and bring some iced coffee or something. Just be with her, okay?" While he was talking, his eyes never left the two men from the coroner's staff who were going about their grim work in the ditch. I noticed John Richard's eyes never strayed toward that spot.

"Look, Marla, Goldy will tell you what's going on when she meets you, okay? I need to go," Tom said in his conversation-ending voice. "She'll be tied up here for about fifteen minutes, so . . . Sure you can get dressed that fast. Yes, Goldy is with me now. No, we're not at home. Marla, please . . . Okay, look, Goldy and I are over on Jacobean, here in the country-club area."

Marla's squawk through the receiver was audible across the porch. Of course Marla didn't need to ask *where* on Jacobean we were. She was the one who had called me seven months ago and in a tremulous, indignant voice, announced the name, address, and all the vital statistics she'd gleaned on John Richard's latest conquest, Suz Craig.

"No, *don't* come over, we've got enough confusion as it is. Goldy won't be here too much longer. . . ." Tom sighed. "Yes," he said finally, "John Richard Korman is here, too. Marla, remember what I said. Goldy will be on her way to the Rodines' place in a quarter of an hour." Then he muttered, "See you later," and disconnected. Well, that was one way to get out of a conversation.

Tom leaped off the porch without explaining where he was going. He stopped to talk to someone from the coroner's van, then hustled back to us. He held up a hand to me: five minutes.

"Okay, Mr. Talkative," said Tom to John Richard. He sounded almost cheery as he snapped the phone back on his belt. "You've been wanting to talk and now you've got your chance. How about telling us exactly what happened here?"

"That's *Dr.* Talkative to you, schmuck." John Richard tossed his head, suddenly calm. His changes in mood, of course, were well known to me. "And I've been Mirandized. I'm not saying another word until I talk to my lawyer. *Just* the way you told me to." Then John Richard turned. His dark blue eyes spit fire at me even as his voice remained hideously even. "But as for you, I *know* you're behind this. One way or another, I'm going to find out how. And if you tell my son about this in any way that makes me look bad, I'll have you hauled into court so fast you'll think our breakup was a caterers' picnic."

Oh, sure, I thought. But I didn't want to hear his empty threats. I was leaving. Of course, I wanted to ask John Richard what kind of "mixing up" he and Suz had done the night before. *Mixing up.* What a euphemism. How about, "I beat up women when they don't do what I want?" In the near distance, sirens wailed. I shivered and wondered about the ID bracelet that Suz had so proudly given John Richard. And why would John Richard think Suz wanted to call *me* this morning? The sirens shrieked louder and a police car, lights flashing, burst into view. I knew better than to try to have any further conversation with John Richard.

The police car squealed to a stop behind the coroner's van. A uniformed policeman and a tall, dark blond plainclothes woman I didn't recognize came up to the porch and asked if I was Goldy Schulz, the person who'd found the dead woman. Was I ready to make my statement? they wanted to know.

Just then, there was one of those unexplained moments of utter silence. The breeze dropped. The coroner's staff in the ditch was still. The speculative buzz on the street ceased. Even the sprinklers stopped their metronomic splatting. Maybe the quiet was in my head. Maybe I was going to pass out.

"Mrs. Schulz?" inquired the tall female officer, who had said her name was Sergeant Beiner. She leaned in close. "Are you all right?"

"Yes," I whispered. "I need . . . need to go get my son."

"Very soon," she replied, as she straightened. Sergeant Beiner was fiftyish. Her six-foot height was somewhat mitigated by a humpback, and her narrow face was actually topped with a rooster-style burst of blond and gray curls. "We're making an exception so you can go in just a few minutes. You *should* be coming down to the department," she added, with a wary glance at John Richard. Then her tone turned sympathetic. "But since you have to go pick up your child, Mrs. Schulz, we'll just ask a few questions now. We know where we can reach you if we need to talk to you some more later. Okay?"

I nodded. "Later," I said dully, "I'll be at home."

The sergeant gently led me off the porch, out of earshot of John Richard and Tom. She motioned for the uniformed policeman to stand by her side as she ticked off her questions: How did you get here? What exactly did you see? What did you do? Did you see anybody driving away? Did you see anybody in the area?

While she made notes, I told her everything: I arrived in Tom's sedan between six-thirty and seven, I saw a body in the ditch; I called 911 and Tom. No one drove away. No one showed up except Dr. John Richard Korman, clutching a bouquet. It was a painful recitation. Sergeant Beiner said she or one of the primary investigators would be by to see me later in the day. I walked unsteadily back to the porch.

"I'm leaving," I told Tom. He stepped off the porch and gave me a wordless hug. I murmured, "I'll be okay" into his chest. Then I pulled away.

Behind me, the grating noises of a stretcher being wheeled across the pavement disturbed the quiet of the neighborhood. Another meow directed my attention to the porch steps. A small calico ball of fur dashed out and clawed at the upended geraniums. It was Suz's cat, Tippy. I snagged the small feline and was rewarded with a scratch on the arm. Tippy, shivering and terrified, then scrambled up my arm. When I tried to coax her down, she dug her claws in and remained poised on my shoulder. Her little body trembled next to my head.

Two more police cars wheeled up Jacobean, red and blue lights flashing. I walked to my van with Tippy the cat perched resolutely on my shoulder. I knew the cat was part of the crime scene. But she would be ignored and abandoned if I didn't care for her. So I took her. Three more uniformed Furman County deputies crossed Suz Craig's lawn to Tom. Two more hauled equipment toward the ditch. No one noticed me.

The video team began to record the scene. I averted my eyes and opened the van door. The cat leaped into the back. I stared at the keys in my hand. My ring was just like Tom's: keys to the house, keys to the sedan, keys to the van. I tried hard to remember what it was I was supposed to do with these keys. *It could have been me.* After a moment of fumbling with the ignition, I started my van, and stepped hard on the accelerator. *It could so very easily have been me in that ditch, if I hadn't gotten out all those years ago.*

The dozen people gathered on porches stared with avid interest as my van chugged down the street. One man shook his head at my noisy progress. His red scalp blazed in the warming sun. Along the street, the velvety lawns glowed like chartreuse carpets.

Suz Craig took my place. But it could so very easily have been me.

Chapter 5

The cat howled the two miles to Hadley Court. I pulled up in front of a three-story, white-brick-and-blue-gingerbread-trimmed Victorian-style mansion that was about as far from a mountain contemporary as it was from Mars. Marla's Mercedes squealed around the corner as I eased to the curb. Behind her tinted windshield I could see she was talking excitedly on her car phone, which she quickly hung up when she spotted me. She threw open her door and came bustling toward the van.

Marla's raspberry-colored sequined sweatsuit did not flatter her portly figure. In one hand she held a covered glass and in the other a paper bag. My dear friend always brought something that she thought would make you feel better. Usually the only thing I needed was to see her, and as usual, the sight of her rushing toward me, her rhinestone-studded sunglasses jiggling up and down on her concerned face, brought a wave of relief.

Wealthy by inheritance, talkative by nature, and pretty in an unconventional way, Marla had endured being married to John Richard for six years less than I had. After John Richard's first few rampages, Marla had also shown much more confidence than I had when it came to ridding oneself of a burdensome spouse. She'd shoved an attacking John Richard into a hanging plant and dislocated his shoulder. She'd then managed to cut the marital knot with great expertise. She and I had become fast friends when her divorce was final, proving that even the worst marital experiences can hold some redemption. Last summer she'd survived a heart attack. Earlier *this* summer, she'd survived a disastrous breakup with the one guy she'd been serious about since divorcing the Jerk. We had a history, the two of us. And I loved her dearly.

"Okay, tell me," she began without preamble when I hopped out of the van to greet her, "are you okay? Probably not," she added with an opulent, scarlet-lipsticked frown.

I fought off an unexpected wave of dizziness. "I don't know. No. Probably not."

"Let's get back in your van, so people don't come out and start asking a bunch of questions. Jeez, this town — I've already had two calls on my cellular." Her brown eyes softened with sympathy and she proffered a plastic-wrapped crystal glass. For the first time, I noticed her hair was damp. "Look, Goldy, I brought you an iced latté. Well, actually half espresso and half cream dumped over ice. Very naughty, but oh so good." She held up the brown bag in her other hand. "And here we have a whole bunch of meds that I just dumped out of my medicine cabinet. They're mostly tranquilizers. Which do you want first?"

"Coffee and downers?" I asked incredulously. I sagged against the van door. I wondered if any Furman County victim advocates carried lunch-bags full of prescription tranquilizers. Probably not.

"Come on, back in you go." Marla hustled me into the van, where the air was even warmer than it was outside. But the interior of my vehicle was familiar and smelled faintly, even pleasantly, of cooked food. The cat was uncharacteristically quiet. I rolled down my window; Marla did the same.

"Just drink this," she commanded, thrusting the glass into my hand. "Tom said to bring you —" Abruptly she stopped. She blinked. "One of my friends on Jacobean called. Suz is *dead*? Are they sure? Lynn Tollifer, you know her? She and her nosy teenage son, Luke, live across the street from Suz. Luke told Lynn that Suz's body was in

68

a ditch at the end of her driveway. Who found her? You?" I nodded and took a tiny sip of the chilly liquid. It tasted like melted ice cream. Marla clutched the top of her frizzy brown hair. "Suz dead! I don't believe it, but I do believe it."

"It should have been me. But he got Suz Craig instead." My voice cracked. I sagged against the headrest. "Gosh, I'm feeling —" John Richard's glare, his anger, haunted me. And I'd had such a strong feeling that he'd been acting, playing a part, but why? And what part? Why come over the morning after you'd had a fight with your girlfriend, bearing flowers, if you'd hurt her badly? If you'd killed her? But he hadn't meant to hurt her badly. At least that's what he always said. He probably hadn't meant to kill her, either.

"Do you think he beat her up so badly she died?" Marla asked.

"Yes, I do. Suz had a black right eye. And bruises on her arms —" I choked.

"Mother of God."

"I don't know what to do."

"Drink your coffee," Marla ordered sharply. "We can talk about all this later. If you don't look better in five minutes, I'm calling an ambulance for you and taking Arch home myself."

The air inside the van, despite the open windows, felt stifling. Marla slid toward me smelling of floral soap and powder. She'd obviously just jumped out of the shower when Tom called her, and I felt a fleeting sense of regret to have caused her trouble. Then the weight of the morning's events smacked me like one of those Jersey-shore waves you're not expecting, and I didn't know whether I wanted the espresso or enough tranquilizers to put me out for a few days.

"Okay, Goldy, look at me," Marla commanded sharply. "Keep drinking that coffee." I took another sip and stared into her large, liquid brown eyes. "Still feeling light-headed?"

"I'm doing a little better," I replied in a voice that didn't even convince me.

"Your first problem is Arch. Think what —"

The sob that nearly choked me turned into another and then a whole barrage that wouldn't quit. Marla hugged me and spoke soft words of no import. Still crying, I glanced up. Gail Rodine was staring out her front window. She probably wasn't expecting to see two women, one with a Mercedes and one with a beat-up van, hugging each other while one sobbed effusively, out in

70

front of her elaborate Victorian cottage. On second thought, Gail Rodine probably was about to call the vice squad.

"I have to get my act together," I croaked.

"Yeah, you do," Marla replied hopefully. "What you need is some medication. Chill you out a little." She thrust the brown bag into my hand and I peered tentatively at bottles of Librium and Valium, foil-encased capsule samples of God-only-knew-what, even a hypodermic. I carefully pulled out the needle, which was labeled Versed. From Med Wives 101, I knew this was a high-potency tranquilizer.

"Where on earth did you get all this?"

"Goldy, with the legion of doctors who are either treating me or going out with me, and an ex-husband who's a doctor, you wonder that? Which one do you want?"

"None. I need to parent, cook, cater, and drive this van without benefit of altered states of consciousness. I won't be able to perform any of those tasks if I'm floating inside a drug-induced cloud somewhere in the stratosphere." And just as uncontrollably as the sobs had begun, they ended, and I giggled. Marla shrugged philosophically, dropped the needle back into the bag, and shoved the bag into my glove compartment. Then she started to laugh herself.

"Look, Goldy, I promised Tom I'd help and that's what I'm going to do. Okay, here's what you tell Arch. You say there's been an incident and his father might be in trouble. Dear old Dad's gone down to the sheriff's department to talk to the folks there. Dear old Dad will be talking to his lawyer over the weekend. With school out, with no town paper until Wednesday, and with the Denver TV stations covering their own murders, Arch won't hear about the arrest except from the Jerk himself, maybe tomorrow." Marla exhaled triumphantly.

"It's going to be awful. . . ."

"Yep," she agreed matter-of-factly. Again she ran her bejeweled fingers through her tangled, damp hair. "But let me clue you in to something, kiddo. You are not responsible for the Jerk's problems. He is. A hard lesson that took both of us a lot of years to learn, but there it is. Right?"

I stared out the window in sullen silence. Hard lesson, indeed.

"Okay now. Next step," Marla breezed on, "who's at home? Somebody to screen your calls? Be with Arch?"

"Macguire Perkins."

"Oh, great. How's he doing? Is the mono over, or almost over, or what?"

"He's sleeping, as usual. Not eating. But

72

he could be good for Arch. You know, be someone to talk to besides me about what's happening."

"Does Macguire do anything that would get Arch out of the house? You know, go out to the movies, whatever?"

"I suppose," I murmured. What did Macguire do? Not much. Virtually nothing at all, to be honest. "He's under doctor's orders to get mild exercise. And for Macguire 'mild' means 'with as little exertion as possible.' I urge him to take a walk most days. Sometimes Arch goes along, and they make it as far as John Richard's office."

"Okay, you'll have to get Arch to go out with Macguire for a stroll today. You want him out of the house for a bit. You know your phone's going to start ringing."

I sighed. "You know you can't make Arch do anything when he has his mind set on something else. Which he will have when he hears this news. Besides, Arch was supposed to go hiking with John Richard and spend the night with him while I worked the McCrackens' Stanley Cup celebration party here in the club."

"Good," said Marla bluntly. I wondered confusedly why everything seemed good to her today. She cast an appraising eye at the Rodines' house. Gail's face was no longer in the window. "I'll call Arch's friend. What's his name, Todd Druckman?" I nodded, and she went on. "I'll ask Todd if Arch can go over and spend the night. That'll get him out of your house. Can Macguire accompany you and help tonight? Is he contagious or anything?"

"No, he's not contagious. But I can assure you he won't have the energy for it." I stared glumly out the window. "How can you talk about all this now?"

"Uh. Let's see. 'Cuz your husband the cop asked me to take care of you?"

I touched her forearm and she tilted her head questioningly. "Is this really happening?" I asked my best friend. "Did John Richard finally kill someone?"

She didn't answer, because at that moment we both heard a very faint voice calling, "Mom?"

Arch had come out onto the Rodines' porch. At fourteen, he was still much shorter than his peers, with tousled brown hair and a generally scruffy appearance. He had changed into khaki cutoffs and a T-shirt printed with the Biocess logo. Biocess was the product of a drug company for which John Richard had been doing endorsements lately. Unfortunately, the only things Arch or I ever got out of John Richard's high-pay-

74

ing endorsements were ugly T-shirts and pens that leaked all over the place. Arch's tortoiseshell glasses winked as he shielded his eyes against the sun and frowned at Marla's and my cars in the street.

"We'll be up to get you in a minute, Arch!" Marla called. "You don't need to come out yet!"

Without replying, Arch turned on his heel and retreated into the house.

"So do you think he did it?" I pressed, not able to let it go. "Do you think John Richard Korman actually, finally, went over the edge and killed someone?"

"Of course I do," Marla replied evenly. "With ten or twelve drinks in him and something to set him off? No question. You said yourself you saw the bruise marks. And the Jerk had something big to set him off, take my word for it."

"What? I mean, besides some money problems."

"He didn't have anything *besides* money problems, Goldy. He and ACHMO are being sued by the McCrackens, and even with malpractice insurance, he's going to have costs. I heard the malpractice people hired an attorney, ACHMO had to hire several attorneys, and John Richard had to hire his own separate attorney. You know how much

75

preparation these trials are going to take. My guess is the financial mess of his lawsuit is eating him alive." She said it smugly. I wasn't the only one who wanted John Richard to suffer. "Look, you haven't had any child support for months, right?"

"Three, to be exact."

Marla raised her eyebrows in mock astonishment. Of course she'd heard me complain about John Richard slacking off in this department numerous times. She went on. "You were so eager to get out of that marriage that you took a one-time financial settlement and minimal child support. Now every time you need something for Arch, like, say, tuition money, you have to go back and negotiate, or should I say *beg*. Right?" I nodded dully and glanced up at the porch. Arch was nowhere in sight. Marla wagged a finger at me to make sure I was paying attention. "My lawyer went for a part of the practice. Ten percent of the gross income per annum. Not that I needed it, but I figured the best way to punish the Jerk was in his pocketbook. If you —"

I interrupted impatiently. "Marla, a woman is dead. Where is this going?"

"To the bank, honey. Back in the good old pre–managed care days, I got sixty to eighty thou a year, a reliable ten percent of six to

76

eight hundred thousand of the Jerk's gyn and baby-delivery practice. But things began to change. With more and more of his patients signing up with HMOs instead of half of them being insured and half paying out of pocket, his income started to decline. He supplemented it with endorsing that designer antibiotic for pregnant women with infections. What's the name of it?"

"Biocess," I supplied.

"Right. Another fifty thou a year there, of which I got a paltry five. Plus he began to work in the hospitals on the weekends, but you know how he hates to have his social life tied up, even if working a weekend shift brought him in another sixty thou a year. All this was getting exhausting for the poor fellow."

"Marla —"

"Wait. Then he got bought out by the AstuteCare Health Maintenance Organization, aka ACHMO, which sounds like a sneeze more than an HMO, but —" She shrugged. "We don't need to be reminded of *that* little transaction, which also brought into our lives the now-dead-as-a-doorknob Ms. Craig."

Poor Suz. An ache pierced my chest.

"Goldy, these days, if you want to have a baby in Aspen Meadow, or if you want to have the Jerk as your gynecologist, you or your husband or your significant other has to belong to ACHMO, yes? I mean, God only knows why any sane woman would insist on having John Richard as her doctor. But he does have his supporters, I suppose. How strong that support might be depends on your willingness to pony up with the cost of ACHMO membership."

"Marla, I know this. And that ACHMO bought his practice for one point one mil, and he bought the fancy new house in the club over by Suz. So what?"

Marla said patiently, "So *I* got a hundred ten thousand when he sold the practice, but in the two years since then I've only received thirty thousand dollars the first year, twenty this year. Don't you get it? His annual income has dropped by more than half. Enough to get him mightily ticked off, wouldn't you say? First I called that new secretary of his, the sweet young thing? You know who I mean."

"ReeAnn Collins," I said. ReeAnn was a lovely twenty-three-year-old who'd been working for John Richard for the last ten months or so. I'd suspected ReeAnn was half in love with him, of course. I'd thought of warning her off, as I always thought I should. But I never did. I hadn't warned Suz Craig,

78

either. A stone seemed to form in my throat.

"ReeAnn didn't know anything about why my reimbursement was dropping off," Marla went on smoothly, "so I called AstuteCare. I demanded to know how much money John Richard was due to get and when."

"Sheesh, Marla."

"Oh, it was fun. I talked to Suz Craig's secretary and then I talked to some guy named Chris Corey, who handles Provider Relations. Corey used to be a doctor, but now he's making it big in administration," she added with a coarse laugh. "He was so-o-o polite, trying to tell me that how much John Richard made was none of my frigging business."

"Yes, I know him —" In my mind's eye, I saw a heavy man tumbling down a flight of steps. "Chris Corey sprained his ankle over at Suz's."

"Yeah, I've seen him limping around. He lives with his sister, Tina, up here. She's one of the women in charge of the Babsie show at the LakeCenter."

I tried to focus. I didn't care about the Coreys. "Are you telling me," I said, "that John Richard has gone from earning up to eight hundred thousand dollars a year down to making three hundred thousand dollars a year?"

"Sad, ain't it?"

"And he supplemented *that* income by endorsing Biocess and working in the hospital. You're saying you didn't like the way your share dropped and you tried to find out if he was stiffing you." What on earth did any of this have to do with the death of Suz?

"Right!" Marla said firmly. "So *finally* I called my *lawyer* about the drop in income and told him about all the people I'd talked to. My lawyer made some more calls and then let me know that the Biocess endorsement was in some kind of limbo. Plus John Richard hasn't yet received the latest bonus he was supposed to get from ACHMO. A bonus in the big fat neighborhood of two hundred thousand dollars. When the bonus does come through, I should see some more cash. I would love to have my cut of that, Goldy. But mainly I did all this just to annoy John Richard, because I knew it would get back to him that I was nosing around. The guy is up to his ears in debt from the good old days, what with payments to *you*, and payments to *me*, and payments on his *condos*, and payments on his new *house*, and payments on his *cars*, and dealing with the *McCrackens*. So. I wanted the Jerk to know I was on his case. I wanted him to squirm."

"And the connection to Suz Craig is . . ."
Marla raised an eyebrow. "Didn't I tell
you? Suz was the one who decided whether
or not he got the bonus."

Chapter 6

Marla and I were prevented from further discussion of John Richard's plummeting finances and mounting problems by the sudden reappearance of my son. Arch bounded awkwardly off the Rodines' porch and frowned as he lugged his overnight bag toward us. I had the sinking feeling that the overnight had not gone well. Marla asked if I wanted her to stay and I said no. After giving Arch a quick, wordless hug and me a bright, reassuring smile, she vavoomed off in her Mercedes.

"Why was Marla here?" Arch asked as he clicked his seat belt in place. He had the thickened voice and strong boy smell that always seems to accompany the morning-after of slumber parties.

"Just visiting," I said lightly.

"Do you think Dad's up yet? I haven't had any breakfast."

"You don't seem very happy," I observed, more as a probe to see if anyone had called the Rodines to report the situation on Jacobean Drive.

"Oh, well." His tone was disgusted. "I mean, we were going to have breakfast, we were supposed to, but then something happened." He shook the hair out of his eyes. "You know Clay Horning?"

"Yes." Clay Horning was the resident hooligan of the Elk Park Prep eighth grade. I kept my opinion to myself, however.

"Clay took half a dozen of Mrs. Rodine's Babsie dolls off a chair. He couldn't understand why Mrs. Rodine had them there. I mean, she never plays with them, but they're on the chairs, on the tables, on the sofas, on the beds, on the bureaus, everywhere! You ask me, Mrs. Rodine is a doll junkie! Anyway, Clay wanted to see how the heads from some of the dolls would look on the bodies of others. He pulled off all the heads and was switching them around — I mean, they pop right on — when Mrs. Rodine had a hissy fit. She swung her frying pan at him. Clay jumped out of the way, but all the uncooked bacon slid out on those headless Babsies. Do you believe that something so *stupid* could ruin a slumber party?" He shook his head. "Some people."

I didn't reply. After a few seconds Arch pushed his glasses up his nose and squinched his mouth to one side. "Mom? I don't mean to complain." He waited for me to speak.

"Are you upset about Mrs. Rodine and the frying pan? Or are you mad that she didn't give me anything to eat? I'm really not that hungry."

"Mrs. Rodine is not an easy person to deal with," I said softly. "But I don't want to talk about her, Arch. Let's just sit here a minute. I need to think."

He shrugged. "Ohh-kay. What-ever."

I watched my son and felt my heart ache with love, with my inability to communicate, and with foreboding. In the last year Arch had finally adjusted to a new family life. He adored Tom, while maintaining a ferocious devotion to his father. But John Richard did little more than tolerate Arch and use him in arguments with me. When Marla's nephew, our much-loved boarder Julian Teller, left for Cornell, the resulting hole in Arch's life had been filled by an adopted bloodhound, Jake. Lately, Arch and Macguire Perkins had become friendly. The two boys liked to listen to music and — as they put it — *hang out* at John Richard's office. All of which now seemed charmingly innocent and faraway. It was unlikely that they would still hang out at the office of a doctor who'd been accused of murder.

Before I could phrase what needed to be said, a forlorn feline howl erupted from the back of the van. Another quickly followed. Arch whirled.

"Mom? Is that Scout? What's going on?"

"No." I sighed. Tippy wanted out. "I'll be right back." When I hopped from the van, Gail Rodine, a top-heavy, matronly brunette, stood glaring on her spacious porch. Holding a clipboard to her chest, she scowled at me, as if my presence at her curb was intrusive. At Gail's side was a tall, similarly heavyset woman with long blond braids. The blonde appeared to be wearing a doctor-type jacket. I yanked open the van's rear door and caught sight of the little calico cat lurking behind my spare tire. "Come on, Tippy," I urged. "Out you come."

Suz's cat did not need to be coaxed. She leaped from the van, crouched on the Rodine lawn, then dashed to one of the blooming pink rosebushes encircling the porch. The cat tried frantically to claw her way up a rosebush. Gail Rodine squawked. The woman with the blond braids swiftly descended the porch steps, arms outstretched. Between Gail's angry yelps, the soothing words the blond woman offered the panicked cat were barely audible. The cat, sensing a friend, leaped from the destroyed rosebush into the open arms of the woman. Then she clawed her way up to her shoulder.

"Mom?" said Arch. "What is going on? Whose cat is that? It looks like Ms. Craig's."

"I'm so sorry," I said, approaching the blond woman, whose hand reached up to stroke the cat on her shoulder. "It's not mine, it's . . . somebody else's." Her wide blue jacket had "Dr. Babsie" embroidered in dark blue script over her heart. "I know you, don't I? Do you practice in our town? I'm Goldy Schulz."

The woman let out a strange, eager laugh. She gave me an intense blue-eyed look. "You're the caterer, right? You're doing several meals for us next week. I'm Tina Corey. Head of the Aspen Meadow Babsie Doll Club. How do you know me?"

"From church?" I guessed, without adding that her face was only vaguely familiar. But St. Luke's had three services each weekend and it was possible to go for years without knowing another parishioner's name.

"Mom?" Arch called from the van. "We need to go or Dad's going to be *really* upset."

I signaled to him to wait. "I . . . I've met your brother, Tina. Chris. At ACHMO. Are you a doctor, too? I mean, it says . . . on your jacket . . ."

She chuckled again. "No-o, this is just the adult-size Babsie-as-Veterinarian cos-

86

tume. Do you like it?"

"I . . . uh . . . sure. I need to go. Want to give me the cat? She's not mine." But when I reached out to Tippy, the cat hissed at me.

"Animals always love me," Tina assured me. "Want me to return her to her rightful owner?"

"Actually," I said, desperate, "if you'd just be willing to take care of her for a while until we can get her turned over to the Mountain Animal Protective League —"

Tina opened her eyes wide. "Never! I'll keep her! I have a bunch of cats already. What's her name?"

"I think the owner called her Tippy."

Murmuring, Tina reached up and gently removed the cat from her shoulder. Gail Rodine glared. "Sweet baby!" crooned Tina, "I'll have you fixed up in no time."

"Thanks, Tina," I said, not waiting for the cat's reply. "See you next week. At the doll show." I trotted back to the van, not daring to glance at Gail Rodine. I hopped back into the driver's seat and cleared my throat. There was no easy way to do this, despite what Marla had said. "Listen, Arch," I said. "Dad's in trouble."

He moved impatiently in the seat next to me. "What?" Behind the thick lenses his eyes grew wary. "Is he okay?"

"Not really. I mean physically he's okay, but —"

"What do you mean, then? Dad's in trouble?" Anxiety cracked his voice. I was desperate to comfort him even as my own voice trembled with each revelation. *Dad's down at the department with Tom* and *Looks like he and his girlfriend had an argument* and *Actually, nobody knows exactly what happened, but Suz Craig is dead.* Arch's reaction — dumbfounded denial — was followed by panic.

"She's dead? Suz is dead? Are you sure?"

"Yes. I saw her body lying in a ditch when I drove by her house this morning. And your dad's under arrest." I took a deep breath. "He's been accused of killing her."

Arch looked out the window. Gail and Tina were seated, conversing, on the porch. The cat was in Tina's arms. "But . . . that doesn't make sense."

"Hon, I know."

He was silent, then said: "When will I get to see him?"

"I'm not sure."

"But, why were you driving by Ms. Craig's house in the first place?"

"Arch, please. I just wanted to avoid taking you to an empty house."

He faced me again. His voice rose with confusion. "Whose empty house? Why? What are you talking about?"

"Dad's! I mean, I thought he might have spent the night at Suz's place and not be home yet! I . . . was just trying to see where he was so I could spare you some pain," I gabbled helplessly. "I didn't know what I was going to stumble on to."

"Well, you didn't spare me any pain," my son said harshly, and turned away from me to stare out the window again.

As I drove the van back into Aspen Meadow, I did my best to act loving and patient. It didn't work. Arch had retreated into silence.

Why did John Richard Korman continue to mess up our lives? That was the question to which there was no answer. My knuckles whitened as I gripped the steering wheel.

At home Arch slammed out of the van ahead of me. Macguire had let Jake into our fenced backyard. The hound howled with delight at our arrival. Anticipating my worry about the neighbors' complaints, Arch became intent on getting Jake back into the house. I sat in the van contemplating Arch's short legs and flapping T-shirt and the crisis that confronted us.

My son would talk to me about how he

was feeling, I felt sure. Only he would do it in his own time. We always worked things out, I told myself. But I felt a twinge of uncertainty. I slid out of the van and trod carefully across the wooden deck I'd added to the back of the house some years before. Suddenly I stopped and stared at the diagonal slats. *The deck, the doggone deck.* Dizzily, I sank down on a cushioned redwood chair.

The deck had been my idea. My present to John Richard on our fifth anniversary. Oh, Lord, why was I thinking about this now? Because everything was erupting: my life, my family, my mind. The world felt like a pinball machine flashing TILT with no way to turn it off.

I gazed down at the deck. I had saved the money out of what John Richard called my "grocery allowance," what I later referred to, once I learned how much money he was really earning, as my "pittance." Naively, I had thought the deck would be a wonderful place for us to gather as a family. I'd even believed that John Richard and I would enjoy watching the progress of its construction. Ha.

I ran my fingers over the smooth redwood railing that always smelled so wonderful after a rainstorm. When the builders started, John Richard had second-guessed and criticized every aspect of the construction. *Why red-wood? It's too expensive. Why do you have to have it so big?* The next day: *Why is it so small? Why don't you add a barbecue?* and despite the fact that he wasn't contributing, he'd yell *This is costing a mint! Do you think I'm made of money?* In the end, he'd declared he was never going to sit out on our lovely redwood deck. So the deck stood empty. To his friends, he'd laughed about my project. He'd called it Goldy's Golden Goof.

After the divorce papers were signed and I had deposited my settlement check, my very first act had been to drive to Howard Lorton Galleries, the most exclusive furniture store in Denver. There I'd impulsively ordered a thousand dollars' worth of deck furniture.

Why rehash old history now? Once again my brain supplied a warning. *Because he's barged into your life again, and it's not just to declare bankruptcy.*

Watch your back, Goldy.

Chapter 7

Inside the house, Arch was on the phone. He looked at me solemnly, then shook his head.

"ReeAnn," he said impatiently into the receiver. Had John Richard's secretary called us? Or had Arch just phoned her? "I don't *know* what you're supposed to tell the patients. Better see who's on call for Dad . . . I don't know! Look, would you please ask him to give me a ring if he phones in?" His voice cracked. "No! How should I know what they're doing to him?" He banged the phone down and regarded me dolefully. After a moment he said, "You look terrible, Mom."

"Thanks."

"Why don't you cook or something?"

I glanced around the kitchen. *Cook or something.* The rows of cupcakes sat waiting to be iced. The remains of my coffee fixings lay in a heap by the sink. Nothing beckoned.

"Mom, please." Arch gave me a quick hug, then pulled back, embarrassed. "It's going to be okay. It's just all a big mistake."

"Oh, honey . . ." But words failed.

"Let me go see if Macguire went back to bed after he let Jake out," Arch announced abruptly. "It's time for him to be up, no matter what, don't you think?"

"Yeah, sure." I shook my head as Arch left to rouse our boarder. To keep from brooding, I made another espresso.

"I'm up, I'm up," Macguire Perkins hollered through the closed door of his room. His muffled voice echoed mournfully down the stairs.

I slugged down the coffee, hauled myself over to our walk-in refrigerator, and stared at the contents. Fixing breakfast for Macguire Perkins — maybe that was a *cook or something* challenge I could handle. Arch was right: I seemed to think more logically when preparing food, anyway. And with Macguire as a buffer, perhaps Arch and I would be able to discuss his father's status as a murder suspect without further fireworks. I heard more banging upstairs.

"I'm up, didn't you hear me?" called Macguire. "Why is everyone tormenting me?"

Good old Macguire, I thought as I got out eggs and butter. With no plans one year after graduating from the same prep school that Arch attended, Macguire had begun the summer working part-time for me. Macguire's father, the headmaster of Elk Park Prep, had agreed to let Macguire live alone in their house on the school grounds for three months. Meanwhile, Perkins senior was off to direct a summer seminar in Burlington, Vermont. When he started as my assistant, Macguire confessed that he was reluctantly trying to decide what to do with his life. What he wanted to do with his life wasn't catering, I discovered after he'd been working in the business a few weeks. Then Macguire made the announcement that he'd decided to become a police detective. Unfortunately, he'd run amok.

Against all advice, Macguire had tried to solve a case on his own. The result was that a criminal had savagely beaten him and — in a raging storm, by the side of the road — left him for dead. Macguire had ended up in the hospital with multiple bruises and lacerations. Unfortunately, that was just the beginning of his medical troubles. After being discharged from the hospital, he'd gone home to Elk Park, where he immediately developed strep throat that quickly evolved into full-blown infectious mononucleosis.

Headmaster Perkins had flown home and asked for my help. Macguire was unable to swallow anything more than liquids and began to shed weight at an alarming rate. During the first three weeks of July, he lost twenty pounds. His doctor said when Macguire finished his antibiotics, he needed rest, support, nutritious food, and very moderate exercise. But Headmaster Perkins couldn't picture trying to help his son get better while the two of them lived out of suitcases in a Vermont bed-and-breakfast, no matter how quaint the setting. That was when Perkins senior begged me to allow Macguire to live with us for the remainder of the summer.

"Just give the kid three squares a day. Or even three cubes. You know, steaks," he'd told me. A square meal or a cube steak? The headmaster thought he was hilarious. For the most part, Perkins senior was merely ridiculous. "Under your care, Goldy dear," he'd announced airily, "I have no doubt my son should recover nicely in a week or two."

I'd said yes, and as a result Macguire Perkins had been living with us since mid-July. But *recover nicely* was exactly what the teenager hadn't done. Of course, our observation of Macguire was inevitably colored by our experience with the now-absent Julian Teller, whose high energy, intellectual sharpness, and enthusiastic affection for our family had been hallmarks of his time with us. Julian

95

had done everything from loving Arch as if the two were the closest of brothers to cooking wildly inventive vegetarian dishes for our family meals. To Julian's surprise but not to ours, he'd been offered a great summer job working in the kitchen of a chic hotel in upstate New York. We felt his absence deeply.

When Tom and Arch and I had agreed to take Macguire in, I'd secretly hoped that Arch would somehow be the beneficiary, because he would have a new friend Julian's age.

Arch, sensing my motive, had mumbled, "It's like when your dog dies, you can't just go out and buy a new dog."

"Arch, give him a chance," I'd protested.

"Trust me, Mom, it's not the same."

But despite Arch's initial reluctance, he'd grudgingly accepted having Macguire as a boarder. Macguire was slow-moving, honest, and sweet. Furthermore, he presented a much more challenging rehabilitation situation than we'd ever faced with Jake, Arch's beloved bloodhound, who'd been fired from law enforcement for being suspected of being unreliable. Which the dear dog wasn't, as it turned out.

The problem with Macguire, however, was that he would not eat. He said he couldn't — he wasn't hungry. Wouldn't or couldn't, the result was the same. The boy would not take nourishment.

In the breakfast department Macguire shunned bacon and sausage; scrambled, poached, boiled, or fried eggs; toast or English muffins; ready-to-eat cereal, oatmeal, or granola; yogurt shakes; fresh fruit of any kind. I had yet to convince him to swallow anything more than orange juice. He claimed his stomach hurt whenever he ate even the smallest morsels. His doctor had proclaimed, "When he gets hungry, he'll eat." In the three weeks he'd been with us, however, that hadn't happened. But I was ever hopeful. Now I set aside the eggs and butter and went back to our refrigerator. There I retrieved a bowl of homemade chocolate pudding left over from a catering job. I ladled spoonfuls of it into a crystal parfait glass.

Arch clomped back into the kitchen after completing his summoning duty, flopped into a chair, and turned doleful eyes to me.

"When do you suppose I'll be able to talk to Dad? He hasn't called his office and ReeAnn is having a fit."

"I don't know," I answered truthfully.

"But . . . is Dad in jail? When will he get out?" Arch insisted.

"Um, I'm not sure. He's probably being processed."

"Oh, great. Like liverwurst."

I let this pass, set the chocolate pudding on the table, and started to mix up a batch of hockey-puck biscuits. If Macguire wouldn't go for traditional bacon-and-egg-type breakfast-taste sensations, perhaps he'd flip for chocolate and biscuits.

While Arch contemplated the table, wrestling with his confusion, I sifted the flour with the other dry ingredients while my food processor cut through the shortening. I mixed in the buttermilk, patted out the dough, cut it into circles on a sheet, and set the sheet in the oven. Then I cleaned the doser and refilled my espresso machine with water. This would be my fourth quadruple-shot of the morning, but I desperately craved the clearheadedness that caffeine usually offered. Unfortunately, such clarity had eluded me ever since my gruesome discovery on Jacobean Drive.

Nevertheless, the coffee-making process gave me time to think about how to deal with Arch. I wished that I hadn't told Marla it was okay to leave. She'd have been able to help me with this minefield of a dialogue, cowardly as that sounded. Arch's questions were difficult to answer, not only because

they were delivered in an alternately pleading and hostile manner, but also because
the answers themselves were sure not to
please him. When would John Richard be
freed? How was I going to tell my son that
bail was not supposed to be granted in capi-
tal cases? Of course, occasionally something
was wrong with the arrest or the evidence,
or the judge had a surpassing reason for
granting bail. Sometimes the suspect's standing in the community was so impeccable that
the judge let him or her out once a huge bail
had been set. But John Richard's reputation
was far from impeccable.

I took a deep breath and poured Macguire
some juice. "Your father's lawyer will go before a judge first thing Monday morning and
at least *try* to get him out on bail. I have to
tell you, Arch, it would be unusual for the
request to be granted. And if bail is set very
high, I don't know if your father has that
kind of cash or equity in his house."

Arch's face darkened and he turned away
from me. On some level he seemed to be
aware of his father's financial problems.
"What about Tom? Are they going to assign
Tom to this case?"

"I doubt that very much," I said carefully.
"It would probably be viewed as a conflict
of interest."

Arch flashed back around. His forehead was so furrowed with alarm that I felt my heart slam against my chest. *You bet it's a conflict of interest,* I could imagine him saying. But to my surprise his distress went the other way. "They're not going to assign Tom? But I thought you said he was the best the department has! If they don't assign Tom, how will we ever prove Dad's innocent?" I was speechless.

So Arch's question hung unanswered as Macguire Perkins galumphed slowly into the kitchen. His yellowed eyes were difficult to look at, as were his hollow cheeks and emaciated frame. When I first met him, he'd been strong, a basketball player and bodybuilder. Now, thin and lethargic, Macguire seemed to teeter on his long legs like a precariously staked scarecrow.

"Well," he murmured without enthusiasm, "how's everybody?"

"Not so hot," Arch mumbled.

Macguire sat down at the table, ran his fingers through his long, unevenly shorn red hair — going to the barber gave him a headache — and stared forlornly at the pudding and juice. Then he sighed and pushed both away. Undaunted, I poured him a glass of milk. He took one sip. When I pulled the hot, puffed biscuits out of the oven, he said,

"I hope you didn't make those for me. Because I can't even look at them. Sorry."

"It's okay," I lied encouragingly, and set the pan on a rack to cool. So much for today's hearty breakfast.

"My dad's been arrested," Arch announced in a tone that said, *Can you believe the injustices of this world?*

"Bummer," replied Macguire. He took another tiny sip of milk, then said, "My dad was arrested once, but he doesn't want anybody to know."

"For what?" asked Arch, who of course wanted to know.

"Drunk and disorderly," Macguire replied matter-of-factly. "It was after my mom left and Daddy-o couldn't handle it."

Arch closed his eyes and shook his head. I turned away and ran hot water and soap into the biscuit-batter bowl.

"I have to cater tonight," I announced. "Stanley Cup celebration party. Marla is calling Todd to see if you can go over there, Arch. Do you feel up to helping me, Macguire?"

"Can I see how I feel later?" His smile was wan. "I want to help. You know folks think that if there's a thin caterer, they won't gain any weight eating the food you serve."

Before I could voice my opinion about this

theory, Arch sighed. "I don't want to go to Todd's," he said morosely.

"Man," said Macguire, "you are in one tight mood, big A. Why don't you go for a walk with me? We'll go visit Kids' Vids if you want, see if they have any cool new games."

Arch sighed again. "It's going to rain. Besides, Dad might call."

Macguire strained his neck to look outside, where the sun shone between a few drifts of cloud. "What, you predict the weather? That's pretty cool." By the door, Jake let loose with another of his howls. "Come on, buddy, we'll go by your dad's office and see if there's any news. We'll even take the dog. If it rains, we'll all get wet."

"Oh, you just want to go see ReeAnn," Arch accused.

When Macguire's jaundiced-appearing face blushed the color of a sweet potato, I knew Arch had found a target. I said, "ReeAnn probably won't be in any mood for company."

"Sure she will," Arch countered. "ReeAnn likes to see Macguire. They took driver ed together, and now she has a Porsche. He's had a crush on her forever. And not even because of the Porsche," he glumly added.

"Gee, Arch," Macguire said, "thank you

for pointing all this out. You and the hound dog want to walk or not?"

Arch regarded me warily from behind his thick glasses. "So can Dad call me from the jail or what?"

"You can call him and then he'll call you back. But I'd say you might be better off waiting. Besides, as you know, he'll have to call his office at some point."

"All right," said Arch, defeated. He took Jake's leash from its hook on the wall and departed.

"So what's Dr. Korman been arrested for?" Macguire asked as soon as the door closed on Arch.

I said, "Murder." Outside, Jake howled with happiness.

Macguire sipped the milk and didn't miss a beat. "Oh yeah? Who'd he kill?"

"Macguire, if you want to go into police work, you need to learn to say, 'Whom did they *say* he killed?' "

"Okay, who'd they *say* he bumped off?"

"His girlfriend. Suz Craig."

Macguire's rusty eyebrows shot up. "Uh-oh. How'd he do it? Wait. How're they *saying* she bought it?"

"Beaten to death, looked like. The technical term would be multiple blunt-force injuries, I think." I had another flash of Suz's bruised and broken body in the ditch.

"Huh," said Macguire. "Too bad." On the deck, Arch was having a noisy heart-to-heart with Jake about the attachment of the leash. "So this dead broad was your ex-husband's chick? Or . . . one of them, anyway?"

I took a steadying sip of coffee. The only activity Macguire energetically pursued during his convalescence was reading Raymond Chandler. Unfortunately, it sometimes took me a moment to translate the private-dick lingo. "Why do you ask that?"

Macguire frowned. "Uh, ask what?"

I said patiently, "Why did you ask if Suz Craig was *one* of his . . . girlfriends?"

"Well, wasn't she? I thought he had a lot of girlfriends."

"Yes," I said cautiously. "But I thought Suz was his *only* girlfriend. His only current girlfriend."

"Oh." He scowled at the milk he'd scarcely touched. "Well."

"Macguire, I've tried to put as much distance as possible between my ex-husband's love life and myself. I don't ask for any details."

"So, what're you saying? You're feeling bad because his girlfriend croaked, huh?"

"Yes." I exhaled. "A woman is dead, and like it or not, at the moment I'm feeling extremely guilty because I never pressed charges against him and got him sent to jail. If I had, maybe Suz Craig would be alive today."

"Don't feel too bad, Goldy." His face assumed its typically philosophical expression. "Nobody can go back in time. It's a bummer, but there it is." He shrugged.

I took another discreet sip of my coffee and bit into one of the biscuits. It was moist, hot, and comforting. "Macguire, do you know if my ex-husband had *other* current girlfriends besides Suz Craig? Did you hear or see something . . . at his office, say? Why did you say 'one' of his girlfriends?"

Macguire scraped back his chair and avoided my eyes. "Uh," he replied slowly, "maybe I should just talk to Tom about it."

"Probably that would be a good idea. But it's unlikely Tom will be assigned to this case."

"Bummer." He sighed.

"Did Dr. Korman have another girlfriend that you know about?"

"Oh, well, no, not exactly. Maybe I'm just imagining things because I was, like, jealous. I just thought . . . that he had something going with ReeAnn."

"You saw John Richard and ReeAnn together? Away from the office?"

"Well, yeah. He was over at ReeAnn's house once, in the evening, when I dropped by to give her a book about Porsches. I mean, I didn't have to take it over. I was like, taking it instead of mailing it because I just wanted to see her. But Dr. Korman was over there and they were cooking out."

"How long ago was this?"

"Oh . . . end of the school year, I think. You know Arch and I walk over to the office sometimes. But ReeAnn and I never talk about any deep stuff while Arch is visiting his dad. Or seeing if his dad wants to visit." He thought for a moment. "But one time I did ask her if she wanted to go to the CD store with me —"

"Macguire."

"Yeah. Well, when we went to the store, we looked at CDs and talked about this and that and I asked ReeAnn if there were, like, any guys in her life at the moment, and she got all secretive and said, maybe. Then I asked her about her job, and she had all kinds of things to say. She didn't like the secretary who had worked there before her, because that woman was fired to make way for ReeAnn. Or so ReeAnn thought."

"Beatrice Waxman."

"She called her Battleaxe Woman. Battleaxe Woman wouldn't help ReeAnn learn the filing."

"Filing?"

"Filing, filing claims, something. But the person ReeAnn really hated big-time was this Craig lady with the HMO. Suz Craig. Some hotshot veep, right?"

"A vice-president, yes."

Macguire shook his head, remembering. "Well, Tom might want to get somebody from the department to talk to ReeAnn about Ms. Craig. ReeAnn was trying to work on billing with the HMO, and Ms. Craig drove her crazy. I'm telling you, I don't know why, but ReeAnn really hated that Craig woman's guts."

Chapter 8

From our front porch I watched thin, sweat-suit-clad Macguire lope painfully down the sidewalk after Arch, who had changed into too-large green Bermuda shorts and a faded green T-shirt — both garments left behind by Julian. With his short arms outstretched and his glasses slipping down his wrinkled nose, Arch tugged unsuccessfully on Jake's leash. The bloodhound's long tawny legs lunged briskly down the pavement. When the unlikely trio spun past the corner store in the direction of John Richard's office, I wearily turned to go back to my kitchen. *Your dad's under arrest.* Despite Marla's beliefs to the contrary, no amount of walking was going to make that better.

At the front door I was brought up short by the security system panel that had been installed two summers previously. Back then, after almost four years of being on my own, I'd begun to go out again. To go out *occasionally*. To go out occasionally with *men*. And just when I'd thought John Richard had mended his ways, his behavior suddenly became a problem. Why should I have been surprised? He hadn't liked the idea of me dating. To demonstrate his opposition to my new social life, he'd threatened a reduction in child support — through his lawyer, of course — and then had taken to driving slowly past our house. Well, I'd been a psych major in college; I knew passive-aggressive behavior when I saw it. Amid the Jerk's protests of uninvolvement — *I never went near your place, bitch* — I'd gotten the system, both for deterrent and for actual security. And by and large, the system had done the trick.

This morning John Richard Korman had once again been utterly adamant concerning his innocence. But we weren't talking about cruising past someone's house or making financial threats. Still, he'd almost convinced *me* he hadn't killed Suz Craig. At least for a brief moment, I'd suspended disbelief and accepted his story. Now, of course, I was equally certain he'd been lying. *They'd mixed it up,* he'd said. John Richard Korman always had an explanation ready for losing his temper and beating the living daylights out of whatever woman was offending him. People couldn't change that much in two years. People couldn't change that much in a *lifetime.* I made a mental note to ask Tom if Suz Craig's house had a security system.

I was about to punch the panel buttons when a sheriff's department car pulled up in front of the house. Two women got out — Sergeant Beiner and a uniformed woman I didn't recognize. I nodded and waved. Of course. Sergeant Beiner had said she'd be coming over later. I would have to answer more questions. Well, maybe they could tell *me* a thing or two.

Sergeant Beiner's step was spry as she strode up our sidewalk. Her high, feathered top of blond-gray hair shook when she asked me how I was doing. When I said I was passable, she smiled briefly, showing slender, yellow teeth, and asked if she could run a few more things by me.

"Deputy Irving will take notes."

Deputy Irving, a curly-haired brunette with a plump face and a uniform that pulled tightly around her midsection, nodded. Deputy Irving was under thirty, with no wedding ring.

"I'm sure you know the questions," Sergeant Beiner began in a soothing, apologetic tone. When she smiled, her face wrinkled pleasantly. "Down at the department, we're aware of your record of detection."

"Thanks," I replied. "I want to help."

"We also remember that you managed to break somebody out of jail once. Somebody who was innocent, as it turned out."

"You have nothing to worry about this time," I assured her. "Would you like some coffee? I've had the equivalent of about sixteen cups today, I think. One more can't hurt."

Both women shook their heads. I invited them to be seated on the porch chairs. When the three of us were settled, Deputy Irving dutifully pulled out her notebook and recorded my name and address. Again I told the sergeant about spotting Suz Craig in the ditch by her home around a quarter to seven and about phoning for medical help.

"Did you suspect she was dead?" Sergeant Beiner asked mildly.

I looked away. "Yes. But I know the drill too, Sergeant Beiner. That's why I phoned EMS."

"A woman on the street named Lynn Tollifer saw you through her front window. She didn't know why you went back to Schulz's car after starting up the street. She figured you were calling about vandalism. Mrs. Tollifer said she couldn't see the ditch from her window. See the body, you know."

"My friend Marla Korman got a call from Lynn about Suz, and Lynn said her son told

111

her about Suz . . ." I paused. "You don't think vandals had anything to do with . . ."

Sergeant Beiner shrugged. "You were there for the arrest." It wasn't a question. She regarded me with the same calm manner that infused her voice. "Of course you've got somebody to vouch for your whereabouts during the night." That wasn't a question, either.

"Tom can vouch for me. He came in at midnight. What exactly did Lynn's son see?"

Sergeant Beiner gave me the same wrinkle-faced smile she had when she arrived at the house. "How well did you know Suz Craig?"

I tried not to envision the pale corpse in the ditch when Suz's name was mentioned. Impossible. "I catered for her once," I replied. "And of course she was my ex-husband's girlfriend. His current girlfriend. Or at least one of them," I added. Deputy Irving scribbled away. "I'm not sure if he had other girlfriends, but he might have. His secretary, ReeAnn Collins, might know. She keeps his calendar. Plus, it's possible Ree-Ann might have been seeing John Richard herself."

When asked, I spelled ReeAnn's name for them.

Sergeant Beiner rocked back in her chair.

"How long ago did you cater this event for Ms. Craig?"

"Little less than a month. July tenth, I think. No, wait, the eleventh. It was a Friday, and the group of people had all been visiting for a week at the Denver office of the AstuteCare HMO. ACHMO."

"What group of people?"

"Human Resources. That's what one of them told me. ACHMO is based in Minneapolis and that's where the team was from."

"Did any of them talk to you?"

I thought back. Steamed trout, vegetable frittata, coleslaw, wild rice salad with porcini mushrooms, fruit cup, chocolate truffles. Everyone had seemed to be in a good mood. "They were happy. Suz seemed pleased, too, with all her landscaping underway. She was pointing out the plants that were being put in as part of a landscaping project. I think it was being done by Aspen Meadow Nursery."

A look passed between the two officers. Sergeant Beiner regarded me with pursed lips, then said, "Suz Craig fired Aspen Meadow Nursery. By all accounts, she was pretty hard to work for."

"Really? Well, I think she fired the nursery because one of her department heads fell down the stone steps. He sprained his ankle, and she mentioned she was going to fire her landscapers." I paused. "Actually, I'm surprised. She seemed so excited about their work."

"Was Suz Craig a demanding client when you catered for her?" Beiner wanted to know.

I thought for a minute. Had Suz been hard to work for? Not even slightly. Although most of my clients were wonderful, I'd had enough horrendous ones to know the type. "I didn't have any problem with her. It was a one-shot deal, though, not a long-term project. If anything, she seemed unusually accommodating." I remembered Suz, her blond ponytail bobbing, her shiny blue silk skirt skimming her knees as she stepped along the newly laid path. "She praised me to the skies for my food, and insisted I go around her property with the guests. She even helped me with the cleanup." When the two policewomen said nothing, I added, "That's unusual, believe me."

"Were these people from Minneapolis still around when she was so magnanimously cleaning up?"

"All five department heads were there. The Provider Relations man left because of his injury. He was the one who fell down the steps. The HR guy asked me for a recipe."

"HR?"

"Human Resources. The head of HR at the Denver office of AstuteCare is Brandon Yuille. Do you know him? His mother died last year, and his father, Mickey Yuille, bought the Aspen Meadow Pastry Shop not long after. Now that Mickey keeps baker's hours, I hardly ever see him. But I'm friends with the Yuilles. We swap recipes and food. I made them some fudge last week and they gave me some Thai peanut sauce." I paused. "So. That's who was there that I can remember."

Beiner raised her eyebrows. "All those people were still around when Ms. Craig was doing the dishes with you?"

"Well, yes."

"Maybe she wanted to impress the Minneapolis people with her versatility. Do you know anything else about her?" Beiner prompted me.

"She was single. Wealthy. Smart. Very pretty."

"Right."

I sighed deeply, because I knew what was coming next.

"Okay, Mrs. Schulz," said Beiner. "You have any idea why someone would want Suz Craig dead?"

If Arch were here, he would say, *"Don't answer, Mom."* And of course, really, I didn't

115

know that John Richard would want Suz dead. But he could lose his temper so easily. Especially if the woman with command of the purse strings had pulled those strings shut.

"My ex-husband, Dr. John Richard Korman, is having money problems. Severe money problems. He's a member doctor of the AstuteCare HMO, they pay him a salary. What I heard was —"

"What you heard from whom?"

"His other ex-wife. Marla Korman. You might want to talk to her. Marla told me that John Richard hadn't yet received his bonus. Apparently, Suz was the one who decided whether he got it or not."

Beiner nodded; Irving wrote and flipped a page.

"Know about her relationships with anyone else? Neighbors? Friends?"

"She was fairly new in the community. To be fair, I think she moved up here to be closer to John Richard."

"What did your ex-husband say to you about their relationship?"

What did he ever say to me about a relationship he was having? *The woman I'm with now is so much nicer/smarter/prettier/more together than you.* I shrugged. "The usual. He adored her."

"Mrs. Schulz? Does your ex-husband have any reason to think *you* disliked Suz Craig?"

I couldn't help laughing. "John Richard believed I was jealous of Suz. Which of course I was not. I really didn't know too much about their relationship. He was going out with her last night, I know that. Then this morning he mentioned that they'd 'mixed it up.' That's one of his terms for beating up a woman. Another one is 'getting physical.' " As if his losses of temper were bouts. "You know that my complaints of his violence against me, including photographs of my face and body, are part of police record."

Her voice a tone lower, Beiner said, "You're saying there's not much to like in John Richard Korman."

"I divorced him."

The sergeant made a circular motion with her finger and Deputy Irving closed her notebook. In the same low tone, Beiner asked, "So do you have a theory on this? I'd really like to know."

Unexpectedly, the old rage surged up. The thought of sitting on my porch and calmly saying, *Yes, I think he beat this woman to death,* made me ill. I clenched my teeth, cleared my throat, swallowed hard. "The facts of the case will tell you what happened," I said finally. "Just beware of John Richard Korman. He's the most accomplished liar you'll ever meet." When no more questions were forthcoming, I asked, "Are we done?"

The two women stood. Sergeant Beiner followed Deputy Irving down the steps. Then she turned back.

"Are you sure you're all right, Mrs. Schulz? You look kind of green around the gills. Do you need a victim advocate?"

"I need Tom."

The sergeant nodded. She said, "I'll call him from the car," and strode away.

Back in my kitchen, I decided against calling Marla. It was getting on to late morning. No matter how difficult, I had to put this catastrophe behind me. I had to do the rest of the food prep for the hockey party. Besides, Marla was undoubtedly on the phone at this very moment, chatting up her country-club cronies to glean everything she could about Suz Craig and her relationship with John Richard Korman. Marla would give me an exhaustive report of her findings before long, of that I could bet the contents of my refrigerator.

I tried to stir the chilled frosting with a wooden spoon. Too cold. I stared at my silent phone. Good old Marla. While I'd done everything in my power to distance myself from John Richard, the fact that we had Arch in common meant I had to deal with my ex-husband, at the very least, on a biweekly basis. Marla, on the other hand, had no children in common with the Jerk, had no reason to see him at all, in fact, and yet she took the greatest delight in following, and reporting on, his every escapade. Her way of despising John Richard was to gloat over and widely publicize each of his setbacks, even if they were slight. And when he had some kind of triumph, like being bought out by ACHMO, her compensation for his good fortune was that she got a cut of the deal.

I set aside the icing, booted up my computer, and studied the menu for tonight's party. The last thing I wanted to do was work an event. My thoughts slipped back to poor, sweet, confused Arch, and I suddenly realized I'd been selfish. *He* needed a victim advocate. I put in a quick call to the office of the therapist Arch had worked with several years ago. An answering machine at the shrink's office picked up. Feeling disconsolate, I left a message saying my fourteen-year-old son was going through a crisis and needed help asap.

Work, I told myself. *You'll feel better.* The kitchen clock was closing in on eleven-thirty. My contract time for the party setup was five o'clock, and I had miles to go before packing up and taking off.

I filled my pasta pentola with water and set it on to boil. Three salads for this evening and one of them was . . . One of them was . . .

One of his girlfriends was . . . John Richard had a girlfriend besides Suz Craig? Black-haired, perky, distance-cyclist Ree-Ann Collins, of all people? Of course, I'd always been convinced that John Richard had fired his previous secretary, stodgy, reliable Beatrice Waxman, and hired nubile ReeAnn, because of the latter's looks. I doubted ReeAnn — whose father, according to Macguire, had promised her a Porsche if she'd get a job — had any prowess with word processing. Or, heaven only knew, computerized billing.

And how did Macguire fit into all this? He'd gone over to ReeAnn's townhouse — another gift from Daddy — at dinnertime, with the flimsy excuse of delivering a book. He'd found John Richard there before him, barbecuing with his secretary. Dinner with the secretary did not an affair make, although with John Richard it probably did. Well, I would tell Tom, as I'd promised Macguire. And I would go over to visit ReeAnn, I suddenly decided.

The hockey-party menu indicated that I had promised Mediterranean orzo salad, a vegetable mélange I'd dubbed Grilled Slapshot Salad, and Vietnamese Slaw, all of which needed to be prepared and chilled. While the pasta was cooking, Marla called.

"That didn't take long," I commented as I began to pit Kalamata olives.

"Give me a break, I've been worried about you. How are you doing?" Her voice trembled with concern. I felt the usual pang of gratitude that she was such a long-suffering friend.

"I'm not doing very well at all." I rinsed my hands. "It's like I'm having post-traumatic stress disorder. Every time I look around this house, something reminds me of the Jerk."

"Take a Valium. Go lie down for a while."

"For crying out loud, Marla, I've got a party tonight."

She paused to take a bite of food: *her* tranquilizer. "Oh, right, the McCrackens' hockey party. You're going to have to wear a T-shirt that says 'I don't know anything.' Otherwise, the guests are going to drive you nuts wanting to know what's going on. Plus

121

Patricia's husband is a doctor, isn't he?"

"Her first husband was. Skip. Skip interned with John Richard and Ralph Shelton. Don't you remember?"

"Not really. That was before my time with the Jerk, honey."

"Well, Skip dumped Patricia when she said she wanted to adopt a child. I got to know Patricia when she was going through the divorce. Her new husband is a dentist. Clark."

"Still, their friends all know the Jerk, so you're going to get a slew of questions."

Ah, Aspen Meadow, which alternated between being intimate and incestuous. "I've already had a slew of questions. The cops just left."

"What did they want?"

"Oh, the usual. What did I see. What did I know about her. What did I know about the two of them."

"Hmph. Have you heard anything else? About the two of them, I mean?"

"No." I sliced the olives into delicate black bits. Then, as usual, my curiosity got the better of me. I murmured, "How about you?"

She took another noisy bite of whatever she was chewing and then washed it down with something liquid. "Well, I've been trying, God knows. I've been waiting ages for the Jerk to get his due, although I'm truly sorry Suz Craig had to die for it." She paused. "Okay. For one thing, John Richard and Suz were at the club bar last night, drinking and arguing almost until the place closed at midnight."

"Aspen Meadow Country Club?" I asked. "Says who?"

"Yes, the country club. You know how John Richard loves to see folks and be seen. And the person who said so was Fay Shelton, current wife of Dr. Ralph Shelton, recently fired by ACHMO by none other than Suz Craig herself." She paused. "Or so I heard. Hold on, there's somebody at my door."

I moved the olives aside and began on some fat, ripe tomatoes that smelled so delicately sweet, I was tempted to pop a couple of juicy red chunks right into my mouth. But the health inspector had recently sent out a sign to be posted in all commercial kitchens: NO SMOKING, EATING, OR DRINKING IN THE FOOD AREA! USE PLASTIC GLOVES WHEN HANDLING RAW MEAT! Across the state, chefs had promptly denounced the first admonition. How were they supposed to serve what they were preparing if they couldn't taste it? A subsequent missive from the inspector allowed as how we could taste with a plastic spoon, which was to be immediately tossed out. As Macguire and Arch would say, *Whatever.*

"Can you believe that?" Marla asked when she returned to the phone. "Frances Markasian from the *Mountain Journal* here at my doorstep already, wanting to interview me about what a bloodsucker my husband was. I told her *ex*-husband and suggested she go back to covering the doll show. Then I got this idea: 'Press Babsie —' "

"Frances knows about Suz? She knows about John Richard's arrest?"

"She knows *all* about it. Maybe she's got one of those police-band radios. More likely, somebody who lives on Jacobean called her. Frances insisted she needed to talk to me. Said it was urgent. What would be urgent about talking to me?"

"What in the world did you say?"

"I told her to come back on Monday," Marla replied gleefully. "I know I'll have more to report on the Jerk's bloodsuckiness by then."

"For heaven's sake." I glanced at the clock. Nearly noon. "Exactly when was Ralph Shelton fired?" I tried to remember the last time I'd catered any event where the Sheltons were present, but drew a blank. I'd known Ralph when John Richard was in

124

medical school with him, and Ralph had a different wife and a daughter I adored. But when your marital situation changes, many of the friendships sadly seem to evaporate. "Where do the Sheltons live, exactly? Aren't they over there near John Richard?"

"Yes, of course. On Chaucer, I think. Ralph's a huge hockey fan so you'll probably see him tonight. Listen, though, here's something else I found out from Fay. Her hubbie, Ralph, wasn't the only one who had problems with Suz Craig. There was a nurse with a gambling addiction. ACHMO didn't fancy one of their RNs taking the bus up to Central City and avidly playing the slots, hour after hour."

"Gambling? Do you know the nurse's name? Would Fay?"

"She didn't say, but I could ask her. On second thought, the word is that Ralph Shelton has a temper, which he usually reserves for yelling at referees at Avalanche games. If I act nosy, he might slam me into the glass. Metaphorically speaking, of course. You're more subtle, Goldy. *You* should go talk to him."

"Oh, sure. What am I, the local gal who deals with bad-tempered doctors?" I heard Tom's Chrysler roll into the driveway.

"How's Arch handling his father being arrested?" Marla asked.

"Wretchedly. He and Macguire are out for a walk now."

"Did Arch like Suz?"

I sighed. "Arch never likes or dislikes John Richard's girlfriends. He just tolerates them. It's a survival mechanism."

"You know he's going to want you to help him clear his dad. You've acquired a reputation as a woman who can nose around criminal cases like that godawful bloodhound of his."

I groaned. "Yeah, sure. This is one criminal case I'm going to keep my nose out of, thanks all the same."

"Listen," she insisted, as I heard Tom's footsteps approach on the deck. His slow trudge signaled that things were not going well. "You could drop by the Sheltons' place on your way to the McCrackens', Goldy. Say you got lost, need directions, and" — here she raised her voice to a trill — "oh, *by the way*, Ralph, old buddy, any ideas about what John Richard and Suz Craig were squabbling about last night? Think he got mad enough at the club bar that he went home and beat her to death?"

"Marla —"

"On second thought, Ralph baby," she trilled, undeterred, "were you so mad at her for canning you that *you* went home and killed her? Keep your hockey helmet on now, Ralph, and your stick down —"

"Please, I *have* to go."

"Promise you'll call me if you have any more post-traumatic whatever-it-is flashes."

I hung up.

Tom lumbered into the kitchen and headed straight for the sink to wash his hands. I suspected it was less because of my careful training than it was his desire to rid himself of whatever psychological muck he was bringing home from the sheriff's department. His face seemed haggard and downcast. My heart sank.

"I'm sorry," I blurted out, "it looks as if you've been dealing with John Richard."

"Don't be sorry," he said as he dropped into one of the kitchen chairs. He had pulled on blue jeans and a navy cotton shirt when I'd called him this morning. Despite the casual clothes, he didn't look as if he'd had anything close to a casual day. He rubbed his eyes, then added, "It's not your fault he is the way he is. Never was."

"He's like herpes," I said. "You just never know when he's going to erupt."

Tom offered no reply. I glanced at him expecting a smile, but his handsome face stayed set in deep thought, his lovely liquid green eyes fixed on the table. I turned back to the orzo salad.

The densely fragrant chèvre cheese fell into appetizing bits as my knife sliced through it. I chopped fragrant fresh basil and crisp stalks of celery, then mixed them in with the orzo. Next I whisked seasonings into balsamic vinegar and began to beat in garlic-flavored oil for an emulsion. When the dressing turned thick and creamy, I poured it over the orzo and vegetables, then stirred it carefully. Although I knew the salad should chill, I was ravenous. I delicately mixed in the chèvre, then reached for a plastic spoon to have a taste. When I put the spoonful into my mouth, the pungent Mediterranean flavors of crumbly cheese and garlic-robed pasta almost made me swoon.

I turned to Tom. "Hungry? I'll bet you haven't had anything besides vending-machine coffee and Danish."

"Sure. I'll take whatever you've got going."

I ladled out a large bowl of the warmly fragrant pasta salad. On a whim, even though it was just past noon, I poured him a glass of Chianti. I figured he needed it. Then I poured myself one, figuring I needed it even more.

Mediterranean Orzo Salad

1 cup (6 ounces) uncooked orzo pasta

3 tablespoons finely chopped red onion

1 cup seeded, chopped fresh tomato (about 3 small tomatoes)

¼ cup chopped celery

2 tablespoons chopped fresh basil (or more if desired)

2 tablespoons finely chopped pitted Kalamata olives

2 tablespoons capers

1 teaspoon "grained" Dijon mustard

¼ teaspoon sugar

1 tablespoon balsamic vinegar

2 tablespoons garlic oil (available in specialty food shops, such as Williams-Sonoma)

Salt and freshly ground black pepper

3½ ounces chèvre, crumbled

Bring a large quantity of water to a boil and cook the orzo just until tender ("al dente"). Drain and allow to cool. Mix the pasta with the onion, tomato, celery, basil, olives, and capers. In a small bowl, whisk together the mustard, sugar, and vinegar. Gradually beat in the oil until an emulsion forms. Pour this vinaigrette over the pasta mixture and season with salt and pepper. Chill the salad. When it is cold, mix in the crumbled chèvre, then serve.

Serves 4

"This is absolutely delicious," he murmured appreciatively after the first few bites. "I'm sure the hockey folks will love it." I gave him a kiss, thanked him, tucked the rest of the salad into the walk-in refrigerator to chill, and turned to the mountain of mushrooms, onions, and zucchini I needed to trim for the Grilled Slapshot Salad.

I said, "Want me to keep working, or do you want me to sit with you for a bit?"

He shook his head. "Think I need my hand held?"

"No, I didn't mean —" I blurted out. But he held out his hand and I took it.

"No. Fault's mine, Miss G. I've been put in the background on this case and I'm blaming you, which I shouldn't. Actually, please stop worrying about *me*. You're the one who should be stressed out. My wife the caterer, the one who refuses to see a victim advocate no matter how bad things get."

"Oh, please."

"*Oh, please,* yourself, Miss G. Talk to me."

I sat at the table across from him and took a sip of wine. Its acrid taste burned into my chest. I sighed. "This . . . event. It's horrid. Whenever I stop chopping or cooking, the memories flood in. I'm desperate to know what's going on. At the same time, I want

131

— I *need* — it to be over."

He nodded. "Makes sense. Should we all go up to the cabin for a while?" Tom's lovely, remote log dwelling outside of Aspen Meadow had flooded this spring, and he'd lost his tenants. Tom and I had scrubbed the floors and walls. Over the Jerk's objections that we were spoiling Arch, we'd paid him to wash the windows. But we hadn't yet advertised for new renters. Maybe going to the cabin wasn't such a great notion. I knew Tom, Arch, and Macguire wouldn't relish being away from our home base for an extended time. And if I stayed up there alone, I'd brood and fret even more.

"No, thanks. I just need to work. Be with you all. And . . . although I know it's going to be tough, I'd like to keep informed on what's happening. Arch is going to have questions around the clock."

His fingers stroked my hair. "Okay. Keep cooking, if that's what you need to do. And I'd be happy to tell you what's going on. It'll make me feel as if *I'm* doing something on this case." He sounded glum.

I frowned at the vegetables. "There's one thing I told Beiner that you should know." I related to him Macguire's suspicion that ReeAnn Collins, John Richard's secretary for the past six months, was romantically involved with him. Tom put down his fork, retrieved his spiral notebook from his back pocket, and made a note. While I heated the kitchen stovetop grill for the Slapshot Salad, I shared Marla's news about John Richard and Suz's fight at the club last night, and that Suz had reportedly fired a doctor named Ralph Shelton and a nurse whose name I did not know.

"Yeah" — Tom shook his head — "there was some kind of problem with this Craig woman being able to keep people. We don't know much yet, but we do know that."

I nodded, then felt a pang of guilt. "Are you sure you want to talk to me about the case? I mean, after what happened last time, when Marla got into so much trouble?"

He looked at me intently. "Miss G. I can't believe you'd really want to get any more involved in this than you are already."

"Excuse me, but my first responsibility is to Arch. Whatever that looks like." I felt the edge creep into my voice and despised myself for it. Tom, after all, was not the enemy. "I'm sorry. I . . . just need to know what's going on. No surprises."

"Some cases have surprises. It's the nature of the work."

"Maybe so, but I need to know the surprises in this case before Arch does."

133

He sighed. I slathered slices of zucchini with a mixture of olive oil and minced garlic. When I laid the glistening wedges on the heated grill, Tom pushed his empty bowl aside.

"All right. Near as they can figure, Suz Craig died between three and five this morning. Rigor hadn't set in when the medics arrived, which is one of the reasons they tried to revive her. There are signs of a struggle in her house, pots and pans strewn about in the kitchen. The guys are out doing a neighborhood canvass asking questions, but so far there's very little."

"Two policewomen were over here."

"Beiner and Irving. They're good." His sandy eyebrows rose. "There was more vandalism in the country club sometime during the night. Looks like kids painting street signs and fences again, but who knows? One possibility is that Suz surprised the vandals somehow, and they killed her. On the other hand, only the club's walls and a few street signs were spray-painted last night. We thought we were dealing with late-at-night vandals, but we may be dealing with early-morning ones. Of course, that wouldn't explain why her kitchen pans were on the floor. Or why she died clutching a gold ID bracelet that said *'To JRK: You're the best. Love, SC.'*" He took a deep breath. "Korman, of

Grilled
Slapshot Salad

2 tablespoons extra-virgin olive oil

Salt and freshly ground pepper to taste

3 large or 4 small garlic cloves, pressed, or 1½ teaspoons finely minced garlic

3 medium-size or 4 small zucchini

8 ounces fresh whole mushrooms

1 sweet onion (sometimes called Mexican sweet onion or Peruvian sweet onion)

2 ears fresh or frozen corn, defrosted

1 tablespoon (or more) sherry vinaigrette (see Exhibition Salad with Meringue-Baked Pecans, page 483)

1 to 2 tablespoons chopped fresh basil

Whisk together the oil, salt, pepper, and garlic and divide it between two 9- by 13-inch glass pans. Slice the zucchini on the bias into ¼" slices, place the slices into one of the pans, and mix carefully with your hands so that all the zucchini slices are lightly coated with the oil-garlic mixture. Trim the stems of the mushrooms. Slice the onion horizontally into ¼" slices. Place the mushrooms, onion slices, and corn into the other glass pan and again mix carefully by hand so that all the vegetables are lightly coated with the oil-garlic mixture.

Oil and preheat the grill. Preheat the oven to 400°. Place the zucchini slices on the grill and cook briefly — no longer than 30 seconds — on one side only. Place the zucchini slices back into their glass pan, cooked side up, and put them into the oven while you prepare the rest of the salad (no longer than 10 minutes). Briefly grill the mushrooms, onion slices, and corn on all sides, until they have grill marks but are not cooked through. This should only take a few minutes. Remove the onion slices and mushrooms and set them aside to cool. Holding each ear of corn perpendicular to the cutting surface, slice off the kernels. Remove the zucchini from the oven. Combine the zucchini slices, mushrooms, onion slices, and corn kernels. Pour the vinaigrette over the vegetables and carefully stir in the fresh basil. Serve immediately or chill for no more than 1 hour.

Serves 4

course, is claiming someone stole his brace-let. He also says he left her house between midnight and one o'clock, after they had that little disagreement you were referring to."

I removed the grilled zucchini slices with their lovely diagonal dark stripes, then placed them in a separate, lightly oiled pan to finish in the oven. "Little disagreement, my Aunt Fanny. John Richard will drink and argue for *hours*. Sometimes he loses his temper right away, sometimes he waits, especially if he's trying to get something out of you. Like a bonus, say." I slipped the pan into the oven. The air was wonderfully fragrant. "I think he just snapped. Beat the daylights out of her, then had no idea she'd walk out of her house and go looking for help. That's my theory, anyway."

Tom shrugged. "He's been unwavering on the leaving-at-one story. But even if he did leave after assaulting her, if she walked out of her house and died from falling into that ditch, he's still our man."

"Tom, if there's something I know well, it's that John Richard lies. He lies so much it's exhausting to try to untangle what he says. This morning, when I saw those roses in his hand, I thought: *This is one of his lies.* It just comes naturally to him. I used to try to figure out why he lied. I thought it was because his mother was an alcoholic or because of the trouble with his father. But that's no excuse. He's still a pathological liar."

Tom actually chuckled. "Yeah, Miss G., they usually are." He pushed his chair out from the table. "How about a hug for a hard-working cop?"

I smiled and dumped the mushrooms on the hot grill, where they made a delicious hissing sound. Then Tom pulled me into his lap for a marvelous, tight embrace.

"Captain called me in for a heart-to-heart," he murmured into my ear. "They're appointing a district attorney's investigator to head the case. But I'm not officially *off* the homicide investigation. I'm just behind the scenes. Can't go anywhere or interrogate anyone or gather any evidence unless I take somebody with me. That's how they avoid conflict of interest."

"I thought you hated that D.A.'s investigator. He's always mooching food. What's his name?"

"Donny Saunders. The laziest guy in a four-state area. And arrogant on top of that." He sighed. "Better go get those mushrooms before they burn."

I jumped up and scooped the mushrooms into a large bowl, then placed golden ears of corn and thick, glistening onion slices on the grill. They hissed and sputtered and filled the kitchen with a divine scent. I flipped the slices and rotated the corn so the kernels browned evenly. When I was removing these, I felt Tom's arms gently circling my waist.

"I'm cooking," I reminded him as I turned off the burners.

He nuzzled my cheek and whispered, "Looks to me like you're almost done. And I'm not hearing Arch, Macguire, and Jake. Can that possibly mean we have the house to ourselves for one brief moment?"

I tried to suppress a smile. I couldn't. "Actually, it does."

He took my hand and we walked wordlessly up the stairs. The bedsheets were cool and inviting. As we began to make love, a warm, gentle summer breeze filled the lace curtains, like a woman's skirt being lifted.

"I love you," I said afterward.

He turned his handsome, wide face to me and smiled. "I love you, too."

"And in case reading ID bracelets has put any doubt in your mind," I added, *"you're the best."*

Chapter 9

Tom kissed me and said that unless I needed him, he was going to catch up on his sleep. I told him to nap away, I still had tons of work to do. Then I tiptoed down the stairs and took the chilled bag of tuna fillets out of the walk-in refrigerator just as the boys traipsed back into the kitchen with Jake. While Arch diligently ran water and plopped ice cubes into a bowl for his bloodhound, Macguire slouched with a gusty, exhausted sigh into one of the chairs. He put his head in his hands and groaned. I ran the water to rinse the fish. I was waiting for Macguire to say, at long last, that he was hungry. He didn't.

"I should go back to bed," he said after another guttural moan. "I'm so tired. Can you do this bash without me?" When I told him I could, he turned to Arch. "Buddy? Thanks for the walk. Sorry we couldn't get over to your dad's office. I'm trashed now, need to hit the sack."

Arch nodded and poured himself a glass of pink lemonade.

"Macguire," I attempted, "please, can I fix you a little something to eat —"

He waved this away and put his head in his hands again, apparently too weary to climb the stairs to his room. I placed the first tuna fillets in a glass pan. Unfortunately, at that moment Murphy's law of telephones kicked in and my business line rang. I begged Arch to answer it so I wouldn't slime the receiver with fish juice. He gave me a world-weary look that immediately changed to one of concern when he realized who was on the other end of the line.

"Oh! Dad! How are you doing? Can I come see you?"

I swallowed hard. Macguire blinked and then blinked again, his expression turning quickly from fatigue to interest. I patted the fillets dry, then washed my hands, trying to decide what to do. Grab the phone from Arch? Write him a note to let me talk? Did I really want to speak to the Jerk? I viciously ground pepper over the fish. But it was too early to marinate the fillets. I dithered, stamped from foot to foot while trying to catch Arch's eye, then snapped plastic wrap over the fish.

"Oh, Dad, I'm so glad you called me. Wow, I'm sorry you have to . . . . Oh, that sounds awful! Gosh, I can't believe . . ."

Saturday, just past noon — less than five hours since the arrest. John Richard had been processed; was he calling me or his son? Had he talked to his lawyer? Why call here? Unfortunately, despite my feelings on the subject, I could not prevent Arch from talking to his father.

"Where's Tom?" Macguire whispered as I forced myself to turn my back on Arch and glare at the menu. I was not going to listen to the conversation. No matter what the Jerk was up to, I still had to finish my next catering task.

I said, "Tom's asleep."

Still the earnest whisper from Macguire. "You should wake him up. He should know —"

"Macguire. If John Richard Korman wants to talk to me, he would have demanded to do so. That's the way he is. But he called our son. They have a right to talk. And as a witness, I *can't* talk to him."

Still, when I sneaked a glance at Arch's freckled face, I was shocked. My son's cheeks, previously flushed with color from his walk with Macguire and Jake, were now translucently pale. A scowl set his face in an expression of worry so deep that I hated John Richard more than ever. How *could* the man drag our son into this? Arch held out the phone.

Goalies' Grilled Tuna

4 (6 to 8 ounces each) fresh
  boneless tuna steaks
Salt and freshly ground black
  pepper
¼ cup sherry vinaigrette (see
  Exhibition Salad with Meringue-Baked Pecans, page
  483)

Rinse the tuna steaks and pat
them dry. Place them in a glass
pan, season with salt and pepper, and pour the vinaigrette
over them. Cover with plastic
wrap and marinate for 30 minutes to 1 hour.

Preheat the grill. Grill the
steaks for 2 to 3 minutes per
side for rare, 5 minutes per
side for well done.

Serves 4

He said eagerly, "Mom, Dad wants to talk to you."

Well, great. I shook my head vigorously at the proffered phone. Arch's eyes flared wide behind the tortoiseshell glasses.

"Yes, yes, you have to!" he whispered fiercely.

I reached for a kitchen towel and grabbed the receiver. "What is it?" I asked in a clipped tone. "I'm not supposed to be talking to you. You must know that. I'm a witness, remember?"

"Witness to what?" His voice grated through the wire. I was sorely tempted to hang up. No matter how hard I tried to put this man out of my life, he always insisted on reappearing, full of menace. At that moment I didn't care what kind of trouble he was in. I didn't want to hear about it. I didn't want to be a part of it.

Arch leaned toward me and whispered earnestly, "You need to help Dad, Mom. Please!" Behind Arch, Macguire opened his eyes wide. He had perked up considerably since the phone call began. If Macguire was thinking about getting involved with criminals again, I'd have the kid thrown into jail myself.

"I'm listening," I said brusquely into the receiver. "But you're jeopardizing your case

145

by talking to me."

"I'll take that chance."

"I have a lot of work to do."

"Well, excuse me for interrupting your cooking schedule," John Richard snarled. "I just need to discuss this mess that *you* got me into. Understand? I'm in a life-threatening situation here. I'm sitting in the jail, I don't know what's going on, and I need you to do something for me. If you hadn't been cruising by Suz's house at that hour —"

"I told you," I said through clenched teeth. Just like the man to make Suz Craig's murder my fault, just because I'd had the bad luck to discover her body. "I didn't want Arch to get to your place with nobody home —"

"Shut up and *listen* for once, Goldy, will you? There's a whole line of thugs waiting to use this phone. I just . . . I can't . . . nobody will *tell* me anything. It's driving me nuts. I need to know what the police have found out about *when* Suz died."

More than ever, his supreme arrogance astonished me. "Even if I knew that" — which of course I did — "I couldn't tell you. Look, I don't think we should be —"

"When she died is important —"

"Why do you think I —"

"Well, I'll find out soon enough," he fumed. "If you want our son to suffer from

146

this escapade, because that's all it is, then just *be difficult.*"

I said nothing. I'd learned this lesson the hard way. You talk, you give him something to criticize. You say nothing, you may eventually get out of the conversation. Without getting hurt.

"Goldy? Are you listening to me? Goldy? Or are you holding the phone away from your ear?"

I smiled at Arch and Macguire, who were both staring at me in consternation. "I'm listening," I replied evenly.

John Richard resumed his fake-earnest tone. "Look. It's just that if I could know the *time* of death right now, instead of having to wait for the damn lawyers to jaw about it, a lot of things could get cleared up. My attorney is hiring his own investigator, and he thinks if we get the right judge there's a chance I'll be able to get out of here on Monday —"

Dream on, I thought. Actually, as I'd told Arch, one in a million chance. I'd heard of it exactly once. So in our state that would make it one in four million point . . . What was our state's population?

"Did you hear what I said?" my ex-husband yelled.

"Monday," I repeated. I glanced at the

tuna fillets and the menu with lists of dishes I still had to prepare for this evening. Actually, I was running a bit ahead of schedule. No way I was telling him *that,* though.

"Okay, now listen up," the Jerk continued, undaunted, "I want you to use that morbid curiosity of yours to check on a few things. First, there's this nurse named Amy Bartholomew. Suz fired her. Now she's doing something with the new health-food store, I think. Also, Suz had an unpleasant visit in July from Ralph Shelton. Do you remember him? She fired him, too. Plus, Suz had some kind of delicate material —"

"Hey! Stop!" I interrupted him. Goosebumps ran over my skin. "I can't do any of that. Even *you* must recognize how inappropriate it would be for me to go poking around —"

"No, I *don't* recognize that —"

"It is hard for me to believe that your self-centeredness extends this far," I snapped. "You cannot possibly think that the wife of a police officer, who happens to be your badly treated ex-wife, should go snooping around —"

"Mom!" Arch's eyes blazed. "Stop it!" he hissed. "You *have* to *help* him!"

"My self-centeredness!" John Richard was shrieking. "My *self-centeredness!*"

This time I did hold the phone away from my ear. Arch pressed his fingers against his eyes and shook his head. The tormented expression on his face made my heart ache. With a ragged breath I said: "John Richard, I need to get off the phone."

His icy tone chilled my blood. "I did not kill Suz Craig. I loved her." He paused, then continued very deliberately, "It's time for you to set aside your *own* self-centeredness. For the sake of our son and his mental health, you need to help me prove that I'm being set up for this damn murder. Do you understand?"

I covered the phone with my hand. "Arch?" I asked with as much calmness as I could muster. My son gave me a defiant look, scowled, and crossed his arms. He was silent. "Would you please go upstairs for a few minutes and let me finish this phone call?" After a fractional hesitation he turned and hurtled out of the kitchen. Macguire made no move to go anywhere except to shuffle toward the walk-in, muttering about needing a Pepsi. "Macguire," I pleaded, "just give me a minute here, okay?"

"I'm not going to bother you," Macguire said innocently. "I just need a pop. Maybe I'll see something in there that will make me hungry. You never know."

"Goldy," John Richard raged, "could you let go of domestic life for a *minute* and listen to me? I did not commit this crime. I left Suz's house at one A.M. When I left, she was fine."

"If you left her house at one and she was fine," I repeated calmly, "then tell that to your investigator. If you have done nothing wrong, then you have nothing to worry about." Then I hung up.

"What's going on?" asked Macguire solicitously. He held a soft-drink can in one hand and the parfait glass of chocolate pudding in the other — the same one he'd turned up his nose at earlier.

I cleared my throat. "Apart from the fact that my ex-husband has been arrested for homicide and my son believes I should try to get him off?" I sighed. My head ached. I sat down, rubbing my temples. "Let's see, the only other things going on are that I've got a big party to cater tonight. Oh, yes, and my son is absolutely furious with me. Apart from that, not much."

"Bummer," said Macguire. He set the pudding aside, untouched, poured the soft drink into a glass, then slurped fizz from the top. "Know what? I don't need a nap, I think. I'll see if Arch wants to talk or listen to music. We'll be quiet, though. We won't

150

bother you, I promise."

I murmured a grateful thanks and stared at the ingredients for a second batch of biscuits. As usual when dealing with John Richard, a sense of unreality closed in. Was I crazy, or was he? He was crazy. No question. A crazy liar, always had been. But then — and this had always puzzled me — how could he be so successful in the rest of his life, the part of his life that did not involve me? He had a fantastic job, lots of money, and a steady stream of girlfriends. People *liked* him. Was it his looks? Well, that was part of it. And he was intelligent. No genius, but he could sound good and fake his way through the situations he knew nothing about. Add to that his great ability to talk and charm his way into people's hearts. And so far he'd been able to lie and cheat his way out of the many, many messes he'd made. And he'd been able to keep the messes quiet.

I did not kill Suz Craig. Yeah, sure. I again measured flour, baking powder, and salt into my food processor, scooped in smooth white vegetable shortening, and let the blade slice the mixture into tiny bits. *Then why were you bringing flowers over this morning? Why* did *she have a death grasp on your ID bracelet? Why are you trying to find out the* time of death? So you can change *your* story? I

151

shuddered. I was *not* going to help him. No matter how manipulative he managed to be. No matter how much he dragged Arch into this.

Poor Arch. I pulsed the processor and watched the blade bite through the ingredients. He wanted so much for me to help his father. But I couldn't. The man was evil. I dribbled in buttermilk until the dough clung together in a ball. I wanted to tell Arch that trying to follow one of his father's lies to get to the truth was futile. You get involved with John Richard, you get sucked into a vortex just like old Captain Ahab, and end up at the bottom of the ocean. As I scooped the silky dough out of the processor, my mind reverted to one of its common themes: How come the evil people in your life don't just *die?* How come the evil people in your life are able to kill smart, promising women like Suz Craig?

Well, the rain falls on the just and the unjust.

Then again, *had* Suz been so smart and promising? Had there perhaps been an evil side to Suz Craig, too? I thought of the rumors Marla had gathered about the dead woman. *No, no, no,* I chided myself. *Don't get into this.* So what if she fired Amy Bartholomew, the nurse who supposedly had gambling problems? So what if she fired Ralph Shelton? I preheated the oven and rolled out the biscuit dough into a soft, rectangular pillow.

Suz, after all, was a boss-type person, and a boss-type person sometimes had to fire people. As sole proprietor of my business, I was thankful I'd never had to perform that particular function myself. I brandished the puck-size biscuit cutter I'd finally found at a baking supply store and cut the dough into circles. Then I arrayed them carefully on a cookie sheet.

I was *not* going to get dragged into this. *Suz had an unpleasant visit in July from* Ralph Shelton. Do you remember him? John Richard's sarcastic voice echoed in my thoughts. Of course I remembered Ralph Shelton the doctor, the hockey fan extraordinaire. We used to be friends. Like John Richard, Ralph had specialized in ob-gyn at the University of Colorado Medical School. Another buddy of theirs had been Patricia McCracken's ex-husband, Skip. Skip had moved to Colorado Springs, and I hadn't seen him in years.

Ralph Shelton. What was his history? I set the timer for the biscuits and thought back. Ralph had divorced his first wife, a petite, very erudite teacher, and over her pained objections, obtained sole custody of their daughter, Jill, who was Arch's age. Problem was, Ralph hadn't been able to take care of Jill when he'd gone on business trips, had late meetings, or had to deliver a baby. So he'd turned to me to take care of his daughter, over and over and over. Meanwhile, Jill's own mother was desperate to have the girl down in her new place in Albuquerque. With mounting problems in my own marriage and young Arch unable to shake a string of ear infections, I'd finally told Ralph I couldn't take care of his daughter three or four times a week. Combined with my separation from John Richard, this had meant the end of the friendship with Ralph Shelton, unfortunately. The worst part was that Ralph had finally sent his daughter to live with her mother in New Mexico. Arch and I had missed Jill terribly. She'd been a fun-loving child with such an infectious laugh that our house had felt empty for weeks after she moved away.

The timer beeped. I slapped the cookie sheet out of the oven with an overenthusiastic bang, then rolled and cut out another batch of biscuits. I stared at the cutter in my hand. I'd been so proud of myself for finding the cutter. When the biscuits were baked, they were the exact dimensions of a hockey puck. Perfect for tonight's party.

Ralph's a big hockey fan, Marla had told me. No kidding. Back in the medical-school days, the only way Ralph Shelton could relieve his academic anxiety was to go to hockey games at McNichols Arena, where he'd bought lifetime season tickets for our ill-fated first NHL team, the Colorado Rockies. I had never understood how Ralph could vent his frustration by cheering for such a poorly performing team. Glumly reporting their losses whenever we got together, Ralph's face had been ruddy and lined. What little hair he had had turned prematurely gray around a widening bald spot. Whether the hair loss resulted from the pain of being a Rockies hockey fan or the prospect of practicing medicine, I knew not. When the franchise had moved on, Ralph had been disconsolate. Whether his enthusiasms had subsequently shifted to baseball, when the new team named the Rockies were swinging bats and setting homerun and attendance records at newly built Coors Field, I knew not. By then, Ralph Shelton had passed out of my orbit. And I'd had my hands too full with the divorce from John Richard to care.

Wait a minute. Sometimes a girlfriend will dye her hair, and become virtually unrecognizable. I watched my oven timer ticking down the seconds until this batch of biscuits would be done. I remembered Ralph Shelton; I'd seen him quite recently. I just hadn't recognized him out of context and with a new look. His bald head had been covered by a billed cap. He'd exchanged his sports-fan garb for gardening clothes. He'd grown a mustache that was prematurely white. I watched my clock. What else? He'd been eager to see what the paramedics were doing. This morning, my old friend Ralph Shelton had been one of the gawking neighbors on Jacobean Drive.

Chapter 10

The food, I scolded myself. *Work!* I perused my recipe for Vietnamese slaw. Napa cabbage, carrots, very lightly steamed snow peas — all these needed to be julienned. When my hand became tired from slicing, I decided to stop and check the phone book. Ralph and Fay Shelton lived on Chaucer Drive, one street over from Suz Craig's street. So what had Ralph been doing up so early this morning? Taking a stroll around the neighborhood? I couldn't wait for Tom to wake up.

The phone rang. Patricia McCracken's voice zinged across the wire. "I can't cancel this party," she wailed.

"You'd better not," I exclaimed as I stared at the mountains of colorful vegetables I'd already cut into uniform thin slices.

"The police have been here, Goldy. I was so nervous about seeing everybody at this party, my first public appearance since I filed the suits, that I took a sleeping pill last night. I don't remember a thing." She took a deep breath and added defiantly, "I didn't kill that HMO lady."

"Oh-kay," I said as I searched my shelves for rice wine vinegar.

"Do you think John Richard killed her?"

"I don't know."

"See you at five then." She didn't wait for me to say good-bye.

What an odd call. I whisked sesame oil with the rice wine vinegar and thought back to the wet spring we'd just come through. I had seen Patricia and her son, Tyler, once, at the library. It had been a momentous spring for our town library, but not because the incessant rain had brought any heightened demand for books. The cause for sensation had been the foxes that had made their den in the rocky hillside behind the windowed reading room. When a litter of five cubs was produced, the births became big-time small-town news. Soon the fox cubs were claiming the early-evening hours to cavort, tumble, and prance through the quartz and granite spillway in full view of an audience of excited children of all ages. Never mind that reading in the high-windowed room became impossible. Any visitor to or from the library was greeted with the same query: "Seen the foxes?"

Paying a visit to the reading room, Arch

and I had encountered Patricia dragging a recalcitrant, whining Tyler with one hand and balancing an armload of Dr. Seuss books with the other.

"Did you see the foxes, Tyler?" I'd asked her son happily. "Are they out tonight?"

Tyler had given me a grumpy stare and let out a wail. Patricia had snarled, "We're not interested in a family of foxes. Not now. Not ever."

Startled, I'd pulled open the massive door to the library for Arch. When he passed by me, he'd mumbled, "What — does she raise chickens or something?"

Not even close, I realized now as I folded the sweet-sour dressing into the slaw ingredients. Struggling with the recent loss of her baby, Patricia hadn't wanted to see the fox cubs playing. The notion of a big, happy family had been slipping from her grasp. I covered the enormous bowl with plastic wrap and popped it into the walk-in refrigerator.

"If you're making so-good food noises, I want some," Tom announced cheerfully as he strode into the room. "Oh, man." He took in a greedy breath. "More biscuits?"

I nodded and removed the last cookie sheet of the golden, puffed rounds, then silently split one, slathered it with butter and blackberry jam, and handed the plate with it to Tom. When he finished, I'd tell him about seeing Ralph Shelton.

While he sat down and began to eat, I put in another batch of biscuits. I iced the dark chocolate cupcakes, which would surround a centerpiece hockey-rink-shaped cake provided by Aspen Meadow Pastry Shop. I placed the cupcakes in covered plastic containers. I wasn't going to brood anymore. I was in my wonderful kitchen, filled with marvelous scents, and feeding the man I loved most in the world. Then I realized he was watching me.

"Tom? What is it?"

"Final batch of biscuits about to come out?"

"In a little bit."

He paused, then glanced at the clock. "How's your time going? When do you have to leave?"

"In about an hour. Why?"

His face grew wary. "I'm worried about Arch."

"So am I. But what makes you mention it? Did he tell you about the phone call?" Doggone John Richard, anyway.

Tom shook his head. "No, he didn't. He didn't say a word. When I went by his room, he was sitting ramrod stiff in his desk chair,

160

staring at nothing. I asked him if he wanted to talk, and he said 'Not to you, I don't.' "

My spirits, briefly raised by my productive work, fell flat. I guessed Macguire had not been successful trying to entice Arch into listening to music. I grabbed a chair and sat. "Tom. Arch wants me to help John Richard. He's desperate for me to prove his father's innocence."

Tom groaned. "Goldy, you can't. I told you I'd keep you informed. But this isn't like that time you found the body in the woods by Elk Park Prep. This time the prime suspect showed up at the scene, started raising Cain, and was arrested. You can't get involved in this: you're a *witness*. Listen, let's get Arch down here to talk —"

I held up a hand to stop him. "John Richard called here about a half hour ago."

"He called here? Wanting to talk to you? Do you know how illegal that is?"

"I told him. He claimed he called to talk to Arch. But then he told Arch to put me on. Even from jail he was his usual manipulative self, whining to Arch and demanding to know from me what time Suz died so that he could use his medical knowledge of rigor mortis to prove he's not the murderer."

Tom chuckled cynically. "That guy. Maybe he was trying to reconstruct his timetable." He frowned. His sandy eyebrows drew into a furry, uneven line. "You didn't tell him anything, did you?"

I shot him an exasperated look. "Of course not."

"I can just tell," he said resignedly, "that this is going to be one holy mess."

"Listen, Tom, remember when I told you about a doctor Suz had supposedly fired, one named Ralph Shelton? What I didn't tell you was about John Richard's and my history with him." Briefly, I summarized how we'd all known one another years ago, when Arch was small. "Anyway," I said, "Ralph's a tall bald fellow with a white mustache. I know he was one of those guys I shooed away from the ditch this morning. I didn't recognize him because he looked so different with a cap on his head. Plus, his hair used to be gray, not white, and he didn't have a mustache."

Tom narrowed his eyes. "You're kidding."

"I'm not. Ralph was there, trying to see what the paramedics were doing. He was wearing gardening clothes and a baseball cap. Your guys must have talked to him in their neighborhood canvass." I thought back to the fashionable camouflage-print pants, wide suspenders, dark billed cap, and

162

handspun collarless shirt Ralph had been wearing that morning. In retrospect, it was perhaps too studied an outfit to have donned so early in the morning. But something else nagged at my memory. What was it? Something about Ralph hadn't looked quite right. What? But my tired brain refused to yield any details.

"I'll check on Shelton," said Tom curtly. "But I do think you need to go talk to Arch. I'll pack this stuff up."

"The last time you packed my stuff I had to make risotto from scratch for a Fourth of July party. As I recall, you thought it would be funny to substitute ingredients on me, so I wouldn't go snooping around in a suspect's house."

He stood and rinsed his dish. "I thought," he said without missing a beat, "that I would be keeping you out of trouble by making you do extra work that time, Miss G. Besides, I apologized and you forgave me. No fair hassling me about it now." He reached into the pantry for several of the large cardboard boxes I used for carting food.

I walked up the stairs, thinking. Shower, change, call Marla — all these I had to do before leaving. Plus talk to Arch, get him smoothed out on his father being thrown into jail under suspicion of committing a brutal murder. Sure.

My son sat slumped in his desk chair. His lank brown hair was uncombed. His glasses perched halfway down his nose. Julian's cast-off T-shirt hung on his motionless body. I longed to hug him tightly, the way I had when he was small and I'd always been able to comfort him.

"Arch. Hon, please. Let's talk."

"About what?" His voice was toneless.

"May I come in?"

His eyes didn't leave the pile of magazines on his desk. He shrugged. "I thought you had a party to do."

"Arch, please, I'm worried about you."

"Yeah, well, *I'm* worried about *Dad.*" He whirled and faced me, his brown eyes ablaze. "You just don't care, do you?"

I sat on the bed. Honesty was the best policy. "You know how when you leave your homework in your room? I don't snatch it up and go running to school to bail you out. It's called being responsible for your actions —"

"Oh, Mom!" he yelled, his tone disgusted. He glared at me. "Don't treat me like a baby! Just don't start, okay?"

"No, then," I said frankly, "I don't care about your father. I only care about you."

"If you cared about me," he shot back

fiercely, "you'd be willing to at least *think* about whether he did this murder or not. Dad isn't lying."

"Did he tell you that he hit Suz the way he used to hit me? He admitted that to Tom and me, you know. That was one of the reasons Tom arrested him this morning. I'm just telling you the truth here, Arch. I'm sorry if the facts are so painful. I don't mean to hurt you."

He pushed abruptly out of his chair. "I need to go. I need to go check some things out."

"What things?"

"There's a nurse who runs a health-food store —"

"Don't you even think about doing your father's investigative errands, young man. His lawyer will hire an investigator on Monday."

"So now you're going to say I can't go to the health-food store?"

"What are you planning on doing there?"

"I don't know yet." He stood in front of the mirror and frowned at himself. Apparently going to the health-food store did not warrant clothes changing or hair combing. "Don't worry, Mom." His voice carried a hint of conciliation. "I'll get Macguire to go with me."

"He's asleep," I said, hoping this was true. I hadn't heard a peep out of Macguire since he'd shuffled out of the kitchen carrying his soft drink.

"I'll wake him up! It'll be good for him to walk again, anyway."

"He'll pass out."

"Mom!" Once again I got the angry, indignant stare. "Will you stop bugging me? Why won't you at least *admit* Dad might be down there in jail for no reason? Whatever happened to *innocent until proven guilty?*"

I rose from the bed, walked to the door, and assumed a quiet tone. "I love you, Arch. I just don't want to see you getting involved in your dad's problems."

He pushed past me. It was an unconscious, but more gentle, imitation of his father's shove by me that morning. "Sorry, Mom. I already am involved. I wish you would help him. He really needs you."

Well, great. I quietly made my way to Tom's and my room to get ready for the evening party. My heart ached.

Fifteen minutes later I'd showered, changed, and punched in a call to Marla's answering machine. When I went out the door, luminescent gray clouds billowed just at the edge of the western horizon. Even this early in August, snow would be falling each morning on the highest peaks to the west. When the afternoon sun warmed and wilted that ephemeral white blanket, the mountain towns on the Front Range would get a brief, deliciously cooling rain. But first the moisture would build into luxuriant cumulus towers that resembled fantastic, brilliant mushrooms. Once these clouds completely filled the western sky, they would spill eastward over the hillsides.

Tom had loaded my supplies and announced that he was going to the hardware store, one of his favorite Saturday-afternoon occupations. He seldom came home with more than a dollar's worth of washers, screws, and nails. Sometimes Arch accompanied him. But I found these excursions deadly boring. Guy stuff. Not surprisingly, Arch had declined accompanying Tom, and my husband had rumbled off alone in his dark sedan.

Arch. I revved the van and backed out of the driveway. It was early, a good thing since I needed to drive around a little bit to think. At the end of our street, I turned and headed along the creek. When I passed Aspen Meadow Nursery on the left and Aspen Meadow Barbecue on the right, I chewed the inside of my cheek. Arch couldn't forsake his father. I didn't really want him to. Despite

167

John Richard's coldly selfish behavior, Arch clung fiercely to the hope of getting love from his other parent. And John Richard spoiled Arch enough with material things — usually when he felt guilty over reneging on a promise — that Arch's longing for a relationship remained like a sharp hunger, seldom fed.

I made a U-turn, drove back through town, and headed up toward the lake. Perched on the edge of the waterfall between the lake and lower Cottonwood Creek, a gaggle of shiny black cormorants arched their backs and eyed the water beneath for fish. Arch used to love to go down to the lake when he was little and feed the waterfowl, now strictly prohibited, as human feeding messed up the birds' willingness to migrate. Arch had known distress back then: the pain of the playground, the agony of his parents' divorce. Then as now, I had tried to soothe and protect him. But his distress this time didn't change the fact that Dr. John Richard Korman, batterer of women, had finally been caught. And then, in front of a street full of nosy neighbors, he'd resisted arrest. I dreaded Arch hearing about *that* scene.

What was painfully inevitable, I knew, was that John Richard would maintain his innocence to his son and anyone else who would listen until the proverbial bovines came home. No matter what he did or what folks he hurt, John Richard would insist to the end that he was not responsible for his actions. Well, we would just see about that.

I passed the lake. In the near distance cars sent up a nimbus of dust as women from the Aspen Meadow Babsie Club drove into the LakeCenter parking lot on their way to set up for the doll show. What Arch couldn't see was that this crime — this *event* with Suz Craig — was going to change everything. The publicity surrounding the arrest, the breadth of the investigation, the preliminary hearing, the trial, the conviction, the sentencing — these would alter his relationship with his father forever. Perhaps it was this coming change that Arch sensed. So he'd plunged into denial. Who wouldn't?

I passed a solitary rower at the edge of the lake and turned the van in the direction of the country club. Since I was still a bit early, did I dare swing by Aspen Meadow Health Foods, to see if Amy Bartholomew, the nurse-without-a-poker-face, was in? No, I'd had enough crime for one day. Besides, Arch and Macguire might be headed over there. If my son thought I was checking up on him, he would have a fit.

Dread made my heart heavy, the way your

chest hurts when an election is going to the wrong people and all you can do is watch the numbers mount. I swung through the entryway to the residential part of the country club, where a crew dressed in white overalls and white billed caps was busy at work eradicating the vandals' painted handiwork from the stone walls. I shook my head. I felt helpless watching Arch's dilemma, which was sure to end worse than any election. The best I could hope for was that it would all be over soon.

It was this idea of expediting things that made me turn onto Jacobean and from there chug left on Sheridan, then on to Chaucer, where I eased up in front of the Shelton place. The house was a massive, out-of-proportion two-story neo-Georgian. White-painted brick contrasted with shiny black shutters and window boxes lush with bright red geraniums and artfully dripping variegated cream-and-green ivy.

What exactly was I doing here? Trying to disprove John Richard's theory, whatever it was, about Ralph Shelton? Trying to remember what it was I had seen this morning? I didn't know. I parked behind the Sheltons' van and hopped out of my own. I knew the rules: Anybody who might testify in a case is a witness. Not only had I witnessed all that had transpired between John Richard and Tom, I'd seen, or thought I'd seen, Ralph Shelton this morning. If I ever had to testify, I didn't want to think about how I could be challenged because of the contact I was now making with Ralph. I also tried not to think about how upset Tom would be with me for making this little sleuthing side trip.

Apart from this morning, how long had it been since I'd talked to Ralph? Too long. I'd last seen his daughter as a four-year-old. Now Jill was a teenager, like Arch. I rapped hard on the elaborate, gleaming brass knocker. Of course, Ralph probably wouldn't even be home. Saturday afternoon on a gorgeous Colorado summer day? He was probably out playing golf.

But he was not on the fairway. Even before the doorbell stopped donging "Three Blind Mice," tall, white-mustached Ralph answered the door. He had changed from the gardening clothes to a collarless navy shirt and faded blue jeans — Calvin Klein at Home.

"What is it?" He stared at me with eyes that seemed to be made of yellow glass.

"Ralph!" I exclaimed brightly. "Ralph, don't you remember me? I used to take care of Jill, about ten years ago."

He pulled himself up. "I am Dr. Shelton."

Always. *Is your first name Doctor?* I smiled. "Ralph, it's Goldy Korman. Now Goldy Schulz. Don't you remember me from all those years ago? I'm a caterer now."

He squinted and cleared his throat. "Goldy?"

"We . . . saw each other in front of Suz Craig's house, when the police were there. This morning. Don't you recall? Over on Jacobean. I didn't recognize you, either. And then I remembered. And after all we'd been through together way back when . . ."

But I couldn't come up with a last-minute lie to push myself into a conversation with this man. Instead, I stared mutely at the right side of his face, where there was a square, expertly cut gauze bandage. I saw again what I'd seen this morning. Just at the upper end of the bandage, under the clear tape, were the beginnings, just the very beginnings, of four vertical gash marks. The kind of scratches that could be made by a woman's nails, when she was fighting you off.

172

Chapter 11

Forgive me, it's been such a trying day."
Ralph's unctuous tone made me even more
uneasy. "I never would have known . . . and
this morning when you were ordering people
around, you seemed so distraught. . . ." He
tilted his bald head and closed his amber
eyes, as if struggling to recall the events.
Then he shook his head. "Terrible tragedy.
The police even questioned me, since I was
out on my walk when . . ." He paused. "But
why are you here now? I mean, if you want
to catch up on old times, then give me a call
and we can set up a lunch or something. . . .
I'll bring some pictures of Jill, she's playing soccer down in New Mexico. . . ." His
voice trailed off. A country-club doctor
choosing to have lunch with a caterer who
was married to a cop? Not likely, regardless
of our history. But Ralph pressed on, with
an eagerness that seemed almost sad. "Actually, I've missed all of my old friends lately,
things have been going so badly . . . and now
this has happened. Should we set up a lunch
right now?" His hand went nervously to the

top button of his shirt. "That would be a terrific idea."

"Oh! Well, actually, I can't make any appointments now, I'm looking for the McCrackens' house." It was lame, but it had to do. "Do you know Clark and Patricia McCracken? Remember, Patricia used to be married to Skip all those years ago. . . ." He squinted skeptically and I rushed on. "I'm catering a Stanley Cup celebration there tonight, at the McCrackens', and I just can't remember exactly where they live, and then I remembered you were such a big hockey fan . . ."

But he had already held up a hand for me to wait. I fell silent as his tall form disappeared down a hallway whose walls were bathed in a vertigo-inducing print of floating cabbage roses. Beyond, I glimpsed a country kitchen with frilly curtains and gleaming copper. I wondered if Ralph had found another job after being fired by ACHMO. If he had not, I doubted he'd be able to keep up life in his old income bracket.

"Twenty-two Markham," he said pleasantly as he returned, waving an engraved invitation. Then he regarded me. "I'm going over there in just a little bit myself. We've remained friends, in spite of everything. It's amazing that she . . . Well. The guests are all going to skate, get another dose of Cup fever. Sound good? But how can you cater at a house you haven't visited?"

I was ready for this one. "Do it all the time. Actually, I thought I knew where the McCrackens' place was. But after this morning my life seems to have turned upside down." I stared helplessly into his yellow eyes, so much like those of a cat. "It's just been a nightmare."

He grinned sympathetically. "Yes, well, I'll just see you over at the McCrackens' place —"

I leaned against the doorframe. "Ralph, can you just show me how to get to Markham? Please? I'm feeling extremely disoriented."

With obvious reluctance, he walked outside and gestured at Chaucer, where, as I well knew, I needed to take two rights and then a left to get to the McCrackens' place. He turned and again squinted. My forlorn expression must have finally ignited a spark of curiosity, for before going into his house, he hesitated.

"How did you happen to come upon . . . Suz Craig . . . er, in the ditch?" he asked abruptly. "I mean, did you drive over it or something?"

"I was on my way to the Rodines' place to

pick up my son and take him to his father. I just saw her there . . . in front of her house. Uh . . . how about you?"

"Oh, I was out for my walk."

I sighed. "I'm sorry for ordering you around this morning. Did you say the police questioned you? I seem to remember them wanting to talk to everybody, you know?"

"Yes, well." He cleared his throat. "You wouldn't believe what they wanted to know from me." He rubbed his bandaged cheek. I felt my own face heat up. "How had I scratched myself, they asked. So I told them what I'm telling you." I didn't like the tone of his voice. Did it mask hostility, or was I imagining things? "Our cat doesn't like to go to the veterinarian's. She scratched me when I tried to put her into the cage."

I nodded sympathetically and thought that Sergeant Beiner was probably on the phone with the veterinarian right now, finding out if in fact Ralph Shelton had just brought a female cat in for a visit. I thanked him for helping me, then backed away. Time to grill fish for the McCrackens.

"So," Ralph said slowly, "the police suspect my old friend, John Richard Korman?" His fingers brushed the top of his shirt, then went to his bandage again. Suddenly, he didn't seem to want me to leave.

176

I shrugged as convincingly as possible. "Who knows? I try to keep up with that guy as little as possible." I turned toward my van. "Thanks for your help, Ralph."

"Wait," he called. "I'm sorry. Of course you have as little to do with him as possible. I . . . I remember how he treated you." I turned back and waited for him to speak. Finally he said, "It's just that I've had such a horrible morning." I pressed my lips together. "I knew her, you know," he said bluntly. Was his voice wistful? Hard to tell. "I knew Suz Craig."

"Really?" I asked. "Oh, right, the HMO. And you're a doc. I hardly know anyone in the medical business anymore. Do you practice in Denver?"

"I *did*. Our group was affiliated with ACHMO. Still is, actually, I'm just not a part of it." He heaved a sigh. "I'll see you at the party later. Sure you know where you're going?" Before I could answer, however, he said, "Good-bye." Then he closed the door.

Well, doggone. Ralph was in some kind of pain, no question, and it wasn't just from cat scratches. I gave the brass knocker one last glance and walked back to my vehicle — in case he was watching through a window — and hightailed it over to the McCrackens' place. Within five minutes I'd eased up to

177

the curb in front of a tall wooden house that had been stained a bilious purple, with shutters painted a dull maroon. They should have photographed this place for a National Hockey League advertisement. Avalanche flags hung from the lampposts along the walk. Oversize Avalanche banners were draped from each upstairs window. The place looked like a sporting-goods store.

When I drove into the McCrackens' driveway, though, I was prevented from pulling up to the back entrance. A rope had been put up around a large, rectangular paved area that had been marked with bright white lines to resemble a hockey rink. I couldn't imagine what my tires would do to all those brilliant chalky lines if I drove over them. I dreaded contemplating how I was going to unload, much less serve.

Clark McCracken, a long-legged fellow with a thin, sweating red face and lots of sweat-streaked brown hair, flapped his arms maniacally as he came loping down the drive toward me. He was wearing a maroon Avalanche jersey, shiny maroon shorts, and stiff, bulky kneepads that made his gait resemble the canter of a crippled race-horse. No question — this man was ready for the end-of-the-driveway game. There was also no question that he wasn't ready for my van to ruin all his chalk marks. I sighed. Unloading a hundred pounds of supplies anywhere near the shortest route to the kitchen was going to be impossible. I rolled down the window and resolved to stay pleasant.

"Need you . . . to park . . ." Out of breath, Clark wobbled, stiltlike. I certainly hoped he wasn't participating for more than five minutes in today's face-off or whatever the hockey equivalent of a scrimmage is. "Park behind the line," he blurted out as he pointed to the closest chalk stripe. He pressed his hair against the sides of his head and gasped. "Then . . . you can walk down with the beer and food to where we'll be playing, with a tray or something."

"Clark," I began patiently. "There is no way —"

"Back up then," Clark interrupted, waving dismissively toward the front of his house. "It'll be okay, the cake's going to come in that way, too. Back to the sidewalk. Open your doors and . . ." He took another deep, agonizing breath and squeezed his eyes shut. "I'll help."

Oh, sure, I thought as I gunned the van in reverse. *And within ten minutes of you trying to help me, I'll be trying to remember the CPR course I took right after Marla had her heart attack.* The van sputtered. I braked a little too hard at the beginning of the sidewalk, a herringbone-brick path that led back to the garishly decorated house.

It was not my place to tell Clark Mc-Cracken that he should not be tugging two fully loaded dollies up his sidewalk so soon before his party. But Clark seemed determined to be as physically involved with the setup for his hockey celebration as possible. I knew what he would do next — splash ice water on his face, comb back his sopping hair, and leap down the stairs to be the official greeter. Then, with an enormous sense of justification, our host would slug down a speedy half-dozen beers before beginning the roller hockey derby in his driveway, which would be followed by a lot more brewskis, a minimal amount of food, and passing out on a piece of patio furniture before I'd finished serving the entrée. That is, if he didn't hurt himself with all the activity first.

On second thought, maybe I should summon an ambulance. Just in case.

"Okay," he said, still panting heavily. "What goes in first?"

Twenty minutes later I was set up in the kitchen. Clark, wheezing from his exertions, made a martyrlike declaration that he was going to light his gas grill — ever a man's job, even if no actual starting of fires was involved.

"Clark," I cautioned politely, "please be careful. There was just a big article in the *Mountain Journal* about how those grills need to be checked —"

Again I got the dismissive wave. "Don't quote Frances Markasian to me, please. I've never heard of mountain moths building nests in propane grills! What will that woman think of next?" He rolled his eyes. "I don't believe a word that crazy woman writes. She's not a reporter, she's a viper looking for a cause. Explosions from moths, give me a break! But don't worry, I'm going to clean the vents. It's my job."

"Just be careful," I repeated gently.

I unwrapped the appetizers for the party: an enormous oval basket of fresh vegetables meant to resemble, as did the rest of tonight's food, a hockey rink. In the place of the goals were baskets of chips, and in the center of the rink-basket I gently lowered a huge crystal bowl of Mexican dip, my own concoction of thick layers of guacamole, cubed tomatoes, smooth sour cream, shredded crisp lettuce, chili beans mashed with picante sauce, sliced black olives, and an ample blanket of golden grated cheddar cheese.

"Ooh, may I taste?" Patricia McCracken cooed as she tiptoed into the kitchen. Her tousle of streaked curls was held back with a twisted headband printed with tiny Avalanche logos. But her fine-featured face was haggard. She wore an oversize Avalanche jersey that reached almost to her knees. She looked like a coed who'd spent the night in a fraternity house, complete with borrowed pajamas and bags under her eyes.

Despite my best intentions to cater this event, I couldn't help but ask what was on my mind. "Patricia, are you sure you want to go through with this? You look exhausted."

"Yes," she said, "I do. Tyler's already over at somebody's house. Besides, what am I going to do, call everyone and say, 'Sorry! Murder in the neighborhood! Gotta cancel!' Oh, gosh, that reminds me, the centerpiece cake's not here yet. Could you call the bakery and find out if Mickey is going to send somebody over with it?"

"No problem."

Patricia extended an index finger to scoop up a bit of dip. I punched in the buttons for the Aspen Meadow Pastry Shop and handed Patricia a small plastic bowl of dip that I had set aside for sampling. She wrinkled her nose and whined, "Is this the same?"

"Patricia, please. Of course." I removed the plastic wrap from the Grilled Slapshot Salad.

"Well, it doesn't *look* the same." She shoveled a pile of dip onto one chip and popped it into her mouth.

"Aspen Meadow Pastry Shop," announced Mickey Yuille in the sad, gruff voice I recognized so well.

"Mickey, hi, it's Goldy Schulz. I'm over at the McCrackens' place and she's waiting for her cake. Can I tell her it's on the way?"

Mickey sighed. "Brandon always insists on helping out with my Saturday deliveries. But now they've had some kind of crisis down at his office, and my other guy is sick, so all the Saturday-afternoon deliveries have been delayed."

I held my breath. Brandon Yuille, head of Human Resources at ACHMO, was already being questioned? By whom? The police? His Minneapolis head office? "We *really* need somebody to bring the cake over," I implored.

"Yeah, yeah, okay. That's what I was going to tell you. Brandon came in late. He's out on his rounds now and should be there any minute. And say! Great fudge, Goldy. Brandon brought me some made from your recipe. Come by and see me sometime. I

183

want you to try out my new cinnamon rolls. They're bigger than the other guy used to make them."

I thanked him, hung up, and unwrapped the biscuits. To Patricia I said, "The cake's on its way."

Using two chips, Patricia scooped up another precariously balanced load of dip from the plastic bowl. "Mm-mm," she exclaimed as she delicately wiped an errant glop of sour cream from the side of her mouth. My words registered and she gave me a puzzled look. "The cake is on its way? So are my guests! We're starting the hockey game earlier than we'd planned, in case we need overtime!" Her voice was full of panic.

"Patricia! Are you sure you're okay?"

"No, I'm *not* okay, thank you very much. Am I ever going to see John Richard in civil court now, do you think? Unlikely. I sold my car to pay my lawyer's retainer. Your ex-husband is sucking me down a drain." She sounded very bitter.

Captain Ahab, I thought again, and cocked an ear toward the hallway. "I think either the cake or some of your guests might be arriving." I loved catering. Occasionally, though, while placating a nervous hostess, I ended up burning the butter or committing some other *faux pas culinaire.* I wanted her to leave the kitchen, but I didn't want to hurt her feelings.

"Clark can greet the guests," she rejoined excitedly. "I want to talk about what happened this morning. What did you see? Were you in on the —"

Mercifully, she was interrupted by dark-haired, handsome Brandon Yuille. Banging through the kitchen door, Brandon balanced an enormous white box on his outstretched arms. The cake. I motioned to the kitchen island and he expertly slid the box to safety. With his eyes twinkling, Brandon swept his long hair off his forehead. Of medium height and slightly — but appealingly — chubby, he wore a loose yellow oxford-cloth shirt with no tie, khaki pants, and loosely tied brown leather boat shoes. He was good-looking and single, although somewhat too young for Marla, much to her chagrin. With a flourish, he opened the top of the cardboard box.

"Oh, Brandon, it's super," I said admiringly. The rink-shaped cake was actually made of two thick layers of ice cream topped with a thin layer of yellow cake. Mickey had icing-painted all the right red and blue lines and the Avalanche logo. He'd even placed tiny plastic hockey players at various places and miniature goals at each end. "The cupcakes will look perfect surrounding it. Let's get it into the freezer."

Patricia was staring at Brandon. "Don't you work for ACHMO?" she demanded suspiciously.

He reddened. "Yes, I . . . I'm just helping my father. . . ." His look grew puzzled. "Wait a minute. You're the one who's suing . . . Oh, I'm sorry, I know you've had a hard time —"

"You all are spying on me," Patricia responded hotly. "Don't think I don't know about all the records you've been trying to get your hands on or have destroyed. You can leave my home now."

"I apologize for coming," Brandon mumbled as he slid the cake into the freezer.

"Patricia, please," I soothed. "Mickey Yuille is the new proprietor of the pastry shop. Brandon works for ACHMO during the week and helps his father on the weekends. Brandon, I'm sorry about this —"

But Brandon's leather shoes were already making squeaking noises as he hastened out of the kitchen. So much for asking him any questions about ACHMO's response to the recent demise of their vice-president.

Patricia sniffed. "If I'd known the pastry shop guy was related to an ACHMO guy, I would have had you make the centerpiece cake." She made it sound as if that was the last thing on earth she wanted.

One of the guests, a slender, energetic woman with curly black hair, crashed into the kitchen. Her blue eyes shone with anticipation as she hurtled toward us. "Listen, Goldy, what's the real dirt on your husband?" Two more women crowded in behind her, whispering and staring at me avidly.

Oh, brother. Every bone in my jaw ached from being clenched. I leaned against the refrigerator and glanced longingly at the fish fillets. Should I pretend I didn't know what was going on? With my *husband? Actually, ladies, my* husband *is a cop who spent the afternoon running errands. That is, after he arrested my* ex-*husband.*

"Out, out, out," Patricia commanded with surprising authority. To my relief, her noisy friends backed out of the kitchen. "And it's her *ex*-husband!"

I could hear a muffled whine: "But we want to hear about . . ." The door closed on them.

"Your poor son," Patricia said, suddenly remorseful. "He must be in agony. And how embarrassing it'll be when his friends start talking about all this. I'm so glad Tyler's not here. I certainly don't want him asking questions. Keep right on with your work,

Goldy. I'm staying with you until Clark starts the hockey game. You need protection from those busybodies."

Of course, she was right. So was Marla. I *should* have worn a shirt that said I DON'T KNOW ANYTHING.

"It's ACHMO." Patricia said it dismissively as I steadfastly organized my supplies. She munched another dip-loaded chip reflectively. "You ever try to talk to somebody on the phone there? ACHMO reminds me of a church I went to once. Everybody hates everybody. The institution doesn't function and it's everybody else's fault. The more you try to replace people, the worse it gets. Better to just burn the place down and start over."

"What do you mean?"

"You know what they did to me," she said. Actually, I had never asked for the litany of volleys in Patricia's negligence lawsuit against ACHMO. I knew she had lost her baby. I was not so interested that I had to hear all the details of the legal battle. Nor did I want to. "You heard ACHMO canned Ralph, of course," she continued conspiratorially. "He'll be here tonight, poor thing."

"I did hear he had been fired." I could sound as sympathetic as the next person. "Did Ralph find a new job?"

188

She nodded. "He was lucky to get something with another HMO, but it's in administration. I'm sure there are many, many people Suz Craig fired," she stated in the same offhand tone. "But two in Aspen Meadow? Please. We should get federal funds." She lifted another chip as she raised an eyebrow.

"The other person she fired is Amy Bartholomew?"

"So you know about Amy. Yes. The woman's a real healer, Goldy. Amy's the one who told me to have this party. Suz lost a gem in her. But Amy sees people at her health-food store now. I don't believe she ever supported six slot machines in Central City, the way they said."

I placed the biscuits on a buttered cookie sheet and covered them with foil to reheat later. "Well," I said hopefully, "the police are bound to sort it out. Maybe you'd like to check on your guests . . . ?"

Unfortunately, Patricia still seemed to be in no hurry to leave. "So are they . . . going to put your husband on the case? The investigator? That would be something, wouldn't it? I can't imagine —"

"No, Patricia." I peered out the window that overlooked the driveway. The male guests had divided themselves into two

189

teams: one wearing T-shirts, the other not. A half-dozen men sat on the wooden retaining wall strapping on in-line skates, while another three — helmeted, padded, bare-chested — were taking tentative gliding turns around the drive. Their faces were hostile and they appeared to be yelling. Hurling insults at each other already? "Uh, do you have a doctor around? I mean, just in case there's a problem with the hockey game outside?"

Alarmed, Patricia stepped up to the window beside me. "Oh, for crying out loud, they've started? Uh-oh, there's Drew Herbert. He's got the logo of the Detroit Red Wings tattooed on his chest." She rapped on the glass. No one outside paid the slightest attention. "Who is . . ." One of the skaters took a spill and Patricia yelped. "Oh, Clark's going to get *us* sued!" With this, she rushed out of the room.

Two nets abutted opposite ends of the driveway. One goal stood by the paved edge that gave way to the sloped front lawn and Tyler's swing set, the other had been pushed up against a high retaining wall made of four-by-fours. Transfixed, I watched from the window until all twelve men were skating at a dizzying speed. Wielding lethal-looking hockey sticks, they bunched and raced, bunched and raced, all the time weaving past one another in furious pursuit of a bright purple tennis-size ball.

The score seesawed between the Shirts and the Chests, with the Shirts leading in high-fives and the Chests in sweat-production. About ten spectators, including the three women who had barged in on me, gathered on the driveway sidelines, hollering and laughing and swilling what looked like large gin-and-tonics in what I hoped were plastic — not glass — cups. What had happened to the beer? Had Clark brought it down to the end of the driveway?

When the score was two to one, a fight broke out over whether one of the Chests had skated out-of-bounds. First two, then four, guys started jostling one another. Unfriendly shoulder shoves accompanied open-mouthed braying.

Squawking, Patricia dashed into the fray. We were still twenty minutes from when I was supposed to bring out the first batch of appetizers for two dozen people. But if this squabble heated up much more, I'd have fewer mouths to feed than I'd planned.

The men argued and gestured with their hockey sticks. *Here!* they seemed to be saying. *No, the ball went out over there!* Two more women, apparently mindless of their own physical safety, rushed in from the sidelines to try to break up the conflict. Patricia stabbed a finger accusingly in her husband's face, while another woman decided her husband needed to have his red face sloshed with gin-and-tonic. When Clark pushed Patricia aside, she turned and stomped back up toward the house. The conflict continued unabated.

Two men popped each other on opposite shoulders while skating sideways and trying to keep their balance. Then one of the Shirts unstrapped his helmet and snapped it upward, smacking it into the nose of his opponent in the melee. The man flailed backward, then did a belly flop forward on the blacktop. The battle ceased briefly while the injured man lay flapping his arms and legs. His squeals for help were muted — probably he had landed on his diaphragm.

Patricia McCracken, her face red and her voice shrill, rushed back into the kitchen. "Beer! Dammit, Goldy! What are you standing there for? Beer! Don't wait for halftime! Take them some beer now!"

I mumbled something about a medic being a better idea than a bartender but scrambled obediently around the kitchen, where I quickly filled a Styrofoam cooler with three six-packs and a shower of ice. Beer didn't seem a very good idea to me, especially on top of all those gin-and-tonics. Still, my contract did not include ground cleanup, if it came to that. I marched carefully down the walk to Clark McCracken, who gestured grandly toward his cement-hockey game.

"Take it down to them! Take it down!" he hollered, his face scarlet with exhaustion and what I suspected was pain. "*Throw* the cans at them if you have to!"

Without Clark, the players had resumed their game, which I found incredible. The Shirts and the Chests were skating around one another with even more alacrity and daring than before. One helmeted player thwacked the ball toward the goal and barely missed the net. Instead, the ball bounced off the retaining wall and smacked one of the female spectators in the knee. Her shrill squawk of pain went utterly unheeded as the skaters bent and swerved around one another to pass a newly produced ball.

"Beer break!" I called as the cans chinked against one another with what I hoped was an inviting sound. But the players could not hear me or the cans as they pushed, grunted, and jostled for position. Clark, somehow revived, whooshed past and waved me down to the sideline. I sighed, heaved the Styrofoam chest above my rib cage, and clinkclomped closer to the players, keeping a wary eye on the game.

Clark bellowed enthusiastically to his fellow skaters: "Hey, guys! A beer break would —"

But I never heard him finish. From the chalked line where I stood, I was suddenly aware of a shift in the game. Like a tornado that had changed direction without warning, a gaggle of sweating skaters loomed. Charging out of the crowd came Ralph Shelton, hell-bent in my direction. I dropped the beers. The Styrofoam chest landed on my feet. Spilling ice filled the air as Ralph Shelton slammed into my stationary, unhelmeted, unpadded body. As he hit me, the look on his bandaged face was a determined, angry grimace, as if he had every intention of killing me.

Chapter 12

There was, apparently, a shortage of doctors. In any event, no one stepped up to offer me help. I lay on the pavement one second, two seconds, three. My eyes felt permanently crossed. As far as I could determine, everyone seemed to be clustered around Ralph Shelton.

I gasped but couldn't bring any air in; the wind was gone from my body. Blood dripped from my forehead. Finally some people moved toward me. Their mouths chattered incomprehensibly. *Move,* I told myself. *Get up.* But I didn't. I couldn't.

I groaned and lifted one shoulder. Pain pierced my stomach and shot up my legs. My calves had been gashed by Ralph's in-line skates. Even more agonizing was my head, which throbbed unremittingly.

As I speechlessly eyed the gaggle now gawking down at me, I was convinced that the cement had cracked my skull. Perhaps I had a concussion. Perhaps my brains were leaking out. Well, I had agreed to cater to a group of hockey fans. I probably didn't have any brains left to leak.

"Goldy?" A strange woman's voice accused me from faraway. "Why did you drop the beer?"

I closed my eyes.

When I opened them again, I was sitting in a gleaming blue-and-white bathroom. I had a vague recollection of someone lifting me and then placing me into this space. I studied my surroundings. Thinly striped blue porcelain tiles covered the floor, ran up the walls, surrounded the tub. Someone had wiped off my legs, arms, and face. The room swam. This was a nightmare, and I was dinner on a Staffordshire plate.

"I won't be much longer," came a comforting voice from the vicinity of the sink. Water was running. I risked eyeing the sink area.

The plump woman who stood beside me was of medium height. Her strawberry-blond hair shone. In the mirror I could see she had a kindly face. Actually, *two* kindly faces. I groaned and closed my eyes.

An impatient, distressed voice spoke from the doorway. "Lucky you're coming around, Goldy." My heart sank: Patricia. This *was* a bad dream. "We're starting on that vegetable basket you put out. Are you all right now? My husband can't put the fish on the grill until you're ready."

"Ready for what?" I muttered as the kindly red-haired lady smeared a gold-colored jelly on my forehead. The jelly looked like Vaseline and smelled like something you'd get in a Navajo gift shop. "What are you doing?" I asked uneasily, even as the comforting warmth of the salve magically removed the throbbing in my head. "Do I know you?"

"Shh, shh." The woman smoothed more salve on my right arm. "Now smear some of this on your other arm." I obeyed. More water spurted from the faucet. The red-haired Florence Nightingale handed me a glassful. "Can you drink some of this and then put this under your tongue?" When I nodded mutely, she shook out a speckled beige tablet from a wide brown bottle that hadn't come from any pharmacy.

"I'm not taking any drugs," I said firmly. Or at least I think I did.

Her laugh rippled off the porcelain walls. "This is about as far from drugs as you can get," she assured me.

"Goldy, did you hear me?" pleaded Patricia, my former friend, my former pleasant client. "We're going to start on your appetizers. Clark's putting on a video of one of the Cup games and I want dinner to be served in forty minutes. If you're still going to cater this party, you'd better pull yourself together."

I clasped the tablet. It was still difficult to bring Patricia into focus. "Ah, do all the skates have their guests off?" I managed. Dyslexic sentence. Still couldn't think right. No wonder press conferences after hockey games were so uninformative. "Ah . . ." I tried again. "Guests have their skates off?"

"Of course they do," Patricia retorted. "You've been in here for almost a quarter of an hour. I'm worried that the grill's going to run out of propane. When that last buzzer sounds, I want these guests to have grilled fish on their plates. Please hurry!" Then she turned on her heel and stomped away. I hoped Clark had put on a video of the last game of the 1996 Stanley Cup. Then we would have dinner in five hours, and I would have the last laugh.

"Don't mind her," said the red-haired woman. "And by the way, I'm a nurse. Put that pill under your tongue. It's a homeopathic treatment for shock and pain."

"What . . . ?"

But I was in too much pain to argue. I obediently slipped the pill under my tongue and got a smile as a reward from my new guardian angel. Doggone if this woman didn't have an aura. On the other hand, maybe my head injury was even worse than I feared.

She said softly, "It's called arnica, from a flower of the same name."

"Who're you?" I managed.

"Ralph Shelton called me," she replied in that mellifluous voice that reminded me of stirred custard. "I live close by." She concentrated her warm brown eyes on mine. "Ralph and I used to work together. He was so worried about you. He told me you were an old friend of his." She added gently, "My name's Amy Bartholomew."

I gagged on the second tablet as Amy patted more of the salve on my right shin. "I thought you . . ." What did I think she was going to look like, Kenny Rogers fresh from singing "The Gambler"? "What's that you're putting on me?" There was a taste of grass clippings in my mouth from the pills. "This stuff in my mouth tastes funny."

"The salve contains goldenseal, olive oil, comfrey, yarrow, white oak bark, and all kinds of other healing herbs. Beginning to feel any better?"

I nodded, then waited for the pain in my head to pulse in punishment for my unwise move. To my astonishment, it didn't. I looked down at my legs: my stockings were torn; bloody scratches crisscrossed my knees. I wished I had a change of clothes, but of course I did not. Amy continued to dab salve on the cuts. When she finished, she told me to hold out my hand. I did, and she shook a handful of the tablets into my palm.

"Take two more now, then another four in half an hour. Then four more every hour until you go to bed. Okay?"

"Okay." I was still trying to calm the chaos in my head. "Do you have a card or something? I mean, so I can pay you? I doubt the McCrackens will cough up the money for your time and supplies."

Amy shook her head and chuckled. "Don't worry about it. Patricia is a customer of mine. Come see me, though, on . . . say, Monday or Tuesday. At the store. I want to take a look at your eyes. You know where I am? By the lake?"

I nodded again. Hesitantly I said, "Do you . . . did you hear about Suz Craig?"

Her face darkened. "Don't bring up negativity now. You can't digest it. You need to get better. Focus on healing."

I sighed deeply. *Focus on healing.* I'd discovered the corpse of a murdered woman, my violent ex-husband was screaming threats from his jail cell, my son was furious with me, I'd been hit in a roller hockey derby, the party I was catering was going down the tubes, and my scratched and bloodied body would be covered with bruises for weeks. *Focus on healing?* No problem.

After Amy left, I ordered myself to stand up. Then I checked in the mirror. Not as bad as I would have thought. There were three separate but relatively small cuts on my face and neck. My right eye was already pink and beginning to swell. My right shoulder hurt. The headache still echoed darkly in the back of my skull. I popped in a couple more arnica tablets and tried to concentrate on setting up the salads.

The guests were fully engaged in watching one of the playoff games between the Avalanche and the Chicago Blackhawks. I scanned the room for Ralph Shelton. Apparently he'd gone home. But questions nagged. Had he deliberately run into me? Had he meant to hurt me? Or was it just difficult to stop on in-line skates? I refused to ponder these questions until I was safely at home. First, I had a dinner to serve.

I tiptoed past the noisy living room to the security of the kitchen and spooned the salads into their bowls. My spirits began to revive as I poured the marinade over the tuna and heated the Mexican eggrolls I'd made the day before. The smell of hot south-of-the-border food was marvelous. I sliced one of the eggrolls to make sure it was suitably hot and crispy, then dipped it into an avocado-lime mixture and took a bite. The eggroll skin crackled around the chile-laden stuffing of chicken, black beans, cumin, and melted cheese. Yum. I was feeling so much better it was amazing. Now all I needed was a Dos Equis, a hot shower, and a leap into bed. Fat chance.

I slipped the biscuits and potato rolls into the oven, passed around the eggrolls, and received a gratifying chorus of *ooh*s and *ah*s and *I'll have another one of those*s. No one commented on my bruised and battered face. I put the fish on the grill and checked on the heating biscuits. Frowning, Patricia devoured half an eggroll. Her face softened. Could she be feeling remorse for scolding me after I'd been slammed nearly senseless by one of her guests? I wondered. Maybe she'd realized I could sue *her*. Maybe she just liked Mexican food. I tested a corner of the grilled fish: flaky and deliciously flavored with the marinade. Apparently I could still do my job correctly.

The guests, some still wearing in-line skating attire, others clad in Avalanche gear, boisterously tumbled out to the buffet line after the buzzer sounded in the Blackhawks game. One or two eyed me curiously, but no one bothered to ask how I was. At this party, they expected injuries. Nor did they ask me what the story was on the Jerk's arrest. Okay by me: the invincible caterer had work to do.

Soon the guests had munched their way through the main course and I put on coffee to brew. Eventually, the guests were drinking their coffee and eating Stanley Cupcakes topped with slices of ice-cream rink, while lamenting that the beginning of the NHL season was over a month away. I glanced at the clock over the kitchen window. Ten to eight. The sun slid slowly behind the mountains. Just above the jagged, deeply shadowed horizon, thin striations of gray cloud lay in perfect, straight lines. *It's a giant comb,* Arch and I would have said, back when he was little. I ran hot water into the sink and put in the first batch of dishes to be rinsed. I couldn't wait to finish this job.

Just after nine o'clock I heaved the first of my heavy boxes across my deck. Tom was waiting. As soon as he saw my face, he shook his head. He opened the back door, came out, and took the box from me. A huge dark green apron swathed his body. He'd been cooking, as usual, because he knew I would not have had time to eat.

"Miss G!" His face furrowed with worry. "What happened to you?"

"Don't ask. It's not that big a deal, anyway."

He sighed. "You get into more scrapes in a day than I do in a year. And I'm the one with the *dangerous* job."

"You've never catered to hockey fans," I muttered glumly.

"True." He set the box on the counter and chuckled as I flopped into a chair. He stooped to give me a kiss, then eyed my cut cheek. Instead he kissed the top of my head.

Later, when we'd brought all the supplies inside, I asked, "Where is the rest of this family?"

He smiled and started the food processor grating potatoes. "Upstairs. Macguire's had quite a day, his most active in the last month. He's had a long shower. But I think he may be running a bit of a fever. Arch took the dog and the cat into his room and the four of them are laughing over doll-collecting magazines."

"*What?*"

Tom deftly beat an egg, dipped in a flour-dusted fish fillet, then rolled it in shreds of potato. I suddenly realized I was starving.

"Don't worry," he went on, "I gave Macguire some ibuprofen. He had an incident over at the lake with Arch. Oh, and Arch isn't going to the Druckmans' tonight, he wanted to stay here and make sure Macguire was okay."

"Back up. What incident? Why were the boys at the lake?"

Tom took a deep breath, not a good sign. "Apparently the health-food store was closed. Macguire was too tired to walk any farther, so the two of them went over to the LakeCenter looking for someone to give them a ride home. One lady — what's her name, Rodine? — said she would if the two boys could bring in some tables. Do you believe that? Why wouldn't she just give the kids a ride home?"

I sighed. "Because she's a gold-plated bitch, that's why."

"Of course Macguire was too weak to lift a table, and Arch was too small, so they asked if they could do something else to earn their ride. So Mrs. Rodine had them carry in some cartons full of boxed dolls. They hauled a crate up on one of the stands inside the LakeCenter while Mrs. Rodine and her pals were yelling directions to some other underlings outside. So Arch and Macguire, trying to be helpful, started to take the doll boxes out of the crate. Once they had them all out, Arch got worried about Macguire, so he went to a soft-drink machine to get the two of them some pops. Meanwhile, Macguire started to take the dolls out of the boxes —"

"Oh, no. No, no, no. The collectors don't want the dolls out of the boxes. The collectors want them NRFB. Never Removed From Box. It makes a huge difference —"

Tom held up a hand. "When Arch came in with the drinks, he tried to warn Macguire, but it was too late."

I repeated, "Too late. Oh, God."

Tom seemed resigned to telling this tale of human folly. Yet his green eyes were merry as he drizzled olive oil on the griddle. "Three women screamed and *chased* Arch and Macguire out of the LakeCenter. Then a guy, one of the helper-husbands, called the sheriff's department on his cellular phone —"

I moaned.

Tom slid the potato-crusted fillets on the hot griddle, where their sizzling sound made my mouth water. "Since I was on my way home from the hardware store, I was the closest." Another smile quirked the corners of his mouth. "So I answered the call. I've done a lot of strange duties in my day. But trying to convince a hysterical trio of women that removing a 1994 Holiday Babsie from its original box is not a chargeable offense — now that was perhaps the most challenging job I've had yet." He chuckled.

I moaned again. "These women didn't actually *do* anything to Arch and Macguire, did they? Why does Macguire have a fever?"

Tom pursed his lips and flipped the fish. "The Babsie ladies chased our boys to the end of the old pier, where unfortunately Macguire lost his balance and fell into the water. A woman in a shell rowed over and held on to him until someone from the Lake-Center could throw out a life preserver." Tom carefully scooped the golden-brown fish pieces into a buttered pan and eased the whole thing into the oven.

I rubbed my aching skull. "I . . . know that doll collecting is a bona fide hobby. Sort of like being a hockey fan. But I just don't understand why these *pastimes* become *manias.*"

"I asked the same question. I might as well have asked the ladies' Bible study to describe the Rapture. One woman told me very seriously that doll collecting was like the best sex you ever had, times ten."

I let that pass. While the fish was baking, I moved — slowly, painfully — up the stairs to check on Macguire and Arch, who both immediately demanded to know why I looked so *awful*. I stalled and took Macguire's temperature. It was one hundred degrees even, not enough to call his doctor, he maintained. Then I told the boys I'd gotten hit by a hockey fan. The fan had been wearing blades, I explained, and I had not.

"*Dude*, Mrs. Schulz," said Macguire admiringly. "You're brave."

"No, just dumb enough to be in his way."

Apparently being with Macguire had worked the kind of effect on Arch Marla had predicted it would. My son did not seem preoccupied with his father and the events of the morning. He didn't even appear to be angry with me. At least not at the moment.

He pointed to the magazine in his lap. "Check this out, Mom."

I bent to look at the page. After a second I moved in closer. I wanted to make sure my eyes weren't deceiving me. A Never-Removed-From-Box Duchess Bride Babsie was selling for twelve hundred dollars. Another one that *had* been taken out of the box sold for six hundred dollars. The dolls had sold for less than twenty dollars originally, and I remembered my little childhood friend in New Jersey who had taken such delight in playing with her Babsies. In the catalog, I saw one that looked familiar from my friend's collection. It was an MIB — Mint-In-Box — Number One Blond Ponytail Babsie. The doll had just gone at auction for six thousand dollars. I felt faint.

"Mom, are you all right?" Arch asked anxiously.

"I'm fine," I assured him. "I've already seen a nurse, and she gave me a homeopathic remedy."

"Homeopathic?" Macguire grumbled. "What is *that?*"

"It means natural," I explained. "Please don't stay up too late. I don't need *both* of you to get sick."

Arch gave me an exasperated look and I closed the door before I could offend him further. Ten minutes later I was scrubbed, robed, and more ravenous than ever. In honor of my service to hockey fans, Tom had named his creation Power Play Potatoes and Fish. He served them with a fine julienne of carrot, steamed baby peas, a small green salad, and southern spoon bread topped with pats of butter. I took a greedy bite of the fish: Tom's pairing of a crunchy potato crust with the delicate texture and rich taste of Chilean seabass was divine, and I told him so. He smiled and told me the recipe was now taped to my computer screen. Then he frowned.

"What was the name of the guy you said hit you?"

"Dr. Ralph Shelton," I mumbled, mouth full of succulent fish. "Remember? I told you about him earlier today. He's an old friend of ours. Used to be with ACHMO, but according to town gossip he was fired by Suz Craig."

"Right. And I was going to check on him, which I did. Which I actually told Donny Saunders to do, more accurately. By the way, did the gossip say *why* this Dr. Shelton was fired?"

I indicated a negative and took a bite of the carrots and peas, celestially fresh, sweet vegetables. The spoon bread was as rich and tender as anything Scarlett O'Hara had ever put into her mouth. I made "mm-mm" noises and Tom nodded in acknowledgment.

"Brandon Yuille, you know him?" he asked, his mind still on work.

"He's the head of Human Resources for ACHMO. He's also the son of a baker in town. He was at Suz's house when I catered over there. I saw him today, but briefly. Why? Have you talked to him?"

"Yeah, a whole team went out to talk to the ACHMO department heads, but most of them are in San Diego at a conference. Medical Management, Member Services, Health Services, Quality Management — four of the six people who had to deal with Suz Craig on a daily basis are gone for the week, although they're coming back early. The only department heads left in town were Human Resources and Provider Relations." He took a breath. "John Richard Korman is absolutely insistent he's innocent. The cops who're questioning him? They're getting real tired of hearing about Suz Craig doing *this* to make enemies, Suz Craig doing *that*."

"I hope they're ignoring him. John Richard Korman is probably the worst enemy Suz Craig ever made. The most dangerous, certainly."

Tom shrugged. "He's the prime suspect, so the department is concentrating on him. But Donny Saunders has asked me to help him out. I agreed."

"So where does Brandon Yuille come in?"

"Korman insists that Yuille and Suz Craig were having some kind of feud. Yuille claims he was with his father at his bakery from midnight to five last night, so he couldn't have killed Ms. Craig."

"You called Brandon?"

"Caught him unawares. He'll probably

211

never talk to me again without a lawyer present. And he's not the most talkative man in the county," Tom observed. "Anyway, he was awfully vague when I wanted to know why Ralph Shelton left ACHMO."

"You asked him that? Brandon was vague or he didn't know?"

Tom's face was unreadable. "Your ex-husband maintains that Ralph Shelton hated Suz, too. I'm wondering if his firing had anything to do with Patricia McCracken's lawsuit against ACHMO."

"What are you *talking* about? I mean, I know Ralph is an obstetrician, but . . ." I felt muddled. It had been too long a day.

Tom stood and picked up my whisker-clean plate. He ran water into the sink, then said, "What I did get out of Brandon Yuille was this: Ralph Shelton used to be associated with an ob-gyn practice down in Denver. Shelton was on call at St. Philip's Hospital when Clark McCracken brought his wife, Patricia, in the night she lost their baby. There she is, losing blood and disoriented and Shelton tells her he's with ACHMO. Even though they're old friends, our Patricia McCracken hauls off and slaps the guy across the face. He fell, and it knocked the wind out of him. That woman's unbelievably strong, even when she's sick."

Power Play
Potatoes and Fish

4 (6 to 8 ounces each) fresh
  Chilean seabass fillets
½ cup flour
2 eggs
4 large russet potatoes
2 tablespoons olive oil
Salt and freshly ground black
  pepper

Preheat oven to 400°. Butter a
  9- by 13-inch baking dish.

Rinse off the fillets and pat dry
with paper towels. Sprinkle the
flour on a plate. Beat the eggs
in a shallow bowl. Peel the potatoes. Grate them onto a
large, clean kitchen towel that
can be stained. Roll the potatoes up in the towel and wring
to remove moisture. (It is best
to do this over the sink.) Divide
the potatoes into four piles.

In a wide skillet, heat the olive oil. Working quickly, dip each fillet first in the flour, then in the egg. Pat half of each potato pile on the top and bottom of each fillet (the equivalent of one grated potato per fillet). Bring the skillet up to medium-high heat. Place the potato-covered fillets in the hot oil, salt and pepper them, and brown quickly on each side. When all the fillets are browned, put them in the buttered pan and bake about 10 minutes, or until they are cooked through. *Do not overcook the fish.*

Serves 4

"But," I protested, "we all used to be close. Besides, Ralph Shelton wasn't the problem. John Richard and ACHMO were."

"That night Patricia McCracken sure *saw* Ralph Shelton as the problem. Then the chain of events goes like this. She files one suit against Korman; she files another against ACHMO. Ralph leaves his practice under a cloud. Our investigation is very preliminary at this point, but it looks as if after that Shelton took an administrative job with another HMO. One named Merit-Med."

I said reflectively, "But Ralph and the McCrackens seem to have buried the hatchet. I mean, he was invited to their hockey party tonight."

Tom grinned. "Yeah, after their little tussle in the hospital Patricia apologized all over the place to Shelton. Maybe she's trying to be sweet to him these days, so that he'll tell her some inside stuff on ACHMO that she can use against them in her suit. I mean, now that he's persona non grata there."

"Ralph seems to stick together with another persona non grata," I commented as I poured two dessert sherries. I told Tom about being tended to by Amy Bartholomew, nurse lately of ACHMO. "She's involved with natural remedies now." That reminded me. I sought out my last four arnica tablets and washed them down with the glass of cream sherry. It may not have been what the homeopaths would have recommended, but I thought it was wonderful.

Tom pulled me into his lap. "Tell me we're going to have a break from talking about this case tomorrow, Miss G. This guy gets arrested first thing in the morning, and it ends up ruining our entire weekend."

It could ruin a lot more than our weekend, I thought glumly, but didn't say so. "You're always telling me how if a case isn't solved in the first forty-eight hours, it's unlikely it'll be solved at all."

"Wait. One more thing. Suz Craig *did* deny Korman his bonus. Late last week."

I sighed. "That's what Marla was afraid of."

"You still don't think this case is solved?"

"I think this case is far from over. But we won't mention a word of it tomorrow. Besides," I teased, "I want to talk some more about the joys of doll collecting. I'm not sure I believe their claims. I mean, *best sex times ten?*"

"You do have to wonder," he replied, deadpan, then led me upstairs.

Chapter 13

You'd think after all I'd been through, I would have slept without a break for twelve hours. Not me. I slept for two.

I awoke at midnight damp with sweat, wrenched from sleep by a nightmare starring John Richard. I'd been jolted awake believing I was Suz Craig, and I was being beaten to death. Perhaps my muscles had cramped after my collision with Ralph Shelton. Whatever the reason, sleep was impossible.

I tiptoed to the kitchen, where I made myself a hot chocolate and topped it with a fat dollop of marshmallow cream. Nothing like chocolate and marshmallow to soothe the nerves. When I was eleven and had failed a social studies test, I'd headed straight to the drugstore and ordered chocolate ice cream slathered with spoonfuls of creamed marshmallow. Did they even make that kind of sundae anymore? I wondered.

I sipped the chocolate, booted up my computer, and started a new file: *JRK ARREST*. I remembered Arch's words: *He* really *needs you.* Well, I didn't care about what John Richard Korman needed. But I was interested in the truth. And I needed Arch to believe I cared about *him.*

It had been a tempestuous day. I had promised Tom we wouldn't talk about the case on Sunday. Still, the information about the crime now bubbling up reminded me of the schools of minnows that can occasionally be seen at Aspen Meadow Lake. If you don't get out your net right away, you're going to lose them.

I began by listing everything I knew about the people involved. Suz Craig had run the Denver office of the AstuteCare Health Maintenance Organization. John Richard Korman, one of the ACHMO providers, had been dating Suz for the past seven months. On the home front, Suz had bought a luxurious house in Aspen Meadow, where she'd been doing an expensive landscape project. On the business front, she had reportedly fired employees without remorse, and refused those she didn't fire their bonuses. And she had presumably enforced the rules of the HMO, which could have had some implications for Patricia McCracken's case. Patricia sure thought so. Maybe I had to find out the details of her case, after all.

QUESTION, I typed. *Why exactly is Patri-*

cia suing both JRK and ACHMO?

QUESTION: Did Suz Craig fire Dr. Ralph Shelton? If so, why?

QUESTION: Was gambling really enough of a reason for Suz to fire Amy Bartholomew, R.N.?

QUESTION: What did JRK and Suz Craig argue about at the country club?

I sighed. How would I get the answers to these questions? And why should I? I saved my file, shut down the computer, and sipped the steamy hot chocolate. The marshmallow had melted into a creamy layer on the chocolate surface. I licked it off carefully, the way a child would. Outside my kitchen window, elk bleated. I did not feel the remotest bit tired. I needed to get some sleep. How on earth could I face church in a state of exhaustion? Then inspiration struck.

Cook! That'll relax you. Put all these people and all these questions out of your head for a while and whip something up. I fingered the containers of Dutch-processed cocoa and the jar of marshmallow cream I'd left on the counter. Why couldn't you put these together in a cookie? Surely there could be nothing like chocolate and marshmallow in a *cookie* to soothe the nerves?

I put some hazelnuts in the oven to toast, then melted a jagged brick of unsweetened

219

Chocolate
Comfort Cookies

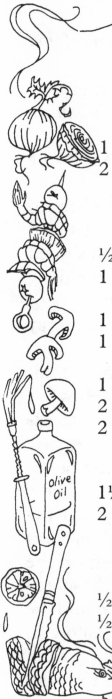

1 cup chopped hazelnuts
2 cups (1 11½-ounce package) extra-large semisweet chocolate chips (Nestle's mega-morsels)
½ cup sun-dried cranberries
1 cup (2 sticks) unsalted butter, softened
1 cup granulated sugar
1 3-ounce package cream cheese, softened
1 egg
2 tablespoons milk
2 ounces best-quality unsweetened chocolate, melted
1½ teaspoons vanilla
2 cups plus 2 tablespoons all-purpose flour (high altitude: add 2 more tablespoons, for a total of 2¼ cups)
½ teaspoon baking powder
½ teaspoon salt

¼ cup Dutch-processed cocoa
1 cup commercially prepared
marshmallow cream

Preheat oven to 325°. Spread
nuts on an ungreased cookie
sheet and roast for 7 to 12
minutes, or until they are
lightly browned and some
skins have loosened. Set aside
to cool.

Butter 2 cookie sheets. In a
large bowl, combine the
chocolate chips, cranberries,
and cooled nuts; set aside. In
another large bowl, beat together the butter, sugar, cream
cheese, and egg until very
creamy and smooth. Beat in
milk, melted chocolate, and
vanilla. Sift together the flour,
baking powder, salt, and cocoa, then add to the butter
mixture. Blend in the
marshmallow cream, stirring

until thoroughly combined. Add the chips, cranberries, and nuts. Stir until well mixed. Batter will be thick.

Using a ¼-cup measure or a 4-tablespoon ice cream scoop, measure out batter and place 2 inches apart on cookie sheets, putting no more than 6 cookies per sheet. Bake 13 to 17 minutes, until puffed and cooked through. Cool on sheet 1 minute; transfer to wire racks to cool completely.

Makes 2 dozen

chocolate in the top of our double boiler. I combined sun-dried cranberries and oversize morsels of semisweet chocolate in a bowl, then scattered the hazelnuts to cool on a plate. I began to feel better. By the time I was beating unsalted butter with sugar and cream cheese, I was humming, and this was a mistake. Jake came bounding into the room on his long bloodhound legs, followed closely by a sleepy-eyed Arch clad in rumpled pajamas. Arch fumbled with his glasses and stared in puzzlement at the bowls, the butter wrappers, and the whirling beater.

"Gosh, Mom! What are you doing? Did you forget something? Do you have to take cookies to church?"

"Sorry, honey, I just couldn't sleep. How about some hot chocolate with marshmallow? That's what I used to have when I was your age and flunked a test. Or when I was your age and couldn't sleep. It always worked, despite what they now say about the caffeine in chocolate."

"Well, I *could* have slept if you hadn't awakened Jake," my son grumbled crossly. He shuffled to the back door and opened it, but the elk had stopped bugling and Jake wasn't the least bit interested in a midnight run. Resigned, Arch closed the door and flopped into a chair. "Sure, I'll have some cocoa, thanks." Immediately he was up, offering Jake one of Tom's homemade dog biscuits. "Yeah, boy, there you go! Don't worry, I'm not going to have a treat unless you do!" The large, tawny dog wagged his tail, licked Arch's face, and whined with canine contentment.

I heated more milk and stirred it into a smooth, thick paste of cocoa, sugar, and cream. In his corner, Jake crunched appreciatively. His dark eyes favored my son and me with loving glances. Arch gave him two more dog biscuits, then watched while I generously glopped marshmallow cream on top of his drink. When I put the steaming mug in front of him, I expected him to pounce on the rich treat as expectantly as I had. Instead, he blew tentatively on the foamy top, then sipped.

"Mom. There's something I need to talk to you about." He put his mug down. "It's about Dad." When my face fell, he quickly said, "Go ahead, make your cookies, it's not important." He added earnestly, "I really mean it, Mom. I don't want to disturb you. Cook, if it'll help you go back to sleep. I just have a couple of questions. . . ."

He had questions, I had questions, everybody had all kinds of questions. My headache returned with a vengeance. I beat the egg and milk into the batter, then added the melted chocolate and vanilla. Once the oven was preheated and the cookie sheets buttered, I measured out what I thought would be a judicious balance of dry ingredients and began to mix them into the batter. These cookies promised to be terrific. But apprehension had drained the joy from cooking experimentation.

Arch said, "So. When was the last time there was an execution in Colorado?"

"Arch!"

"No, really, just tell me. And . . . was it by lethal injection?"

I sighed and scooped the batter onto the cookie sheets. "No, the last execution used the electric chair. And it was over thirty years ago, I think. Law enforcement in Colorado has switched over to lethal injection. But they've never used it."

"The death penalty" — his voice cracked — "is for first-degree murder, right?"

I slid the cookie sheets into the oven and turned. "Arch —"

"Just tell me."

"Yes, for first-degree murder. But —"

"Are you going to help Dad?" he demanded.

His question stung. I set the timer and tried to think of what to say. Finally I asked,

"What would you like me to do?"

"Oh, you know," he replied earnestly, "that stuff you do sometimes, go around asking questions, like that. Try to help with the investigation the way you do with Tom."

"Tom's off this case, and I'm a witness. Which is supposed to mean that I don't go around talking to people connected with the case."

"You did when you found that guy's body out at Elk Park Prep and when that lady was killed in the parking garage."

"Those were different. I didn't see any suspects, and I certainly didn't witness an arrest for homicide. And besides, those things happened when I was pretty ignorant about law enforcement."

His thin body sagged. "So that means no." His tone turned morose. "If Dad does get out of jail on Monday the way he thinks he will, I think I should go live with him. Until the trial. I mean, it might be the last time I would see him."

I couldn't believe we were having this conversation, in the middle of the night, in the warm security of our home, here in our warm kitchen. In the extremely unlikely event that John Richard got out of jail anytime before his preliminary hearing, I couldn't imagine that he would *want* Arch to live with him.

Whatever punishment I had envisioned for the Jerk during all these years, it hadn't looked like this. It hadn't looked like losing my son.

"Arch," I said quietly, "are you threatening me with moving out? 'Cause that's what it sounds like."

"Mom! Of course not! I'm just trying to do what's right here. He *is* my father."

I struggled for clear thoughts and the right words. "Okay, look. If I can talk to some people . . . and those conversations would help lead to justice . . . *Justice*, I'm talking, Arch, not 'getting somebody off.' There's a difference."

"Yeah, yeah, truth, justice, and the American way. Courtesy of SuperMom."

"Arch!"

"Okay, okay."

"If I could talk to some people but not jeopardize my position as a witness, would you stay here at home? Your dad's really not . . . set up to take care of you. And I would worry about you."

He nodded, whispered "Okay," and drank his cocoa in silence. Then he sniffed, mumbled, "Be right back," and left the room. Jake, ever faithful, scrambled after him. I took the cookies out of the oven and set them on racks to cool.

When Arch returned, he clutched a wadded-up tissue. I couldn't tell if he'd been crying. "I was just thinking, Mom." He'd changed his tone, a clear indication that he wanted to discuss a new topic. "You said you were having a cup of hot chocolate to drink right now, because you couldn't sleep? But when you can't sleep, you should go out for a drive. Don't you remember? That's what you used to do when I was little. When I couldn't sleep, you took me out for a drive, and you said it made you sleepy, too."

"Oh, hon —"

"You probably don't remember, but you *used* to say that driving me around was like having hot chocolate when you were little. The rhythm of the car put me to sleep the way the hot chocolate did you. Even if it was the middle of the night, if I was fussy, you would take me. I don't remember the drives, I just remember you telling me we used to go."

I nodded and checked the cookies; they were almost cool. I remembered the drives, all right. And I hadn't taken them just because Arch was fussy. Time and again, I'd gripped that steering wheel the way fear had clutched me. Rocking over bumpy mountain roads, I'd been desperately trying to figure out a way to escape from my life, from John Richard Korman's abuse, and a marriage I just couldn't hold together anymore. I had been lost in the worst way, and it had taken years to get my *life* on the right road.

Now I packed up the cookies, stacked all the dirty dishes in the sink, and threw away the ingredient debris.

"A drive sounds like a great idea," I told my son. "But what do you say we get some sleep first?"

Arch agreed. For once, he wasn't in the mood to taste my new cookies, and neither was I.

Chapter 14

I begged the Almighty to help me rest up before church began the next morning. Finally I fell into a restless slumber at dawn. Tom woke me, bearing a cup of steaming espresso.

"If you want to make it to the late service," he advised gently, "we need to get a move on." As I struggled upright and promptly winced, Tom added with concern, "Sure you don't want to just stay in bed this morning?"

I assured him I was just stiff. Plus I'd been up during the night cooking. He shook his head and began to massage my aching shoulders. My lower back was still in spasm, and my right ankle throbbed. After drinking the espresso, I checked the ankle. It was ominously blue-black. I limped into the bathroom to take a hot shower, dabbed bits of makeup over the scratches on my face, and finally felt ready to get spiritual succor. While Arch rummaged through the clean laundry for a pair of pants, I tiptoed into Macguire's room. His forehead felt hot, but he moaned a refusal when I suggested his seeing a doctor. I begged him to take a couple more ibuprofen, which he did. By the time I closed his door, he was asleep. Damn Gail Rodine for making Macguire fall into the lake over her damn silly dolls.

When Tom, Arch, and I arrived at the massive oak entryway to St. Luke's Episcopal Church, the two men in my life held the doors ajar chivalrously. I hobbled through. When the sea of faces turned to appraise my entrance, I immediately realized we'd have done better asking for communion to be brought to the house. For the infirm, having the sacrament delivered was a common enough practice. But it wasn't a very common practice for a caterer who'd been trampled by an inebriated hockey player the same day her ex-husband was arrested for murder. So I hadn't thought of it.

Still, I should have known what kind of spectacle, and fuel for gossip, my bruised self would present. The ripple of whispers rose to a wave. Marla, wearing a lilac-print designer sundress, bolero jacket, matching purple earrings and high heels, immediately bustled over.

"I don't think they're staring because they want to book a buffet brunch," she confided.

"Gosh, Marla. Thanks for the news flash."

The choir shuffled into the vestibule. I took advantage of their arrival to whisper to Marla, "I told Arch I'd ask around about John Richard."

Her taupe-and-lilac-shadowed eyes widened at my confession. "Bad move, Goldy Schulz."

Tom guided us to a pew at the back and the four of us squeezed in. Marla hugged Arch and palmed him two Cadbury bars, which he stuffed into his pants pocket. If Marla's cardiologist ever X-rayed her Louis Vuitton handbag and discovered the bulges were chocolate bars and cream-filled cupcakes, he'd probably have cardiac arrest himself. She leaned close to me.

"Check out who's visiting. I'm an Episcopalian, so I can't point."

It took me a few seconds of scanning the pews to locate Chris Corey, his sister, the cat-loving Tina, and Brandon Yuille, sitting together on the opposite side of the nave. Tina had already told me she was a parishioner. Brandon attended occasionally. I'd never seen Chris at St. Luke's before.

"Probably here to plan Suz's memorial after coffee hour," Marla whispered. "Anyway. As long as you're poking around, have you heard anything new? And what happened, did you lose a fight with your blender?"

I glanced quickly at Arch. My son always made a good, but not perfect, pretense of not listening to adult conversations.

"No and no," I whispered back to her. She opened her mouth, probably to ask another question. Mercifully, the opening bars of the processional hymn rang out. "I'll tell you all about it later."

As much as I tried to concentrate, my eyes wandered back across the nave where Tina and Chris sat with Brandon. As the Old Testament lesson was read, I tried to recall when I'd seen Tina attending church, if ever.

To my horror, I giggled. *Stress.* I gulped and caught a glimpse of Marla's puzzled face, as well as the sudden confused looks from the two Coreys and Brandon Yuille. Well, great.

As we rose for the reading from Luke, I thought of what Marla had said about why two ACHMO department heads would be in church this morning: all the other department heads were away in San Diego. Chris and Brandon were indeed probably here to make funeral arrangements for Suz Craig. Suz had no relatives to perform this task, and Arch had told me that Suz was a nominal Episcopalian. Arch had also reported that Suz had accompanied John Richard on his rare appearances at St. Luke's. Of course,

John Richard did not go to church so much to worship as he did to brag about or show off whatever new possession he had, be it car, condo, or concubine.

Stop. In any event, our priest, now delivering his homily, liked to think of St. Luke's as a happy, if not always harmonious, family. Supposedly only family members could use the church building, even if they were dead. You couldn't be baptized, married, or dispensed to the Hereafter unless both you and the people making the arrangements were church members. So it looked as if Suz belonged to St. Luke's, albeit posthumously.

Man, what was the matter with me? I squeezed my eyes shut and focused on the intercessions. A woman prayed for the repose of the soul of her neighbor, Suz. By the time I opened my eyes, the woman's prayer had ended. I had not seen who it was. Brandon quietly echoed the supplication for Suz, then offered a plea for his father, who spent many hours alone. My mind took off again. Brandon had been at the bakery with his father from midnight to five? Sounded like a weird explanation of your whereabouts, even if your father *was* a lonely widower. The idea of *spending many hours alone* made me think of John Richard, who, I was willing to bet, was not attending chapel this morning in the Furman County Jail.

During the offertory, two visiting bagpipe players sounded the mournful notes of "Amazing Grace." While one of the choir sopranos sang the lyrics, my brain reverted to Ralph Shelton. Why had I had the strong feeling Ralph was hiding something when I went to his house? He'd been so hesitant, as if he wanted to talk to me but was afraid to. At the words, "I once was lost, but now am found," I glanced over at Arch. Tears slipped out of his eyes. My heart twisted in my chest.

Forget hugging him. Forget asking what was wrong. I knew better than to treat a fourteen-year-old boy in a way that would embarrass him. Still, it had been years since I'd seen Arch weep openly. I rummaged through my handbag, found a paper napkin, and wordlessly handed it to him. Without acknowledging me, he snatched the napkin. Tom patted my shoulder. Marla shook her head.

During the final hymn, Arch decamped to the men's room. As soon as he left the pew, Marla leaned over. "We should skedaddle before the horde descends on us during the coffee hour. Let's see if Brandon Yuille or the Coreys will talk to us. As ex-wives of the accused, we can say we have the right to know why he might have killed their boss."

"I don't want to leave Arch. . . ."

Marla said, "Arch'll be better off with Tom than with you right now. Think about it. Tom should take him down to the jail for visiting hours." She addressed Tom: "Can the Jerk see Arch today?"

Tom ignored the perplexed glances we were receiving from the people in the pew in front of us and nodded. "Let me take him down to see his father, Miss G. It'll be okay," he reassured me.

My sore shoulders slumped in defeat. Arch returned. The four of us bowed as the cross went by. Then we waited endlessly for the choir, bagpipe players, and priest to process out. When I finally told Arch that Tom would take him to see his dad while Marla and I ran a few errands, he brightened. I was surprised. I'd have thought he'd have responded with apprehension. It seemed I was past knowing what my son needed.

Marla pinched me and I scooted out of the pew, ignoring my aching body. I was feeling every hour of my age today. Once we were outside, she used her sixth sense — the one that fed on gossip — to locate Brandon Yuille and Chris and Tina Corey, who were standing by a pine tree at the edge of the parking lot.

"Yoohoo!" Marla called. "Need to chat for a sec!"

Brandon waved unenthusiastically while Chris, his ankle still in a cast, shifted the weight of his cumbersome body and forced a smile. Brandon, ever sharp, wore khaki pants and a military-style khaki shirt. Tall and heavy, Chris Corey had an enormous potbelly and pale hair and beard. He looked like a young blond Buddha, or rather a young blond Buddha who wore a white dress shirt and gray slacks, and limped. What I'd liked best about Chris when I first met him was that he didn't insist anyone call him doctor. His rumbly baritone had reminded me of a physician from our family's distant past. But when I'd asked him if he'd ever treated us — a pediatrician who'd treated Arch, maybe? — he'd said no. Maybe Chris reminded me less of Buddha than of Santa Claus. When he smiled, his blue eyes crinkled. Apparently, Tina, a female version of her portly brother, hadn't been able to find a Babsie-goes-to-church outfit. She wore a severe black cotton suit, and her hair was twisted back in a tight bun.

"I know you two probably don't want to talk right now," Marla gasped to the men, out of breath from her brief but determined trek across the gravel-covered lot. "Actually, we don't either." She feigned a sadness as fake as squirt butter. "It's just that we *have* to. . . ."

"It's okay," Chris replied amiably, tugging on his blond beard. "It's a tough situation. But we can't visit for long. We're here to plan the funeral."

"We can't talk very much at all," Brandon added, his voice tight. He flipped his long, dark bangs out of his eyes. "The priest just has to finish talking to the coffee-drinkers."

I nodded. The coffee hour was always the time when our pastor had to field questions that fell under the general rubric of pastoral theology. In actuality, coffee-hour questions rivaled anything Ann Landers had ever had to face. *Is God punishing my neighbor with cancer? My son baptized his anole lizard and then the lizard died. Can you give it a Christian burial?* For our spiritual leader, discussing Suz's memorial service might prove to be something of a relief.

Marla plunged right in. "If our ex-husband goes down for murdering his boss, it's going to be bad for us, you know. Much as we don't mind the Jerk suffering, we'd like to know why he killed Suz Craig."

Chris, Brandon, and Tina stared at Marla, open-mouthed.

"That's not . . ." Chris began. "You can't

expect us to discuss —"

"Oh, yes, we can," Marla continued brazenly. "You guys are department heads with a big corporation. You need to be responsive to the public, or at least to the ex-wives of the guy who's been charged with murdering your boss. So what we've heard is . . . there were problems with firing at that HMO. Were there problems in the Human Resources department, Brandon? Did everybody hate her?" When he gaped blankly at her, she turned to Chris. "Can you answer our questions? Please?"

I was embarrassed. This wasn't asking a few questions. This was grilling, with no hot dogs in sight.

"Ah." I leaned in for a few confidential, lighthearted words with Tina Corey. "That doesn't look like a Babsie outfit that I recognize. Let's see . . . could it be . . . Babsie-as-a-Choir-Director?"

Tina's face became rigid. "I don't know what you're talking about."

"Goldy, please," interjected Chris, "could you not —"

"Babsie-as-Altar-Guild-Director?" I attempted, undeterred.

"Be *quiet*," said Tina.

Startled by her harsh tone, I pulled back. Apparently, Babsie wasn't a churchgoer.

"Sorry," I muttered. "Er, how's the cat?"

Tina's face remained stonelike. She said nothing. Maybe the cat had run away, and she blamed me. I wished I'd kept my mouth shut. Some people just can't shoot the breeze when they're about to plan a funeral. I shot Marla a pleading can-we-leave glance.

Chris squinted over Marla's shoulder and waved to the priest, who was heading our way with a worried look on his face.

"We don't want to cause a ruckus," Chris said soothingly.

"Then answer my questions," Marla insisted.

"Yes," Chris said softly. "There were problems at ACHMO. It was not a happy place to work."

"You all look so solemn. People are wondering what the five of you are discussing out here," our priest said, joining us.

"Nothing," Marla said gaily. She always sought gossip but rarely shared it when there was no hope of reciprocal dirt. She tugged me away and I muttered good-byes to the two men and Tina. Marla pulled open the door to her Mercedes. I got in on the passenger side. After the van, sitting in the low-slung four-wheel-drive Mercedes always made me feel like an astronaut en route to Uranus.

"I can ask Brandon Yuille and Chris Corey a few questions if I want," Marla said defiantly as she slammed her door and prepared to blast off.

"Yeah, right. You can see how well it went."

"Tough tacks." She revved the car and zoomed out of the lot, then slowed behind a van crammed with tourists from Kansas. "So who should we be talking to if you're going to help Arch? And what are we supposed to say? Or haven't you figured that out yet? 'Hi, we're the two ex-wives of the doctor who's been busted for murder! Can we come in for tea and a little interrogation?' "

I sighed. "Let's go talk to Frances Markasian. You said she came to visit you, why didn't she come to visit me? I think she lives in the Spruce apartments."

Marla pressed the accelerator. "Now *there's* an upscale address."

The Spruce apartment building was a four-story stucco edifice that had probably been constructed when Aspen Meadow was rapidly expanding in the sixties. *Spruce up* was just what the building owners had not done, unfortunately. The seventies had seen the apartment house, which sat perched on a hill overlooking Main Street, painted a blinding yellow. I was willing to wager there'd been no repainting since. Warped and rotted cedar-shake shingles curled on the roof or lay helter-skelter between the crab-grass and the drooping lodgepole pines that flanked the building. Marla pulled the Mercedes next to a wall of yellow cinder blocks that marked off the front parking area. I didn't see Frances's Subaru, but knew there was another cracked-asphalt blacktop behind the building where the residents kept overflow cars.

"Tell me again why we're here," Marla said doubtfully.

"All this happened to John Richard yesterday," I reminded her. "You know Frances Markasian. She's a fast and efficient snooper. If somebody knows anything, she will."

"All I know is that she's also covering the doll show at the lake," Marla grumbled. "Maybe she's doing a story on Coroner Babsies."

The elevator was out of order. We walked up the stairs to apartment 349, the Markasian residence, and knocked. No one home. An elderly man came out into the third-floor foyer and unabashedly watched us as Marla rapped harder. The elderly man cleared his throat.

"Hey, you girls!" he snarled. His white hair

had been brutally shaved in a crewcut, and his deeply lined face looked malevolent. "What do you want? You're not more of them, are you?"

I held my index finger up to Marla: *Let me handle this.* To the elderly gent I said pleasantly, "More of whom?"

He made an impatient gesture. "Parade of people all day. That woman's not a reporter, she's a bureaucracy. Get out of here, you're ruining the place."

I felt my cheeks redden.

But Marla wasn't merely blushing. She was purple with rage. "Cool your jets, fella! If we want to look for somebody, we'll look, you got it? We'll knock on every door in the place if we want to. Ever heard of freedom of the press? Do you know where we can find Frances Markasian?"

"Look, you two!" he cackled. "You want stories on your dolls? Grow up! Dolls for grown women," he spat. "You want Frances Markasian, go down to the lake and find her!"

I was ready to retreat, but Marla insisted on having the last word, as usual. She wagged a lilac-painted nail at the man.

"Watch your mouth, please! Collecting is a venerable hobby. And it's a smart investment! Not only that, but you're rude!"

"I may be rude, but I'm not crazy!" he cackled before disappearing into 350.

Marla shot after him and I had to limp along behind her to catch up. Fortunately, the man's apartment door slammed before Marla could force her way in for a confrontation. Marla rapped hard and repeatedly on his door. Squeals of "Shut up!" and "Go away or I'll call the cops!" issued from other apartments. But our white-haired, unpleasant critic did not reappear.

Chapter 15

In the afternoon sun Aspen Meadow Lake shimmered like sugar on ice. Several dozen cars in the dirt parking area made me wonder if there was a waiting line for skiffs and paddleboats. We got out of the Mercedes and approached the LakeCenter's front door.

The LakeCenter was a jewel of that architectural species known as "mountain contemporary." Constructed of row upon row of massive blond logs, wide, soaring trapezoids of glass, polished plank flooring within, aprons of flagstone without, and topped with a phenomenally expensive all-weather shingle roof, the structure was the glory of the Aspen Meadow Recreation District. The interior consisted of a huge space, fancifully called "the Ballroom," and a more intimate adjoining space known as "the Octagon." Both rooms provided unequaled views of the lake. There was a kitchen, too. I would be working there when I catered to the Babsie people. Alas, the kitchen afforded no scenic vista.

Unfortunately, the LakeCenter was locked up tight. We rounded the building, looking for Frances Markasian and any evidence of the doll show. The cormorants paddled furiously along the lake's edge. When they dove for fish, they would stay underwater for so long it seemed impossible that a land-based animal would not drown. But then, miraculously, the sleek black birds would pop back up, triumphantly clasping tiny, slithering fish in their beaks.

When we came up on the boat-rental shop, we found that it was indeed open. Thirty or so people waited for skiffs.

"A land-office business," Marla commented, "despite the fact that it's on the water."

"But no Frances," I pointed out.

"Think we should go talk to those other people John Richard mentioned, Ralph Shelton and Amy Bartholomew? And how'd you get messed up, anyway?"

"I'd rather not see either of them just yet. Ralph Shelton banged into me yesterday at the McCrackens' party. Literally. Amy Bartholomew patched me up. Before Ralph used me for a landing pad, I tried to ask him some questions about Suz. He didn't have much to say. Ditto with Amy, except I got some New Age gobbledygook about Suz

Craig's negative karma. I don't want to ask them any more questions until we know better what we're looking for."

"What exactly are we looking for?" Marla said as she vavoomed the Mercedes.

"I wish I knew."

"Speak for yourself," she shot back. "We know the Jerk did it. I'm looking for lunch."

"Hold on a minute," I replied. "Frances hates to cook. She's a cheapskate, but every now and then she shows up at the Aspen Meadow Café, especially if she's doing an interview and the paper is springing for the meal. With any luck, we could run into her there."

We trekked over to the café, but Frances Markasian was again nowhere in evidence. So Marla insisted on treating me. With the Jerk finally in jail where he belonged, she claimed, we should have every manner of salads to celebrate. Using her best queenly manner, she waved at the waitress and announced: "Bring 'em all." Soon platter after platter arrived: roast beef salad, pasta salad, corn and pepper salad, fruit salad, and an arugula salad with toasted walnuts that I went wild for. I knew from experience that I'd never get the recipe from the café chef, so I made a mental note to reinvent it in my own kitchen, using some meringue-baked pecans I had frozen. Not one to neglect balance, Marla ordered a bottle of champagne and hot popovers to go with our salads.

I laughed at her indulgence. Really, I'm extremely fortunate that I have both Marla and Tom to be sure that I'm regularly fed as well as loved and fussed over. For someone in the food business, such care is a rare treat.

Marla claimed to want none of the leftovers. When our waitress handed me the bulging bags of goodies, I observed, "Our family will have enough here for a week."

"That's the idea," Marla replied happily. "Besides, dealing with the Jerk, you're going to need all the help you can get."

When she was signing her credit-card slip, a newly arrived group of diners caught my eye. I grabbed Marla's arm. "Hey, check it out."

She followed my gaze. We watched Frances Markasian trying to decide which of the outside patio tables would suit. With her were Chris Corey and his sister, Tina. Tina had changed into some kind of costume. This time, I was *sure* it was a Babsie outfit.

"Do you know why Tina changed into that getup?" I asked Marla, who made it her business to know as much as possible about the lives of Aspen Meadow residents.

"The costume? Who knows. Tina is an aide at Aspen Meadow Preschool. She's the head Babsie-club organizer, too, so it might have something to do with the show starting. Maybe Frances is interviewing her."

Tina now sported the same long blond pigtails she had at Gail Rodine's house yesterday. She wore a frilly lace blouse and a royal-blue vest with matching skirt, both covered with a lace-edged, snow-white apron.

I said, "For the doll show I've mainly been dealing with Gail Rodine. She's in charge of hospitality and security." Marla made a face. I pushed my chair back. "I promised Arch I would help him. Let's go crash their lunch."

"Mah-velous," she said. "I love crashing anything."

Frances was peering into the café for a waitress. As she did so, she impatiently tapped one foot. The foot was encased in a duct-tape-wrapped sneaker. Her black trench coat was, of course, unnecessary in the August heat. But Frances was (or fancied herself) a high-powered investigative reporter temporarily trapped in Aspen Meadow, Colorado. With long, wildly frizzy black hair, skin of an unhealthy pallor, thrift-shop clothes, and a chain-smoking habit that would undoubtedly blacken her lungs within

249

a decade, she at least knew how to *dress* the part.

Frances's ambition in the county was legendary. She went after every crime and disaster story like a starving wildcat pouncing on its prey. Her headlines were certainly creative. In May we'd had I-70 DRIVER SHOOTS ROADSIDE BUFFALO IN COLD BLOOD! June had seen EXPLOSION IN MOTH-INFESTED PROPANE GRILL SAILS PRESIDENT OF KIWANIS INTO CREEK! Readership of our town paper had tripled since Frances had come on staff two years ago.

"Hey, Goldy," she said amiably as we neared her table. She pushed the black frizz from her forehead. "I've already been by to see you today, but you weren't home. Do you know the Coreys? Chris is head of Provider Relations with ACHMO — the AstuteCare Health Maintenance Organization in Denver. And this is his sister, Tina. She works at Aspen Meadow Preschool and presides over the local Babsie doll club."

"Good to see you, Frances. And I know both Coreys," I replied. "In fact, we've already chatted this morning."

Chris brought his unwieldy bulk to a standing position, balancing awkwardly on his cast. His pale beard bobbed as he greeted us.

"We're sorry to disturb you," Marla lied in a breathy gush.

Frances rumbled a laugh and lit a cigarette. "No, you're not sorry. Anyway, this is great. I'm absolutely *desperate* to talk to Goldy. Sit."

Tina nodded at us. Her cold manner had changed completely from her behavior at church. She blushed. If I'd been wearing her outfit, I'd have blushed, too.

Gaping at Tina, Marla said, "Well, Heidi, where'd you leave your sheep?"

Chris smiled indulgently, but the color deepened painfully on Tina's neck and cheeks. She lowered her head and smoothed the frilly apron. I knew better than to ask about the cat again. Frances scowled in the awkward silence. This was not a good way to start a lunch-crashing, no doubt about it.

"Wait a minute," I said enthusiastically. "I know that outfit, Tina! It's the Icelandic Babsie!" Tina raised her head, grasped a blond pigtail, and gave me a shy smile. "I'm catering the doll show," I reminded her, since she seemed not to have remembered me at church. "Do you remember me from the Rodines' place yesterday?" I shook

Tina's limp, fleshy hand. "Do you remember me?"

Tina regained her composure. "Of course. You gave me my new kitty."

Finally, we were on solid ground. Maybe she just didn't discuss dolls or cats at church. "That cat sure took to you," I said warmly. Tina beamed.

Under her breath Marla muttered, "Gosh, Goldy, run for office, why don't you?"

Our waitress reappeared, and Chris announced that he was treating everyone, what would we like? Chris, his sister, and Frances ordered sandwiches. Marla, suddenly the picture of charm, said she'd love some fudge meringue pie. I went for Linzertorte and iced coffee, trying to think of how to ask Frances my questions about John Richard. *What have you dug up? Are you on to something? Exactly why did you want to see me this morning?* Lucky for me, Frances pried so blatantly that we were spared subtle inquisition. Instead, she plunged right in.

"Hey, ladies, think your mutual ex-husband will grant me an interview from behind bars?" Her slightly yellow teeth flashed in a wide, crooked smile.

"I don't know," I answered sincerely.

Marla said, "I'll pay for you to do the interview, if you get a photo of him in an orange suit that you publish in the paper."

"Has it been hard, or are you two just *loving* this?" Frances wanted to know, with her usual sensitivity.

Marla shrugged.

"I wouldn't say I'm loving it," I told Frances tartly. "A woman is dead. Plus my son's suffering pretty badly, especially after his father called from jail yesterday. Arch is down there visiting him right now."

Too late, I realized I should have kept my mouth shut. Frances and I were friends, but nothing came before a scoop. She dug frantically in her voluminous black handbag, yanked out a pen and a grimy pad of paper, and began to scribble. "What did Korman say in this phone call that upset Arch?"

"Nothing! Please, stop taking notes. For crying out loud, Frances, this is *personal.*"

Chris mumbled, "Maybe we should talk about something else, Frances. I don't think —"

She gestured imperiously. "It's always personal for somebody, Goldy."

"Don't give me that low-brow journalistic jive. Please. If you want me to stay here and visit, promise not to print anything about my son."

She kept on scribbling, pursed her lips, and pushed her hair out of her eyes. "Okay,

I won't if you'll let me run some stuff by you. Besides, I'm sure you'll want to hear all I've learned about this Craig business. Chris here" — she flapped a casual hand in his direction — "is an insider. There's all kinds of scuttlebutt. You know this town. Once something happens, it's like a . . ." She closed her eyes and sought the perfect simile. "Like a . . . volcanic energy erupts around the desire to know what's going on."

Chris took a deep breath and shifted his weight uncomfortably. Tina sipped some water. Marla, of course, was all ears. But Mount Saint Frances calmly lit a cigarette. My attempt to ask Frances a few delicate questions was going awry pretty quickly.

"Run some stuff by me?" I echoed. "Such as?"

"Okay, this is top secret. If somebody comes up to the table here and wants to know what we're talking about, we say I'm interviewing Tina for the doll show."

"So what are you running by me?"

"ACHMO is planning a raid," she informed me blithely, her tone a shade lower. "On John Richard Korman's office. Tomorrow morning."

Marla shrieked with glee. I said, "A raid? Frances, what on earth are you talking about?"

Our food arrived and I was thankful for the momentary distraction. A raid? What were they looking for? And why would ACHMO raid anyone's office? This could not be true. I assumed an expression of polite interest and, because the waitress hovered over us, attempted to change the subject.

"How's your ankle coming along?" I asked Chris. "I should have asked after church."

He smiled shyly. "I'll be kicking field goals in no time."

Frances took three bites of her sandwich, pushed it away, and relit the half-finished cigarette she had carefully squashed out when the food arrived. "So. You want to hear about the raid or not?"

"Yes, yes, yes," urged Marla, eyes sparkling.

"Why don't you just tell the police about it?" I asked. The Linzertorte was delicious, a crunchy crust covered with jewel-colored raspberry jam. "A raid by the HMO has *got* to be illegal, Frances."

"But it isn't." Chris's surprisingly powerful baritone commanded attention. "We do it all the time. Usually we call first, which is what we'll do tomorrow. We come in to check information in the files."

"*What?*" Marla exclaimed. "What about patient confidentiality?"

Chris readjusted his ankle and went on. "Marla. Goldy. May I call you by your first names?" Frances nodded, I noticed, before we had the chance. "It's in our contract," he continued. "We can visit any practice we own. A nurse, a doctor, someone with medical training who's working for the HMO, comes in. It's not really a *raid*." He grinned indulgently at Frances, who was lighting her second cigarette. "We just want to check how certain procedures get billed, and we do it by going through individual files. The provider's office has to let us have what we want."

Well, my curiosity was piqued, no question. John Richard in jail and ACHMO was going to crash into his office to go through his *files*. Small wonder that Frances was interested, too.

"What are you going to be looking for tomorrow morning? Something related to Suz Craig?" I asked mildly.

"And may I come?" demanded Marla.

Chris's reply was matter-of-fact. "No, oh, no. And actually, Suz is — was — the one who ordered this visit. It's been planned for a while, but we were waiting until Korman was called out on a delivery. Now we've got a perfect opportunity to go in. And it's not what the Medical Management person will *say* she wants that matters. Or what I say, as head of Provider Relations. Since she's a nurse and I'm a doctor, that's how ACHMO gets around the patient confidentiality issue. But in this case what we *say* we want and what we'll *actually* be after are two entirely different things."

"What is it you'll actually be after?" I inquired innocently. "And why are you telling us this?"

Chris tugged on his beard. "What we'll be looking for are personal notes from Korman about the McCrackens' suit. At least, that's what Suz, and now the chief honchos at ACHMO, want us to be looking for. And those *would* be illegal for ACHMO to lift. The corporation is trying to cover itself, and it's taking the opportunity of Korman being out of the way to be thorough. Frances will tell you about it. She's going to write an article exposing the whole thing."

"Frances is going to write an *exposé?*" I said, wide-eyed.

"Imagine that," commented Marla. "And will this exposé help or hurt the no-good doctor in jail for murder?"

Frances scowled as she crushed out her cigarette and lit another. She muttered, "The timing could be a little better. The angle I'm going to be looking for is: Did Korman have a clue that Suz Craig had this raid on his records planned?"

"What do you get out of this, Chris?" I asked. "Don't you still work for ACHMO? Won't this article get you into trouble with them?"

"I want people to know what the HMO is up to," he answered darkly. "You shouldn't be able to just go through people's files whenever you want. And Frances is going to keep my identity a secret. I can't afford to lose my job."

"But ACHMO wouldn't have killed one of their own, would they?"

A pained expression wrinkled the heavy folds of his face at my question. "I don't think so. Neither does anyone I've talked to. You can imagine, Goldy, all of our phones have been ringing off their hooks ever since the captain down at the Furman County Sheriff's Department called ACHMO's chief honcho in Minneapolis yesterday. One of my higher-ups at corporate called and said now was the time to go through Korman's records, the way Suz planned. So that's why they're sending me in tomorrow — to find any personal notes Korman might have left in his office." He paused and blinked at me. His eyelashes were so pale, they were invisible. "Everyone at ACHMO is convinced your husband beat Suz to death."

"He's my *ex*-husband," I said quietly. Why did no one seem to remember this?

"My ex-husband, too," said Marla defiantly. "So get your facts straight before you go off insulting us."

Frances leaned affectionately toward Chris and whispered something in his ear. Tina fluffed the lace on her Icelandic Babsie blouse. And I sat back and thought that now I had one more thing for the sheriff's department to ask John Richard: *Know anything about Suz's dirty little scheme to betray you?*

"Look, Goldy," Frances said, "there are two things we want to talk to you about. First of all, Patricia McCracken. Seen her lately?"

"As a matter of fact, I catered a party for her last night."

"Is that where you got banged up?"

I nodded and pretended not to notice the way the two Coreys stared at my face. I concentrated instead on the sky, where layers of pink cloud were again gathering in the west.

Frances persisted. "Now we all know Patricia got dumped by a doctor, then married a dentist. She doesn't have the kind of money she used to, since there are at least fifty dentists in Aspen Meadow. Back in the old days she had a way of displaying the three things she bought with her divorce-from-the-doc settlement: a too-large diamond ring, a sapphire bracelet removed and perpetually left behind in exercise class, and an always-filthy white Triumph whose leather seats her son, Tyler, had smeared with fingerpaints when he was a toddler."

"She just sold the Triumph to pay her lawyer's retainer," Marla interjected. "Everybody in town knows that."

"Have you met Tyler?" Frances asked, unfazed. "He's a five-year-old monster."

"I know him," Marla said. "He's a brat."

"Oh, no," said Tina. They were her first words in a while. "He's extremely creative. He used to help me with the hamsters. He just has a lot of energy, that's all."

Frances raised an eyebrow at me.

"Yes, I've met Tyler," I replied. "Arch baby-sat him a couple of times when Tyler was younger. But the kid was so hyper that Arch said he'd never go again, no matter how broke he was. Last night the McCrackens took Tyler over to a friend's house rather than risk him wrecking their party, which got wrecked anyway," I muttered, thinking of the hockey free-for-all and my aching bones.

"Uh-huh," replied Frances, bored. She fished in her purse again, pulled out a can of Jolt cola, and popped the top. She was never without several cans, and given its triple-caffeine hit, I doubted she ever slept at all. Now she took a long swig, then dragged on the cig. I wondered if her doing an article on HMOs would have any influence on her unhealthful habits. Somehow, I doubted it. The cigarette dangled from her mouth as she handed Chris the Jolt and pawed again through her purse for another notebook. She retrieved it, flipped a few torn and curled pages, and announced: "Okay, here it is. Our Patricia begged Dr. John Richard Korman to stick her in the hospital when the placenta previa was causing problems in the pregnancy. But ACHMO wouldn't cover it. ACHMO said Patricia should rest right in her own snug little bed until she was ready to deliver. With all of the McCrackens' money tied up in their heavily mortgaged house and Clark's mostly off-again dentistry practice, the prospect of an open-ended hospital stay was enough to conjure up bankruptcy. So Patricia peddled her jewelry," Frances added with relish. "The diamond ring and sapphire bracelet paid for a one-month hospital stay that ACHMO wouldn't spring for plus babysitting for Tyler. She couldn't sell the Triumph because she would have had to buy a new car when she had the baby, and the Triumph had depreciated too much even to give her a down payment. And little Tyler's finger-painting on the white seats didn't exactly add to its value."

Frances looked at me as if expecting praise. I looked back at her in silence. Marla rolled her eyes.

Frances sighed. "So she sold the jewelry and stayed in the hospital until she ran out of money. Then she checked into a low-cost suite near the hospital, you know about those? She put that on her credit card." Frances raised her eyebrows, pressed her lips into a grim line, and flipped another page of her notes. "But it wasn't enough. She lost the baby at seven months. Talk about bitter — that woman's saliva could pickle a turkey."

"Frances," I chided. "You don't have children. You can't imagine the loss —"

"Yeah, yeah, yeah. So Patricia McCracken went nova. She sued Korman. She sued ACHMO. Her lawyers accepted the cases on contingency. Patricia took out a second mortgage on their Keystone condo and sold the Triumph after all, to pay the other legal fees. She didn't care what she spent, as long as she brought John Richard Korman and ACHMO to their knees. You can't sue an HMO for malpractice. So she's trying to sock them with negligence, for even having Korman as a provider. What Patricia *didn't* tell me, but I was able to find out from another source, is that our very same Mrs. P. McCracken was arrested last week for smashing flagstones in Suz Craig's driveway."

I sat up straight. *"What?"*

Marla murmured, "For heaven's sake, Goldy, what good is it to have you married to a cop if he doesn't even keep us supplied with news of local crimes?"

"Ah," said Frances. "Marla and Goldy are finally interested. You know how angry that woman was? I'll tell you. She was screaming about how if she couldn't have her baby, 'some conniving coldhearted childless bitch' " — she glanced at her notes, "and I quote, 'isn't going to entertain with a big patio paid for with blood. With BLOOD!' "

"But Patricia McCracken was in Keystone last week," I pointed out.

"Not the whole week she wasn't. Anyway, after the arrest, Suz Craig didn't press charges. But Ms. Craig did get a restraining order against Patricia, who agreed to undergo psychological evaluation. She also agreed to enter grief therapy for people who've lost their babies before delivery, as soon as she returned from a planned trip to Keystone." Frances slapped her notebook shut with a triumphant *thwack*.

"Except for the flagstone story, did you get all this from Patricia?" I asked.

"Of course I did," Frances responded hotly. "What the hell kind of reporter do you think I am? And I had to give Tyler all the candy corn I usually keep in my purse to keep him from crawling all over me."

Marla said, "Candy corn? Is that the best you could do?"

Tina Corey *tsk*ed.

To Tina's brother I said, "How come ACHMO doesn't recommend hospitalization for placenta previa?"

"I don't make the rules, Goldy. Some MBA does. What ACHMO did wasn't illegal, unfortunately."

I turned back to Frances. "But if Patricia is suing, isn't there some kind of gag order on her talking to you?"

"Gag order? Are you kidding?" Frances pulled out another cigarette and lit it with the end of the one she was finishing. "That woman is dying to have her story published in the most incendiary manner possible. The only reason she talked to me was that the *Denver Post* and *Rocky Mountain News* weren't interested. And coupled with what I know about ACHMO swooping into the Jerk's office to search for notes on the case

. . . well." She inhaled in a satisfied manner. "ACHMO is going *down*." She smirked at me.

I had the sudden feeling I needed to get home and check that Arch had survived his jail visit. "Well, we'll see. Marla, are you ready?" Without waiting for a reply I said, "We need to fly, Frances."

"Hold on, you haven't told me anything yet about Suz's murder. I don't want to talk to you just about Patricia McCracken." Frances began to rummage in her purse again while Marla popped a last bite of pie in her mouth. "Look, I've got a few things to show you."

"Frances, I can't *tell* you anything. You must be able to understand that —"

Her nicotine-stained fingers held out three newspaper clippings. Reluctantly, I took them. Marla peered over my shoulder. Frances swiped the hair out of her left eye and demanded curtly, "Tell me if either of you know either of these guys in the first one."

Two smiling men held up glasses of wine to the camera. MERITMED HMO CELEBRATES NEBRASKA SUCCESS. Well, bully for them, and I hoped they were quaffing an Omaha vintage. But there was no doubt that I knew one of the two men. In fact, I had seen him yesterday, up close and personal. The caption read: "Ralph Shelton, M.D., and Mark McCreary, Chief Executive Officer, MeritMed, observed the company's success in the Cornhusker State." I checked the date: May 14.

I tapped the blurry images. "Ralph Shelton used to work for ACHMO, now he works for MeritMed. So what?"

Frances blew smoke in a steady stream off the patio. "MeritMed has an office in Denver." She squinted at me; I shook my head. "In March Ralph Shelton was fired from AstuteCare by Suz Craig."

I looked at Chris. "You want to tell us a little more about those problems with firings?"

He shrugged. Marla demanded, "Do either of you know *why* Ralph was fired?"

Chris shook his head. "Not yet."

While Marla read the first article, I perused the second piece. It was much shorter, with no accompanying photograph. It was an announcement from a paper in Vail.

Dr. John R. Korman will address the Colorado Association of Obstetricians tonight at 8 P.M. on "Postpartum Use of Antibiotics." Summit Stag Hotel, across from Vail Valley Medical Center.

The article was older than the first, dated in early January.

"Frances," I asked, perplexed, "why are you showing us this? I don't know John Richard's schedule. He goes to these conventions if it means he can ski and whoop it up. The only times I know what he's up to is when we have to change our visitation arrangements with Arch."

Airily, Frances waved this off. "Do you know your ex-husband's relationship with a drug company named Bailey Products?"

"Yes," interjected Marla, her voice sour. "John Richard travels around, or he used to travel around, touting their product. Something called Biocess. How do you know about it?" When Frances glanced at Chris, Marla pressed, "Do you know what happened to the Biocess endorsement money?"

Frances nodded. "Yeah, I found out from Ralph Shelton, who also used the stuff in his practice. Ralph's old buddy John Richard Korman pushed Biocess from Portland, Oregon, to Portland, Maine. At least until recently. Check this out."

I took the article Frances now proffered, and again Marla read over my shoulder. This was from a newspaper in Omaha, and like the first clipping, was also dated May 14. The headline ran: MEDICAL CONFER-

ENCE ATTENDEES WARNED OF ANTIBIOTIC'S POSSIBLY LETHAL SIDE EFFECTS. I skimmed this one, too, which basically said that an HMO executive was warning his colleagues in other HMOs that in the course of their standard audits, his organization had found that Biocess had been linked to one death from liver failure, and several cases of negative side effects, plus higher costs postpartum. I skipped to the end of the article, where a Bailey Products spokesperson said that an Adverse Event Form had been filed with the FDA and that Bailey had put the use of Biocess on hold until they could do more studies of the antibiotic.

"Hmm," I said noncommittally, and handed the article back to Frances.

She took it and said, "So Biocess, Korman's much-loved designer antibiotic, was discovered to cause liver damage. And the cornucopia of goodies from Bailey Products available to John Richard Korman was suddenly empty."

"There's your answer to what caused that blip in income," I told Marla.

Frances went on. "Now you two, of all people, should know Korman's financial situation had become really, really bad. In fact, everything was about to come crashing down on his head. And think how much worse it would become if Suz Craig denied him a big fat bonus. Which she did."

I said to Chris, "Why did Suz deny the bonus? Why would she?"

"Legitimately?" he asked with a frown. "We send out questionnaires to a sampling of a doctor's patients. If we get even one serious complaint, the bonus is automatically denied. Or if a doctor refers patients to specialists too much, or if he refers too little, the bonus is denied. If he hasn't seen enough patients or cut costs over the past year, the bonus is denied."

"Now that's what I call both a carrot and a stick," Marla murmured.

I said, "Look, Frances, we both knew he was having money problems." But truly, neither Marla nor I had known the full extent of the problems.

"Yeah, yeah," Frances was saying. "And now ACHMO is going to raid him. And you know they'll make him the fall guy for the McCracken mess if they find one scrap of paper they can use to blame him for the whole thing."

I asked Chris, "You mentioned that you'd be looking for what you called 'personal notes' that John Richard might have made when you go in tomorrow. What kind of notes?"

Frances eagerly interjected: "They're looking for anything John Richard might have written to cover himself, like 'I told Patricia that my recommendation was for her to go into the hospital. But then I had to tell her that the HMO vetoed it.' Or like 'Told P. McCracken today that HMO had denied her hospital stay because they're penny-pinchers. Cheap sons of bitches!' " she finished with a flourish.

I addressed Chris Corey. "Do you think there were such notes? And exactly who is going in looking besides you and the Medical Management lady? Somebody who represents Suz's interests in protecting ACHMO?"

Chris leaned forward. "Korman and ACHMO are not exactly on the same side on these suits, you know. If Korman kept notes to try to cover himself, ACHMO wants those notes very, very badly. If Korman criticized the HMO to a patient, he violated the terms of his contract with us. Worse for AstuteCare, if the HMO recommended bedrest at home while Dr. Korman claims *he* recommended a hospital stay or she'd lose that baby . . . Well, you can see what would happen to the malpractice suit, and how bad

ACHMO would look. ACHMO needs to know what he's thinking, what he's done." He shook his head glumly.

"Something else," Frances said. "Chris tells me ACHMO was considering putting Korman on probation as a provider, just for being sued for malpractice."

Marla erupted in a gale of laughter. As Frances lit yet another cigarette, I wondered how ACHMO was reacting to the Jerk being accused of murder.

Frances exhaled and went on. "Plus, if Korman was saying one thing to Patricia McCracken and another to ACHMO, then ACHMO claims they can put him out the door. And, believe me, if Korman got kicked off the ACHMO provider list, he'd have *nothing*, since he sold his practice to them. And the person deciding about his probation is Suz Craig. Or should I say *was* Suz Craig?" she concluded gleefully.

"Why don't you talk to the police?" I asked with a glance at Chris. He shook his head sadly. "Why tell me?"

Frances quirked her bushy black eyebrows and, true to form, ignored my questions. Of course I already knew the answer: Because she wanted a story. "Listen," she demanded, "did Korman give either you or Marla anything to keep? Like any files or packages or notes on the McCracken case? I won't be able to nab ACHMO without something concrete."

Again Marla burst out laughing. "He gives me any files, he knows I'm going to shred them. Goldy might smoke them in her barbecue."

"Are you kidding?" I protested. "I'd put them through the vegetable shredder."

Frances shook her head. "Okay, okay, it was worth a try. But think. You probably heard the story about Suz and John Richard arguing at the club Friday night. After what I just told you, wouldn't it make sense that they argued about *money?* He says he needs his bonus, she says he'll be lucky not to be cut off by ACHMO completely. Goldy, does Tom know yet what they were fighting about?"

"I'd like to stay married, thanks, Frances." I'd had enough. "Okay, Marla, I really need to get home. I'm worried about Arch."

"I'm with you," she said heartily, and took a last sip of coffee. We shook hands with Chris and Tina, thanked them for treating us to dessert, and started to leave.

"Hey! Hold on!" Frances cried as she nipped along behind us. "I need to know what Korman called about from jail!"

I finally managed to get Frances to let go

of the Mercedes door handle by promising to call her if there were any momentous developments in the case of John Richard. "Momentous developments" to me meant anything the Furman County Sheriff's Department public information officer was about to announce to all the newspapers, but I did not make this clarification to her.

Frances's black coat billowed out behind her and the smoke from her cigarette whipped away as she strode back to the café for another Jolt cola. I would call her if *I* wanted to know something. But next time I'd be careful not even to mention Arch.

Chapter 16

At home Macguire announced he was having trouble swallowing. His fever had abated somewhat, but he still would not eat a morsel. I made him some soft-serve strawberry Jell-O. After three bites he announced he needed to go back to sleep. Well, great.

I perused the contracts for the doll-show meals that Gail Rodine and I had worked out. Babsie-doll collectors were apparently as paranoid about getting mayonnaise on those itsy-bitsy plastic high heels as they were about having their dolls taken out of their original boxes. So the Babsie-bash organizers, despite the fact that they were expecting over two hundred people per day at the show, had only sold tickets for forty box lunches on Tuesday. Then on Wednesday a sit-down breakfast for the executive committee and helpers — twenty people — would be followed that evening by a concluding barbecue, for which the show organizers had sold sixty tickets. All the meals would be served on the LakeCenter patio picnic tables. A guard would be stationed at the back door so that not a smear of barbecue sauce could touch a single doll's ponytail. Best of all was that Gail Rodine's down payment would provide the first installment of Arch's fall tuition at Elk Park Prep, an expense John Richard was supposed to cover. The likelihood of *that* happening was now as slender as spaghettini.

Arch, Tom, and I had takeout Chinese food that Tom had insisted on bringing home. I was both curious and apprehensive to hear the details of their afternoon. *How did your father look in an orange suit? Was he handcuffed?* And most important: *Did he say he did it?* But Arch mumbled that he didn't want to talk about it. I was bothered that he was so very subdued. While we were doing the dishes, I brought Tom up to date on all I had learned from Frances and Chris Corey. He placed the last serving spoon in the dishwasher, washed his hands, and took some notes that he said he'd pass on to the D.A.'s investigator. Then he set his notebook aside and told me that Arch hadn't uttered a word all the way home.

"Did you see John Richard, too?" I asked him.

Tom shook his head. "Miss Goldy, you'd better prepare yourself. This is a classic lose-lose situation. Tomorrow John Richard may get out on bail. It's a long shot, but . . . The county judge who's coming up on rotation? Name's Scott Taryton. Taryton's stated publicly that he's tired of all the mollycoddling women are getting these days. For mollycoddling, read *rights*."

"Oh, don't —"

Tom held up a fleshy palm. "Listen. A female judge down in Denver let a first-degree murder suspect out on thirty thousand dollars' bond last summer. The woman had shot her husband, alleging abuse. Taryton blew a gasket when that judge granted bond. We've been waiting for some kind of retaliation from him. Setting bond for a man implicated in a murder — especially one stemming from a domestic dispute — would be just his cup of tea. John Richard could be it."

"But isn't there a law about not letting murder suspects out?"

Tom scowled. "Oh, sure. Murder suspects, according to state law, need to be held without bond until a hearing on the evidence. But after bail was granted last summer for that other suspect, the upholding of that particular state law has become fuzzy. Fuzzy enough for Taryton to do exactly what he wants."

"God help us."

"Taryton's no friend to women," Tom concluded grimly.

It was no wonder that I once again had trouble sleeping. The insomnia came despite an expert shoulder massage from Tom and a late-night phone check from Marla — did I want help from her for any of the doll-club events? I thanked her and said I would be fine; I needed the work to keep my mind occupied.

I fell asleep dreaming of dolls bearing trays of grilled burgers. At two I awoke with my heart hammering. *Bam, bam, bam,* John Richard used to hit me. He'd shake me and then strike my face with his fist. I'd try to get away or fight back. No use. *Bam.* One leg, the other leg, my back. He was a great believer in symmetry.

I shuddered and crept out of bed. Then I took a shower to relieve my cramping muscles. I toweled off and listened for noise in the house. Had I awakened anyone this time? Apparently not. I dressed silently — sleep was now impossible — and suddenly remembered Arch's advice: *You should go out for a drive. That's what you used to do when I was little. When I couldn't sleep. . . .*

Should I? Well, why not. I found my keys and purse and tiptoed out onto the back deck. Overhead, shreds of cloud drifted across a river of stars. The air was warm. A sudden *bleat! bleat!* accompanied a rustling of leaves. A wave of panic swept over me. Then I saw a dozen elk moving slowly under the pine trees. It *was* a one-in-ten year for the big animals.

I sat in the van and wondered how long a drive I needed to make to get tired enough to go back to sleep. I didn't have anyplace to go. But even as I turned the key in the ignition I knew where I was headed.

My van engine sounded loud on Main Street. All the stores, of course, were dark, from Darlene's Antiques & Collectibles to the Doughnut Shop. A breeze washed through the aspen trees lining the street. Cottonwood Creek splashed and rumbled, while a cloth sign advertising Aspen Meadow Barbecue flapped like a forgotten flag. Gone were the rows of motorcycles ordinarily parked at acute angles in front of the Grizzly Bear Saloon on summer evenings. They had roared off into the night hours earlier, and the saloon was engulfed in darkness.

The van chugged past the spotlight trained on the waterfall emptying out of Aspen Meadow Lake. The cormorants had abandoned their perch, and I wondered fleetingly where the birds spent their nights. The Lake-

Center roof twinkled with a string of Christmas lights that our recreation district board had insisted would give the place a festive look year-round. They'd been right.

The small shopping center housing one of our two grocery stores was also dark, except for the Aspen Meadow Pastry Shop, where, I was sure, the ever-industrious Mickey Yuille was making cinnamon rolls for his Monday-morning customers. Perhaps Brandon was there keeping him company.

At the entrance to the country club, a dark car sat under the streetlight. Its door read MOUNTAIN SECURITY, but no one was inside. Perhaps the fellow had succumbed to sleep and was lying across the front seat. I was tempted to find out how ticked off he would be if I blasted him with my horn.

I turned onto Jacobean and glanced at the clock on my dashboard. Eleven minutes from our house to Suz's, no traffic. The streetlights cast a neon glow on the asphalt and all the mown lawns. The yards were perfect except for Suz's. There, mounds of topsoil lay untouched, and yellow police ribbons were pulled taut around the crime scene and the house.

Even though it was only one day after the murder, the sheriff's department could not afford to put deputies in front of the house.

I pulled up slowly by the ditch and glanced again at my dashboard clock. Thirty-two minutes after two. John Richard's place onto Kells Way was three blocks in one direction, then another two around a curvy road that cut a circle through the club's residential area, then two more blocks in the direction of the golf course. His house was on the downhill side of the road leading to the course. I wondered if there were police ribbons around it, too.

When my van accelerated noisily down Jacobean, I saw a curtain being drawn back in the Tollifers' front room. A yellow trapezoid of light framed a figure peering out. Apparently, I wasn't the only one with insomnia tonight.

A scant six minutes later I turned onto Kells Way. Here the streetlights were tucked into the tops of lodgepole pines. The light that fell on the asphalt shifted and swayed with the movement of the trees. Six minutes to the street sign — but how long to his driveway? I let the van drift down to the curb in front of the mammoth mock-Tudor residence that John Richard occupied all by himself. It took only a few seconds. I cut the engine and rolled down the window. Was I feeling tired? Not even remotely. So much for Arch's prescription for insomnia.

The wind picked up. Wind chimes on a nearby deck swirled and tinkled. The sound filtered through the rush of clicking aspen leaves. I breathed in the sweet summer air and wondered if John Richard had a window in his cell.

Okay, now, *think*. If John Richard had left Suz's house around one A.M., as he claimed, then he could have been back at his place before one-ten. Say he went inside. Had a few more drinks. Decided to go back and finish their argument. This was a possible reconstruction of events, but not a likely one, given his violent way of finishing things once he'd started them.

My neck stiffened and I tried to get comfortable. The pain in my shoulders had subsided to a mild ache. I reached for a tablecloth I kept stored in a plastic bag behind the passenger seat. I shoved aside the earphones and wires of Macguire's Walkman and pulled out the damask cloth. Tucking it around me, I tried to envision another way of timing Friday night's events.

No matter how much other people may not have liked Suz, John Richard was the one who'd been with her, arguing with her at the club, possibly about his terrible financial situation. Say he'd fought with Suz at her home, left her dead or near dead, then had gone back to his house around three or three-thirty A.M. This, I thought, was a more likely scenario. It fit the way he acted. Once he was enraged, it could have taken him several hours to work his way through it. What had Tom said? *Near as they can figure, Suz Craig died between three and five . . . Rigor hadn't set in when the medics arrived.* If John Richard left Suz sometime after three A.M., then everything fell into place.

The breeze died; the rustle of leaves and pine needles stopped. In the distance a car rumbled around the club's circle. A wide swath of light swept the end of Kells Way. Then there was sudden quiet.

Say John Richard's fight with Suz had gone on and on. She screamed and contradicted him. The argument became violent, with pots and pans being used for weapons. Then Suz finally got the usual *bam bam bam.* Then more arguing and maybe another horrible whack. Then he left in a huff, with her hurt and screaming. She would have cried for him not to leave her in such a state. Then she stumbled outside for help, fell into the ditch, and died. All this would explain why rigor hadn't set in until just after seven A.M.

There was a noise on the street that was not from a tree, a car, a herd of elk, a sprinkler system, or a set of wind chimes. My heart stopped. Someone whispered with loud insistence.

"Hey, man! Aren't you *done* yet?"

My spinal column turned to ice. The voice was about fifty feet away, on the same side of the street where I sat in my van. Whoever this was, he or she or they must have come along after I'd parked my vehicle, during that ten minutes when I'd been sitting deep in thought.

I cut my eyes both ways, without moving, but could make out nothing. Kids sneaking home after hours? Car thieves? Burglars? If a couple of guys were going to rob a private residence, I didn't care. I just didn't want them to add *assault of caterer* to their list of crimes.

"No, man, I'm not *done!*" came the urgent whispered reply. "This fluorescent stuff is dripping all over the damn place! Plus, I'm almost out! So hand me another can and shut up!"

There was grunting and clinking. "I'm tired of doing a good deed, man!" was the bitter response. "That security guy comes this way right on the hour!"

"I told you to shut your mouth, or the neighbors will get him here even earlier!"

"But it's almost three!" his partner insisted. "He's going to be here any second!

We need to split! Just *leave* it!"

My dashboard clock said 2:52. Eight minutes until the security guy showed up . . . if he did. Ever so slowly, inch by inch, I leaned forward to look out the windshield. If I could see them, I could figure out how to drive off without incident. Kells Way was a dead end. If these two guys — whoever they were, whatever their intentions — were in front of me, I could rev the ignition, throw the van into reverse, and zip backward up the street. If they were *behind* me on Kells, I could make a U-turn and accelerate across someone's driveway to get past them.

Spotlights shone down on the homes, driveways, and lawns on each side of the street. John Richard's house boasted spotlights above the garage that did not quite illuminate the two darkened stories of the rambling, beamed structure. Nothing out of place appeared on his blacktop. Then I noticed several cans that looked as if they'd been discarded to one side of the driveway. Farther over, almost to the stone entryway that was topped by an expansive burgundy awning, I could see the bottom of a ladder. Why would John Richard have left a ladder out? He hated doing home repairs.

Inching forward slowly in my seat, I strained my eyes to see more. A figure was moving through the trees. Then I made out someone on the ladder. A car door slammed, and the movement under the trees abruptly stopped.

"Hurry *up*, man! What're you doing, getting high on fumes?"

This whisper came from high on the ladder. From the same direction as the car door, a motor started up. Someone was going somewhere. The guy under the trees scrambled up the ladder rungs, and I heard the unmistakable *hiss-s-s* of a spray-paint can.

It was the country-club vandals.

The car that had started around the circle above Kells revved and moved. Was it the security man? I couldn't tell. Headlights coursed along the left side of the street, the dead end, then John Richard's house.

One of the vandals was at the bottom of the ladder. The other was at the top. Young men, lean and tall, dressed in dark colors. In the approaching headlights a dripping, crooked word painted in brilliant yellow appeared above them.

KILLER

Chapter 17

I shivered again. Perspiration sprouted on my forehead and palms. The vandals who had caused so much property damage in the club area were spray-painting their verdict on John Richard's house. Or maybe it was something they'd seen. Well, I'd forgotten the cellular phone and couldn't call the cops. So these guys would have to make their point to law enforcement on their own. I was getting out of here.

I pumped the accelerator, turned the car key. The motor strained, didn't turn over, died. I'd flooded the engine. I turned the key again, didn't pump the gas. This time the engine whined and died again. Footsteps thudded across John Richard's lawn. Dammit all, anyway.

Frantically, I rolled up my window. But I couldn't reach across in time to close the one on the passenger side. A lanky figure in a black ski mask pulled up the lock, wrenched open the door, and scrambled in. I could smell the sweat on his body. *They're kids,* I told myself. *Don't panic.* Behind the black mask the vandal's eyes glared menacingly at me. He grabbed my upper right arm.

"Get out of the car," he hissed angrily. "And shut *up.*"

"Let *go,*" I said evenly, tugging away from him. "I was just sitting here because I went out for a drive —"

His fingers bit into my arm. "Shut up and *get out.*"

"Stop pulling on me and I will," I replied in a quiet, nonthreatening voice that I hoped didn't betray how furiously my heart was hammering. To my astonishment, the figure in black loosened his grip slightly. I shed the tablecloth and hopped awkwardly onto the street.

"Watch her," Vandal One ordered Vandal Two. In the streetlight I could see Vandal Two was brandishing a tire iron. "I gotta check her van," the first guy said. "See if she's got some kind a weapon or night-vision camera in there."

"That's ridiculous, of course I don't," I snapped. "I'm just a caterer." I strained to see up the street. The passing car had disappeared without turning down Kells Way. Where was the security man?

"Oh, yeah?" said Vandal Two, a smirk in his voice. He twirled the tire iron inexpertly.

"Kinda early for fixin' breakfast, wouldn't you say?"

"Listen, guys. The man who lives here, the guy who was arrested? He's my ex-husband."

"Really," said Vandal One. He spat. "What, this guy's in jail, you've got an old key, you figure you'll go in and pick up a few things while he's not around?"

"No. That's not why I'm here."

Vandal One leered ominously. "Then why *are* you here?"

When in doubt, tell the truth. "I couldn't sleep. I went out for a drive."

Vandal Two's eyes sparked behind the mask. He raised the tire iron. "You'll sleep if I knock you over the head."

The words were out of my mouth before I could pull them back. "Hey, tough guy! I thought you were so worried about the security man driving up!" This warning earned me a rude shove on the shoulder. I stepped back and said, "Why're *you* here?"

Vandal Two stabbed a finger at the house. "Can't you read? We know he did it."

In the darkness it was almost impossible to see the ugly yellow word. "Ah. Killer. How do you know that?"

"Wouldn't you like to know. We see lots of things."

I shrugged. But if these two knew anything about the attack on Suz . . . "How —"

"Wait a minute," exclaimed Vandal One, "you said you're a caterer? I read about you."

I said mildly, "And you are . . . ?" When he didn't answer, I went on. "So why are you so certain my ex-husband killed her?"

"You think we have time to tell you anything?" erupted Vandal Two. To his compatriot he urged, "Come on, let's get out of here."

"I'm married to a cop," I announced hastily. "If he catches you, he'll ream both of you out so bad you'll get a life sentence for shoplifting when this is over. Both of you," I added, stalling for time. Where in the world was that security guy, anyway? "But if you'll talk to me about why you think my ex-husband is guilty —"

The guy with the tire iron waggled it in my face. "I know why you're here. Insomnia, my ass. That doc goes down, I'll bet you inherit this house. You're too shy to gloat over your loot in the daylight, but you just couldn't sleep until you got a good look at your new place."

I was tempted to ask: Just how much of that paint did you inhale, anyway? But there was no telling these two anything. No telling them that, come those circumstances, Arch would inherit. Not that my son would want this enormous place. Not that my son would want anything besides having his parents alive and well and out of jail. But I needed to know if they had seen something Friday night. And where was the security man? Why did no neighbors seem to hear me out here arguing with vandals?

I made a decision. The vandals probably wouldn't hurt me, despite the pop Vandal Two had given my shoulder. These two were cowards, which was why they defaced other people's property at night. Still, they were angry young cowards, so I would have to be careful.

I took a tentative step toward my van. "I want to go home. Are you going to tell me why you think my ex-husband murdered that woman? Or do you want the cops swarming all over here tomorrow with their fingerprint equipment? Actually," I said offhandedly, "they'll probably do that, anyway. A murder investigation is a whole different ball game from cleaning up graffiti, guys."

Vandal Two lifted his chin mockingly. "You're just dying to know, aren't you?"

"Yeah. I am."

Vandal One pressed forward. "We saw him," he said, his mouth so suddenly close to mine, I trembled in spite of myself. His breath smelled of potato chips. "The Korman guy left that night in a white Jeep. He's gone two minutes and then comes back in the Jeep, only slower this time."

"What time did he do this leaving and returning? Where were you when you saw all this?"

"Oh, bitch, what do you think I am — Rodney King with a videocamera?"

"Rodney King didn't videotape —"

"Shut up," growled Vandal One. "The doc leaves in his Jeep. About ten minutes later he drives up again, but the lights are off."

"What do you mean, the lights are off? And was it two minutes or ten minutes? Are you sure it was Korman? Was it a white Jeep or a silver one? He has one of each."

"Look, it was a white Jeep. And it happened. He drove away fast and came back slowly, with no lights. He knocked on the side door and what's-her-name yelled at him a little bit. Then she let him in."

Vandal Two hissed, "Suck it up, man, somebody's coming! We gotta split!"

The tire iron clanged to the pavement. The boys bolted. I peered up Kells Way into the glare of headlights. The approaching car was not the security car. The driver stopped, opened a mailbox, and stuffed in a newspaper. This person didn't bring security; he brought the news. He would be no help. Spooked by some ambushes in Denver, the newspaper delivery folks now wouldn't stop if you were bleeding your guts out in six feet of snow. But I didn't need this person's assistance.

I whirled and peered into the shifting light of the yards. The vandals had vanished. They had found a magical way of disappearing through people's property. From what vantage point had they watched Suz Craig's house the night she died? The two guys hadn't seen me drive down Kells Way. Perhaps they'd been vandalizing the club road signs on an adjoining block when I'd parked.

The metallic slap of mailboxes being opened and closed punctuated the night air. There was no sign of the security man and no sound of a pickup truck or some other vehicle being driven away. Where had the vandals gone? I had no idea.

It was time to boogie.

By the time I drove past the security car with its still-dozing watchman and arrived home, the dashboard clock read three-forty-five. Time flies when you're avoiding insomnia. I shivered my way into pajamas, eased into bed, and slid my arms around Tom's warm body. No use waking him. A reasonable morning hour would be a better time to tell him all that had happened.

But I'd awakened him anyway. He turned over and mumbled, "Where in the *world* have you been, Miss G.?" I shushed him gently and curled in closer. But he took my cold hands in his warm ones. "I went downstairs looking for you . . . then I saw the van was gone. Honestly, I've been a wreck."

I wove my cold legs through his deliciously warm ones. "I couldn't sleep, so I went for a drive. I wanted to . . . to *time* the driving distances over by Suz Craig's. How long from Suz's house to John Richard's, you know. But" — I hugged him tight — "I ended up interrupting a pair of vandals spray-painting John Richard's house. You're not going to believe it, but these guys were painting the word 'Killer.' So I talked to them —"

"*What?*" Tom extricated himself from my embrace, threw off the sheets, and turned on the lamp. Soon he was dressed in a terry robe and had one of our zillion leaky Biocess pens poised over his trusty spiral notebook. He said, "Would you care to make a quick statement, Mrs. Schulz?"

I sighed, then told him all about the vandals on Kells Way. I included their rude shove and their nonvideotaped account of how they'd seen John Richard drive away from Suz's house in his Jeep that night and then return very slowly, lights out. "They thought I was in front of John Richard's tonight so that I could steal something from inside the house. Or to gloat over inheriting the place."

Tom tapped his notebook. "You didn't hear them drive away? But yet you say they were afraid of the country-club security man. Who never showed up."

"Maybe they hid in their car or their truck," I offered.

He scowled. "Maybe. More likely, they're teenagers who live right there somewhere. They probably took off on foot or on bike, figuring they could come back later for their paint and ladder." After a moment of pondering, he turned off the light and pulled me close.

I murmured, "I'm sorry I worried you."

His breath brushed my ear. "Please don't do any more middle-of-the-night neighborhood prowling, okay? Can we get you a prescription for sleeping pills? It'd be safer."

"No, thanks." I hesitated. "Tom. It takes almost ten minutes to get back to John Richard's house. These guys couldn't tell me if it was ten minutes or two minutes between when he roared off and when he returned.

And why would he drive back so soon? He never recovers from a fit of temper that fast."

"Haven't a clue. I'm going back to sleep. But I want a promise from you. A couple of promises, actually."

"Name them."

"Miss G. You seem determined to poke your nose into this. Maybe you doubt Korman killed the woman. Maybe you're trying to help Arch. But you're snooping around. Don't disagree." When I nodded, he went on. "Okay, promise me: You won't go down to that ACHMO office. You won't break into John Richard's office and go through his files. You won't break into Suz Craig's house or John Richard's house. We — official law enforcement — will go to the offices and interview the people. We will go through the files, search the houses, all that. Okay?"

"What *can* I do?"

"Do what you always do. Talk to people. Feed them your great food. And *try* to stay out of trouble. Promise?"

I sighed. "You drive a hard bargain, cop."

He sighed too. "Let's just say I love my wife. And I want to keep her alive."

The next morning, Monday, I was sleeping so deeply when Tom left that he didn't bring me coffee. I didn't even hear Arch go out, although he left me a note taped to the computer saying he'd be back from his friend Todd's house by dinnertime. I banged around the kitchen making espresso and toasting homemade bread. I started a sponge for the brioche I would use for the doll people's box-lunch sandwiches. No other catering assignments loomed, so I checked that I had the right smoked meats and cheeses, plus some almonds, lemons, and seedless raspberry jam. I wanted to start experimentation to make my own Linzer tarts. I reread the last line in Arch's note: *You* promised *to help Dad, Mom.*

Right. Help him without visiting the ACHMO office, without breaking into Suz's or the Jerk's house, without sneaking into the Jerk's office to go through files. How about this: I could visit John Richard's office and *not* poke into files. Couldn't I?

I put in a call to Tom's phone and got his machine. Any leads on the vandals? I wanted to know. Or on anything else? Call me back. After I finished breakfast — crunchy toasted Anadama bread thickly slathered with butter and apple butter — I checked on Macguire. He was sleeping. I felt his forehead. The fever seemed to have broken.

His yellow-flecked brown eyes opened wide when I withdrew my hand and he groaned. "What's up?"

"Not much. I just wanted to check on you. Any chance you'd want to walk over to John Richard's office with me in a little bit? ReeAnn will probably be there."

It's amazing how energizing infatuation can be. With much groaning, Macguire roused himself, showered, shaved, and dressed. When he shuffled into the kitchen, his white cotton T-shirt and dark jeans hung so limply on his emaciated frame that I found myself begging. After all, it's my profession to *feed* people.

"Please, Macguire. *Please* eat something. Let me fix you some juice and toast. People love my homemade bread and —"

"No. Thanks." He surveyed the kitchen dispiritedly, then looked at my anxious face and relented. "Okay. I'll have a little glass of juice and a piece of bread. Don't toast it, though. Toast is too crusty. Hurts my throat."

He swallowed less than a quarter-cup of juice and nibbled a third of a slice of crustless homemade bread. At least it was something.

When we walked through the door of John Richard's spacious, all-beige office fifteen minutes later, ReeAnn Collins was in a state, and it wasn't a good one. Holding the lengthy phone cord in front of the marble counter, she paced across the deep-pile carpet, complained into the receiver, and gestured furiously with her free hand. Her buxom figure was shown off to splendid advantage by a size-too-small white T-shirt and clinging black biking shorts. Her curly black ponytail and long, pouffed bangs bobbed as she bent from time to time to whack at magazines that spilled from the beige-painted tables.

"First Judy calls in sick. She's a nurse, but she can't tell me what kind of sickness she has. So here I am, left to do everything, and then the sheriff's department calls and says don't touch anything. They're on their way." She nodded us distractedly toward the waiting-area chairs. "Then *ACHMO* calls," she continued into the phone, "and says don't give anything to the *sheriff's department.*" I sat down and wondered, as I always did, how hugely pregnant women could ever extract themselves from these deep, soft couches once their appointment time arrived. ReeAnn stormed on. "ACHMO says the files belong to them, and if I give the sheriff's department anything, I'm in deep yogurt. So then they say they're on *their* way." She set her heart-shape, usually quite pretty face into a pout as she listened to the advice from the other end of the line. She examined her black-and-purple-painted nails and sighed. "Okay. Bring your bike rack. Noon." She slammed the phone down and examined us bitterly. "What do *you* want?"

Macguire tucked his chin into his neck and gabbled something unintelligible. Poor kid. Aside from ReeAnn's plentiful figure and pretty face, I couldn't figure the attraction. Maybe it was the black-and-purple nails.

"ReeAnn," I reassured her, "we're here to help you. You see, I talked to somebody from ACHMO after church yesterday, and after what happened to Ms. Craig —"

She stabbed a dark fingernail at Macguire. "Are you the one who told the cops I didn't like Ms. Craig? Because they came to my place yesterday, you know."

"Er, I, no —" Maguire stammered. "I guess I —"

Before he could continue his feeble protests, ReeAnn pointed the fingernail at me. "Uh-huh. And you, Mrs. Ex-Korman Number One, exactly how're you going to help me? My boss is behind bars and the cops think I hated his girlfriend? What're you going to do, hire a temporary nurse to come in and help out? Call all the expectant women and recommend other doctors to them? You going to loan me some money from your catering biz when I don't get paid this week?"

"ReeAnn, you're upset. Please call me Mrs. Schulz. Or Goldy."

"*I* know," she said spitefully. "You're here about money. That's what Mrs. Ex-Korman Number Two is always calling about."

I replied calmly, "I'm not interested in money, or at least only marginally. Listen, do you know *why* the ACHMO people are coming today?"

She sighed dramatically and looked away. "I never know. One week it's 'Let's see how you're billing ultrasounds.' Then they pull out ten records of women who've had ultrasounds. If one of the patients happened to say, 'Oh, my, I'd like to have an ultrasound because I'm worried about the baby,' and the doc writes that in the woman's file, you can kiss your reimbursement good-bye."

I said, "Hmm." Chris Corey had explained that the HMO came in to the doctors' offices to check billing, but I still didn't know the reason. "Why does what the patient says about the ultrasound matter?"

"Be-cause," she supplied impatiently, "if you want to be sure ACHMO is going to pay for the ultrasound, there has to be a *medical* reason for the test. And the ultrasound has to be the *doctor's* idea, understand? Even if it's the patient's idea, we have to dress it up like the doctor figured her life was in danger if she didn't have an ultrasound. Otherwise, ACHMO doesn't fork over the money for the ultrasound. Understand? Welcome to the world of managed care, Mrs. Ex-Korman Number One."

This was going to be fun, I could tell. The phone rang. ReeAnn dealt with the problem — a woman seeking an appointment — by referring her to another doctor. Then she turned back to us.

"So what do you two want, anyway? To talk about ACHMO coming? I don't have time."

I said bluntly, "Do you think my ex-husband killed Ms. Craig?"

My question seemed to surprise her. She pursed her lips and opened her eyes wide. Macguire watched her in enamored awe. Then she reached back to twirl her ponytail while she considered. "He could have," she replied noncommittally.

When she didn't say more, I prodded, "How about Patricia McCracken? Do you think she could have lost her temper with Suz Craig?"

ReeAnn snorted. "That's just as likely." The phone rang again. "Listen, I'm sorry, I really don't have time to chat —" I waved

301

to her to answer the phone. ReeAnn disposed of this caller by advising her to give the pharmacy a ring.

"Where's Patricia McCracken's file?" I asked as soon as the secretary was not-so-ready to chat again.

Her laugh was derisive. "You gotta be kidding if you think I'm going to show you a patient file."

"I don't want you to *show* me anything," I replied patiently. "What you might want to do is try to find something. It's what the ACHMO people are going to be here looking for. It could be a letter, a note, something about the McCracken suit. If John Richard wrote a few lines to himself about Patricia McCracken's care and the ACHMO people take them, it *will* adversely affect me and my son. John Richard could be found at fault in the malpractice suit and we'll lose financial support. Actually, what I really wanted was for Patricia to win her suit."

ReeAnn shook her head vigorously; the ponytail bobbed. "You've *already* lost financial support," she said scathingly. "He was thinking you were making so much money from your food business, he didn't have to pay anymore. And then when Bailey Products dumped Biocess . . . It's been awful. And he works so *hard*," she whined. "And what'll happen to *me* if they try him for killing her?"

I took a deep breath. I'd always suspected that ReeAnn and John Richard were cut from the same self-centered cloth. Now I was sure of it. But had ReeAnn and the Jerk been romantically involved in the few months she had been working for him? Could ReeAnn have been jealous of Suz Craig? Jealous enough to kill?

"My son," I said with a smile, "is extremely upset about his dad being in jail. So I promised him I'd ask around to see if there was anything to clear him, okay?"

"Uh, ReeAnn, remember?" Macguire interjected feebly. "Remember when you mentioned you were involved in a project with the HMO? Something to do with Ms. Craig? Remember, you called her Ms. Crank? That's probably why the police came to visit you."

"That woman was a first-class bitch," ReeAnn spat. "And that's exactly what I told those cops. I did call her Ms. Crank. And you know what Ms. Crank's favorite saying was, don't you?" Macguire and I looked at her expectantly. She raised her voice and trilled, " 'I don't *do* — I *delegate*.' "

"Oh, yes," I mumbled, remembering that that was precisely what Suz had said to me regarding the preparation of food for her business lunch. "I guess I did know that. But she did help me with the dishes when I worked for her, and she could have delegated that —"

"Cheap!" ReeAnn fumed. "I finally told her, 'Don't tell me to *do* another thing, okay? *Delegate somewhere else!* I don't work for you!' "

"What exactly did she want you to —"

I was interrupted by a knock at the door, followed by the entrance of Brandon Yuille. Today he wore a loose blue oxford-cloth shirt with no tie, navy pants, and Top-Siders.

"Hey-ho, we're here!" Brandon's cheery greeting was more along the lines of *How soon will Christmas dinner be ready* than *This is Eliot Ness, get up against the wall.* "Hey, Goldy! What're you doing here? I forgot to ask you yesterday, did you try that Thai sauce I gave you?" His whole attitude was much brighter than when I'd seen him after church. Behind him, however, Chris Corey appeared even glummer than he had the day before.

"Ah, no," I replied, "not yet."

"Well, then, why're you here?" Brandon asked again, still smiling.

"I'm just looking for some of Arch's, er, homework papers."

"In August? Isn't school out?"

"They've been missing for a long time."

ReeAnn slapped a pile of files down on the counter and shot me a knowing look of exasperation.

"Well, boys, here's a batch of D & Cs for you to look through. Did I guess right?"

"Nah, we need C-sections," Brandon announced brightly. "They've been missing even longer than homework papers." His laugh was infectious, and I found myself smiling in spite of myself. To ReeAnn he said, "Should we start in there?" He motioned down the hall to the filing office.

"That sounds just great." ReeAnn didn't do sarcasm well. "As if I had some choice, right? I've got to stay here and do the phones."

"Here's the list of the files we'll be looking for," Chris said meekly as he squeezed his pudgy body behind the counter and consulted a clipboard. He waited a moment until Brandon was out of earshot. I nipped over to the counter. "Did you do a dummy duplicate of Patricia McCracken's file?" Chris asked ReeAnn urgently.

"Yes," she whispered back. "Just the way you told me. I've got the original up here." She pointed to a shelf. The phone rang; she snatched it.

"What?" she squawked. "It's *your* turn to bring lunch! You think I can handle one more thing today? Forget it! Tuna sandwiches!" Then she slammed down the phone. It didn't sound as if she got along very well with whoever it was.

I said, "Chris! I thought you wanted ACHMO to be caught trying to take the file!"

He harumphed and readjusted his capacious belt. "If Brandon takes the dummy with McCracken's name on it before the police get here," he whispered impatiently, "then they'll still be committing an illegal act. And with ReeAnn keeping the real file, your husband's lawyer can still have the information he needs."

"He's my *ex*-husband, okay?" I hissed fiercely. "And I thought you said it would be a Medical Management lady coming here today. What has Human Resources got to do with checking billing? Does Brandon ever do that?"

Chris shrugged grandly. "They're scared." And then, balanced precariously on his cast, he lumbered off after Brandon.

"Don't remove anything, fellas!" I called after them. "My husband's a cop and I'll tell on you!" To ReeAnn I said softly, "The sheriff's department is on its way?"

"Supposedly." She eyed the telephone on the marble counter, as if debating which friend she should complain to next.

"Uh, I guess we'll be going," Macguire announced. His face was as sallow as I'd seen it since he'd been living with us. Despite his words, however, he didn't seem to have the energy or the will to move.

"ReeAnn," I whispered as I scooped up the back copies of *Architectural Digest* she'd spewed on the floor during her first manic phone call. "Can we please talk for a few minutes? It's for Arch."

"I don't know where his homework is."

"Please."

"I have to answer the phone."

"I know you were romantically involved with my ex-husband," I improvised. When I said this, ReeAnn shot Macguire a withering look. "It's okay," I added.

"I'm involved with somebody else right now, not an old geezer. And I was with *him* all Friday night. My new boyfriend can vouch for me, and I told the cops that, too."

"Fine." I tried to think. "Just tell me — What was Suz Craig working on that she was trying to delegate? Delegate to you, I mean? It seems odd she'd ask you to do work for her, when she had a whole army of secretaries to choose from at ACHMO."

ReeAnn snorted again, her trademark. "I'm not a secretary, I'm an *assistant*. And the stuff Ms. Crank had me do was penny-ante. 'Make our dinner reservations.' 'Call Aspen Meadow Nursery. Get them to come out and fix my steps.' "

When she seemed reluctant to go on, I prompted, "That's it?"

"Well. Not exactly." She bit the inside of her cheek, then confided, "It's what John Richard told me she tried to delegate to him that was really weird, if you want to know the truth."

"The truth would be great."

She leaned close. "She wanted him to put some stuff — I guess it was papers or something — in a safe place, somewhere the ACHMO people couldn't find them."

"What stuff? How do you know it was papers? The kind of papers they're trying to find now?" Suddenly I remembered what John Richard had said to me on the phone: *Suz had some kind of delicate material.* . . . What material? I'd thought it related to Ralph Shelton, but was that wrong? "Are you sure it was papers?"

She shrugged indifferently. "Who knows?" The phone rang. ReeAnn answered it and started to redirect another patient. To my surprise Brandon Yuille suddenly appeared at my side. He flashed me his movie-star smile.

"Goldy? May I talk to you for a minute?"

"More Thai sauce?" I said brightly.

"Please. Just right outside the front door. Just for a sec, if you don't mind."

I walked outside with him. I'd tell him what he wanted to know — maybe — if he'd answer a couple of questions, too. I made my voice pleasant. "Brandon, I was wondering . . . Was Suz Craig as hard to work for as some people say?"

His fine-featured face bloomed pink. "Some people thought she was . . . difficult." His tone grew guarded.

"So, what people are we talking about?"

He brushed my question away. "Goldy, there's something important I need to ask you, but it's . . . delicate." Man, they all loved that word, like they had to rinse out some lingerie. "You know how folks going through a divorce will sometimes hide assets from each other? Like money?"

I laughed. "Of course I do. Who's getting the divorce?"

He squirmed. "I . . . can't say. But you know about hiding assets?"

"Sure. One person in a marriage hides assets, the other gets to hire a forensic accountant, as I had to do, to go through the books of the person doing the hiding. Sometimes you find the stash and sometimes you don't. Lucky for me, I did."

Brandon's eyes, ordinarily deep brown, turned almost black. His voice became painfully earnest. "I promise, Goldy, if John Richard has given you anything to hide . . . we . . . I . . . need to know."

I almost laughed again. I imagined a list of intimate — make that *delicate* — questions: Have you had cosmetic surgery? Do you dye your hair? How much do you weigh? which could develop into How much money do you make? Now, apparently, to that invasive list I could add: Has your abusive ex-husband given you anything incriminating to hide?

"Brandon," I said with equal earnestness as the phone pealed again inside, "if my ex-husband had given me a bald eagle that he had shot and stuffed, I wouldn't tell the ACHMO honchos."

Brandon Yuille, my foodie buddy, turned on his heel and strode away. I immediately felt bad. I liked Brandon; I didn't want to alienate him. From inside the office ReeAnn said, "What? Who? Yeah, she's here. Goldy!"

When I went back into the office, Chris Corey had not reappeared and Macguire was still slumped in one of the chairs looking catatonic. As soon as Brandon found out the call wasn't for him, he brushed past ReeAnn on his way back into the file rooms.

"Man!" ReeAnn exclaimed, gesturing with the phone. "What is *his* problem? Anyway, the phone's for you."

I sighed and walked back to the counter. "Yes?" I said tentatively into the receiver.

"Miss G." Tom's warm, calm, reassuring voice. "I had a feeling you'd be over there. Bad news, I'm afraid."

"Go ahead."

"I warned you. The judge did it. John Richard made bail. He'll be out in two hours, probably back up in Aspen Meadow by noon."

"No."

"Yes. Now listen, you're a witness in this matter. He's been warned not to talk to any witnesses, but you know how poorly this guy follows directions. If he shows up at the house, or does anything to try to contact you, you ignore him, understand? Call us. We don't want this case ruined before it even starts."

"Okay." My voice was on novocaine.

"Goldy? Don't want to press a point here, but you're in danger. You found the body. You saw him drive up with the flowers.

You're the main person who can testify about his physical abusiveness. He's in some kind of mental state, and he may just want to rid himself of you altogether. Is Macguire there? I thought we agreed you weren't going to go poking around through files."

"I'm just here at the office for a few minutes. And I'm not doing any poking through files. The people poking are the ACHMO folks. Are your people on their way? ReeAnn said they were."

"They should be there in five minutes. Be sure you're in your kitchen in two hours, okay? I'm warning you, Goldy. I don't want you hurt. Okay, please put me on with that secretary so I can get her to kick those ACHMO guys out until our people get there."

I handed ReeAnn the phone, then told her that Macguire and I had to go. She tossed her ponytail in a suit-yourself gesture. But Macguire and I were not going straight home. We had someone else to warn.

Chapter 18

As we drove away from the office, I waited for a barrage of questions from Macguire. Ordinarily, the teenager took great interest in criminal cases. But he regarded me dully when I said we had one further stop to make.

"You don't want to go right home?" he asked. "You're always talking about how dangerous the Jerk is."

"I promised Arch I'd ask a few questions."

He shrugged and was silent. When we rounded the lake, spumes of dust were rising from the LakeCenter parking lot. The doll-show organizers had arrived. Without enthusiasm, I realized I needed to talk to them, too, before I went home, so that made *two* stops. I pulled into the lot of the sleek wood-paneled Lakeview Shopping Center, a two-story, L-shaped constellation of boutiques and offices that had recently been constructed on the old site of a gaudy saloon. Before the saloon went bankrupt, it had boasted a Vegas-style light display arranged in the shape of a covered wagon that appeared to roll from one end of the building toward the lake. But drunk wannabe cowboys exiting the saloon frequently thought the neon wagon was going to roll over them. Numerous car accidents had ensued. The sheriff's department had ordered the light display turned off, and that had been curtains for the saloon.

I parked in front of Sam's Soups, which had a For Lease sign in its darkened window. Food service in Aspen Meadow is always a touchy business, and Sam's alternately gluey and thin soups had not been a local hit. Next door to Sam's, Aspen Meadow Health Foods had held on, but only by going through a number of permutations. Up until a few months ago, my friend Elizabeth Miller had offered everything from twenty-pound bags of millet to gallon jugs of soy milk. Elizabeth had sold the store to Amy Bartholomew, R.N., late of the AstuteCare HMO and new purveyor of homeopathic remedies.

Only she wasn't purveying at the moment. Amy's paper clock sign indicated that she opened at eleven. It was barely ten. Not only that but Amy had scribbled "Most Days" on the clock's center. Great. I glanced across the road at the LakeCenter.

"Mind if we drop by over there?" I asked Macguire, pointing at the LakeCenter. "I

314

just want to see how they need me to set up for the breakfast Wednesday."

"Sure." He gave me a weary smile. "I'm not ready to go back to bed yet. I feel as if I spend my life between the sheets." His face was cadaverous. Poor guy. I felt terrible that ReeAnn Collins had treated him so offhandedly. It's difficult to take cruel treatment from a member of the opposite sex, especially from someone you care about. At nineteen, I'd been some kind of basket case myself when it came to relationships, and I hadn't been struggling with mononucleosis and a flaky, egotistical father in the bargain.

"We'll come back over here when the proprietor opens," I promised. "You want to rest for a minute before we go talk to the Babsie Bash ladies?"

"Whatever," Macguire repeated, apparently too tired to think of anything new to say. He stared glumly at the lake, a meadow of sparkles broken up by paddle- and sailboats. I wondered how Tom thought I'd be protected from the Jerk with poor, listless Macguire accompanying me. *He's out.* I shivered. But I shook this off, the same way I always tried to rid myself of thoughts that included the Jerk.

Soon we were back in the van, rocking over

dirt potholes, past the boundary of the municipal golf course, and into the wildflower-rimmed lot of the LakeCenter. After I parked, the two of us walked toward the large log building, where men and women with plastic-coated badges that said DEALER were carting boxes of wares inside.

"Gail?" I said when we approached.

Gail Rodine, in conversation with a uniformed man, lifted her chin in acknowledgment. Actually, her chin was about all I could see of Gail's face. She sported a floppy-brimmed hat that sprouted feathers in every direction and might, I reflected, serve well as a centerpiece for the annual Audubon banquet. Her mid-thigh-length dress was a glittering black-and-white-striped affair. Where did this woman get the money for her hobby? The LakeCenter was not a cheap space to rent, and I was not a cheap caterer to hire. The local Babsie club must get a cut of the profit made from the sale of dolls, and that percentage must be considerable.

"I'll be with you in a moment," she announced, and continued her low murmur with an older man in a gray security uniform that hugged his belly like a sausage casing. The man's complexion was splotched, his nose was bright red, and his silver-gray hair lay in flat, greasy curls against his head. He punctuated every few sentences of Mrs. Rodine's with a hiccup. He was not the sort of security guard to inspire confidence. Still, I stopped a respectful distance away from their conversation. Despite the fact that Arch had spent the night at the Rodines' house, Gail and I did not move in the same social circles, as we both well knew. Wealthy folks are very conscious of service-sector people who are intrusive. Macguire held back another ten feet behind me. I think the memory of the women chasing him to the end of the dock two days before made him less anxious to be sociable.

Gail Rodine motioned me forward as she announced crisply to the guard: "And this is our caterer. She'll be here to set up the box lunches tomorrow, and our breakfast on Wednesday just before nine o'clock." She cocked an eyebrow at me, as if daring me to contradict her agenda. Actually, I needed to get in closer to eight on Wednesday. But before I could utter a word, Gail noticed Macguire. Her face stiffened with anger.

I tried to sound reassuring. "Gail, we're just here today to check that the ovens are working and to see where you want the buffet to be. Plus, day after tomorrow, I need to get in closer to eight or eight-fifteen. Would that be okay?"

317

She lifted her chin, and I had a glimpse of a hooked nose and an auburn-lipsticked mouth with a cruel slant. "Eight will be fine. You said 'we.' Is this . . . person . . . your assistant? If so, you may come in now, he may not," she proclaimed imperiously. "That boy has already made our lives quite difficult here. And we're preparing to take our morning tea break. The break will be held in the same place as the brunch."

"Okay," I managed to choke.

"Well, then." She bristled impatiently. "Come and see what I'm talking about."

Gail marched ahead of me down the path. Ordinarily, I adore my clients. They're happy to book me. They enjoy planning the menu. They rave about the food I lovingly prepare. Ordinarily, things end happily, with future bookings in sight. But sometimes you can sense when things are going to go badly. Gail had been cruel to the kids at Arch's slumber party; she'd been mean to Macguire when he'd merely tried to help. I'd just seen her give the security guy hell and I could feel that I was next in line, right before the tea break. I tried to wipe from my mind a sudden vision of Gail Rodine bobbing in a lake of Orange Pekoe, with her Babsie dolls tied around her neck. I suppressed a groan. Behind me,

Macguire turned and shuffled back to the van.

I followed Gail past the bored-looking, slightly ripe-smelling guard — after all, what kind of drinking stories could he get from protecting dolls? — and into the kitchen. The large and serviceable space was as I remembered it: two ovens set against one wall, a sink overlooking the parking lot. Two lengthy counters separated the kitchen from the ballroom. These counters doubled as a snack bar in the winter months, during skating season, but would serve for me as a prep area. I checked that the ovens worked and looked briefly into the ballroom, where dealers were cracking open long tables and setting up tiers of empty shelves for their displays.

"In the morning," Gail explained grandly over the bustle of dealers, "I want all the food out back. Nothing can touch the doll displays, remember. You can wheel the food trays out through here."

She swished toward the wall beside the kitchen, then expertly opened a door in what looked like a solid block of logs. The door — actually a rectangle of sawed logs that snugged into the wall — gave out on the flagstone patio on the side of the structure. Gail moved outside. She briskly pointed out the grill for Wednesday's final meal, the picnic tables on the deck overlooking the lake where dining would take place, and the tall doors between the ballroom and the deck.

"No dolls beyond this point, unless they have been purchased," she said firmly. I smiled, nodded, and wondered how Macguire was doing. After promising Gail that I'd be back the next day with the box lunches, I zipped back to my van.

Macguire, chin in the air, mouth open, had fallen asleep with his head cocked against the neck rest. There was no way he could have been comfortable.

When the van jolted out of the dirt lot, he was startled awake. He blinked, then muttered, "Uh, I'm ready to go home."

"Just one more quick stop. I promised this nurse I'd be in to see her today. Plus I want to warn her about my ex-husband being released from custody. He mentioned her on the phone from jail. I should let her know he might show up."

"Then I'd better go in with you," Macguire said wearily. "If your ex has already gotten up here, you'll need backup."

We bumped back over the potholes, pulled into the Lakeview lot, and parked in front of the health-food store next to a Harley-Davidson. An Indian cowbell attached to the door gonged as we entered. Inside, ruffled green gingham curtains framed the windows. The pinewood-paneled walls were hung with pictures of the Maharishi Mahesh Yogi and other dignitaries of the vegetarian world. The distinctive smell of exotic herbs and incense that permeates most health-food stores enveloped us.

Even though the store had only been open ten minutes, two people had preceded us. One was Patricia McCracken, whose pear-shaped body was stuffed into a white tennis dress that contrasted with the more exotic surroundings. She sat at a table with Amy Bartholomew. Amy sported a green-flowered Indian dress embedded with spangles. The other person in the store, a black-leather-clad burly man with shoulder-length, curly black hair, studied two shelves stacked with brown bottles. An array of silver rings spilling down his left ear flashed in the sunlight whenever he leaned forward to study a label.

"Even in disguise," Macguire whispered, "I don't think Korman could look like that."

"You're right," I whispered back.

At their table Patricia and Amy were in intimate communication. Patricia's voice cracked with pain; Amy's voice exuded its liquid warmth. After nodding briefly to acknowledge our arrival, Amy directed Patricia

321

to hold a bottle to her heart with her left hand. With her right hand Patricia was told to press her forefinger and thumb together in an okay sign. Then Amy asked a question and gently pried apart the fingers of Patricia's right hand. "Six a day?" Amy murmured, and pulled. The okay sign opened. "Eight a day?" It opened again. At twelve a day Patricia's fingers wouldn't budge. Amy wrote on a yellow pad while Patricia wrote a check. A novel approach to prescription, this.

Patricia gave me an apologetic glance as she exited. "Do you still hurt from Saturday?"

"I'm fine," I told her, not quite truthfully. "But listen. John Richard's out on bail. I don't think he'd come after you, but when he loses his temper with women . . . Well. Be careful."

Patricia's face tightened and she swore under her breath. Then she shook her head and moved away from me without asking another question.

Amy was already eyeing Macguire by the time the cowbell rang behind Patricia. After an appraising squint, she moved to Macguire's side. The thin teenager towered over her.

"You're not well," she murmured.

"Yeah, lady. Really."

"I'll be with you in a sec."

Macguire nodded without interest. He stopped in front of a rack of magazines. Amy slipped over to the shelves, where she seemed to know exactly what the Earring King wanted. I watched her hand him a large cellophane bag filled with lots of small cellophane bags, each of which was crammed with multicolored capsules. I could imagine Frances Markasian's loud headline: COP'S WIFE ARRESTED IN HEALTH STORE DRUG BUST.

The Earring King glared at me. "What're you staring at, woman?" he demanded.

"I'm sorry," I stammered. My mouth had gone dry.

"Edgar, you need to transform that anger," Amy gently reprimanded the man. "It's blocking you."

Emanating hostility that showed no sign of being transformed, Edgar slapped down some dollar bills for his cellophane bags, mumbled that he didn't want the change, and clanged through the door. A moment later a motorcycle engine split the silence. Amy shook her head of red hair.

"Cancer," she said sadly. I didn't know if she meant the disease or the astrological sign, and wasn't about to ask. She looked at me and said, "How's that shoulder?"

"Fair."

"Let me treat your friend and then you. How's that?"

"Well . . ." How was I supposed to say this? *My ex-husband called from jail. He suspects you of killing his girlfriend. Or he wants to pin the murder on you. Now he's on the loose and may come looking for you, Amy. Better pack up your alfalfa sprouts and hit the trail.* "I need to talk to you without interruption," I said somewhat lamely.

"No problem," Amy replied brightly, and blithely turned the door's paper clock to CLOSED.

Amy beckoned to Macguire. He shuffled behind us as she led the way to the back of the shop, where small tables were sandwiched between two refrigerated cases that held plastic bottles of chlorophyll and other substances I wouldn't want to ingest. Next to the bottles were plastic bags of adzuki, black, and pinto beans, a few tired-looking carrots, and a small selection of packaged grains. Macguire flopped into a chair and I sat next to him. Amy clasped one of Macguire's hands in hers; he immediately withdrew it. I had the same discomfiting sense I'd had in the McCrackens' bathroom — that Amy was way ahead of me, and I wasn't sure I wanted to catch up.

"Perhaps you should just treat me," I told her. "I don't really have any authority to —"

But Amy was absorbed with Macguire's eyes. He turned his face away from her and rubbed his temples. She said, "What do the M.D.s say?"

"The . . . Oh," I faltered, "well, Macguire has mononucleosis, and he . . . what worries me is that he doesn't have any appetite. The doctor has said he should be getting better, but . . . Anyway, he's staying with me until his father gets home later in the month, and I'm not sure his father would approve of —" I was yakking away. Why did this woman always make me yak?

"Macguire?" Amy asked in her kind, melted-milk-chocolate voice. "Do you want to be healed?"

Macguire tilted his head skeptically, glanced swiftly at Amy, then stared at the floor. "I guess."

"Okay. Just relax." She had him remove his watch. Then she touched his head with first one hand, then the other.

"What are you doing?" I blurted out.

She replied without looking at me. "I'm reading his aura."

Oh, *that!* I reflected. *Of course.* Marla and I would have to offer it in Med Wives 101.

Amy took a small flashlight from her pocket, then opened and smoothed out what looked like a paper diagram or chart of some kind. "Look at me." This Macguire did, and for the next five minutes Amy shone the flashlight in his eyes and consulted her chart. When she'd made a few notes, she rose and briskly began to gather supplies. A bottle of chlorophyll. Five brown bottles of pills. Cellophane bags similar to the ones the Earring King had purchased. Then she commenced the same drill she had with Patricia: Macguire held the medicines to his heart, and Amy asked questions and tested the response by pulling apart his fingers pressed in the okay sign. I kept an eye on the door, in the remote case the Jerk showed up.

Finally Amy seemed happy with a combination of three bottles of pills, two cellophane bags, and the chlorophyll. She asked Macguire if he wanted her to run through putting together his twice-a-day regimen. As usual, he replied dully in the affirmative.

"You'd better watch this, too," she told me, and then showed us the sheet. He was to take ten capsules twice a day, plus a teaspoon of chlorophyll dissolved in a cup of cold water. Yum-*my!*

I pointed at the capsules. "What's in these?"

"Shark cartilage," she replied, "pau d'arco bark, essiac tea, rosehips —"

A vision of Macbeth's witches rose before me. "Okey-doke," I interrupted her, before we could get to eye of newt.

"Are you ready for me to take a look at you?" she asked.

"Sure," I said enthusiastically. What did I have to lose?

While Macguire dutifully swallowed his capsules with a glass of springwater spiked with chlorophyll, I got the same flashlight-in-the-eye treatment he'd received. Again Amy consulted her chart.

"Hmm," she said. Then the beautiful brown eyes and faded-freckled face regarded me sadly. She bit the inside of her lip and then made her pronouncement: "You're depressed."

Great, I thought, *got herbs for it? Prozac bark?* Instead I said, "Since it's truth-telling time, Amy, there's something I really need to talk to you about."

"Your ex-husband. Dr. Korman."

"How did you know?"

She smiled. "I may run a health-food store, but I don't live in the next galaxy. Suz Craig and I didn't get along, as you said you knew,

327

when I helped you out at the McCrackens' house. What, you think Dr. Korman is going to come gunning for me? I was a victim of Suz's nastiness, so now I'm a suspect in her murder? Is Dr. Korman trying to say I killed her?"

Without warning, I felt infinitely dejected. Maybe it was Amy's suggestion that I was depressed; maybe it was my acknowledgment of the truth. A woman was dead. If my ex-husband had killed her, he would pay. But so would my teenage son, who would pay a long-lasting price in emotional pain. If John Richard had not killed Suz, then finding out who did would be left to the D.A.'s investigator, Donny Saunders. Saunders, who, last time we'd met, had informed me radicchio was the name of a mobster. No wonder my spirits were low.

"Let's get you some herbs for that depression," Amy said decisively. She moved to the same area of the same shelf where she'd pulled down the bottle for Patricia McCracken. Hmm.

And then I, too, went through the drill of holding the herbs to my heart and having my fingers pried open. Within five minutes I, too, was swallowing mammoth capsules whose ingredient list included only three things I recognized: bamboo sap, ginger rhizome, and licorice root. It didn't sound like a mixture I'd use in a cookie.

"So is Patricia McCracken depressed, too?" I asked Amy. "About losing her baby?"

Amy lifted her eyebrows. "Wouldn't you be?"

"Depressed enough to get really angry with Suz Craig?"

"Who knows? Suz distressed a lot of people."

"Including you." When she gave a single nod, I swallowed, then said, "Why'd she fire you?"

Amy smiled placidly. "Is that what Suz said, that she fired me? No. That's what she always said when people couldn't get along with her . . . that she fired them, as if they were the incompetent ones." She shook her head gently. "I quit ACHMO. My payout from the pension plan helped buy this shop."

"Why'd you quit?"

"Why'd you divorce Dr. Korman?"

"Because he abused me."

"Aha! Same here. Only Suz Craig didn't abuse people physically. She beat them up *mentally*." Amy said it as if it were a disease. "When I left, I thought, now why did that take me so long?"

"Meaning . . . ?"

She frowned and pondered my question. For a long minute she was silent. Then she answered, "AstuteCare has been in Colorado for eight years. I was with them from the beginning, moved up to Medical Management. There was a group of department heads, including Brandon Yuille and Chris Corey, who also lived in Aspen Meadow. We worked as a team. Suz joined ACHMO two years ago. It was the beginning of hell."

Hell. Interesting. "Why? What did she do to change things?"

"We used to have a weekly meeting to discuss problems we were having. What we needed in the new Provider Relations Manual, that kind of thing. Suz would scream and yell. 'What's the matter with you people?' was her favorite. And then she'd viciously attack every person in the room for being stupid, lazy, incompetent. Or, in the case of Chris, fat. 'How's a tub of lard supposed to set a model for health?' Suz used to yell at him. You get the idea. Brandon Yuille's father, who'd just lost his wife, was remodeling and reopening the pastry shop. Suz was on Brandon's case constantly about being there on the weekends instead of working overtime for her. She claimed Brandon came in too tired to be of any use, because he was up all night baby-sitting his father, on and on. It was none of her business that Brandon's father was a widower and alone and desperately needed his company. But she *made* it her business. She made his life miserable."

Aha, more hell. "Wasn't there anybody you could complain to?"

She shrugged. "It was coming to that. A group of them was trying to go over her head."

"And did they? And to whom?"

"They talked about it. But I'd had enough. Her cruelty was unbearable. I couldn't stand it anymore. The last — no, let's see, the *next-to-last* — straw for me came about five months ago when I was negotiating to buy this store. I saw the store as a long-term project for my retirement. Originally I was planning just to have it open on the weekends, until I could build up the clientele over about a ten- or fifteen-year period, when I retired from ACHMO. But Suz never wanted you to be in charge of your own destiny. *She* wanted to be in charge of your destiny."

"She knew you wanted to open this store?"

Amy smiled sadly. "Suz made it her business to know personal details about the people who worked for her." She shook her head. "Anyway. One of the ACHMO doctors had a gambling problem. Suz asked me — privately, mind you — to follow the guy to the casinos in Central City, see what he was up to, and try to talk to him. See if he'd go into some kind of self-help group, therapy, whatever. If I did, she said, she promised to co-sign one of my loan applications. I didn't feel good about it" — she shrugged — "but if one of our providers had an addiction that would negatively affect the care he gave, I believed I should help find that out. So, I agreed to follow him."

"So you don't gamble?"

She laughed softly. "No. I followed this provider of ours to Central City and found him playing slots. I watched him for two hours, then confronted him. He convinced me to dance with the one-armed bandit for a while so I could see how much fun it was. I dropped eighteen dollars in quarters into two slot machines and never made more than a dollar. Then I convinced this guy — a pediatrician, if you can believe it — to have some coffee, to talk to me. Over coffee he said he wasn't going to quit gambling. I was wasting my time. Suz got rid of that doctor and now he's in Utah, leading rock-climbing expeditions. Different kind of gamble, I guess. Then Suz spread it around that *I* had the gambling problem. At that time people were bidding for this store space and I was working feverishly on loan applications. Because I hadn't succeeded in rehabilitating the pediatrician, Suz refused to co-sign for me, and I didn't get my loan. When I confronted her about trying to destroy all my plans for the future — to destroy *me* — she claimed I was paranoid."

"And so you quit."

Amy looked away for a moment. Then she said, "Well, not just then. You know how it is with institutions you're involved with. Institution of marriage, institution of the job, institution of the church. At first you're doing work you love and everybody's nice. Then maybe the work gets boring but you like the people so much you don't want to leave. Then some of the good people leave and you think, well, it's not as good as it used to be but it's better than going out there looking for something new."

I looked over at Macguire, who was perusing a magazine on nudist colonies.

"Pretty soon," Amy went on, "there are only a handful of people you like, or a handful of *things* you like, about the institution. Then bad things begin to happen. In our case at ACHMO, we got Suz Craig, a female

333

vice-president we didn't like. She came in and made us all miserable. And although we got a great deal of camaraderie out of talking about her behind her back, it was scant comfort."

"I still don't understand why someone didn't complain."

She sighed. "There was talk of it, but you know, who was going to bell the cat? Human Resources? Brandon Yuille is so terrified of losing his job that he wouldn't even join in on our gossip. Poor guy, he had enough to deal with with his mother dying."

"Was she covered by ACHMO?"

"Don't know," Amy replied. "Brandon talks a blue streak about food and always brought us goodies, but about his personal life he was extremely closemouthed."

"How about Chris Corey? Did he hate Suz Craig, too?"

"We all hated her, Goldy. She tormented Chris for being overweight and for being late on his deadlines. She used to say that this wasn't a waiting room where he could be an hour late for all his appointments. And so on and so on. She was cruel and spiteful and manipulative. Plus she was ruining the HMO with the way she was handling cases like Patricia's. She wanted us to find dirt on the people suing, without realizing how that kind of activity could backfire. An HMO can't survive bad publicity. People just won't sign on."

"So if you didn't leave when she refused to co-sign your loan, why did you finally leave?"

"You know, I never could figure out if Suz wanted me to leave or wanted me to stay. If she wanted me to leave, why didn't she just let me buy my store? If she wanted me to stay, why did she threaten to use the gambling issue in a way that would hurt me? I'm telling you, the woman was just *mean*." She sighed. "The *very* last straw for me was when we had a team meeting and in front of all my colleagues, Suz told me I was over the hill, didn't know the first thing about healing people. She even said I didn't dress like a professional."

I couldn't help it. I eyed Amy's shapeless, spangled dress-that-could-double-as-a-nightgown. She laughed.

"Don't worry, Goldy, I didn't wear this kind of thing to work. But I wasn't going to wear short wool suits that came up to my behind and didn't even keep my legs warm in a Colorado winter."

"So you . . ."

"I went home after the public dressing-down Suz gave me and I looked in the mirror, hard. I asked myself, 'Are you happy?' And the answer was such a resounding 'No' that I went in the next day and quit. Then she threw a fit about my quitting. She swore she'd tell anyplace I applied that I had gambling problems and couldn't hold down a steady job. 'Who am I going to hire in your place?' she wanted to know, after screaming at us for weeks that we were expendable. I just listened and kept telling myself, 'In eight hours, Amy, you will never have to listen to this tyrant again.' Because that's what Suz was — a tyrant."

"And so you just walked out."

"Yup. Cleaned out my desk, took my two weeks of vacation as my notice, and that was it. I never looked back. I had some savings to tide me over, used my pension payout to buy the store instead of getting a loan, and now I'm doing what I love." She smiled. "By next year I may even be showing a profit. I'll start some new pension savings."

I looked at the brightly decorated store, the sparsely filled shelves of herb capsules and poorly stocked freezer, the "health" magazines that included the soft-porn rag Macguire was finding so entrancing. But the place, like Amy, had . . . well . . . the place had an aura. And the aura was one of happiness. Aura! Yikes! Listen to me!

"You know what I'm talking about," she insisted. There was a slightly accusatory tone in her voice. "You opened your catering business after being married to Dr. Gorgeous. You must be ecstatic to be free of him."

"It's . . . well . . ." From the wall, the Maharishi beamed down at me. "It's *nirvana*," I admitted.

"Then you know what I'm talking about."

"I do. But now Dr. Gorge — John Richard has been charged with Suz Craig's murder and my son is suffering like you wouldn't believe. For my son's sake, I need to find out if his father really killed her."

Amy considered the green gingham curtains at the front of the store for a long time without replying. Then she said softly, "I believe in the forces of the universe, Goldy. He who has sinned will sin again. The truth will all come out. You need to trust."

"I do trust, Amy. But to everyone's astonishment, John Richard Korman is out on bail. He may come looking for you, want to ask questions, and then lose his temper. It's the control freak in him. Very predictable. Anyway, I'd feel better if you weren't alone. Can you get somebody to work in the store with you? At the very least, keep the phone handy in case you have to dial 911."

I reached out for her hand. "John Richard called me from jail. He wanted *me* to come over and investigate you."

Amy pulled her hand away from mine. Her voice grew chill. "Is that why you're here?"

"Amy, please. I know this man. I'm here to warn you. He was involved with ACHMO, you were involved with ACHMO, and most certainly you didn't get along with Suz." I paused. "John Richard thinks you might have killed her, and that you've set him up to take the fall for you. Believe me, he's not a person you want to have gunning for you."

She shook her head as she ran her fingers through her shiny red hair. "These people," she muttered sadly. "I swear."

Chapter 19

Jake's earsplitting howls greeted Macguire and me before the van turned into our driveway. The cause for this canine distress was the arrival of Donny Saunders. The investigator for the Furman County district attorney sat on the top step of our front porch. Well, well, it was about time.

Donny boasted slicked brown hair, a prominent nose and forehead, and an arrogant, horse-toothed smile he displayed whenever he stole the credit for a major bust. The closest Donny Saunders usually came to an arrest was sending seized material to a lab. Most recently, a uniformed officer had discovered twenty-five kilos of cocaine during a speeding stop. Donny Saunders had filed the report and then brayed endlessly afterward about making the biggest drug seizure in the history of the county.

At the sight of him, I took a deep breath. A good investigator would have been at my door no later than Saturday afternoon, right after I'd discovered the body of Suz Craig and been questioned by Sergeant Beiner and her assistant. Two days had now gone by. The fact that Donny was finally paying me a call was not a good sign that the crime was being efficiently investigated.

"Hey, Goldy, how you doing!" he greeted me. "Got anything to eat? I'm starving! And you better do something 'bout that dog!"

I struggled to appear friendly even as I gagged at Donny's Vegas-style suit of shiny blue fabric that shimmered and glinted as he swaggered toward us. I introduced Macguire, identifying him only as a houseguest.

"I'll need to talk to you alone," said Donny with his usual smug self-importance as I opened the front door. What a hospitable statement.

"Gosh," murmured Macguire in a hurt tone, "that's the third time today people haven't wanted me around when Goldy Schulz talks to them. Do I have b.o. or something? Guess I'll just go sit by myself. Wait till it's time to take ten more herb capsules." Before I could soothe his feelings, however, he plodded to the backyard to reassure Jake. After a moment the howls ceased. Unfortunately, *my* torment was just beginning.

"I've got a lot of cooking to do," I warned Donny. "I'm doing a big event tomorrow."

The enormous shoulder pads inside Donny's sapphire suit rose ominously when he shrugged. "Not to worry! How would I bother you? Cook away, little lady! A woman's place is in the kitchen! Ha! Ha!" His good-ole-boy tone made me grit my teeth. "But say," he bulldozed on, "you got anything good to eat that's, you know, ready?"

I closed my eyes, tried to count to ten but only got to four. I remembered my promises to Arch on the one hand and to Tom on the other. Maybe I could actually learn something from Donny. But I doubted it.

I suggested a cheese sandwich and Donny eagerly accepted. He quickly added that bread kind of stuck in his craw and he'd need three or four beers to wash the crumbs down. My hopes for our conversation sank to a subterranean level unavailable to geologists. But since the brioche had completed its first rising, I removed it from the refrigerator along with a six-pack of Dos Equis. I punched down the cold, silky mass of dough, set it aside for its second rising, and proceeded to make Donny a sandwich of thickly sliced homemade bread, pesto, fresh tomato, and chèvre. He asked for his second beer when I placed the sandwich in front of him. I handed him the cold bottle with the hope that it might loosen his tongue to share information I hadn't heard yet. I dreaded to think, though, what my husband would say about my plying an investigator with brewskis in the middle of the day.

"Say, this is pretty good!" Donny mumbled, mouth full. He took another enormous bite and munched thoughtfully. "Whaddaya call this white cheesy stuff?"

"Chèvre."

His horsey teeth pulled into a wide grin. "Nah, Goldy, that's a *truck*."

I forced a smile. "What do you want to talk about, Donny?"

"Okay," he said seriously, wiping his mouth and then using his napkin to blow his nose. "Few things." He swigged the beer. "Suz Craig. You found her."

"Yep." I decided I'd better cook. Otherwise the temptation to lose my temper might be too great. "I sure did find her." I took out a cutting board and a zester and ran the tool down the side of a lemon. Zest strands curled outward, sending a fine, pungent mist of lemon oil onto the board. "I saw her in a ditch as I was driving down the road just before seven last Saturday."

"And she was your ex-husband's girl-friend."

"She was, indeed." I minced the zest, then

retrieved a coffee grinder that I used exclusively for pulverizing fruit zest and nuts. "Haven't you read my statement?"

He gestured with the now-empty beer bottle and unsuccessfully repressed a belch. "I took a look at it. Now, what we need to establish here is John Richard Korman's prior patterns. You know, his similar activity. How he used to beat you up. How he almost killed you. That's the way I'll build my case." He eyed the Dos Equis carton longingly, but I ignored him. "Goldy," he continued, gushing with sincerity, "I've seen *lots* of criminals like this before. Once they do it, they get a taste for it. They keep doing it. Until they kill somebody."

"Wait, Donny. What about the autopsy results?"

"Coroner's office should have 'em at the sheriff's department by the time I get back to the office. But don't you worry your pretty little head about that. So, when was the last time John Richard Korman clobbered you?"

I took a shaky breath, remembering. "Seven years ago. He broke this thumb" — I gestured — "in three places not too long before we divorced."

"Okay, I'll have to check what the pathologist says about Suz Craig's hand, if there're any contusions there. If we're lucky, maybe

343

he broke her finger, too. How would Korman attack you? You don't mind me asking?"

"He'd grab my arms, shake me very hard. He liked to punch me in the face, even though most high-income abusers are devious enough to avoid the face. I usually ended up with a black eye."

"Which eye?" He was not writing.

"The right. Which was the black eye on her, too, I noticed."

"You're correct there, little woman. Okay, now when he clobbered you, would he knock you out right away? Or would the fight go on for hours?"

I gripped the knife. Recalling these events never became less painful. "It depended on how angry he was," I said softly. "But, Donny," I couldn't help interjecting, "what about the facts of *this* case? Since I never pressed charges, a judge may not allow all this. Have you talked to anyone down at Suz Craig's office? At ACHMO?"

"Oh, yeah. I was down in Denver talkin' to some execs at the HMO this morning —"

"Which execs?" The only ACHMO executives in town had been busy raiding John Richard's office in Aspen Meadow. Had the rest of the department heads returned from the San Diego conference?

"Well . . . talking to Suz Craig's secretary, actually, 'cuz most of the rest of the guys are off on some trip. But you can learn more that way. Those gals really know what's cooking, if you know what I mean." He winked.

"Ah." I put down the knife and zapped the lemon zest in the grinder. Then I pulverized the blanched slivered almonds and piled them into a pale mound. "So. What did Suz's secretary have to say?"

"Well . . ." He reached for another beer, pried off the top, and took a long swig. "I really shouldn't say."

"Why not? Maybe I could help you. Fill in the blanks."

He harumphed, popped the last of the sandwich into a corner of his mouth, chewed, and licked his fingers. Sometimes I wondered if the only decent food Donny ever got was when Goldilocks' Catering got mired in one of his investigations. "I'm telling you, Goldy, nobody likes Korman. But nobody liked that Craig woman, either. I mean, *nobody*. You know, you'd think people wouldn't speak ill of the dead. But get right down to it, I'm surprised nobody did her right there in the office. Course, they didn't have the pattern, like our Doc Korman."

345

I beat unsalted butter with sugar, egg yolks, vanilla, and lemon zest; measured out flour and the other dry ingredients, and then mixed them with the creamed mixture to make a nutty, buttery, heavenly-smelling dough. "Have you been looking at any other facts of the *case,* Donny?"

"Tha-a-a-at's why I'm here, right?"

I wondered briefly if I could nip out for one of the tranquilizers Marla had given me. Maybe Amy's herb capsules had sedative powers. But no — there was a chance Donny's boastfulness would win out and he'd tell me what Suz's secretary had had to say. If I didn't appear too eager, that is. So I concentrated on the question of how to provide a high ratio of tart raspberry jam to cookie dough. Scooping the dough into cupcake pans and then topping them with spoonfuls of jam would work. I ignored Donny and set about buttering a pan.

He continued eagerly. "You listening? You wouldn't have believed how much that secretary, name of Luella Downing, hated Ms. Craig. Luella was in some kind of state this morning."

I *tsked,* but continued assiduously spraying a pan.

"See," he persisted, "this Luella resented Ms. Craig 'cuz Ms. Craig had made it her

Babsie's Tarts

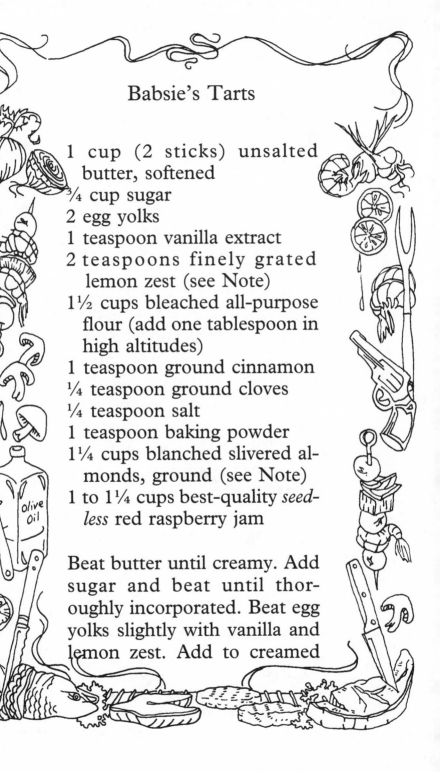

1 cup (2 sticks) unsalted butter, softened

¾ cup sugar

2 egg yolks

1 teaspoon vanilla extract

2 teaspoons finely grated lemon zest (see Note)

1½ cups bleached all-purpose flour (add one tablespoon in high altitudes)

1 teaspoon ground cinnamon

¼ teaspoon ground cloves

¼ teaspoon salt

1 teaspoon baking powder

1¼ cups blanched slivered almonds, ground (see Note)

1 to 1¼ cups best-quality *seedless* red raspberry jam

Beat butter until creamy. Add sugar and beat until thoroughly incorporated. Beat egg yolks slightly with vanilla and lemon zest. Add to creamed mixture, stirring thoroughly. Sift dry ingredients together, then stir into creamed mixture. Stir in almonds.

Preheat oven to 350°. Spray two nonstick cupcake pans with vegetable oil spray. Using a 2-tablespoon scoop (or measuring out in 2 tablespoon increments), place one scoop of batter into each cupcake pan. Pat the batter gently to cover the bottom of each cup. Do not indent the dough or the jam that is to be cooked in the center will leak through. Place 2 teaspoons of jam in the center of each tart.

Bake for about 15 minutes, until the batter has risen and turned golden brown around the jam. After the pans have been removed from the oven, use a sharp knife to loosen the edges of each tart. Allow the tarts to cool in the pan until cool to the touch, at least 1 hour. Using a kitchen knife, gently lever the tarts out onto cookie racks and allow to cool completely. You may serve them plain, or sprinkle with powdered sugar and serve with a scoop of best-quality vanilla ice cream.

Makes 2 dozen

Note: Citrus zests and nuts are easily ground in a *clean* coffee grinder.

business to know some money details of Luella's divorce." I looked up from the pan and raised my eyebrows. Donny smirked triumphantly. "I told Luella I wouldn't prosecute or nothing." I hid my exasperation and nodded knowingly. He went on. "Come to find out that Ms. *Craig* knew *Luella* had liquidated her IRA and put the money into her *parents'* account so's Luella's *ex* wouldn't find it. Our Ms. Craig used that info to get Luella to shut up about the taping."

I dropped the pan on the counter. "Taping of what?"

He held up a hand. "I'm getting there. And don't worry, I checked to see where Ms. Luella was over the weekend, just in case she'd gotten it into her head to off her boss over the IRA stuff. Luella was organizing a rummage sale for her parents' church in Aurora. The story checks out — Beiner went to the church and interviewed the parents."

A minute amount of admiration for Donny wormed its way into my brain. "So . . . what was Luella taping?"

"Luella wasn't taping. Suz Craig was. Any meeting in her office." He lowered his voice. "Like the frigging White House, you asked me. See, nobody but Ms. Craig and Luella knew. Luella says if she'd dropped the dime on her boss, she would have lost her job and possibly her IRA bucks."

"Does Luella know what was on the tapes? Did she transcribe them?"

"No, oh, no. Luella just happened to discover Ms. Craig loading a fresh tape into the machine built into her desk. See, one time Luella walked in on Ms. Craig without knocking, checking on some correspondence or something, and saw her fiddling with this machine. Luella says, 'What in the world are you doing?' That's when Ms. Craig says, 'You tell anybody about this and I'll fire you and tell your ex where your IRA dough is.' The one thing Ms. Craig told Luella was never to touch the machine. The boss lady told Luella she taped the meetings to cover herself. She also labeled the tapes and put them in a locked cabinet."

"Good Lord. So what happened? How were they discovered?"

"When Ms. Craig turned up blue in a ditch, somebody called Luella. Turns out Luella was already home from the rummage sale. Soon as Luella heard her boss was dead, she called corporate HQ. Somebody was there even though it was Saturday. Luella hollered, 'You guys need to know about these tapes and go get 'em before the press gets hold of 'em. Old Suz Craig was such a bitch, there's no telling what's on those tapes.' Corporate HQ has a cow and sends two guys to Denver Saturday night. They're scrambling like mad to break open her locked cabinets when somebody tips off the sheriff's department. They show up with a search warrant and seize the tapes they've found, plus use Ms. Craig's keys from her house to search all the office cabinets for more."

"You learned all this from Sergeant Beiner? Or from Luella Downing?" I asked suspiciously.

"Little of both. My job, you gotta put everything together."

"And why do you suppose Luella is spilling her guts to you?"

His eyebrows lifted. "Hey, Goldy! Ace caterer amateur detective! Wake up! Luella shouldn't have called Minneapolis first, she should have told the *cops* about the tapes first. This morning Luella's suddenly got a big case of remorse, ooh, ooh, she meant to tell us, but she didn't want to lose her job, see, is what she's saying. Meanwhile, our department takes an inventory. Looks like *one* day's tapes are missing, and the people at ACHMO swear they don't have a clue where they are. So, bit later in the morning, the sheriff sends a team back up to Suz's house. They turn up nothing."

"Sheesh."

"So I'm thinking about your ex-husband, see. I'm thinking, why did he and Suz Craig have that catfight on Friday night? And then I think, the missing tapes, of course! John Richard probably has them."

What? I pressed my lips together and turned away. I had to think. *Delicate material,* John Richard had said. I nudged soft scoops of dough into each cup. And what had ReeAnn said? *She wanted him to put some stuff . . . in a safe place, somewhere the AstuteCare people couldn't find them.* I ladled tart, inky jam on top of each dough disc. At John Richard's office this morning, Brandon Yuille had asked me the same question: *If John Richard has given you anything to hide . . .* I popped the cupcake pan into the hot oven.

"What could be on the tapes?" I asked, perplexed. "And who could have them?"

"Well, now, those *are* the questions, aren't they? The execs are scrambling like crazy. Where're the tapes, these powers-that-be want to know. And, believe me, this morning? *All* the ACHMO secretaries were pulling up the wall-to-wall trying to find the damn things. Meanwhile, back at the ranch, since Suz Craig's house has turned up nothing, the duty judge gives our guys a search warrant for *Korman's* house. No tapes, but somebody messed up his house *bad* with paint —"

"One day's tapes . . . What day? What folks met with Suz Craig that day?" I interrupted.

"Luella's trying to reconstruct that." He shook his head and burped. "Korman doesn't have anyplace he hides things, does he?"

"He's compulsively neat. And he's just sold his place in Keystone." I chewed the inside of my lip. "He hasn't been to his condo in Hawaii since June. I guess he could have stashed the tapes there. But if they're in Hawaii, what would happen if Suz wanted them back?"

"Man, would I love it if the department sprang for a trip to the islands! Damn! You got another beer?"

"Donny. Are you driving?"

He pulled his chin into his neck. "Well, yeah, but you don't need to worry about a coupla beers, Goldy, I can handle it. And don't worry, I'll call out to Hawaii for a search warrant. Now, how 'bout —"

"Let me fix you some coffee. You know my husband's a cop. I wouldn't want you having an accident after drinking beer at our house. It'd look bad."

"Okay," he said reluctantly, eyeing the

espresso machine on my counter. "Only don't give me any of that cappuccino crap or I'll barf."

I fixed Donny plain black coffee, which he slurped noisily. The nut-scented Linzer tarts resembled circular stained-glass windows when I removed them from the oven. Since they would go in the doll-show box lunches, I decided to call them Babsie's Tarts. While I was placing them on a rack to cool, I asked Donny if there were any suspects besides John Richard. He said not since Luella's alibi had checked out. I asked him if they'd caught the vandals who'd defaced John Richard's house, and he said, "Oh, do they think it was vandals?" Finally I asked him if he knew about the bonus John Richard was supposed to get, but didn't.

"Yeah, yeah. That's part of my theory. The Craig lady didn't approve the usual bonus for Korman, so he didn't have any money, and so he wouldn't give her the tapes he'd hidden, and so they argued and he killed her." He turned the corners of his lips down, shook his head. "It was his pattern," he concluded smugly. "Say, those smell awful good."

I put a warm, crumbly Babsie's Tart on a small plate and handed it to him. "Ah . . .

did you find out why exactly Suz didn't give him his bonus? Did Luella clue you in on that?"

He placed the small tart in his mouth, lounged back in the chair, and held up one finger as he chewed. "Billing," he said finally. "He didn't bill right. I'm going to *really* grill Korman's secretary about that. You know, about whether Korman and Ms. Craig ever argued about bills. Plus there's a malpractice suit outstanding against him. The HMO didn't like that, or the fact that they were being sued by the same patient. So our doc was in hot, hot water. Boiling. More reason to kill Ms. Craig." He glanced at his watch. "Talk about billing! I need to see a couple more people today or the department will have a fit over the hours I submit."

"How come?"

"Well, usually I bill by the hour, but they've been saying I'm too thorough with each person and spend *too* much time investigating. Whoo-ie! Now I bill by the people I talk to. Plus, even though I have a photographic memory, I have to write up a report on each interview. And believe me, those reports can be a bear, you're typing 'em up the middle of the night."

"I'm sure you can manage it," I said reassuringly as I escorted him to the door.

"I wouldn't mind the typing so much," he said disconsolately, "if only I didn't get so hungry."

So I gave him another tart. Donny Saunders may be a pig, but I can never resist a hungry soul.

To my surprise, Arch called and asked if Todd could spend the night. I said yes, and was further pleased when Arch asked for his favorite dinner, baked potatoes with a variety of toppings. I was hopeful that fixing the potatoes would help me reflect on Donny Saunders's visit. Tapes? What tapes? And where were the missing ones? I'd learned just enough to be frustrated. If Frances Markasian ever did a story on the waste of taxpayer money, I'd point her in the direction of old Donny.

I filled a wide frying pan with extrathick bacon slices, and for some reason thought of the composer Schoenberg. Schoenberg had been quoted as saying that his music contained all his secrets. His compositions held the key to unlocking the inner workings of his soul. You just had to know how to listen. Somehow, all the information before me might contain enough data to unlock the secret of what had happened in the early hours of Saturday morning. I just didn't know how to decipher it.

The phone rang. It was the therapist's office calling to say I'd be getting a call later in the day about scheduling Arch. Apparently there was no way the temporary secretary could do anything now. I sighed and said I'd be waiting for her call.

I trimmed crisp green broccoli for one of the potato-toppings and thought of Arch. He and Todd were planning an extended "jam" tonight. Jamming, I'd learned, was not about food, but about music. Fine with me. I wanted Arch to have a regular social life instead of fretting about his father. Truth to tell, though, it pained me that I couldn't relate to the music that today's fourteen-year-olds liked. I'd faulted my parents for finding the Rolling Stones execrable. But the Rolling Stones made *music*. What Arch and Todd listened to was just *noise*. Well, I thought with a sigh, *Schoenberg's* mother probably had trouble with her son's music. Come to think of it, I thought as I retrieved a dozen fat Idaho potatoes from my pantry, Schoenberg's music pretty much sounded like noise to me, too.

As I washed and pricked the potatoes, I remembered to call the town veterinarian. I was still wondering about the scratches on

Ralph Shelton's face and if they'd truly come from his feline. The veterinarian's receptionist said that under no circumstances could she tell me anything about the care of Ralph Shelton's animals. Patient confidentiality seemed alive and well these days, if you were a cat. Well, maybe Tom would know.

I placed the potatoes in the oven, then kneaded the brioche dough gently, divided it, and set it into loaf pans for its third and final rising. By the time Arch, Todd, and Tom arrived home, I'd put the loaves in the oven and finished making the dinner. Todd Druckman, who was baby-faced and slightly pudgy, and had hair that was even browner and straighter than Arch's, pronounced ours the best-smelling kitchen he'd ever visited. A pile of baked potatoes invited slashing and filling. I pointed to where the boys could choose from a vat of creamy cheese sauce bubbling on the stove, broccoli florets heaped in a steaming pile, and a mountain of hot, crispy bacon that beckoned with its mouthwatering scent. The real surprise occurred, however, when Arch, Todd, Tom, and I were bustling around setting the table. We didn't even notice Macguire entering the kitchen.

"Hey!" he said. "What smells so great?"

For a moment we were all speechless.

Macguire, hungry? Then Tom winked at me. "What is it Cinderella's godmother says? Sometimes miracles take some time?"

I looked at my watch. "Yeah. Six hours. That's when we left the health-food store. Amazing." Macguire still shuffled and his body was achingly thin. But healthy color infused his cheeks for the first time in a month, *and he wanted something to eat!* Both were momentous developments. I offered a silent prayer of thanks.

The potatoes were indeed out of this world: each flaky bite was robed in golden cheese sauce and melded stupendously with the tender broccoli and crunchy bacon. Macguire, to my amazement, slowly ate two potatoes slathered with toppings, then laughingly pronounced himself so full his stomach ached. Tom, Todd, and Arch cleaned every last bite from their plates. Our meal was full of companionship, good food, and laughter. I never once thought of the corpse I'd found in the ditch.

Arch broke the spell of family life. He said suddenly, "I wonder what they're having at the jail tonight."

"Hon," I replied gently, "your dad's out on bail. This morning we —"

"You found out this morning that he got out? And you didn't call me at Todd's?"

"I thought . . . if your dad wanted to call, he would —"

"And you probably wouldn't let me talk to him!" He looked accusingly from me to Tom. "And I'll bet you haven't done anything today to help him, either!"

"Excuse me, young man, but I *have too done something* —"

But before I could finish my sentence, Arch threw down his fork and ran out of the room.

Tom shook his head. Todd looked bewildered. I silently put a half-dozen Babsie's Tarts on a plate, handed Todd a six-pack of soft drinks, and told him to go on up and see what he could do. Todd took the plate along with the pop cans and gratefully excused himself.

"Maybe I should go, too," Macguire announced in a guilty tone, and left. Minutes later I saw the light on the phone flash red, indicating that Arch was making an outgoing call from upstairs. The call did not last long. Probably Arch had called John Richard's number and left a message on his machine. My mind immediately leaped to a fresh question: If the Jerk wasn't home to answer his phone, where was he?

Tom said, "Let me do the dishes, Miss G."

"You do everything," I said, disconsolate. "Bring home take-out. Do the dishes. Put up with us. Put up with *me*."

"You make a great dinner," he countered as he started hot water running in the sink. "And you're the one who tries to do everything. You can't make everything go smoothly."

"At least I'd be a better investigator than Donny Saunders."

Tom chuckled. "Sorry, Miss G., but that's not saying much."

While he was doing the dishes, I asked him about the tapes from Suz Craig's office. He said the department was listening to the tapes they had found and making an inventory of them. I told him about the discussions I'd had with Amy Bartholomew and ReeAnn Collins. He nodded and didn't take notes, indicating he'd already heard similar information at his office. Then he punched buttons on the espresso machine. A few moments later he placed a demitasse of crema-laden espresso in front of me and sat down across the table.

I sighed. "If I drink this, I'm going to be up all night."

"Aw, drink it. You're going to be up all night anyway. You're going to be up every night until this is over. And trust me, Goldy, these things *always* come to an end. One way or another."

I closed my eyes and sipped the rich, satisfying espresso. When Tom placed the last dish in the dishwasher, I slid the golden-brown brioche loaves out of the oven and placed them on racks to cool. Their rich, homey scent bathed the kitchen.

Tom said, "Let's take some cookies out on the deck. I want to talk to you about the autopsy, but I want to be somewhere the boys won't hear us."

"Chocolate, coffee, and death. Dark topics all."

We stretched out on one of my fancy deck-furniture couches that had been in disuse for so long. The night air was sweet, mellow, and filled with the buzz of unseen insects. Just above the mountains' dark silhouette, Venus glowed like an ice crystal.

We savored the Chocolate Comfort Cookies in silence, curled together in each other's arms. The cookies were chock-full of fat chocolate chips and crunchy toasted hazelnuts. The sun-dried cranberries gave a delicious, tart chewiness to each bite.

I asked Tom if the cops had called Shelton's veterinarian and he said yes. The scratches on Ralph Shelton's face had been inflicted by his cat but were minor. Then

Tom sighed. He asked, "Did you also know Suz Craig had a cat?"

"Yes, a shy calico one named Tippy. Saturday morning, right after you went to talk to the deputies, that cat jumped into my arms. I know Tippy was part of the crime scene, but I was afraid she'd get trampled if I abandoned her. I left her with Tina Corey. Why?"

He didn't answer right away. I snuggled in close and just enjoyed his warmth.

"Here's what we found out today," Tom said at length as he massaged my back. "Suz Craig's security system was turned off. Also, Suz Craig didn't die from falling into the ditch. She died of a subdural hematoma. No blood, because she was hit with her cat's scratching post. It's a solid metal cylinder covered with carpeting. You know what a subdural —"

"Yes. A blow causes bleeding into the brain. The bleeding brings on death."

"Right. It takes eight hours for lividity to fix, and she'd only been in the ditch two, maybe three hours before you found her. It's very unlikely she could have gotten the fatal blow there. So somebody put her outside. Why, we don't know. We're still waiting for the drug screen to come back; that'll take a few days."

"Yes, I remember."

Tom continued thoughtfully. "Here's the odd thing. She definitely has the same pattern of bruises that you used to have when John Richard attacked you. If he'd beaten her up and killed her immediately, the bruises wouldn't have shown up on the corpse. Bruises take about three or four hours, minimum, to develop, unless the victim's one of those rare people who show a bruise within an hour. So what happened between the time Suz Craig got beaten up and the time she died of a blow from the cat's scratching post? And how did she get into that ditch?"

"The vandals say John Richard left that night and then came back. Or somebody in a Jeep just like one of his, no lights, came there."

"Yeah." Tom sighed wearily. "I know what they said. We're checking to see if any white Jeeps were rented anywhere in the Denver area. And we've got the drug screen to wait for. Plus the skin under her nails has been sent to a crime lab. So we'll know more by the end of the week. If it's Korman's skin, at least we'll have him for assault."

But not necessarily for murder. Would he walk? I didn't want to think about it.

As Tom had predicted, I did not sleep

well. At one point I crept down to the kitchen and typed into the computer my own notes on what ReeAnn Collins, Amy Bartholomew, Donny Saunders, and Tom had told me. I didn't have a photographic memory. But then, after what I'd been through when I lived with the Jerk, I'd prayed *never* to have a photographic memory.

Chapter 20

Despite the fact that Tuesday morning dawned with a bright sun and jewel-bright hummingbirds whirring past my downstairs windows, I did not feel the least bit cheered. Tom had left early. I went through my yoga routine trying to empty my mind — not easy. Today, among all the other crises, I was set to begin catering to the doll people. I'd read recently about the necessity of going into a zone of enjoyment when doing your work, especially if you expected to derive pleasure from your career over the course of a lifetime. I tried to see the zone and imagine Gail Rodine not in it.

I sliced the cooled brioche loaves and then began making the box lunches. Each lunch would contain four sandwich triangles: cucumber, smoked salmon, Swiss cheese, and the pesto-tomato-chèvre combination that Donny Saunders had gobbled up so ravenously. I shuddered and fixed myself an iced lattée. Something Donny had said kept swimming up just below my consciousness as I smoothed cool mayonnaise over the bread slices and laid out the sandwich fillings.

When I finished wrapping the sandwiches, I tucked a miniature bottle of white wine, wrapped cheese straws, a cup of plum, orange, and banana fruit salad, and a plastic bag with a Babsie's Tart and a chocolate cookie in each box. As I closed the last cardboard box, my eye fell on the computer. Computer, disks, tapes. Tapes. *If Luella had told anyone about the taping, she would have lost her job.* How significant were these meetings that Suz had taped? I didn't know, and I'd promised Tom I wouldn't go nosing around at ACHMO. I put in a call to Brandon Yuille's office. I would apologize for snapping at him at John Richard's office, then pump him for info. When his assistant asked suspiciously who was calling and I told her, I had to wait two minutes for her cold response that Mr. Yuille was unavailable. I asked if I could call back at a more convenient time. She responded icily that there just was no convenient time. Fine. I hung up and called Chris Corey's office.

His secretary put me right through. "Goldy!" His deep, rumbly voice sounded surprised. "What's going on? Korman hasn't come over to bother you, has he?"

"He wouldn't dare. Listen, Chris, something one of the investigators said has been bothering me." I hesitated, remembering I'd promised not to mention that Luella was the one who had spilled the beans to Donny. "It relates to what we were talking to Frances about Sunday at the café. You said ACHMO was going into John Richard's office looking for notes about the McCrackens' suit."

"Well . . . yes."

"It's just that I heard there were some missing tapes, too."

Chris grunted. "Don't remind me."

I persisted innocently, "What's going on? Why would Suz keep tapes of meetings in her office?"

He lowered his voice. "Look, Goldy, it's a huge crisis. Everybody's upset about it. Nobody seems to know *why* she was taping in her office. *Secretly* taping. Makes it much worse."

"You say that as if there were other taping systems."

"Yeah, sure. The microphones in our *main* meeting room are sound-activated, and everybody knows that everything *there* gets taped, then transcribed so we have accurate minutes for each meeting. It could have been Suz was afraid of industrial spying, and that's why she did some kind of backup taping in her office. Maybe she kept the tapes locked up there and took them from her office to her home or wherever because some threat had appeared."

"Did she know about your work with Frances?"

"Not unless Frances told her, and that's unlikely."

"Who could be doing spying that would make Suz worried?"

"Look. Our meetings are confidential, Goldy, and if another HMO like MeritMed is trying to find out the details of our expansion plans, there could be hell to pay. And with legal action outstanding against us, the thought of having tapes of other in-house meetings floating around where anybody might get their hands on them is causing mass paranoia in corporate headquarters, believe me."

"Are you sure Suz had them?"

"No! What sends shivers up the bowels of HQ is that somebody Suz *fired* might have them. If anyone besides Luella knew Suz was taping, there could have been motivation to get in and steal them, especially if they might prove something against ACHMO. Plus," he added darkly, "they're panicked that Patricia McCracken might have them somehow. That woman's gone a little bonkers. It wouldn't surprise anybody here if she'd managed to steal the key to that cabinet, break into the office, and swipe the tapes from one of the days when Suz met with our lawyers about the McCracken case."

"So you don't even know what day's meetings are missing?"

He groaned with frustration. "We're trying to reconstruct, but it's a huge mess. We should know today. We're supposed to have security, but you know how that goes. Anyway, Goldy, speaking of meetings, I've got to go to one now. Damage control. Good luck with whatever it is you're working on."

"I'm not really working on anything, Chris. It's just that my son is very upset. I promised him I'd try to help his dad, much as I dislike the man."

I hung up and packed the lunches between freezer bags guaranteed to keep food cold. When I was almost done, Macguire came down to breakfast. His transformation was remarkable. His cheeks were genuinely pink. There was a spring to his only slightly wobbly step, and he had a broad smile on his face that made me laugh.

"Let me fix you some toast," I offered. "And some eggs, maybe?"

"Sounds great." While the frying eggs sizzled in the pan, Macguire dutifully washed down his ten herb capsules with water turned a science-fiction green by the chlorophyll. "Todd and Arch are still asleep," he announced. "I'll wake them up at ten. They listened to music until three A.M. I'll fix 'em breakfast, too. Toast, probably." His grin warmed my heart.

I thanked him for tending to Arch and Todd, declined his offer to help load my supplies, and hauled the first cardboard box out to my van. When I came back into the kitchen, my phone was ringing.

"Goldy, my God, I'm so glad I got you." Ralph Shelton's voice sounded exhausted and strained. "Look, I'm terribly sorry about running into you at the McCrackens' party. I just got out of control on those blades. Are you all right?"

"Sure, Ralph." No use troubling him with a litany of my lingering aches. "Thanks for calling."

He hesitated. "I just need to talk to you for a minute. Remember when you were over here asking how to get to the McCrackens' place?"

"Yes. What's the matter?"

"Well. I was supposed to drive to Omaha this morning, but they got word that . . . Oh, God, I need to know if you know anything about these tapes that Suz Craig was making. Please tell me, Goldy, I'm leveling with you.

As an old friend."

I took a deep breath. "Why do you care about them?"

His voice wavered, as if he were about to cry. "Because I went in to see her last month, on the fourteenth to be exact, and . . . I just can't let anyone know what we talked about. Please, Goldy, help me. Suz was trying to destroy me. Do you have the tapes? Does John Richard? Are they at his office? Or his house? I've already driven past Suz's house and there's that damn yellow tape all around it —"

"Ralph, calm down. First tell me — exactly why were you fired from ACHMO?"

For a moment I thought he wouldn't answer. But then he sighed. "Patient complaints. No sexual misconduct or anything like that. It's just that I have a terrible bedside manner. I always have. You can imagine how that can kill you in ob-gyn. So. I was offered an administrative job with Merit-Med. I took it."

I recalled Suz's secretary, whom Suz had kept in line with threats. "Was Suz threatening you in any way?"

He hesitated. "You've learned a lot, haven't you? She did threaten people. Yes, I was one of them. But it was all . . . exaggeration. I left before she could ruin me," he concluded darkly. "But if someone gets hold of those tapes . . . Oh, God," he moaned.

"Did you . . . were you . . . did you do something to Suz Craig?"

"Of course not, what the hell do you think I am?"

Well, that was what we didn't know, wasn't it? "I honestly don't know where the tapes are, Ralph. And John Richard's out on bail. You could give him or his office a call. But his secretary is frantic with the mess, and there's no telling what kind of emotional state John Richard is in. If I were you, I'd stay away from both of them."

"Yeah, well, you're not me."

At the LakeCenter the Babsie-doll show was in full swing. The security guard, even more hung over today than before, grunted a question about whether my assistant would be helping me, because he had strict orders not to let "that young fellow" near the dolls. I kept my patience and told him my assistant would not be accompanying me today. The armed guard escorted me past the display tables, where shiny arrays of statuesque, ultraslender, elaborately coiffed Babsies in lacy, sequined gowns elicited choruses of oohs and aahs from the crush of excited visitors. Even I was impressed,especially when I saw the price tags.

At the appointed time, I passed out box lunches on the patio to women clutching blue lunch tickets. While they ate, I indulged in a more detailed tour of the show. One table was dedicated solely to Holiday Babsies from 1990 to the present. All the dolls belonged to Gail Rodine. All were marked "Not for Sale." The costumes were festive and fantastic: tiny rhinestones glistened above shimmery red and green taffeta gowns; white furs set off dark velvet evening dresses. Another table featured Babsie as astronaut, Babsie as veterinarian, Babsie as a prima ballerina, Babsie horseback riding, Babsie walking her poodle on the Champs-Elysées, even Babsie as President. All that was missing was Babsie as Elvis. A long aisle was devoted to Babsie accessories. I looked with awe at teensy-weensy toreador pants; high heels; sequined leotards; compartmentalized Babsie suitcases; flip-curled wigs in blond, black, brunette, and red hair; and sexy lingerie that befit the Babsie Massage Parlor. As Donny Saunders would say, *Whoo-ie!*

The few attendees not indulging in box lunches were cooing over a table on the far side of the ballroom. When I joined them, I realized their drooling wasn't from craving my cucumber-brioche sandwiches. Their eyes were greedily fixed on a display of a single Babsie. I stared at the display: Babsie in a "Japanese exclusive" gown. I didn't know if that meant the gown was made or sold in Japan or both. No matter. I was transfixed by the miniature image of a fashion plate.

Babsie's blue eyes, rosy cheeks, and bow-shaped mouth were demure, and her long, perfect blond coif did not reveal a single flyaway strand. The bodice and skirt of the tiny full-length gown were made of snowy white satin, and the toes of itsy-bitsy pink high heels peeked out at the hem. A hot-pink embroidered chiffon overskirt pouffed and swirled above the white satin. A miniature stole of the same pink fabric hugged the doll's shoulders, while a choker of minuscule pink pearls decorated her neck. *Very nice,* I thought appreciatively, *the sort of thing you'd wear to an inaugural ball or a royal wedding.* Then I looked at this Babsie's price tag: three thousand dollars. When the woman next to me asked if I didn't think it was just unbelievable, I said, "Yes, incredible beyond words." Never let it be said that I was a caterer who couldn't appreciate her clients' hobbies.

The first woman said, "The dealer said to me, 'How can you refuse this adorable doll?'

Now I feel as if this poor doll is a refugee who will starve if I don't buy her!" A tear slid down one of her cheeks.

A second woman whispered, "I've got a spy in France. You should see my phone bills. But when the French Babsies come out — you know, the ones we can't get? — I have my spy get it. She airmails it in a plain brown wrapper. For security. It costs me, but it's worth it."

John le Carré, eat your heart out. I tore myself away from the dolls and returned to the patio. In a large plastic garbage bag I collected dirty cups, wrappers, used plastic spoons, and empty miniature wine bottles. Suddenly the cormorants near the shore rose in a frenzied flutter, and I was dimly aware of a distant *wap wap wap wap wap*.

I sat on one of the patio benches and squinted at the sky. *Wap wap wap,* louder and louder. In the summer, this was the most dreaded sound in Aspen Meadow. It was the Flight-for-Life helicopter. Usually the only time you heard it was when someone, frequently a child, had drowned, fallen while rock climbing, or been lost for hours after straying from a wilderness hike.

I trotted to the Dumpster near the lake and lofted in the trash bag. The helicopter circled near Main Street. That was odd. The copter appeared to be hovering over Cotton-wood Creek, not too far from our house. I reached into my apron pocket for the portable cellular phone I took to events and shakily punched in our number, reminding myself that not all disasters in Aspen Meadow had to involve me.

One second, two seconds, three . . . then the phone connected and Arch answered on the first ring. "I'm okay, Mom."

"How did you — ?"

"Are you kidding? All you do is worry about me. I heard the helicopter a minute ago and called Marla to make sure she wasn't having another heart attack. She'd already found out what was going on. Somebody was in an explosion. A grill at the park blew up. They think some mountain moths built a nest in the vent. Then when the person lit the propane, the grill exploded, just like Frances Markasian wrote about in the paper. Oh, wait, there's the other line. Maybe it's Marla again."

I watched the slow sweep of the second hand on my watch while I waited for Arch to come back on the line. As usual, I tried to reconstruct where Tom was —

"Oh, Mom," Arch said, his voice subdued. "Marla says that, you know, she survived the explosion, but she's burned and bloody —"

"Who survived, Arch?" I was frantic. "Marla?"

"Oh, no, Mom. The person trying to light the grill . . . the person who got hurt . . . It was ReeAnn.

Chapter 21

I asked Arch how Macguire was doing. He was asleep. I asked if Arch had heard from his father. He said no. I told him to make sure that all the windows were closed and that the security system was armed. And stay inside, I said. It wasn't a logical order, it was an emotional one, a fact my son hotly pointed out. I told him I'd be home in less than an hour. Then I disconnected and called Tom.

He wasn't at his office. I checked my watch: two o'clock. Rather than leave a message, I redialed the department and asked to speak with Sergeant Beiner. When she answered, I identified myself and told her what had happened.

"Hold on," she said. In the background she rustled paper. "This ReeAnn? Korman's secretary, right?" I insisted that this accident involving ReeAnn had to be related somehow to Suz Craig's murder.

Calmly, Sergeant Beiner said, "How?"

I bit the inside of my cheek and watched the cormorants land back on the lake. A hummingbird soared and then dipped to sip the nectar from a nearby poppy.

"How," I repeated not so patiently to Sergeant Beiner, "could an accident involving ReeAnn Collins relate to Suz Craig? John Richard might have thought she killed Suz and decided to punish her. Aah . . . maybe somebody thinks ReeAnn has possession of something incriminating."

"Hmm," said Sergeant Beiner, clearly unconvinced.

I told her I knew about Suz secretly taping meetings. I added that Donny Saunders and Chris Corey had reported that some tapes were missing. Maybe somebody thought ReeAnn had them. Maybe Patricia McCracken or Ralph Shelton or *somebody* was so desperate for the missing tapes that they had tried to blow ReeAnn up. Sergeant Beiner said that these people had all known ReeAnn for some time, why do something to her *now?*

"I don't know," I replied persistently. "Maybe because of the tapes. But there is a connection, I'm certain of it."

"Goldy," advised Sergeant Beiner, "take a breather."

"Please help me," I begged her. "I know you usually keep the families of those affected apprised of the progress of an investigation . . . Can't you please help us, just so we'll stay informed and my son won't have so much anxiety?"

For a moment she was silent. Then she said tersely, "Patricia McCracken I don't know about. She called this morning to get an update on the criminal investigation so she can decide what to do about her civil suits. I just called her back an hour ago. Now" — there was a rustle of pages and I knew she was consulting her notes — "Amy Bartholomew was interviewed by Donny Saunders this morning. Ms. Bartholomew told him she was leaving to go camping alone for a few days in the Aspen Meadow Wildlife Preserve, and that *you* were the one who told her to get away for a while. Maybe she didn't go, but I don't think that she had any grudge against ReeAnn Collins that was life-threatening. Do you?"

"I guess not."

"As for Dr. Korman, he's out on bail, as you no doubt are aware. You might want to put your efforts into recalling that judge in the next election." She paused. "I don't know about Ralph Shelton. We'll have somebody go up and talk to him. But I have to tell you, it's going to be a while."

"Okay." I felt defeated, not because I wanted Amy or Patricia or Ralph or somebody at ACHMO or even John Richard to have hurt ReeAnn, but because I was completely confused. I mumbled an apology to Sergeant Beiner for bothering her and hung up.

I raced back to the LakeCenter and finished cleaning up the box lunches. Occasionally, I reflected as I stooped to pick up the last of the trash the visitors had left, I have a great culinary idea that fails. But before I know things aren't going to work out, the inspiration stokes my energy and makes my brain fire on all cylinders. Blue cheese pizza was the product of such thinking. Coffeecake swirled with frozen pitted Bing cherries was another, as was sausages baked with apples and hominy. They were all failures. I'd gagged on the too-salty pizza. The coffeecake turned first inky, then mushy, then inedible. And when Arch had had two bites of the sausage concoction, he'd asked if we could go to Burger King for breakfast.

Most of my food ideas and experiments succeed. But it's hard to bear that in mind when the failures occur. And instead of responding to these setbacks with an optimistic, Thomas Edison–style, now-I-know-what-doesn't-work attitude, I usually feel frustrated and angry that I spent time and money on ingredients yielding such disasters.

Worse, the anguish accompanying the failures always plunges me into a psychological well of uncertitude. Questions like Are you really in the right line of work? and Who do you think you are, anyway? taunt me. Eventually, of course, I always pull myself together, toss the messes in the garbage, and go on to the next concoction.

It was that pulling-together time that I now longed for. Poor ReeAnn.

When I pressed the buttons on our security system and entered our home, the warmth inside brought a small lift in my spirits. It's not so bad, I told myself. ReeAnn was alive, if injured. I was upholding my promise to Arch. I was trying to find out what really had happened to Suz Craig. I didn't want to clear the Jerk, I didn't even care if anything *ever* exonerated him. But I did want to know what had happened, and why, so that when they hauled John Richard off for an extended prison stay, I could tell Arch with a clear conscience that I had done my darnedest.

I called Lutheran Hospital and asked to check on the condition of ReeAnn Collins. Since I was not family, I was told, the information could not be divulged. Upstairs, Arch and Macguire were listening to what could advisedly be called music. Macguire showed me a huge box of imported chocolates that

Marla had brought over. She'd told the boys she was going down to Lutheran Hospital to check on ReeAnn personally, and she'd call me later. I knew she'd get the info. When Marla told people she was a family member, they rarely argued.

The boys offered me a wrapped Mozart-kügel and I took it. It was somewhat ironic that the only way these two would acknowledge the classical masters of music was through candy. Within moments more chocolate bulged in their cheeks and noise blared down our street. I thought again of Schoenberg's mother and retreated hastily to my kitchen.

I booted up my computer and went through the file I'd opened on the circumstances surrounding Suz Craig's death. What significance could ReeAnn have to the murder of Suz Craig? What was the link? I couldn't see any, apart from the fact that ReeAnn had known all about the Jerk's affairs, and probably a great deal about Suz's as well.

I scrolled back through my computer file and reread an early entry, where I summarized the catering job I'd done at Suz's house in July. It had been a clear, sunlit day, with clouds piling up over the mountains to the west and birds flitting among the blue campanula and columbine. Suz had been nervous about the appearance of her yard with its unfinished landscaping. She'd fretted about the weather, since she hadn't wanted the ACHMO honchos to be soaked by an unexpected mountain shower. She'd shown little interest in the food preparation and presentation. To me this said: Career woman whose postcollege path did not detour through the kitchen. Which was just fine. That kind of client uncritically appreciates my work, even thinks of it as a kind of magic. Suz had appeared cheerful, but she had not really enjoyed the food. And when Chris Corey had fallen down the steps, she'd been distraught.

All of this begged the question I'd never thought to ask in the first place: Why had the Minneapolis people been visiting in July? The people at the party had certainly made no mention of an annual review, audit, or meeting. In retrospect, that seemed strange. When I'd asked one visiting staff member what had brought him out to Denver, I'd received a noncommittal response along the lines of "Fighting fires." Exactly what kind of fire? Suz's guests had all been from Human Resources at ACHMO headquarters, that much I knew. I did have a foodie buddy in the Denver ACHMO HR office. But the last time I'd seen Brandon Yuille, at John Richard's office, he had been upset with me for not telling him where the Jerk would hide something. Now I realized he'd probably been referring to the missing meeting tapes, as well as notes about the malpractice and negligence suits. I felt guilty all over again for snapping at him, and resolved to be reconciled before asking him more about Suz.

To keep my promise to Tom, I knew I couldn't pay Brandon a visit at the ACHMO office itself. Not that they'd let the ex-wife of the man accused of murdering their vice-president through the doors. So instead I phoned Brandon's office and again identified myself: Goldy Schulz, the caterer, the *friend of Brandon's*. Once more Brandon's secretary was either well-trained or just her usual wary self. She asked the nature of my call.

"I need to apologize to him for a misunderstanding we had. Also, I'd like to talk to him about a lunch I catered a while ago," I replied. I avoided mentioning the name of Suz Craig. "We talked about Thai food and fudge, remind him of that. I have a couple of questions about the event itself."

There was a pause. "Aah," the secretary said finally, with mock regretfulness, "it looks as if Mr. Yuille will be in a meeting for the next three days."

"Don't they ever take breaks?" I asked good-naturedly. "This won't take long."

She didn't respond immediately. I had the feeling she was looking straight at Brandon, who was vigorously shaking his head. At length she stiffly announced, "I can connect you with Mr. Yuille's voice mail, if you'd like."

I assented and briefly told the recorded voice that I was trying to help my son deal with his father being arrested by keeping him informed about the murder investigation. Could Brandon forgive me for being short with him at Korman's office? And could he satisfy my curiosity, tell me why the Minneapolis HR team at Suz's house had come to Denver in the first place? Finally, did he happen to know if anyone had it in for John Richard's secretary, ReeAnn Collins, who'd just been badly injured in a barbecue incident?

Well, I thought as I hung up, *that ought to either ruin our friendship or take it to a whole new level.* I had the disconcerting feeling that I'd been too pushy. Moreover, whether any useful information would come out of my requests was, it seemed at this point, extremely questionable.

I wanted to cook. But my growling stomach announced I was too hungry to concentrate. I'd had nothing to eat in the last eight hours except a piece of toast, coffee, and a Mozartkügel. Looking around, I dove into the container of Chocolate Comfort Cookies like a madwoman. Although I've read accounts of how addicts heighten their drug experiences, in my opinion nothing beats a large mouthful of dark, velvety chocolate on an empty stomach. I closed my eyes, bit into the cookie, and waited for the rush. An ecstasy of shivers began in the small of my back. I sighed with chocoholic contentment. Now I was ready to face whatever the rest of the day cared to deliver.

According to my catering calendar, the following morning — Wednesday — Gail Rodine's doll-club board of directors wanted a fancy breakfast by the lake. I'd promised her baked scrambled eggs with cream cheese and shrimp, fruit kebabs, honey-cured ham, and an assortment of breads. My supplier had delivered the meat last Friday. I heaved the plump, bone-in ham onto the counter to check if it had been spiral-cut as I'd ordered. It was, and would only need heating in the morning. The eggs and shrimp I would assemble at the LakeCenter, but the breads needed to be organized today.

I had two large loaves of the brioche left

over from the box lunches, plus several dozen dark pumpernickel rolls that I'd made and frozen particularly for this event. But one more bread was needed to round things out. Experimenting to put together a delectable new bread for an upscale breakfast? *Please don't throw me in the briar patch.* Thomas Edison, here I come. I knew I could do it. I scanned the walk-in pensively.

In the use-up-stray-ingredients economy that good caterers invariably subscribe to, I noted egg whites left over from making the Babsie Tarts, a couple of oranges that I'd ordered along with the lemons, and several unopened jars of poppy seeds. I pounced on these ingredients. I'd assemble a cakelike orange poppy-seed bread. Or die in the attempt.

As always, cooking lifted me from the doldrums. While the egg whites were whipped into a froth, I measured the dry ingredients and then delighted in the fine spray of citrus oil that slicked my fingers when I scraped the zest from the oranges. Outside, the sun shone brilliantly in a deep blue sky and a warm breeze swished through the aspens. I opened the window over the sink. The boys' music reverberated along the street. Out back Jake howled an accompaniment. I smiled. If the music made the boys happy, I wasn't going to say a thing.

I was folding the poppy seeds into the batter when John Richard Korman jumped in front of the window. I screamed and dropped the bowl in the sink. The bowl shattered. Jake howled. Locked out back, the dog couldn't help me. I'd disarmed the security system. I hadn't turned it back on. Oh, God.

Unthinking, I wheeled around wildly for the phone. But by then John Richard had pulled off the screen, reached through the window, and grabbed my wrist.

"Let go!" I cried as I wrenched my hand back. "Go away!" I screamed. He lurched up through the window, with my wrist still in a death grip. His free hand slapped my face. He smelled like whiskey.

"Shut up!" he growled. "I'm telling you, Goldy," he said in a menacing voice as I opened my mouth to scream again, "shut the hell up. I want to talk to you. I want to talk to Arch. Let me in."

Instead I pushed hard to try to get him out. Mercilessly, he twisted my wrist. I cried out in pain. Again he told me to *shut the hell up*. Then he yanked my hand over the window frame. Blood spurted from my forearm where the skin scraped against the metal. Poor Jake howled to no avail. My abdomen pressed painfully against the sink. My feet barely touched the floor.

"Who wrote that shit on my house?" He twisted harder on my wrist. "The neighbors say you know. Who was it?"

"Vandals." I put my free hand on my face, trying to protect it from another slap. "Vandals. The sheriff's department doesn't know who they were. They can't find them. This isn't a good idea," I warned him. "Just go away. I promise I won't tell Tom."

"Why didn't you open your door when I knocked?"

"I didn't hear you."

"I *said,* 'Why didn't you open your door when I knocked?' "

"I told you . . . agh . . ." Pain shot through my wrist again. "I didn't *hear* you."

"Bullshit. Listen. I didn't kill her, Goldy." With his other hand he seized my chin and forced me to look in his eyes. "I did not kill Suz Craig. She'd been *repri-manded*" — another tug on my arm made me squeal — "by the Minneapolis people and faced being *fired.* We had a *fight,* but I didn't *kill* her. *They* killed her." His fingers bit into my wrist so savagely that I whimpered.

"Tell the cops," I gasped. "Tell . . . your lawyer."

"I did! I just wanted to tell *you!*"

392

His handsome face twisted in rage. I knew he would hit me again. I was panicked about the two boys upstairs. I couldn't let Arch see us like this again. I wouldn't let the Jerk *hurt* me like this again. Stunned with pain, I frantically searched for something — anything — to rescue me. There was no knife in sight.

Through gritted teeth he said, "I want to talk to that kid you have living here. Perkins. I think *he* painted my house."

Pain shot through my arm. I squirmed to get some leverage against the sink.

"For-*get* it!" I screamed. With my left hand I seized the heavy piece of ham on the counter. I swung the meat up, then down on top of John Richard's head. The meat glanced off his forehead and his eyes rolled up in his head. Releasing my wrist, he stumbled backward.

I lurched for the phone, dropped it, retrieved it, pressed 911. I shouted that I had an intruder, my ex-husband, John Richard Korman.

I screamed, "He hurt me! I'm bleeding!"

"Is he there now?" The 911 operator spoke calmly.

I scrambled for the window in time to see John Richard, one hand clutching his temple, limping toward the street. "Yes, yes, but he's

393

leaving! Hurry!" I yelled. "Quickly! Come and get him and take him *away!*"

But I already knew it was too late. The Jeep roared and he was gone.

Chapter 22

I closed and locked the window. Outside, Jake had not stopped his incessant howling. I let him in through the back door. He bounded over to me immediately, whining, putting his muzzle up to my face, trying to lick it. I floundered into the bathroom to wash the blood off my arm. Unfortunately, the sound of sirens brought Arch and Macguire rushing down the stairs.

The bloody fingers of my left hand pressed the lock on the bathroom door. I couldn't talk to anyone just yet. When the boys called, I responded by saying I'd be there in a minute. I looked dreadful. My face was blotchy; my right cheek bore the scarlet imprint of John Richard's hand. I turned the cold water all the way up and splashed and resplashed my face. It had been a long time since the Jerk had treated me like this. Our house boasted a security system, a bloodhound, and a live-in policeman. None of these had helped.

Would we ever be safe?

★ ★ ★

The next hour passed in a daze. At my insistence, Arch and Macguire went back upstairs. The two policemen who came to the door, both deputies I did not know, asked if I could tell them where John Richard had gone. I gave them his address in the country club and begged not to have to go down to the department to make my statement. The deputies instructed me to write down exactly what had happened. As I was scribbling, one of the cops called Tom, who was not at his desk. The other took the ham into evidence. I almost laughed, but I couldn't stop trembling enough to do so.

By contacting and attacking a witness in the homicide investigation in which he'd been charged, John Richard had gotten himself into deep trouble. When the sheriff's department located him, they would arrest him again. Somehow knowing this did not make me feel much better. All I could think of was Arch.

I took a shower, changed into fresh clothes, and searched for my son. I found him on a portable phone in his room. Judging from his confidential tone, he was talking to his buddy Todd. When I knocked on the door, he quickly disconnected.

"May I come in?"

396

I could tell he felt horrible. His voice cracked when he whispered, "Mom, are you okay?"

"No, hon, I'm really not."

"I didn't even have a chance to see him."

"I know."

Arch slumped morosely on his bed, his lips pressed together. Finally he said, "I just feel as if it's so hopeless. You promised you'd help him and —"

"I *have* tried to help him," I interrupted, careful to keep my tone soothing. "Not because of anything good he's done, but because I promised you that I would —"

"Excuse me, Mom, but you have *not* helped him. He says he didn't kill Ms. Craig. I believe him."

"Arch, please. I have spent the last three days on the telephone asking questions, going around talking to people, and —"

Behind the glasses, his eyes burned ferociously. "And what have you found out? Nothing!" Guiltily, he softened his tone. "I know you want him to go to prison. In your heart."

Poor, miserable Arch. It didn't help that he was probably right. I did want John Richard in prison, where he couldn't hurt another woman. I said patiently, "I am waiting for people to call me back. I can't make people talk to me."

He got up and slid halfway under his bed. When he inched back out, he was clutching his backpack. "Sorry, Mom, but I'm going to live with the Druckmans for a while. At least until Dad's hearing. Todd's mother said it was okay." He opened a drawer and began pulling out shorts and shirts. "If I hadn't been here, Dad never would have come around and started hitting you. He was probably looking for me."

"Honey, please, please don't go."

"This way," my son continued, avoiding my eyes, "we won't have another big mess with the police coming over. Please leave my room now, Mom."

He'd ordered me from his room. He wouldn't speak to me. He refused to even *listen.* I retreated to my kitchen, where I sat in silent shock for ten minutes. Then I called the Druckmans to apologize for my son being a freeloader and to see if I could at least bring over some food. Kathleen Druckman assured me that she was happy to have Arch for as long as he wanted to stay. I didn't need to deliver any meals, either, she said with a laugh, she'd be insulted. She and her husband would even take Arch down to the jail to see his father. And was it true that John Richard had knocked me unconscious with a whole poached salmon? I said no, thanked her again, and hung up.

Macguire had left a note taped to my computer: *Going out for a walk, hope you're okay. See you at dinner. Can we have pizza?*

Not even Macguire's renewed appetite cut through my misery. When Arch slammed out the front door, I almost burst into tears. Instead, I dialed Tom's number.

It was four o'clock. He wasn't there, so I left a very brief voice-mail message. John Richard had been here. Both Arch and I were okay. If he wanted more information, he could talk to the officers who, I hoped, would have arrested John Richard by the time he got this message.

The memory of the Jerk's slap rushed back into my consciousness. But what had he shrieked about Suz Craig? *She'd been reprimanded.* For what? I put in another call to Brandon Yuille. He was the Human Resources person, after all. Unfortunately, he again refused to speak to me except through his secretary. I told her to ask Brandon if the ACHMO bigwigs were about to fire Suz Craig and if so, why. And remind him, I said, that I was sorry we'd had a misunderstanding. Also that I had a close personal relationship with the investigative journalist of the *Mountain Journal* and she'd just love to start bothering him for an interview. I hung up with a bang that did nothing to improve my mood.

I cleaned up the mess in the kitchen left from my fracas with the Jerk. To fulfill Macguire's request, I mixed up some pizza dough and set it aside to rise. I called my supplier to see about replacing the ham and got her machine. Then, because I couldn't think of anything else to do, I started over on the orange poppy-seed bread.

This time, just as I was again at the fateful point of folding in the poppy seeds, the phone rang. I thought it might be Marla or Tom or even Brandon Yuille getting back to me, but I was wrong. To my surprise, it was Patricia McCracken.

"Well," she demanded breathlessly, as if none of the sorry events of the last three days had ever transpired and we were still happy confidantes, "what have you found out?"

"About *what?*" I gently scraped a poppy seed–speckled pillow of the light, moist batter into a buttered and floured loaf pan.

"About John Richard, silly! Has he gotten himself into any more trouble?"

"Like what?" I really did not want to discuss this. Any info I gave Patricia would be all over Aspen Meadow in an hour, given her feud with the Jerk. At least she hadn't heard the crazy story about him hitting me with a salmon.

"My neighbor's son was driving by the park when the helicopter came down. I heard ReeAnn was burned over three-fourths of her body," she continued. "Was she with John Richard? You don't know what happened with that, do you?"

This was the woman who had complained so bitterly to me about our community's obsession-with-disaster? Incredible. Some people just can't see themselves as fostering the very problem they're griping about.

"I can't talk, Patricia," I responded. "I need to finish making some bread."

Bitterly, she said, "You're not much help," and hung up.

Not much help. Well, wasn't that what everyone was saying about me these days? I slid the bread into the oven, then rebooted my computer and added *According to the Jerk, Suz was reprimanded by ACHMO HQ* honchos to my list of what I knew about her. A brief time later, I took the golden-brown bread out and placed it on a rack. It perfumed the kitchen with its rich, orangey scent. Macguire arrived home as I was feeding the dog and the cat. I assured him I was just fine and told him I'd be kneading cloverleaf rolls in no time. He looked skeptically at the slap marks on my face and the thick bandage I'd placed over my forearm. But unlike Patricia McCracken, he was too polite to say anything.

Tom arrived shortly after six, bearing vegetarian calzones and a deep-dish sausage pizza. He unloaded the food, gently examined my face and arm, and cursed John Richard. He carefully punched down the mass of pizza dough I'd already made, zipped it into a heavy-duty plastic bag, and popped it into the freezer. When he finished unwrapping the Italian feast, I felt tears prick hard.

"Please, Goldy, don't, don't," he crooned as he gathered me up in his arms. "What you've been through . . . I'm so sorry I wasn't here. I feel like I failed you."

"You didn't."

"I did."

"Oh, Tom. Arch has gone to live with the Druckmans until John Richard's hearing."

"He'll be back," he said confidently.

I let him hold me. "All this food," I muttered finally, "it's going to get cold."

He held me out at arm's length. His warm green eyes gave me a skeptical look. "That's what I brought my convection oven into this house for, remember? You like pizza, don't you? Even if it's pizza made by somebody else?"

You like pizza? "Sure," I said uncertainly, and sat down at the table while Tom preheated the oven and opened a bottle of Chianti. I shivered. *Even if it's pizza made by somebody else?* Tom had gently asked.

My afternoon encounter with John Richard had brought another assault of memories I thought I'd repressed. One time, I *had* tried to serve pizza made by somebody else. Arch had been three months old and sick with a painful ear infection. Exhausted from being up with him all night and then all day, I'd ordered a pizza for dinner. John Richard had thrown a fit, of course. He'd torn the pizza into bits and dumped them in the garbage disposal. If he'd wanted take-out pizza, he'd shouted, he would have stayed single.

Without being asked, Macguire set the kitchen table. Not one of us mentioned my son. Arch must have told Macguire his plans to live with the Druckmans. Again, Macguire was too polite to mention it.

The strange thing about going through a difficult time is that eventually, you get hungry. The Italian sausage on the pizza Tom had brought home provided a sharp, juicy complement to the crunchy crust. The calzones were so stuffed with steaming tomatoes, onions, peppers, and cheese that it was hard to take a bite without making a mess. By the time we finished eating, my mood had lifted somewhat.

"Something I need to discuss with you all," Tom said in the gentle voice he used whenever he needed to drop a bombshell.

I said, "Uh-oh."

"The deputies couldn't find John Richard," he announced matter-of-factly. "He wasn't at his house. There's an APB out on him, but you need to know he's at large."

"That sucks," Macguire said.

"It's probably just as well Arch is at the Druckmans'," Tom continued. "Here at home, we need to keep the windows shut all the time. Turn on the attic fan if you need ventilation. But the security system stays *armed.* I mean it."

I rubbed my temples and tried to give myself a silent pep talk. No uplifting thoughts came. When Macguire offered to do the dishes, Tom and I consented gratefully. Upstairs, the Chianti and relaxing meal finally took effect. No matter how bad the news is, not only do you have to eat, you eventually have to sleep. I hadn't slept well since I'd discovered Suz Craig's body. I yawned.

"Put on your pajamas," Tom ordered with a loving smile, "and let me rub your back."

"It's not even eight o'clock."

"Miss G., let me take care of you. No fussing."

I winced as I pulled the pajama sleeve over my bruised arm, then remembered the arnica and antidepression herbs from Amy Bartholomew and slid the tablets and capsules onto the table next to the bed. Before I could take any, though, I had to ask my husband a few questions.

"Tom," I said as I lay carefully on my stomach, "where could John Richard be?"

"Aw, he's someplace he thinks is safe. With friends, probably. I don't think he'd dare come after you. Not after today."

"Beg to differ." After a moment I said, "Arch doesn't think I'm looking into the charges against his father. After all I've done, that almost hurts more than anything."

Tom's large hands pressed and massaged my aching body. "He's a kid, Goldy. He just doesn't understand. Cut him some slack."

"I've cut him tons of slack. He just hasn't cut any for me."

Tom chose not to respond to this. Under his hands my weary muscles began to relax. I felt my eyes closing.

"I've got something else to ask you," I said weakly.

"I wish you wouldn't talk."

"Has anybody at ACHMO told you Suz

was about to be fired? Or why?"

He chuckled. "Korman sure claimed that in his interview. But he was the only one who mentioned it, and he can't prove a thing. Everyone else swears her job was secure."

"Ah," I said. I downed the herb capsules and slipped the arnica under my tongue. A few minutes later, I did not resist when sleep claimed me.

I awoke at two A.M. in such a state of alertness that I felt sure Arch had come home, the security alarm had gone off, or either Scout or Jake was scratching to go out. None of these was the case. I looked out the window: the night was still. No breeze or rush of creekwater was audible, of course, as every single window in the house was locked up tight. I turned on the dresser light and saw a note from Tom.

Miss G., Arch called before he went to bed. You were sleeping so soundly I didn't want to wake you. He wanted to tell you good night and that he loved you. Also, Marla phoned. ReeAnn C. is banged up pretty good but they think she's going to pull through. T.

Peachy. But it was not worries about Arch or even ReeAnn that had awakened me. It

406

was something else.

If Suz Craig was about to be fired, or was even in danger of being fired, how could that relate to her being murdered? And why had Brandon Yuille, my buddy-in-Thai-food, refused to answer any of my calls? Was he still annoyed about our conversation at the Jerk's office, despite my apologies? John Richard was on the loose, but I doubted he was watching our house. I slipped on jeans, sneakers, and a sweatshirt. During the day, Brandon could refuse to return my calls all he wanted. But at this hour, I knew exactly where to find him.

Chapter 23

The Aspen Meadow Pastry Shop had undergone a sea change since Mickey Yuille, my old master baker friend, had bought it, refurbished it, and hired an energetic cleaning service. Lacy, pristinely white European-style curtains now hung in the windows. The glass display cases, formerly messy with weeks of fingerprints, gleamed spotlessly in the dimmed light of the cozy dining room. The former owner had offered a hodgepodge of almost-stale cookies and partially baked pastry shells. These had been replaced by appetizing rows of truffles, chocolate-dipped macaroons, and French cream cookies so buttery, they gave new meaning to melt-in-your-mouth.

Since it was a quarter past two in the morning, I stopped lusting over the offerings in the dark shop-front and looked for movement in the kitchen. An oblong of yellow light illuminated Mickey hustling back and forth. As I sidled across the front window to get a better view, I caught sight of Brandon. He sat at a long table, gesturing as he spoke earnestly to his father. The back door had been left partially open, probably to bring cool night air into the oven-heated space.

I nipped past the comics shop, the insurance agent's office, and the Christian Science Reading Room. I rounded the back of the building and came noiselessly up to the back entrance with its open door. Mickey *had* suggested I come by for some fresh, hot cinnamon rolls. Now the unmistakable scent of that most prized of spices, Indonesian cinnamon, came wafting out into the darkness. I pushed the door open and stepped inside.

"Howdy all," I said brightly, as if I customarily popped into closed bakeries at two A.M. "I had insomnia, so I just thought I'd drop in."

Mickey, balding, shrunken, but with a smile so endearing he always reminded me of a stuffed troll, looked up from the thick layer of golden dough he was rolling out. "Goldy! So glad to see you!" He set aside his marble rolling pin and bustled forward to embrace me. He smelled marvelous, sweat mixed with spice and flour. His long white apron dusted my outfit. I grinned and returned his hug, then looked over at Brandon. His handsome face was no longer set in its usual impish expression. He looked as if a monsoon had arrived at his doorstep.

"Morning, Brandon," I said pleasantly. "So glad I could run into you here. I've been trying to call you to apologize for our misunderstanding at my ex-husband's office."

His shiny dark hair fell in his face and he immediately brushed it back. "Sure, okay, no hard feelings," he mumbled without visible enthusiasm. "Glad to see you."

"Coffee, coffee, let's have some fresh," said Mickey, obviously glad of my company, even if his son was not.

"Why didn't you answer my calls?" I asked Brandon as I sat in one of the chairs at his father's worktable. Out of earshot, Mickey ran water and measured out ground coffee.

"I can't call you back," Brandon rejoined. "They are watching me every second. I'm afraid every call of mine is monitored. . . ."

"Who's 'they'? Who would monitor your calls?"

Brandon's handsome face screwed up in dismay. "The same guys who were here before, from the headquarters office of Human Resources. They've come back in from Minneapolis until the preliminary hearing with your ex is over. I'm telling you, Goldy, it's a bad scene."

"You think that's a bad scene? My fourteen-year-old son has *moved out* until the preliminary hearing. That's how ticked off with me he is over this case. I want to find out what the *hell* is going on with my son's father a whole lot more than your corporate bigwigs do." He said nothing. "Please, Brandon. Please help us."

Brandon exhaled unhappily. "Whatever I tell you, you've got to say you didn't hear it from me."

"Brandon, for heaven's sake! You didn't participate in any illegal activity, did you?"

His smile was a younger, less wrinkled version of his father's. "Of course not. No illegal activity. I didn't even kill Suz Craig, as is believed in some circles."

"What circles?"

His face turned pink. "Oh, you know. The gossip mill."

"Was she about to be fired by ACHMO when she was killed?"

His father reappeared with the coffee. It was marvelous, dark and hearty. We took grateful sips and showered praise and thanks on Mickey.

"You all go ahead and visit," Mickey told us. He eyed the rectangle of dough. "I gotta work."

"Can't we help you?" I offered. Cloth towels shrouded the domed top of another enormous bowl of risen dough.

"Naw, naw," Mickey replied, waving a

411

floured paw. "The priest is doing grief work with me. Says I gotta work. Stay busy. Best antidote. I like having you here, though."

I looked back at Brandon, who shrugged. He murmured, "Just let him. He knows what he needs. I'm here for company. When I help him, it's usually on the weekends."

"Was Suz about to be fired?" I asked Brandon again. "Or had she been submitted to some kind of disciplinary action?"

Brandon sipped his coffee and was silent. For a moment I feared he'd decided not to answer. "Not exactly reprimanded. She was . . . being observed. In her dealings with people." I waited for him to go on. He shifted in the wooden chair. "Headquarters had had a lot of complaints." He seemed to go into a trance as he watched his father spread butter on the rolled dough.

"Complaints from whom?" I prompted.

Brandon blinked and shrugged. "Everybody who'd ever had to work with Suz Craig."

When he seemed in danger of going into another trance, I said, "Amy Bartholomew said the same thing. She said Suz set a trap for her. Amy wanted to control her own destiny, as she put it, and Suz had other ideas. Suz accused Amy of compulsively feeding the slots up at Central City. Then Suz tried to make it impossible for Amy to buy the health-food store."

Brandon's eyes were on his father as he sprinkled dark cinnamon sugar over the golden dough. "Yeah, I know. I'm the very young, very unsuccessful head of Human Resources, remember?"

"Amy said Suz criticized you for spending too much time here with your father and for coming into the office too tired to do good work. She criticized Chris Corey, too."

"Oh, boy, don't remind me." He looked at the ceiling. "Chris was putting together a new Provider Relations Manual. He's very thorough, and Suz kept changing the language of certain guidelines. It was her fault he missed the deadline. But she threw a fit anyway, in front of everybody."

"Did she criticize Ralph Shelton?"

"Of course," he said simply. "She told us she was putting together a file of patient complaints, plus a critical letter from her, into a packet to go to MeritMed."

"Why would she do that? He already told me that was why he was fired."

"Who knows? Plus, Goldy, I'm not convinced she should have fired him. Every doctor gets unhappy patients. Last year, the state board of medical examiners received over seven hundred and fifty complaints. Eighty-five percent were dismissed." He sighed. "And then Shelton was so pathetic, calling each of us after she fired him, to see if we could stop her from sending the packet of complaints on. We all suspected Shelton was trying to renew his old friendship with Korman to get *him* to prevent her from sending the packet to Shelton's new employers at MeritMed. But apparently Korman repeatedly gave Shelton the brush-off through that cute secretary of his."

"Sort of the way you gave me the brush-off today."

"Sorry. I really *was* in a meeting."

"Did Suz criticize and threaten John Richard, too?"

Brandon's large brown eyes and narrow face suddenly seemed overcome with sadness. "She could be the warmest, most loving person you could ever imagine." He paused and looked away. "She could also be vicious. Every day when I drove into that parking lot, my stomach would clench. What kind of mood was she going to be in today? What would she try to do to me? How could I fend her off?"

"Did she want to have control over John Richard?" I persisted.

He frowned, then shook his head. "Who knew? He didn't share much with us, you know, the administrators. Suz's control of *information* was what concerned her, and she was good at it." His forehead wrinkled. "I did hear that Korman's billing was problematic, and that he didn't automatically qualify for a bonus he was expecting."

"Who told you those tidbits?" When he shrugged, I went on. "Where do the ACHMO honchos come in? Why were they here last month? One of them told me they were fighting fires."

He sighed again. "I might as well tell you. *We're* the ones who complained about Suz to headquarters. Naughty us. Amy didn't tell you about that?"

"She said something was planned."

"The department heads did an end run. We called Human Resources at headquarters. 'This woman is killing us,' we said. 'You have to get rid of her.' "

"Wow."

He jabbed the air with his finger. "But listen! HQ is always telling us: 'Our vision is to build a cooperation-based organization! We want to have open lines of communication! Call on us *anytime* for help!' " His scowl deepened. "Did that ever backfire."

"How?"

"They came, they listened, they left. You catered a nice lunch for them their last day,

415

after we'd been meeting with them all week telling them how horrid our boss was. That next-to-last day, guess what? They met with *her*."

"Uh-oh."

" 'Uh-oh' is right! Open communication? Sounds more like *betrayal*, don't you think? They told Suz, 'Brandon Yuille says you criticize him too much. He can't get his work done hiring new people if he has to listen to complaints about you all day.' And to this Suz said, 'You know, Brandon's just lost his mother. I'll take him out to lunch this month.' "

"Oh, no."

"Oh, yes. The very last day, those HR people had the nerve to tell us about their conversation with her, and all she'd promised. They said they'd solved our little *personnel* problem. So you can see why our lunch showed a few cracks of tension."

His father slid a baking sheet from one of the large black ovens along the wall. Inside I could see flames. I had a fleeting vision of Hansel and Gretel.

Brandon went on. "And then the following week Suz called each of us in. To me she said, 'You ever complain about me again, I'll fire your ass so fast you won't know what hit you. I'll make sure you never get another job in Human Resources anywhere in Denver, or anywhere in the country, in an HMO.' " His laugh was empty. "Then you won't believe what else she said. 'Brandon, I swear I'll have your medical records altered so it says you've got cancer just like your mother.' "

"Oh, come on. Surely —"

"Come on yourself. You don't think she had access to our medical records? How naive are you?"

"I just can't believe it."

"Goldy, believe it."

At this point Mickey interrupted us by setting blue plates of hot pastries in front of each of us. He beamed like a magician.

"Oh, my gosh," said Brandon, "bear claws."

I did not know if this Danish-style pastry shaped like a giant claw was indigenous to the Rocky Mountains. I'd never heard of it before moving out here. I bit off one finger of the almond-paste-filled delicacy. Butter oozed between the flaky layers. A light, sugary glaze and crunchy sliced almonds complemented the rich filling. Another luscious reason to live in Colorado.

"Thank you so very much," I told Mickey. "You can't imagine how much I appreciate this."

He poured me more hot coffee. "Of course I do. Food-service people are the last ones to sit down and actually enjoy *eating* anything. Besides, I love the company, as Brandon can tell you. I'm about to make some sour-cream cakes now. . . . You two need anything else?"

"Thanks, Dad. No," said Brandon warmly as he squeezed his father's hand. For the first time I noticed the bags under Brandon's eyes. His schedule must be brutal, I thought. He'd told the cops he went to bed at eight P.M. every night so that he could be here by two A.M. It wasn't a regimen I would want to follow on any long-term basis, especially since I'd tried it for the last few nights and now felt like a walking zombie.

"I'm going to leave in a few minutes," I told Brandon. "I think I understand better now why everyone, especially my ex, had trouble with this woman. It's hard to believe that Suz would threaten you with changing your medical records, though. Couldn't anybody call her on trying to intimidate people? It sounds so much like blackmail."

Brandon chewed the last of his bear claw. "Great idea, Goldy. Now we know those meetings she had with us in her office were taped. When I called headquarters the week after HR left, they said to me, 'You get proof she's threatening you and we'll fire her.' Not that I would trust them. But I checked the labels on the tapes Luella Downing found. None were from the Monday after the HR people left, when Suz went on her threatening rampage."

"That's it?" I said, astonished. "Monday — what would it have been, July 14? The tapes from that day are missing?"

"Why? You know where they are?"

"No," I said with a sudden yawn I couldn't suppress. "I don't have a clue."

When I crawled back into bed at four, Tom rolled over and said, "I'm beginning to think there's someone else."

I started to laugh and couldn't stop. They were the kind of giggles you get when you're very young, at camp or a slumber party, and can't contain, no matter how valiantly you try.

"Uh-huh," he said. "You got another statement to make? Some wrongdoing you encountered out on your prowls?"

"I can't . . ." I said between giggles, "help it . . . if I can't . . . sleep."

"Soothe me, then. Tell me where you went."

"To the pastry shop. Had a bear claw.

Sorry, I didn't bring you any."

He put his arms around me and growled. "Promise me the next time you go on one of these excursions, you take me with you. I feel like a kid who always gets left behind."

I snuggled into his arms. "Okay. Whither I go, thou goest. Or words to that effect."

"So did you find out anything about Korman at the pastry shop?"

"Sort of. The missing day's tapes are for July 14, when Suz Craig called in all the employees who'd complained about her to HQ and threatened to fire them. She must have met with other people that day, too, like Ralph Shelton. So . . . if you had tapes of yourself blackmailing people, where would you hide them?"

"I'd destroy them."

"Oh, cop, you're a lot of help."

Chapter 24

My yoga regimen that morning was made more difficult by the phone ringing insistently at six o'clock. I pulled myself out of a contorted asana with the hope that this was the sheriff's department calling to tell us they'd captured the Jerk. No such luck: over the wire came the commanding voice of the much-dreaded dollmeister, Gail Rodine.

"The board doesn't want you to use the grill tonight for our final dinner," she announced without a hint of apology for calling so early. "I mean, after what happened to ReeAnn Collins, we just . . . feel it's too dangerous."

Thinking of the mountains of hamburgers I had made and frozen, and the bags of chicken breasts I had been planning to marinate, my heart plummeted. I could never get them *all* grilled at home and reheated at the LakeCenter, without ruining them. "What would you like, then?" I asked carefully. "It'll be impossible to order in more food supplies before tonight."

"Well . . . what do you already have on

hand? Anything that you could grill, say, at home and then heat up?"

"Some I could do," I said confidently. "The last thing I want is for a client to be worried about preparation. But what I have on hand . . ." I mentally weighed the chicken. "If I grill the chicken I have, it will only feed half your folks. I'll have to make . . ." I mentally scanned my refrigerator. "I'll prepare a Camembert pie to fill things out. It'll contain shrimp and vegetables, too." From under the rumpled covers Tom's sleep-worn face appeared. I held my hand over the receiver and mouthed, "Client needs whole new dish for tonight."

"Macguire said he wanted to help you," Tom replied as he rolled back under the sheet. "Give him some chopping to do. He's worried about how depressed you are about Arch. He really wants to go back to being your assistant."

"Goldy?" Gail Rodine. "Goldy, are you listening to me? How much extra is this going to cost?"

"I do want you, the board, and the guests to be comfortable, Gail —"

"Don't worry," she said, clearing her throat, "I've already called a Denver caterer, and he said no one could meet our needs for a fancy dinner by five o'clock tonight without an exorbitant surcharge."

"Gail, please —"

"That's ridiculous!" she shrieked into my ear. "I told them, 'You don't want us to get blown up by a propane grill, do you?' "

"The Camembert pie retails for approximately forty dollars. You're already getting grilled Chicken à l'Orange and rice. I can add a tossed salad of field greens and perhaps a molded fruit salad, if I have time. Plus vanilla frozen yogurt with those chocolate cookies you had in your box lunches. There's only a five percent surcharge for changing the menu at this late date."

"Fine, fine, put it on our bill." She rang off.

"I'm afraid to ask what that was about." Tom's voice rumbled as he headed for the bathroom.

"Woman doesn't want to stage her last barbecue tonight," I said as I groaned before starting a final stretch. "Doesn't want to end up like ReeAnn."

"Figures. Hey, let me see that." He walked over to me, a manly vision in T-shirt and cotton undershorts. He touched my arm. "My God, Goldy! Look at that bruise! I *swear* I'm going to kill Korman myself, one of these days."

I twisted and frowned at the black-and-blue mark that had formed on my lower arm from being banged around by John Richard. I hadn't noticed it until now. "Oh, well. Say, do you want to go back to bed?"

He smiled at me but touched the bruise gently. "Does it hurt?"

I gave a doctor-style shrug. "I'll live, if we have a roll in the hay first."

He obliged, and we had a wonderful, warm, intimate time. Sometimes the best thing you can do in the morning is go right back to bed.

After a while Tom said, "I'm going to help you with this breakfast, and go in late. By the way, I bought you another spiral-cut honey-cured ham. It's in the walk-in."

I grinned and kissed him. "You're marvelous beyond words. And thank you — I'd love the company this morning."

I fixed myself an espresso while Tom took his shower. Because the hospital had rebuffed me, and because it was too early to call Marla, I made a quick call to the sheriff's department: ReeAnn Collins was out of danger and recovering from third- and second-degree burns. John Richard Korman, unfortunately, was still at large. And no, the duty officer informed me, Korman had not shown up at the Druckmans' house.

I sipped the espresso and wondered how Arch was doing. He'd only been gone one night, but it felt like an eternity because it was so open-ended. *I'm going to live with the Druckmans for a while. At least until Dad's hearing.* I got out leeks, tomatoes, and cream cheese, then retrieved two large bags of shrimp from the freezer. When Tom appeared in the kitchen, with his hair freshly washed and a tiny glob of shaving cream stuck under his ear, I was doubly glad he had decided to stay. Nothing like loneliness and a violent ex-husband on the lam to make one brood.

"Give me a job, Captain Cook," Tom demanded merrily after he'd chugged down the espresso I'd given him and heard the news about ReeAnn and the Jerk. "The less savory the job, sir, the better."

That was easy: I despise poaching and shelling shrimp. Now I not only needed the shellfish for the doll-club board breakfast, I needed them for the dinner, too. "If you could cook and shell all that shrimp, I'd be eternally grateful."

He eyed the bulging bags and chuckled. "Aye-aye, sir."

I started on a brioche-style dough that would form a delectable top crust for the dish

I'd decided to call Collectors' Camembert Pie. While we were both working, Macguire made a sudden appearance in the kitchen. I glanced at the clock: not even seven. "This is unexpected," I remarked. "What's up?"

"Give me something to do," he said bravely, his voice still thick with sleep. "I want to help."

I cut a glance at Tom, who resolutely bent over the shrimp. These two had conspired to cheer me up, no question about it. Fine. To Macguire, I pointed out the plump tomatoes to be seeded and chopped, artichoke bottoms to be trimmed, asparagus to be steamed and sliced, Camembert to be thickly cut, and Parmesan to be grated.

"I'll worry about putting it all together when I get home," I said with a smile.

"Uh," said Macguire, "that's a lot of food for breakfast, isn't it?"

"It's for dinner, Macguire."

"Oh." He rubbed his eyes. "Well, can I go back to bed until about ten and start chopping then?"

I laughed. "Of course." When he had hauled himself back upstairs, I beat the eggs for the main course. "Tom," I said thoughtfully as I chopped tomatoes and leeks, "what's the time frame for John Richard's trial?"

"Preliminary hearing should be in about another three weeks. The county's prosecuting attorney needs to see if there's enough evidence to go to trial. As soon as the drug screen's done and the skin and hair under Suz Craig's fingernails are analyzed, they'll know more than they do now. But as you know, there's already a lot of evidence against him."

"What about the vandals?"

"No sign of them. They could be anybody. They could have been hired by somebody sympathetic to Suz Craig."

"Hmm, I don't think so." I melted butter, put in the chopped leeks, and stirred the gold-and-green mixture. The aroma was deliciously sharp and fresh. "I guess it's conceivable that someone rented a white Jeep. Someone who knew what kind of car John Richard drove. The person would have to live close by."

Tom expertly drained the shrimp and ran cold water over them. "The only people connected to the case who live *very* close by are Patricia McCracken and Ralph Shelton. Patricia says she was asleep and her husband backs her up. Ralph Shelton says that after he and his wife got home from the country club, they went to bed. The wife says he was next to her in bed the whole night. But she admits she's a sound sleeper."

"Lucky her." I stirred the bright red tomatoes into the bubbling mass of butter and leeks, then gently stirred in the eggs. "I wish I knew why I can't find out what's going on inside ACHMO."

His voice quivered with anger. "I wish *I* knew why I can't seem to protect you from that violent ex-husband of yours."

"Not to make any excuses for him, but the man can't deal with frustration. Especially when he's had a few drinks. Maybe he knocked on the front door the way he said he did. But just because I didn't answer right away is no reason to lose his temper."

Tom shook his head, then measured out the shelled shrimp I needed for the breakfast dish: Doll Show Shrimp and Eggs. I stirred in the shrimp, then removed the pan from the heat. At the LakeCenter this morning I would add the cream cheese chunks to the eggs, vegetables, and shrimp, then bake the dish for a short time, just until the cheese melted and the ingredients had all melded into an irresistible mélange.

"Why don't you just bake it now?" Tom, ever the efficient cook, wanted to know.

"You can't put the dish in too early or it won't come out right."

"Ah. Well. If I leave now I'll be exactly an

Doll Show
Shrimp and Eggs

1 teaspoon Old Bay Seasoning
8 large frozen easy-peel shrimp
3 tablespoons butter
¼ cup chopped leek, white part only
⅓ cup chopped fresh tomato, seeds and pulp removed
6 eggs, slightly beaten
   Salt and freshly ground black pepper
3 ounces cream cheese, cut into ¼ inch cubes

Preheat oven to 400°.

Bring a pint of water to boil and add the Old Bay Seasoning and the shrimp. Cook the shrimp until they are *just* pink. *Do not overcook the shrimp.*

Drain and peel the shrimp, then cut each one in half. Melt the butter in an oven-proof skillet, then add the leek and tomato. Sauté gently for about 5 minutes, until the leek is softened.

Pour the eggs into the leek-tomato mixture, season with salt and freshly ground pepper, and cook over medium-low heat, stirring occasionally to prevent browning, until eggs have almost congealed but still have some liquid left. Stir in the shrimp and the cream cheese. Bake in the oven for about 10 minutes, or until cream cheese is melted and eggs are completely congealed.

Serves 2 to 3

Collectors' Camembert Pie

Crust:

1/3 cup milk
2 tablespoons butter
2 teaspoons sugar
2½ teaspoons (1 package) dry
   yeast
¾ teaspoon salt
1 egg, slightly beaten
1½ teaspoons oil
1¼ cups flour (or more)

Heat the milk, butter, and sugar until the butter is melted. Remove from the heat and set aside to cool slightly (to 105° to 115°). Stir the yeast into the milk mixture and let it stand for 10 minutes. Stir in the salt, egg, and oil. Add the flour ¼ cup at a time, stirring well, until each addition is thoroughly incorporated and dough holds together well. Turn out onto a lightly floured board and knead for 10 minutes, adding small amounts of flour if necessary, until dough is smooth and satiny.

(Or use a dough hook and knead in a mixer for the same amount of time.) Place the dough in an oiled bowl and turn it once to oil the top. Cover the bowl and set aside to rise at room temperature until tripled in bulk (about 2 hours). Punch the dough down, roll it into a rectangle approximately 9 by 13 inches, and place it in a jumbo-size zippered plastic bag. Refrigerate for up to 6 hours. When you begin to prepare the pie, remove the bag from the refrigerator to allow the dough to come to room temperature.

Filling:

1 tablespoon Old Bay Seasoning

36 large (1½ pounds) easy-peel shrimp

8 ounces fresh asparagus, trimmed

1 pound fresh tomatoes, cored and seeded

1 pound canned artichoke bottoms (5 or 6 per can)

2 12-ounce wheels (1½ pounds) Camembert

1 cup mayonnaise

2/3 cup freshly grated Parmesan

2 teaspoons pressed garlic (4 to 6 pressed cloves)

¾ teaspoon dried thyme, crumbled

¾ teaspoon dried rosemary, crumbled

¾ teaspoon dried oregano, crumbled

In a wide skillet, bring a quart of water to boil and add the

Old Bay Seasoning. Add the shrimp and cook until *just* pink. *Do not overcook the shrimp.* Drain the shrimp and discard the cooking water. Peel the shrimp and set it aside until you are ready to assemble the pie.

Slice the asparagus spears into thirds. Slice the cored and seeded tomatoes into eighths. Drain the artichoke bottoms, trim them of any rough edges, and slice each artichoke bottom into sixths. Scrape most of the rind off the Camembert and slice each wheel into sixteenths. (You will have thirty-two pie-shaped pieces of cheese.) In a small bowl, thoroughly combine the mayonnaise, Parmesan, garlic, and herbs.

Preheat the oven to 350°. Butter a 9- by 13-inch glass

pan. Assemble the pie by placing half of the shrimp in the bottom of the pan (three rows of 6 shrimp each), then evenly layer half of the asparagus, half of the tomatoes, half of the artichoke bottoms, and half of the Camembert over the shrimp. Using a small spoon, dab half of the mayonnaise mixture over the Camembert layer. Repeat the layers in the same order, ending with the last layer of shrimp. Carefully place the brioche dough over the top and cut several vents to allow steam to escape.

Bake for 45 minutes, or until dough is golden brown and filling is hot and bubbly. Allow to cool slightly before serving, about 5 or 10 minutes.

Serves 6 to 8

hour late. Think you can handle the rest of the morning?"

"With you for a helpmate, my dear sir, I can handle anything."

He sighed skeptically. "Just be careful, Miss G., please?"

"Yessir. Now, please, go serve and protect and don't worry about me, okay? Stop crime. Make America safe for the consumption of apple pie. *My* apple pie."

After he left, I brushed my fingers thoughtfully over the ugly bruise on my arm. Something I had seen and something I had said were working their way into my consciousness. It takes at least three hours for an injured area to turn black and blue, I knew that from Med Wives 101. As well, alas, from personal experience.

But black-and-blue marks didn't form on a corpse, as Tom had pointed out. Suz had had a nasty blowout with John Richard, and she'd had the exact pattern of bruises he usually inflicted. He'd even *admitted* they'd had a fight. Yet he was equally adamant that he'd left her alive after their argument and gone home. And really, the way he'd acted at my window yesterday was more typical of him: He got frustrated and he blew up. Then he either beat you until you submitted, or until something else stopped him, like the hanging plant Marla had whacked him with once, or the ill-fated ham I'd cracked over his head yesterday.

And Suz hadn't accidentally fallen into the ditch. She'd been beaten to death with a metal scratching post and then her body had been dumped into the ditch. It didn't make sense.

Even if someone else had killed her and wanted to put the blame on John Richard, *how could he or she even know Suz and the Jerk would be together that night? How could he or she know he'd lose his temper?* And even if the Jerk had beaten Suz up, a killer wanting to pin the murder on John Richard would have had to wait *until the bruises formed* so that it looked as if John Richard had not only beaten her but finished her off. Like the timing on the egg dish I was preparing, the killer's timing would have to be perfect.

And then I remembered what I'd said to Tom: *You can't put the dish in too early or it won't come out right.* If John Richard had not murdered Suz Craig, then whoever had had taken great pains to plan it.

I glanced at my watch: seven-forty-five. I quickly packed up the ham, the eggs, and the breads for the breakfast, which was scheduled to start at nine. This last day of the doll show would begin at eleven. The doors would close at four so that the ballroom could be cleaned. Then the show would reopen at five and close at seven. The final dinner for the board and their guests was set for eight o'clock, to take full advantage of the magical evening light on the lake.

I slipped my cellular phone into my pocket, but not before I'd taken note of three numbers: Patricia McCracken, Frances Markasian, and Lutheran Hospital, in case ReeAnn Collins was well enough to talk. Regardless of the fact that I had catering to do today, I had a crime to try to solve. My heart ached. I wanted Arch home. I wanted to know, once and for all, what had happened in Saturday's early-morning hours. And I was going to find out. For Arch, and for me.

Carefully, I scanned our garage and my van's interior. No Jerk. Where could he be? Twice during the short drive to the Lake-Center I had the discomfiting feeling that someone was following me. But my rearview mirror yielded nothing unusual, and even when I pulled onto the shoulder of the lake's frontage road, no one else stopped. I put it down to nerves.

At the LakeCenter the portly, disheveled security guard again looked and smelled like the "before" picture in an advertisement for

Alcoholics Anonymous. His disheveled gray hair was a mass of greasy curls; his red-veined eyes resembled a back-roads map of Utah. In the trash can next to him three empty whiskey pint bottles looked incriminating. As before, I felt sorry for him. And like any kind-hearted caterer, I asked if he wanted some coffee and toast once I got the board's breakfast under way.

"Wha . . . ?" he slurred. "Break . . . fast? Oh, yeah. Sure, coffee. Put some brandy in, you got any. 'Kay?"

So much for good deeds. I sighed and asked if there was any way he could open the side door for me.

"Yeah, sure. Pull your van 'round the far wall. It's 'kay. I can't leave the front for more than a minute to help ya, though. Gotta protect the damn toys. I'll open the door from inside, it's 'kay, I can trust ya. Right?" He burped and disappeared to open the side door.

While the oven was preheating for the eggs and ham, I sallied back and forth to put down an extension cord for the large coffee urn and set out the silverware and plates. The morning was quite cool, and the warming promise of the large coffeepot gurgling on one of the picnic tables seemed especially welcome. The pussy willows beside the lake path shifted and whispered in the breeze. A red-wing blackbird warned its compatriots of my presence by squawking and raising one wing. I smiled, sliced and arranged the bread, then poured the juice. When I'd given the guard a large mug of coffee and put the eggs and ham in the oven, I dialed Lutheran Hospital and asked to be put through to ReeAnn Collins. If she was not well enough to talk, I would not press her.

A man, sounding too old and serious to be ReeAnn's unreliable boyfriend, gruffly answered the phone. I identified myself and asked to speak to Ms. Collins. The phone was handed across.

"Helloo-oo!" a woman cooed merrily.

"R-ReeAnn!" I stuttered. "It's Goldy Schulz. You sound so — good! I was sorry to hear about the accident."

"Yes," she said with unusual pleasantness, as if she were enjoying the attention. "Right now I've got bandages on my body from the burns. I can't do much moving yet."

"I'm so sorry this happened to you."

"Well, you know, I got thrown into the creek by the explosion. The doctor told me it was a good thing, getting cold water on the burns right away. Anyway, I'm in excellent physical shape. Even though I was numb, I managed to paddle over to the creekbank. Everybody was pretty impressed. Plus now I'm on painkillers," she added with a giggle. "Beats working, that's for sure. Gotta roomful of flowers from my boyfriend. Plus, I've met a couple of cute interns, if the b.f. doesn't work out."

"ReeAnn," I whispered with relief.

"Plus," she continued gaily, "there's a cop at the door and one here to answer the phone, 'cuz the sheriff's department figured out there was explosive in the grill."

"What?"

"Oh, I forget what kind it was. The boy-friend feels guilty." She sighed. "Somebody *supposedly* from his bike shop called and said 'Forget the sandwiches.' Then whoever it was set up our lunch for twelve-thirty. I was going to get there at noon, dump charcoal on the grill, get it started. I got to the park, dumped on the charcoal, and the grill went ka-boom. Total bummer. So," she said in a hungry-for-news voice, "how's John Richard? Have you gotten any money? Think he's going to be able to give me my last pay-check?"

I swallowed. "You haven't heard from him?"

"Are you kidding?" she scoffed. "The only people I've heard from are my boyfriend, my mother, and the damn ACHMO people.

They still seem to think I've hidden some tapes of theirs. I told them what I've always told them: Go to hell. Now the sheriff's department screens my calls. So have you gotten your money or not?"

"No, I haven't gotten it." I thought again about my speculation concerning timing. What had John Richard and Suz been arguing about Friday night at the club? "Ah, ReeAnn, if it's not too much trouble, do you remember if there was something that happened on Friday, some negative thing that could have set off a fight between John Richard and Suz Craig?"

"How could I forget? It was the last day I worked with him. That Friday, a FedEx came. When I opened it, I thought, Uh-oh, the doc's going to be ticked off now! First the condo in Keystone, now he's gonna lose the one in Hawaii!"

"And the FedEx was . . ."

"A letter from Suz Craig's office at ACHMO. Saying no bonus this year. He went ballistic."

No kidding. But this was interesting, since I was thinking about timing. The no-bonus notice hadn't come by postal service — too unpredictable as to arrival time. Nor had the denial of bonus come as a phone call — too easily argued with. Whoever had sent the letter had sent it FedEx, so he or she could be absolutely certain the message would arrive on a certain day, and virtually guarantee a conflict.

"What did the letter say?"

She sighed impatiently. "Something about how we hadn't done the billing properly or consistently or within their guidelines or something. And he wasn't going to get his bonus. That's it. At the bottom, it said, 'signed for and on behalf of Suz Craig.' I told him it was because she was afraid to sign it!"

"Who signed it for her?"

"Didn't say. I couldn't tell, anyway, because John Richard snatched that letter away and started to have one of his fits."

I gritted my teeth. I checked the timer for the eggs: one minute to go. The doll collectors had gathered outside and were drinking their juice and pulling large cups of coffee for themselves from the silver urn. "ReeAnn, look, I just have one more question for you, and it has to do with Suz Craig." She groaned. "I'm just trying to figure out about that night, Friday. Was there any reason they were going out? Did they have a standing date for Friday night?"

"Oh, now that I *do* remember, because Ms. Crank was always wanting them to celebrate their little anniversaries. First month of going out, they exchange balloons; second month, they buy each other workout clothes; on and on until they've been going together six whole months, then she gets a fur coat and he gets an ID bracelet, for God's sake. Pullleeze."

"And Friday night was . . ."

"August first? The Month Seven anniversary, where have you been? I think she wanted tickets to Bermuda, but instead she got herself killed. What can I say? She should have given him the bonus. Oh, man, listen to me. I need another painkiller." Chortling, ReeAnn hung up.

The timer beeped. I took out the casserole and had a taste with a small plastic spoon. The silken texture of the eggs, combined with the tomatoes, leeks, hot, barely melted chunks of cream cheese, and seasoned poached shrimp, was divine. I carried the pan out and placed it next to the warm ham and baskets of bread. The doll board members included Tina Corey dressed as Sea Queen Babsie and Gail Rodine in a formidable wide-brimmed hat covered with netting. They all piled up their plates with food and talked excitedly about what a smash their opening day had been. I was surprised to see Frances Markasian, her wild black hair and ratty trench coat at odds with the perfect coiffures, stylish clothes, and occasional doll costumes of the board members, at the end of one of the picnic tables. She whispered to me that she was covering the show for the paper.

"I'm telling you, Goldy," Frances said as she shoveled up a heaping forkful of eggs, "I'm going to have to do a bikers' convention next, to recover from this."

"I need to talk to you," I whispered back. "I'm just about done serving here, and I was going to call you today, anyway. I have some information and some . . . lingering questions about Suz Craig's murder."

She brightened. "You promised you'd share stuff with me and you're actually going to do it? Wonders never cease. These eggs are yummy."

"Thanks. I'll give you the recipe. Want to talk?" I asked conspiratorially.

She dropped her fork, eased off the picnic bench, and shouldered her huge purse. "I need to take notes while we talk. Let me meet you in the kitchen, before I die of ecstasy."

Chapter 25

"I've been thinking about you a lot lately, Goldy," Frances announced when she'd heaved herself up on one of the counters, armed with her notebook, a newly popped Jolt cola, and a cigarette strictly forbidden by the signs posted everywhere in the LakeCenter. She blew the smoke in a rolling stream out the kitchen's open window. "With all that John Richard's up to, it's almost as if you're being punished, too. I heard he beat you up and then skipped. Any idea where he is?"

"No. And if those women catch you smoking around their precious dolls, you'll be punished so badly you'll never be able to say the words 'Bail-Jumping Babsie' again."

She shrugged. "Aw, you're breaking my heart." The cigarette dangled from her thin lips. "Spill it. Tell me everything you've got. I've got a police band radio, remember. How badly did John Richard hurt you yesterday?"

"I'm okay," I said briefly. "You remember who Ralph Shelton is?"

"Course I remember. I may have been

covering the doll show, but I haven't been covering it from Peoria. He's the guy, the ob-gyn doctor, who got canned by Suz Craig. I went over to his house. Asked him about the scratches on *his* face and he said it was from a cat, then slammed the door in *my* face. The vet wouldn't talk to me about Shelton's cat."

"Yeah, I know. Have you discovered anything about what was going on between Ralph Shelton and Suz Craig?"

"I thought you got me out here to tell *me* stuff."

I took a deep breath. Brandon Yuille hadn't told me I couldn't share what he'd divulged; I just couldn't say he was the one who'd given me the info. "Apparently, there were patient complaints outstanding against Shelton. Not only did Suz fire him, she was trying to use the complaints to poison his future at MeritMed. Or so I heard."

Frances made a quick note. "Very good, Goldy. Who'd you hear that from?"

"Can't say."

"Was it Chris Corey?" I shook my head. She smiled. "Well, I *had* heard about the patient-complaint action, and how Suz planned to use it, from Chris Corey." Another stream of cigarette smoke swirled out

447

the window. "What else have you been able to get?"

"That's it." Which, of course, was not true.

She inhaled reflectively. "Chris also told me Ralph Shelton had an appointment with Suz Craig in her office on Monday morning, July 14. What were the two of them going to talk about, do you know? This patient-complaint packet?"

Monday morning, July 14. The missing day in Suz's secret tapes. On that Monday morning, *what* had Ralph Shelton talked to Suz about? Had Ralph received some of Suz's wrath that day, too? I had no idea. *Could* the Jerk have Suz's tapes from July 14? Had whoever tried to blow up ReeAnn thought the Jerk had given *ReeAnn* those tapes? Didn't know that either, and I certainly wasn't going to start speculating with Frances. We were friends, but there are some things you just don't share with a journalist.

"I still think Korman did it." Frances stopped scribbling but held her pen poised. "I'm just looking at ACHMO for my other story. But you're really into this."

I slumped against the counter. "It's awful."

Frances energetically stubbed out her cigarette in the sink, then slapped her notebook closed. "Two things, Goldy. You seem very stressed. It's your involvement in this case."

"Oh, gee, Frances, how would you like it if your violent ex-husband was accused of murder? How would it feel if he came over and tried to beat you up before escaping to God-knows-where? Relaxing? Besides, I'm asking questions to soothe Arch, I told you."

Frances swept a dark mass of frizzy hair off her forehead. "Know what, Goldy? You need a hobby."

I said glumly, "Cooking used to be my hobby."

"Naw, you need something else. It *is* like you're being punished, you're so obsessed with this case. You need to get some distance."

I grabbed a box for the dirty breakfast dishes. "What would you suggest, Frances, doll collecting?"

She burst out laughing and jumped off the counter. "Now *you're* punishing *me.*"

It took a solid hour to clean up after the breakfast. By the time I finished, I felt as drained as the empty silver coffee urn. But the breakfast had been a success. When the doors opened for the hordes waiting to get into the doll show, I was glad I could slip out the side exit and avoid the stampede. I hustled to my van. A phone call to the McCrackens wouldn't do. I stepped on the gas and headed toward the country club. I wanted to see Patricia in person.

She was pushing Tyler the Terrible on their swing set constructed on the sloping backyard beyond the driveway, scene of the infamous roller hockey game. For a moment I stood watching them, unobserved. It had been a long time since I'd seen Patricia look happy. Her face was relaxed, her arm movements enthusiastic and graceful. She and Tyler were wearing matching navy sweatsuits. With each tug on the ropes she cooed to her son, a blond little fellow whose round face and squeals of laughter showed he was loving every minute. I almost hated interrupting them. On the other hand, unlike Patricia, my son was estranged from me, and I had information to gather before Arch and I could be reconciled.

"Howdy!" I called, and stepped carefully down the embankment. "I was in the neighborhood! Thought I'd stop by!"

Patricia smiled unenthusiastically and allowed the swing rope to go slack, which caused Tyler no end of grief.

"Keep swinging," I told her, once I was beside her. "Don't disappoint him."

Obediently, she started pushing again, but less energetically, so that Tyler again squawked.

"Do you want me to do it?" I suggested. "I felt bad about not being able to talk to you yesterday when you called. So I just thought I'd come by. Sort of for an update."

She brightened and moved aside so that I could push Tyler, who gave me only one command: "*Really* hard, okay? *Really* hard."

"Okey-doke," I agreed, and gave him a good push as Patricia flopped onto the grass, watching us. Tyler squealed with delight. "Hey, buddy!" I called to him as he lofted up over the hill. "I'm a swing pusher from way back! I'm the queen of the swing pushers!" I gave him another vigorous shove and he yelped happily.

"Be careful," Patricia cautioned.

"One of the reasons I'm here is that I want *you* to be careful," I said in a normal voice so as not to frighten Tyler. "John Richard is out on bail. And now he's disappeared."

She lifted her pale eyebrows. "I took tae kwon do before I got pregnant and after I got out of the hospital. Have a red belt, black stripe, now. I can take care of myself. What's the other reason you're here?"

"Well, I was just thinking about John Richard's finances."

She wrinkled her rabbitlike nose. "He had to auction the condo just . . . what? In the last ten days."

"But why auction it at all? See, he hadn't gotten news about his bonus yet —"

Patricia perked up. "Bonus? Did he not get a bonus from ACHMO?"

"Apparently not."

Patricia's grin was wide. "I may be able to use that in my suit."

"Anyway, I'm just wondering . . ." I gasped from the exertion, but Tyler crowed with delight. "You said you'd give me the details at the hockey party, but everything got so crazy . . ."

She smiled wickedly. "Oh, I *do* know why he had to auction the condo, Goldy. My husband said it was almost as if I'd planned it, so I could make Korman miserable."

I inadvertently stopped pushing and the swing knocked me in the abdomen. I recovered, but Tyler howled. I pushed again, a tad more moderately. "Why did he have to auction off his condo?"

She squinted at me. Keeping track of Tyler's trajectory so I wouldn't get whacked again, I couldn't return her look. "Because of his legal bills. Have you ever been sued?" When I shook my head, she said, "You're looking at ten thousand just to get started.

At least fifty thou to keep your lawyer going. Sure, he had malpractice insurance, but it didn't cover everything, not by a long shot. He just didn't have the cash he needed." She plucked a piece of grass from her skirt. "I was so happy when they auctioned off that condo, you can't imagine." She chuckled, then stood and brushed the rest of the grass from her skirt. She walked over to spell me with the swing pushing. "Goldy, listen. I may *wish* I were God," she said very deliberately. "Unfortunately, I'm not. But let me tell you. John Richard Korman hasn't begun to suffer for what he did to me. And he won't be able to escape, no matter how hard he tries."

As if in agreement, Tyler emitted an ear-splitting yowl. I fled.

I called Macguire from the cellular once I'd roared out of Patricia's driveway. To my astonishment, he answered on the first ring.

"Goldilocks' Catering!" He brightly launched into my official greeting. "Where Everything Is Just Right! Whaddaya-want?"

"Macguire! Please don't say 'whaddaya-want?' to potential clients. It sounds unprofessional."

"Oh, *Goldy!* Sorry! No problem. Listen, I'm chopping all these vegetables. They look

453

good, too! Think you should slip a little chlorophyll into the filling?"

"No," I said firmly. "Listen, did Arch call?"

"No, but that therapist's office called you back and said everyone's on vacation. You want a therapist for Arch, you're going to have to use a referral to someone in Denver."

Great, I thought. First, of course, I'd have to convince Arch to come home.

"Also," Macguire went on, "Mrs. Druckman called. She's taking Todd and Arch down to the Natural History Museum. Oh, and Marla called, too. She was on her way to Denver to see ReeAnn, wanted you to come have lunch with her, just so you could relax! But it's too late now, she's gone."

"That's okay, I'll come home."

"No, don't! Let me finish what I've got going here. If you come home, you'll just mope around about Arch. You should go out for lunch! How about Aspen Meadow Barbecue? My buddies and I think it's great. Plus, you've got that dinner tonight, you might as well get some food now! Have a bowl of chili and a beer! Relax and leave the chopping to me!"

"Macguire —"

"Oh, oh, *scrrk, scrrk*" — he started making fake squishing noises — "you're breaking up, you know, it's those *scrrk scrrk* cellular phones *scrrk!*" And he disconnected.

"Macguire," I said to the dead phone, "I've seen you do this trick before." But I smiled anyway and dutifully headed the van in the direction of Aspen Meadow Barbecue, famed creekside hangout of construction workers, truck drivers, wannabe cowboys, and assorted tough guys, all of whom had the single-minded intention of getting completely smashed at lunch. An outdoor dining area separated the hard-drinking crowd inside from tourists and the occasional brave group of ladies coming for a luncheon get-together on the water. The last time Marla and I had eaten there, she'd told me that the de rigueur item for the crowd inside was extra hot chili consumed with shots of tequila.

But Marla wasn't with me today, I remembered. I sighed. Did I really want to have lunch out alone? Macguire was doing the prep for the dinner tonight, and I could use a break. Across the street from Aspen Meadow Barbecue was a banner draped across the wooden sign of Aspen Meadow Nursery. It advertised a perennial-and-bush sale. I thought of Frances's admonition: *You need a hobby.* Well, maybe I'd go scope out the shrubs before braving the rough lunch crowd at Aspen Meadow Barbecue.

I wandered through sparsely stocked aisles and finally decided on some Fairy roses. The bushes featured lovely pink blossoms and were guaranteed hardy at our altitude, a key asset. As I loaded them into the van, I pictured Tom getting a huge kick out of my sudden interest in things horticultural.

Wait a minute. I stopped dead and looked again at the carved sign: ASPEN MEADOW NURSERY. In the list of questions I'd entered into my computer about Suz Craig's murder, had I even thought to look into these people, *also fired by Suz Craig?* No. Well. No time like the present.

I hustled back inside and told the cashier that on second thought I'd like to have my yard landscaped. And I wanted to have the same person who'd done Suz Craig's in the Aspen Meadow Country Club. Suz had raved to me about the great work he'd done.

The cashier's face fell. "Uh, you sure?"

"Absolutely."

"Well, Duke's out in the yard. Big blond fellow. Better go catch him, he does an early shift, then goes out with the guys for lunch on Wednesdays, then he goes home and sleeps. I have to tell you, Duke didn't like that Craig woman. You might want to find somebody else, if she was your friend. He

456

had a big grudge against her. Still does, even if she's dead."

Yes, yes, I thought, *take a number and get in line.* The cashier pointed me in the direction of the nursery's yard, which was on the same side of the street as Aspen Meadow Barbecue. The man at the yard gate pointed to a Paul Bunyanesque, platinum-haired giant who wore ear protection and drove a Cat loaded with mulch. The gate guard waited until the Cat had turned in our direction, then waved to the giant, whom I assumed was Duke. Duke dumped the mulch in the waiting bed of a truck, then chugged over to us. He flipped a switch and the engine died. He hopped out of the Cat and loomed over us — he was at least six foot six — and asked the gate guard what he wanted, for crying out loud. The guard jerked his thumb in my direction.

Duke turned his attention down to me. His dark blue eyes were not friendly. The bus-yellow ear-protection device dangled from one of his meaty hands, and I had the feeling that if he didn't like what I had to say, he'd pop it right back on. I looked way, way up at him.

"Ah, I understand that," I began sincerely, "you did some landscaping for Suz Craig. I thought it looked great."

457

"Yah, what about it? You a friend of hers?"

"Well, sort of —"

"Okay, see ya later," he said abruptly, and snapped the ear protection back on.

"Wait!" I yelled. Duke scowled, opened his eyes wide, and tugged off the metal ear muffs.

"I gotta go, lady. I'm going out to lunch in a few minutes and I need to finish this load. You want a landscaper, ask the people at the nursery to give you a referral someplace else. I don't want to work for nobody who liked that woman. Got it? See ya later, okay?"

"Well, hold on," I said, desperate now. "Just talk to me. I don't really want landscaping. I catered for Suz Craig and I'm having some problems —"

Duke smirked knowingly. "Ah, she stiffed you, too, huh?"

"What?" Then I understood. Suz Craig had refused to pay him for his work. I assumed a sad expression. "We had terrible problems," I confided.

Duke looked at the sky and shook his blond head. "Honestly, people like that —"

"You heard she was killed."

"Yah. No wonder."

"So you thought she was hard to deal with, too. I'm just wondering if your story is similar to mine."

"I'll tell ya, I'd have to be half plastered to tell my story about that woman. But then you wouldn't be able to shut me up."

Inspiration struck. I asked, "How quickly can you finish your load?" He grunted something unintelligible. Undaunted, I went on. "How does tequila and chili sound? My treat."

Duke grunted again, something that I decided to take as a yes.

I said, "Let's do lunch."

Chapter 26

Inside Aspen Meadow Barbecue, there was only one free table. I quickly nabbed it for Duke and me while scoping out the restaurant's interior. All I needed now was someone I knew informing my new drinking buddy, Duke, that my husband was a cop. That could put a chilling effect on our lunchtime chat. But of the two dozen men ranging from scruffy to burly at the bar and tables, no one looked familiar.

Once Duke had seated himself and called greetings to a few of his pals, I slipped over to the bartender. "Two tequila doubles for my friend, but just give me water, because I'm driving us home. When I signal, bring us the bottles. Put water in mine. I can't drink, but I don't want him to feel as if he's drinking alone."

The bartender, who sported a stiff handlebar mustache, squinted at me appraisingly. "You trying to keep him away from the wheel, or you trying to get him into bed?"

I pulled a twenty-dollar bill out of my pocket. "Just please do what I ask."

He palmed the bill in a way that suggested he'd been bribed before. "I'll give you something besides water, to look more realistic. Tell you the truth, I'm glad somebody's driving Duke home. Every Wednesday I gotta call somebody from the nursery to take him."

Soon Duke and I were crying "Skol" and clinking our first glasses. I took a tentative sip of what turned out to be flat Mountain Dew.

"Whatcha drinking?" Duke wanted to know, his tone already mellowing from defensive to chummy.

"Different kind of tequila. Lime-flavored." We chugged our second shots companionably and I sneaked a peek at my watch. Just past noon. I needed to be home to put together the doll club's dinner no later than three. Subtracting time to get Duke back to his place, that gave us about two hours. I signaled to the bartender to bring us the bottles. The man was so inventive, I had no doubt he could provide a suitable container for my Mountain Dew.

Duke smacked his lips. "Ah. Well. So. What happened to you with that woman? You trying to get money out of the will? That's what I'm doing. Lawyer says it'll take at least a year 'cuz a the criminal investiga-

461

tion. My plants'll croak by then." He shook his head unhappily.

"No! Actually, see, I have a different kind of problem. My ex-husband's the one who's been accused of killing her —"

Duke grinned broadly. "Oh, boy. Mind if I smoke? It's not tobacco, it's a clove cigarette. Heard of 'em?"

"No, but go ahead." In a minute the spicy smoke rose in a cloud. I gagged but plunged onward. "I catered for Suz Craig, even though she was my ex-husband's young, blond girlfriend. No grudges, you understand. But now her death has made a real mess for my family. You know, everybody blaming everybody. So my problem is that I keep looking back at what happened and thinking, How could I have prevented this?"

The bartender arrived and winked at me. He set a tequila bottle in front of Duke and a black ceramic decanter in the shape of an Aztec goddess in front of me. Cute. Then the waitress arrived and Duke informed her that we wanted two bowls of their hottest chili. I thought longingly of a crisp, cold arugula salad and how well it would go with iced coffee.

"What could you have done to *prevent* it?" Duke now repeated incredulously, shaking his big head. "Nothing. Not a damn thing.

Some people are just that way. Bossy, impossible to please. Nothing you do is right for them. I always want to ask new clients, Are you an asshole? 'Cuz if you are, I'd like to know up front. Save us both a lot of time. But, a'course, the nursery owner won't let me." He shook his head again.

"How was Suz Craig bossy to you? She seemed to like the landscape work you were doing when she showed it to me."

Duke raised his bushy blond eyebrows, then tilted the tequila bottle toward his glass. "Oh, sure, she lied. You think everything's fine, when all the time she's getting ready to axe ya. But plain and simple? The woman was a bitch. Too damn smart. Never had to learn how to deal with regular people. Tolerance, you know? She didn't have none. Patience neither." He quaffed another double shot. "For example. She trips on her in-grade steps made outa four-by-fours, the ones she ordered, and all of a sudden she wants new steps. Only she wants flagstone this time."

"Flagstone," I repeated. "Like the patios?"

"Yah. So we order more flagstones and put 'em in the garage with the stuff we've hidden from the vandals. We build the steps. She doesn't like the way they look. Fifteen thousand dollars and two weeks' work time

463

from my crew, and she says, Take out the flagstone, I want granite. Where'm I supposed to get granite steps? I say, Ya want an escalator? I know a guy."

"Someone did fall down the steps and sprain his ankle," I pointed out.

The tequila bottle was rapidly emptying. "Oh, I know, believe me. Big fat guy, shoulda watched where he was going. But it isn't just them steps. She wants white tea roses alternating with pink musk mallow. This is a harsh, dry climate, I keep telling her. Ya want tea roses, ya need Florida. Even if ya put in rugosas, ya need irrigation. Fine, she says, just do it. So we put in a water tank and a drip system. But then she doesn't want to *see* the water tank, right? So we have to wait to put in the rugosas and mallow until a picket fence goes up. And then she says, Ooh, ooh, I need stepping-stones around the picket fence. I say, How 'bout marble? And she gets all huffy."

Our chili arrived. One bite of the fiery concoction almost sent me running for the creek with my flame-spewing mouth wide open. Instead, I drank deeply of the Mountain Dew, right out of the Aztec goddess decanter.

"Damn," said Duke admiringly.

I ripped into several packages of saltines,

dumped them over the chili, and ate cracker crumbs as I unabashedly wiped tears from my eyes. When I could finally clear my throat, I asked, "So what finally happened?"

He stopped shoveling chili into his mouth, chewed, and considered. "After all her complainin' and moanin' and us tryin' to accommodate her? One day we show up as usual, though I'm thinkin' I'm going to have to give my crew a year's worth of free beer to keep 'em on this job, and she comes out and says we're fired. The fat guy's fallen down the steps and she doesn't want to get sued. I say, Fine, lady, we just need our tools, and she says, Make it snappy."

He ate more chili. I filled his two double-shot glasses. He drank, then sighed. If the chili was scorching his throat, he gave no sign of it.

"Down by the picket fence there are the rugosas and musk mallow that we just planted. But doggone if she hasn't put in a friggin' half-dozen *marble* stepping-stones, next to the plants, around the fence. Did she do it herself or hire somebody else? I say, Hey lady, who did this? I was only kidding about the marble, I say, and she says for us to get out pronto and send her a bill." His face turned morose. "So the nursery, you know, it takes them about a month to itemize the bill. She hasn't even gotten our bill and she's dead." He ate more chili without a wince, then slugged down another double shot.

"What a mess," I said comfortingly.

Duke shrugged. His eyes had taken on a wet, bleary look. "I asked the cops . . . I said, Could we at least have our plants back? Because I figure we earned them." He drained another shot glass. "They said . . . You know what they said to me?"

"Probate."

"Yah, they said I'd have to wait until probate was over. Until the investigation was done. I said the plants would be dead by then. We never put a pump in the irrigation system." He scraped the last spoonful of chili from the bowl, poured another double shot of tequila, and downed it. How many had he had? I'd lost count at ten. "Some night when I'm trashed? I'm going to go back over there. Dig up those plants we put in. Nobody'll miss them. Pee on her patios, too, while I'm at it. Matter of fact, I should go right now." He regarded me sadly. "Wanna come?"

I said no thanks and paid the bill. By the time I'd deposited Duke at his apartment — he lived in the same complex as Frances — I'd come up with some more questions. But

Duke was no help. He stumbled to his door and declared he was ready to dive into bed. At least he didn't ask if I wanted to join him for that, too.

It wasn't too surprising, I thought as I turned the van in the direction of home, that Suz had been so demanding about the land-scaping. In the case of the catered lunch I'd done for her, I realized in retrospect, she'd been eager to make nice and accom-modate the ACHMO people from head-quarters. She'd wanted to seem calm and flexible in front of her own department heads. But landscaping was something you had to live with and look at every day, sort of like your bathroom or bedroom. Still, why fire the nursery just because Chris had fallen down? Had Suz found somebody else to do the work for her? Somebody she liked better?

I pulled over on Main Street. It was only one-fifteen; Duke had gotten drunk a lot more quickly than I'd hoped. Cooking could come later. At that moment Macguire was right: I couldn't quite face going through our door knowing my son wasn't there. I called Tom on the cellular phone, fully expecting to get his machine.

"Schulz," he answered gruffly.

"Hi. Remember Suz Craig's tiff with the

landscape people? Did she hire somebody else after that?"

"Well, hey, Miss G., how's it going? Did you hear we found C-Four in that grill? We put two uniforms on guard at ReeAnn Collins's room." I said I knew, but that my urgent question at the moment was about Suz's landscaping. Tom repeated, "The landscape people. Aspen Meadow Nursery?"

"Somebody new."

"Not that we know of. I mean, nobody's come forward saying they need to be paid except for Aspen Meadow Nursery."

"No bills at all? No mail from, say, a construction company, an independent builder? Somebody in the marble business?"

He laughed. "What in the world are you up to?"

"Nothing. Just trying to fill the time between catered events."

After I hung up, I sat in my van and brooded. Suz Craig had squabbled endlessly and bitterly with Duke and his crew. Then she'd fired them, but only after Chris Corey had fallen. Why? Why hadn't she fired them when the first problems erupted? And then Suz had put in some marble stepping-stones that Duke had suggested in jest? Why?

Oh, Lord. Why, indeed.

Why would Ms. "I don't do, I delegate"

Craig fire her landscapers and put in some stones herself? Because she'd needed to. I made a careful U-turn on Main Street and headed back to Aspen Meadow Nursery.

When I got there, I knew exactly what I wanted. Did they have a cap, a workshirt, work gloves, and a gardening apron emblazoned with the words ASPEN MEADOW NURSERY and their plant logo? The cashier gave me another one of her quizzical looks but said the owner had always told her that if customers wanted something, even if it was the funny-looking rock bordering the parking lot, sell it to them.

"The shirt might not be clean," she said apologetically.

"The dirtier the better. And I'd like a shovel and a spade, too."

I put it all on my credit card and raced home. In the kitchen Macguire stood back triumphantly from the mountain range of neatly chopped tomatoes, artichoke hearts, and steamed asparagus. Platters were heaped with sliced Camembert and grated Parmesan. I thanked him. Again I was aware of how much better he looked: healthy skin color, shiny-clean red hair, straight posture, a frame that looked as if it had gained at least five pounds in the last two days, bright eyes, and, best of all, a huge, happy smile. No question about it, I was an herb-treatment convert.

"Great job," I told him.

"Need any more help?" he asked energetically.

I surveyed all the work he had done. "Absolutely not. Thank you many times over."

"Two more things," he said secretively, then opened the walk-in. He retrieved a pan of grilled chicken. "I followed your recipe for marinating and grilling this chicken. Just a few minutes in the oven and it'll be ready. I already tasted it. Juicy, succulent, tangy sauce, all that great stuff you always say. I'm a success! I can cook!"

"Macguire, I don't know what to say —"

"Hold on, look at this." He pulled out an enormous Bundt cake pan and held it out carefully for my inspection. Suspended sections of grapefruit glistened inside clear gelatin. "It's from the *Fanny Farmer Cookbook*," he said proudly. "Grapefruit molded salad. No mix. I made it myself."

"You're wonderful. And you really *can* cook."

"Oh, and Arch called just when the Druckmans were getting ready to go to the museum. He was, like, whispering into the phone that the food's not so good over at the Druckmans' place. They should be back by

Grilled Chicken à l'Orange

Marinade:

Zest of 1 medium orange
Juice of 1 medium orange (approximately ⅓ cup)
1 teaspoon dry mustard
Tiny pinch of cumin (optional)
2 tablespoons red wine vinegar
⅓ cup olive oil

4   boneless, skinless chicken breast halves

Sauce:

2 tablespoons butter
2 tablespoons flour
1½ tablespoons sugar
¼ teaspoon cinnamon
¼ teaspoon dry mustard
2   tablespoons red wine vinegar
1½ cups orange juice

In a 9- by 13-inch glass pan, make the marinade by combining the zest, juice, mustard, cumin, if using, and vinegar. Whisk in olive oil. Spread out a sheet of plastic wrap approximately 2 feet long and place the chicken breasts on it. Spread another sheet of plastic wrap over the chicken breasts. Using the flat side of a mallet, pound the chicken breasts between the plastic to an even ½-inch thickness. Remove the plastic wrap and place the chicken breasts in the marinade. Cover and allow to marinate for 30 minutes to 1 hour.

When you are ready to cook the chicken, preheat the grill. Then prepare the sauce. In a wide skillet, melt the butter over low heat and stir in the flour. Cook this roux over low heat for a minute or two, until it bubbles. Add the sugar, cinnamon, mustard, and vinegar and stir until well combined. Whisk in the orange juice, bring the heat up to medium, and stir until thickened. Lower the heat and cover the pan to keep the sauce hot while you grill the chicken.

Grill the chicken just until cooked through, 3 to 5 minutes per side. *Do not overcook the chicken.* When serving, place the grilled chicken on a heated platter, pour some of the sauce over it, and pass the rest of the sauce.

Serves 4

now, so I'm taking him some of the burgers you made for the barbecue-that-isn't-happening tonight. Is that okay?" When I nodded, he added, "Maybe Arch'll come home sooner than you think."

"Maybe."

Together, we packed the food for the doll people's dinner into my van. When Macguire had left with the bag of burgers, I made sure the security system was armed. Then I hightailed it to Suz Craig's house. I had half an hour before I needed to set up at the Lake-Center.

In the van I fumbled with the buttons on the Aspen Meadow Nursery shirt, then tied the apron around my waist and stuffed what I could of my curly hair under the cap. It was too bad the van said GOLDILOCKS' CATERING on the side, but I hadn't thought the Aspen Meadow Nursery cashier would want to loan me one of the nursery trucks.

I assumed a confident, businesslike expression, then hopped out of the van, carrying my shovel and spade. Walking quickly across the lawn, I rounded the house, which still had yellow police ribbons taped across each door. Lucky for me, I knew where the picket fence was. And just as Duke had indicated, next to the roses and musk mallow, gleaming white marble stepping-stones were set around three sides of the fence.

I dug under the first stone and upended it, then dug into the loosely packed soil underneath. Nothing. I set to work on the second and again encountered only dark, loamy dirt underneath the heavy stone. The third and fourth stones were the same.

Exhausted, I leaned back on my heels and wiped my brow. A cool mountain breeze ruffled the tree branches. Without warning, I saw a furtive movement by the next-door neighbor's garage. I held stock-still and waited, but nothing appeared.

I gazed back at the mess I'd made of the path around Suz's small picket fence enclosing her water tank. Two more stones to go. The fifth stone yielded nothing. Under the sixth and final stone I hit the real pay dirt. Under a loose inch of soil was a heavy-duty zippered bag. Inside were four audiocassettes.

Chapter 27

Using my teeth, I wrenched off the work gloves. I shakily unzipped the bag and removed the tapes from their plastic boxes. To my surprise, they were labeled: Corey, Yuille, McCracken, Shelton. And every one was dated Monday, July 14. I shoved the tapes back into the plastic bag, folded the bag under my right arm, picked up the shovel and the spade, and scampered back to the van. I threw the bag of tapes onto the passenger seat, dumped the tools into the back, and jumped into the front seat.

As I was ripping off the nursery apron and shirt, I wondered how I was going to listen to the tapes. I wanted to hear them immediately, but I *had* to cook if I was going to get my job done. Sitting in my van attending to my tape player wouldn't get the Babsie-doll people's final meal prepared. Then I remembered what I'd first grabbed when I was looking for my tablecloth the night I encountered the vandals. I pawed wildly behind the driver's seat and pulled out Macguire's Walkman.

I shivered as I faced forward. I glanced in my rearview mirror. Why had I sensed another movement close by? Had someone sprinted across the street behind my vehicle? I set the earphones on my head, put in the McCracken tape, revved up the van, and accelerated down the street.

Voices crackled at a slight distance from the recording device. The first audible words were from Suz Craig. It was startling to hear her voice. *"Minneapolis says we're going to have to settle, but I wasn't ready to give in. . . . Chris? Didn't she have an abortion a few years back? Anything we could do with that?"*

Chris Corey's rumbly voice was unmistakable: *"Not an abortion. Her primary-care physician gave her a referral to a psychiatrist. Anxiety. Don't know if we can use it. Or how."*

Suz snapped, *"Put in a call to that Markasian woman, see if she can run something. God knows, I live in that town now, I have to read that local rag. Markasian's gone on and on about McCracken's damn suits. Now she can run an anonymous-source article about McCracken having emotional problems. That'll balance things out. Make her do it, or we'll pull our tasteful little ACHMO ad from that damn paper."*

The meeting was interrupted by a woman

buzzing Suz to say that Ralph Shelton had arrived. The tape ended. A car behind me honked impatiently. I'd have to wait until I arrived at the LakeCenter before putting in another tape.

At the waterfall between the lake and Cottonwood Creek, the cormorants perched and preened and regally surveyed their domain. I would miss them when summer was over. Similarly, I would miss the red-winged blackbirds, noisy heralds of my arrival at precisely four o'clock at the side door of the LakeCenter. The guard, sitting in desultory fashion on a trash can, waved me over. I was willing to bet there was nothing about his guarding sojourn in Aspen Meadow that *he* would miss.

I pressed the rewind button on the Walkman, took the headphones off, put on my catering apron, and made my first trip through the side door. A cleaning crew of four — two men and two women — were buffing the highly polished wood floor and gently dusting the tables and displays. At my van, I slipped the Walkman and bag of tapes into my apron pockets. Then I hauled in my second box of supplies. When one of the cleaning women happened to glance up at me, I quickly turned away. I would listen as I worked. After schlepping my boxes into the empty kitchen, I laid out all the ingredients. I slipped in the next tape, marked "Shelton," and began to layer vegetables over the shrimp.

Ralph and Suz exchanged a cold greeting before getting down to business. *"You can't hurt me like this, Suz."* Ralph Shelton's frightened voice shook.

"Excuse me, Ralph, but I can. Know what a group of people from a California church congregation did? Drove two hundred miles to tell another congregation not to hire the priest they were firing. These folks didn't trust the bishop to tell the church considering their old priest that this was a cleric with a credit-card problem. Thirty thousand in debt, to be exact."

There was a pause, then Ralph spoke. *"If you . . . if you . . . go to MeritMed with these complaints about me, which are totally frivolous, I'll tell everybody about your unauthorized use of patient files. Confidential files, mind you."* He tried to sound more confident. *"And that's* not *a frivolous complaint."*

"You helped me get some of those files. You wouldn't dare go public. If I go under for using files, you're coming."

"I don't care." His voice was on the brink of tears. *"You have no reason to be so cruel."*

This was followed by the sound of a door slamming.

Wow. I put in the tape marked "Corey."

Suz's voice began. *". . . you know I've told you how being so fat is unprofessional. And being ungrateful to me isn't going to get you anywhere, either."*

Chris Corey's voice rumbled, *"I'm a physician. I don't appreciate being humiliated in meetings. I'm tired of it."*

"Really?" said Suz. *"You think complaining behind my back is going to do any good?"*

"That wasn't my idea," intoned Chris.

"Don't bring Brandon into this. What do you think, that if this job doesn't work out, you'll go back to being an orthopedic surgeon? You can't just waltz back into being a doc, Chris, you're as rusty as an old knife. Face it, you're finished as an M.D."

"I am so unbelievably tired of listening to you —"

"Something else. You don't think I know all about your sister? Multiple-personality disorder, goes into trances when she's stressed? Tell me, is she Tina when she's taking care of stray animals and dressed up like a doll? Or is that Mary Louise, so prim and proper, who goes to church and doesn't know a thing about dolls? You know I have access to her files. I know everything. Think the school where she works wouldn't like to know about her long history of emotional instability? Think about leaving this job, or criti-

cizing me again to Minneapolis, and your sister's secret is all over the place."

Chris's voice quickly pleaded, *"Don't do that. Tina has only shown two personalities. She's not violent. She's no danger to anyone. She's suffered so much . . . and now her personality's fragmented . . . I take care of her. Please don't hurt her."*

"I just want a fair shake," Suz said firmly. *"You've got a problem, come to me, got it? Those are the rules."*

End of tape. Multiple-personality disorder, good Lord. Actually, I should have suspected something at church. There, I'd asked Tina about a doll outfit and the cat. She'd acted as if she hadn't known what in the world I was talking about. I'd put it down to stress over planning Suz's funeral. But I hadn't been talking to Tina; I'd been talking to Mary Louise. I shuddered to imagine the humiliation that Tina Corey would undergo if the administration at Aspen Meadow Preschool, much less the rest of people in town, found out about a history of psychological problems. For starters, she'd lose her job. Then she would be shunned. Whatever Tina's problems were, if she was functional and her brother was taking care of her, they were certainly none of Suz Craig's business. I placed the Camembert slices over the vegetables, slipped in the fourth tape, and began on the last layers of the pie.

"You called them." Suz Craig. *"You set up the appointments. You got people to betray me. How do you think I'm supposed to feel?"*

Brandon Yuille's voice was the clearest yet. *"Suz, I had to, I had people coming to me day and night complaining about working with you. I couldn't just ignore them."*

"Brandon, you could have talked to me —"

"I tried to talk to you. Before and after —"

"Before and after we broke up?" Suz's laugh was sour. *"Maybe I didn't notice, what with all that passion."* Brandon said nothing. *"Look, I know you're hurt that I started going out with Korman, but he and I are right for each other. You're too young."* Suz made *young* sound like a dirty word.

No wonder Brandon had blushed when he'd told me how caring Suz could be. I suddenly realized why Brandon wasn't talking on the tape. He was crying.

"Brandon! Why did you call Minneapolis in? To punish me? Because it worked."

I heard a sob. *"I was trying to do my job."*

"Well, don't do your job so well, okay?"

"I am going to do my job," he said defiantly. *"I'm in charge of Human Resources. Don't tell me not to do my job."*

482

"Your job? Your job? You drag your sorry ass into this office late, day after day, looking more tired than a nomad lost six weeks in the desert. You're not doing your job! And you don't find me complaining about you, do you?"

"You're the only one . . . who seems to mind that I don't look good." I heard him blow his nose. He cleared his throat. *"And I thought you didn't care about how I looked anymore."*

Her voice was cruel. *"Listen. If you call the Minneapolis people again, you'll be very sorry. I'll fire your ass and have your records altered so they say you have cancer. You'll never get another HR job in Denver. You won't be able to stay near your father. Something else. You don't think I know your father supported a blond nurse down in Denver while your mother was sick? You think people in Aspen Meadow would want to know their beloved pastry-shop owner two-timed his wife who was terminal with cancer?"*

Even on the tape I could tell Brandon was startled. I could imagine his sparkling dark brown eyes and enthusiastic smile dimmed with pain. *"My mother . . ."* — his anguished voice was just above a whisper — *"was barely conscious for the last three months of her life. That other woman was her nurse."*

"An ACHMO nurse. Your father slept with her."

483

"You're insane."

"He's lonely, Brandon. During the day I'll bet he's lonely all the time."

And that was the end of *that* tape. Sheesh! Again I was stunned that Suz Craig had had the audacity to make these tapes. And to threaten people like that? Incredible. I could certainly see why she'd felt she had to hide the tapes from July 14. These cassettes were much more incriminating of *her* than they were of the people she was attempting to blackmail. Although someone hadn't thought so. Were there any tapes of the Jerk visiting her office?

I nudged the brioche dough over the pies and slid them into the ovens. They were the kind of concoction you could serve at room temperature or reheated. The final job was to prepare the promised salad. Macguire had filled several large zippered bags with freshly washed bunches of arugula and other delicate field greens. Before leaving home I'd snagged a jar of homemade sherry vinaigrette and packed up a batch of crusty, meringue-coated pecans.

By the time I had the salad assembled, the pie crusts were golden and puffed. The melted Camembert filling, with its garlic-and-herb seasoning, smelled heavenly. I carefully removed the pies and placed them

Exhibition Salad with Meringue-Baked Pecans

Pecans:

1 egg white
¼ teaspoon cinnamon
¼ teaspoon salt
⅓ cup sugar
4 tablespoons melted butter
2 cups (½ pound) pecan halves

Preheat the oven to 325°. Butter a shallow 10- by 15-inch jelly-roll pan.

Beat the egg white until stiff. Mix the cinnamon and salt into the sugar. Keeping the beater running, add the sugar mixture, 1 tablespoon at a time. Fold in the melted butter and the pecans. Spread the pecan mixture in the prepared pan and bake for 15 minutes.

Remove the pan from the oven. Using a spatula, carefully flip the pecan mixture one small section at a time. When all the pecans have been turned over, return the pan to the oven. Bake an additional 15 minutes. Watch them carefully — do not allow them to burn. Cool the pecans on paper towels.

(Only 1 cup of pecans is used in the preparation of the salad. The other cup can be eaten as a snack or frozen in a zippered plastic bag. These pecans also make a wonderful holiday gift.)

Sherry Vinaigrette:

1 teaspoon Dijon mustard
¼ teaspoon sugar
1 tablespoon best-quality sherry vinegar

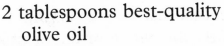

2 tablespoons best-quality
   olive oil
Salt and freshly ground
   black pepper

Whisk together the mustard,
sugar, and vinegar. Whisking
constantly, dribble in the olive
oil. Add salt and pepper to
taste. Makes ¼ cup.

Salad:

2 cups (2 ounces) fresh
   arugula
6 cups (6 ounces) of a mixture of fresh radicchio, en-
   dive, and escarole

¼ cup sherry vinaigrette
1 cup sugared pecans

Wash, dry, and trim the
arugula and the other greens.
Tear them into large bite-size

pieces. Just before serving, toss with the vinaigrette. Sprinkle the pecans over the top and toss again. Serve immediately.

Serves 4

on the counters to cool. I'd reheat them, along with the chicken, just before the closing supper.

I stared at the four tapes on the counter. I needed to do something with them. If Suz Craig had felt they were so incriminating that they should be buried, then I certainly didn't want to keep them. ReeAnn had gotten herself blown up, I was willing to bet, by someone who thought she had these very tapes. I didn't want to have them in the LakeCenter kitchen, in my van, or even in my home. I wanted them to be in a safe place until Tom could get them. But where?

As I scanned the ballroom, I couldn't get the nasty, threatening voice of Suz Craig out of my head. What would she have been able to find out about me? I wondered. If she'd married John Richard, she could have gotten hold of Arch's records from when he was in therapy after the divorce. Maybe she would have used them to gain a reduction in child support, or for some other, more sinister intent. I shuddered. I needed to call Tom. In my haste, I'd forgotten the cellular in the van.

While I was trotting back to my vehicle, I realized I now had to turn this whole thing over to Tom. I'd tried to sustain my relationship with Arch by fulfilling a promise to look into the case of the murder of Suz Craig. John Richard had been accused and appeared, for the most part, guilty. But the case had been more than a can of worms. It had been a tankful. With the tapes I'd discovered, and the physical evidence that would soon come back from the crime lab, Tom would help Donny Saunders figure out what had really happened to Suz.

Still, I couldn't help wondering how someone could have known, or could have taken the time to find out, what he or she had to know to plan out the murder of Suz Craig. *You can't put the dish in too early or it won't come out right.* Timing was everything. Not only would the killer have to know all about Suz, he or she would have to know all about John Richard's financial situation, what kind of car he drove, the ID bracelet, everything. And, most obscurely, the killer would also have to know under what circumstances John Richard used to beat me, what triggered his abusive rages. He or she would have to know about Suz and John Richard's monthly anniversary celebrations and that getting the Jerk totally frustrated would set him off — like lighting a fuse. The killer could get him frustrated by sending him notice of a failure to receive a bonus, when he was already deep in financial hot water.

But it all seemed like a terribly long shot. There was still a slim chance that John Richard wouldn't lose his temper, no matter how provoked.

In my van the cellular phone was bleating insistently. I grabbed it and flipped it open, but whoever it was had hung up. Arch? I called Tom but got his machine. I told him about the tapes and that he should send somebody up to the LakeCenter to retrieve them. Then I picked up the large plastic container of cookies.

The cleaning crew had left by the time I reentered the LakeCenter. The floor gleamed like a mirror and the thousands of little Babsie faces smiled beatifically at me. My cellular squawked again. I thumped the container of cookies down on the counter and reached for it.

"Goldy? Where've you been?" It was Frances Markasian. "I've been trying to reach you for hours! What'd you give me this number for if —"

"Spare me, Frances."

"What happened?" she cried. "Where are you?"

"I'm at the LakeCenter doing a catering job for the doll show. What do you want?"

"One of my sources told me a woman with

a van was snooping around at Suz Craig's house, digging around outside. Was it you? What did you find?"

"Nothing. And who's your source?"

"Suz's neighbor, Lynn Tollifer. She saw your van and called me. Did you find those tapes?"

"Frances, you're too much."

"Well, I didn't, I mean . . . I'm coming over. I want those tapes!"

"Forget it! The cops get them —"

"So help me, Goldy, I'll strip that van of yours and pull every pot out of that Lake-Center kitchen, I'll —"

"Cool it, Frances, I don't have the tapes," I lied.

"You're lying, I swear. I'm in a meeting, and my editor won't let me leave. But I'll be over there in half an hour, so help me —"

I disconnected.

Oh, brother. Wait a minute. This place had a live security guard. This place also had vigilante collectors if the guard couldn't do his job. Again, I scanned the LakeCenter ballroom. Where could I put the tapes, in a place that would take Frances forever to find them? The table full of Holiday Babsies looked the most promising. They all belonged to Gail Rodine, and she wasn't selling. I'd stash them in the doll boxes, call

492

Tom again, and have the cops figure it all out.

It was unlikely that I'd have the place to myself for long, so I raced across the ballroom to the right display and slipped one tape each under the skirts of Holiday Babsies from 1991, 1992, 1993, and 1994. There were at least thirty dolls there. Gail Rodine lived in Aspen Meadow, and when she took the dolls back home, Tom could get the tapes without much trouble. He wouldn't be happy about it, though.

When I tucked the flap of the last box into place, I heard a loud thump at the front of the LakeCenter. My skin turned cold. The Jerk. Had I locked the side door? I couldn't remember. I trotted toward it. Unfortunately, the slickly polished floor was as slippery as a skating rink. I skidded sideways, desperately twisted to regain my balance, and finally managed to land with a crash on both of my hands. I yelped with pain. By the time this case was over, I'd be covered in bruises from head to toe.

I tried to roll over and was only partially successful. My back seemed to have regained its flexibility, but the only thing really paining me now was my left hand, in particular, my left thumb. Broken in three places by the Jerk, and destined forever to give me trouble.

493

I looked at my aching thumb. I looked at it and looked at it, and I had a dawning sense of horror. *You'll be throwing pizza in no time,* the orthopedic surgeon had told me after a particularly savage beating had brought me to the hospital along with the broken thumb. He knew the pattern of bruises inflicted by the Jerk because he'd seen them before. *I'll be kicking field goals in no time,* he'd promised, much later. *What do you think . . . you'll go back to being an orthopedic surgeon?* Suz had said. *Your voice sounds so familiar,* I'd said. *Did you treat Arch?*

No. He'd treated *me.* A long time ago. He could plan the murder because he knew exactly what to do and how to make it look as if John Richard Korman had done it.

At that moment the side door of the Lake-Center swung open and Chris Corey appeared, a heavy, bearded study in fury. He saw me on the floor, holding my aching thumb. He snarled: "I see you're still good at getting yourself injured! How's the thumb? And while you're telling me, give me those tapes!"

Chapter 28

I scrambled to my feet. Pain shot through my body, but I had to think. The front door to the LakeCenter was locked; the back door was locked — for security. Somehow I had to get out through the entrance where Chris Corey stood.

"I don't have them," I replied shakily.

"I know you do! I paid that kid, Luke Tollifer, to watch Suz's house. Where are they?"

"In the car, in the car! My van!"

"Show me!"

I made my way to the door, thinking I might be able to slip past him and run. Before I could squeak by, however, he grabbed my left hand, and then my thumb. Cruelly, he twisted it behind my back. I yelped. At the same time, I noticed the cast on his ankle had mysteriously vanished.

"Where's your phone?"

"In . . . in my apron pocket."

He felt inside my pocket with his free hand, tugged my phone out, and sent it skittering across the shiny floor. "I want the tapes, then I'll leave. Walk to your van, get those tapes, then I'm gone. Scream, and I swear to God I'll hit you harder than I did her."

Oh, God. Fear washed through my body. My feet slid out from under me. He wrenched me up off the slippery floor.

"Please, Chris, don't," I gasped. "Think about what this is going to do to you. To Tina."

"Yeah, yeah. 'Think about Tina' is what I should have done before, huh? Move."

"Okay, okay," I gasped. My thumb throbbed in agony. I feared I'd pass out. Chris pushed me forward through the threshold of the side door. I looked back at him, insanely confused that his limp had also disappeared. As he fiercely nudged me along the log wall, a gaggle of red-wing blackbirds erupted from the wetlands bordering the LakeCenter.

I looked around wildly for help. The parking lot was empty except for my van. Where had Chris parked? I thought about screaming. But who would hear me? We were hundreds of yards from the road, even farther from the Lakeview Shopping Center.

As we rounded the building, Chris pushed me along the sidewalk toward the parking lot. I caught a glimpse of a car on the far side of the building — the side opposite the kitchen. Of course. He'd driven up quietly and parked away from the kitchen. And naturally he knew how to be quiet; hadn't he approached Suz's house in the darkness and quiet, in a Jeep just like John Richard's?

The guard was no help. Chris had clobbered him — the crash I'd heard at the front — and he lay sprawled next to the trash can.

"Where are the tapes?" Chris asked as we neared my van.

"Aah . . . aah . . ."

He wrenched my thumb brutally. "Where?"

"I can't . . . think . . . if you're hurting me," I protested in a low voice. I was using negotiating skills I had learned long ago, to keep John Richard from hurting me. When he relented a bit, I said, "Aah . . . under the . . . passenger seat. It's a tight squeeze, you'll never be able to reach. Better let me . . . get them."

The first cars of the doll people appeared at the far end of the dirt-road entryway to the LakeCenter. *Stall, stall,* I thought desperately. Chris wrenched open the passenger-side door and pushed me inside, still gripping my thumb.

"You have to let go of me," I gasped. "Or I can't get them." I tried to think. Where was my tire iron? Did I have any spare kitchen utensils anywhere, something I could use on him? He shoved me into the van on my stomach. But at least he relinquished his death-grip on my thumb. I reached under the seat with my numb left hand. Nothing, of course. "Hold on," I called. "Just a sec."

He yanked back on my legs so violently that I thought I would break in two. I landed half in, half out, and on my side.

"Help!" I screamed. I had no idea if the doll people were even within earshot. "Somebody! *Help!*"

Chris picked me up by the waist and threw me on my back on the passenger-side seat. Then he flung his whole, heavy body on top of me. His fleshy hand clamped over my mouth. I kicked wildly. But with him on top of me and outweighing me by a good one hundred and fifty pounds, I had zero leverage.

"Shut up!" he breathed. His hand tightened on my throat. Panic shot through me. He was going to strangle me. I'd never see Arch again. Or Tom. I thrashed wildly. Chris's hand slipped off my throat. The glove compartment banged open.

Marla's bag of drugs fell onto the van floor.

Oh God, help me, I prayed as I strained under Chris's weight. I groped desperately.

Keep calm, keep calm, keep calm. I reached into the bag, found nothing, scrabbled around frantically. Then my fingers closed over what I sought. I popped off the needle cover.

Chris had grabbed my throat again. He squeezed. With every ounce of strength I had left, I stabbed him with Marla's hypodermic of Versed. I pushed down on the plunger, hard.

Stunned, Chris squealed with pain. His hold on me relaxed momentarily. He screamed again and hauled back to tear the needle from his body. I scrambled through the open door. By the time I was outside, Chris was stumbling dazedly down the parking lot, toward the LakeCenter and his car.

I watched him, open-mouthed, gasping for breath. Was he going to just . . . take off? Was he so big that a dose of a superpotent tranquilizer had no effect on him? He faltered, appeared to trip, and then staggered forward.

"The Babsies!" I screamed at the large group of beautifully dressed women who were sashaying across the lot toward the LakeCenter door. "That big blond man! He's stolen them!" I pointed at Chris. He turned to stare open-mouthed at me, not comprehending. He was slowing down, no question. But he was only twenty feet from his car. "The Babsies!" I shrieked again at the women, gesticulating wildly. "That man knocked out the guard! He's going to take the dolls!"

The women started to trot. Chris gaped at them. Then he turned and floundered toward his vehicle. The women picked up speed.

"No, no!" he cried as the first doll collector attacked him. "No!" I heard him shout when two more women jumped on him. Bellowing in astonishment, he staggered forward. Then, under the onslaught of furious Babsie protectors, he fell to his knees.

I walked shakily back to the LakeCenter to call the sheriff's department. Chris Corey wasn't going anywhere.

Chapter 29

Tom, as it turned out, had been up at his cabin. Empty since high creekwaters had flooded the first floor with two inches of water, unrented since Arch, Tom, and I had spent several weekends scraping off dried mud, the cabin now awaited a professional interior paint job. When Tom drove up and parked half a mile away, then used a little-known path through the woods to approach the place from the back, he had a hunch that the cabin held a squatter — one of the very few people who knew about the flood damage and the time we'd spent cleaning the place up. Unfortunately, John Richard hadn't figured that Tom would be able to take him so easily. By the time Tom arrested the Jerk again, Sergeant Beiner had appeared at the LakeCenter and arrested Chris Corey.

That night, Chris confessed to the murder. He had wanted to end the torment of working for Suz Craig. He remembered how John Richard had attacked me; he had waited for the right time — the silly monthly anniversary. He had stolen the ID bracelet when John Richard was helping a woman with an induced delivery that had been scheduled — and approved — by ACHMO. Finally, he had written the bonus-denial letter. The drug screen on Suz's body fluids indicated that she, too, had been the recipient of a high-potency tranquilizer: morphine. Once Chris had primed John Richard to beat Suz, all Chris had to do was go to Suz's door pretending to be distraught and wanting to talk things out. He'd offered to treat her contusions, then he'd given her a shot much like the one I'd given him. He'd waited until the bruises from John Richard appeared. Then he'd killed her by whacking her with the carpet-covered, solid-metal scratching post. Finally, he'd laid her in the ditch, with the bracelet as the nail in John Richard's coffin. And then he'd gone back to pretending to be a helpful, sympathetic guy, complete with a fake cast.

He just hadn't figured on the tapes. Luella Downing had called him, as well as Brandon, on Saturday to tell him about the existence of Suz's secret taping. He'd used the visit to John Richard's office to look for them. ReeAnn — his ally — had told him she didn't have them. In desperation, he'd tried to blow up ReeAnn — he'd learned she was meeting her boyfriend for an outdoor lunch — because he had a feeling she'd stolen the tapes from John Richard. But just in case she hadn't, he'd paid Suz's nosy teenage neighbor, Luke Tollifer, to watch Suz's house, which is how he found out about my digging effort.

That evening the results came back from the crime lab: the skin and hair under Suz Craig's fingernails belonged to John Richard Korman. John Richard was charged with first-degree assault and tampering with a witness. They're talking about a plea bargain, but it looks as if he'll face at least two years in prison.

After the police hauled Chris Corey away from the LakeCenter, Sergeant Beiner took the briefest of statements from me and seized the tapes I pulled from their hiding places in the doll boxes. Gail Rodine, looking on, glared. I'd never get a Babsie booking again as long as I lived. I somehow managed to finish the dinner for the doll people. Happily, the preparation was easy; I couldn't have handled any additional grilling.

On Thursday morning, the day after Chris Corey was arrested, I saw Frances Markasian at Suz's memorial service. Afterward, we talked. I wanted her to leave Arch out of any article she wrote about the case and Chris's arrest. She felt terrible about being duped by Chris, and apologized for yelling at me about the tapes. Of course, I forgave her. Frances said she'd already talked to Brandon Yuille about an exposé on Suz's use of confidential medical files. Brandon had told Frances to tell me Ralph Shelton had agreed to cooperate; he would try to get Amy Bartholomew to help, too. I accepted Frances's promise to keep Arch out of her wrap-up article on the case.

Unfortunately, Tina Corey's mental illness did get leaked, and not just to the *Mountain Journal*. Both the *Denver Post* and *Rocky Mountain News* reported on her history of multiple-personality disorder. She went into a stress trance and ended up in the psychiatric ward of St. Joseph's Hospital. No visitors allowed.

On Friday afternoon, Arch came home. Tom had called him and they'd talked for over two hours. My son was having a hard time, as was to be expected. Macguire picked Arch up at the Druckmans', then drove him to the Coreys' house, where they helped the Mountain Animal Protective League load up Tippy the cat and Tina's other pets into a van, so the animals could be delivered to foster caretakers. But back at home, Arch was dejected. Even when Julian Teller called, saying he was coming for a visit, Arch did not appear cheered. Macguire offered to talk to him up in his room. After the two boys went up, Marla phoned and told us all to sit tight, she was bringing us take-out Vietnamese food for dinner.

Tom and I sat together on the couch. He pulled me close, and I felt the tension that had knotted my body for the last week begin to ebb. He said, "The only thing I can't understand is why you just wouldn't let Korman take the fall for this. I'm glad we've got the right guy, don't get me wrong. But you've wanted revenge for so long. Don't deny it now, I can read you better than you think, Miss G. Plus, this seemed like a perfect opportunity to get Korman sent down. And not just for a year or two."

I sat for a long time, thinking, enfolded in his arms. "I couldn't sacrifice Arch. Just to get my revenge, I mean. Chris Corey wanted his revenge on Suz, and his sister got trampled in the process."

"God," he said, "I love you."

"Mom?" Arch's call came from the bottom of the stairs. "Mom?"

I stood up. "Yes, hon."

He wore a crumpled khaki shirt and baggy black shorts. I wondered if he'd had a shower in the time he'd been at the Druckmans' house. Even his glasses were smeared.

"I'm sorry."

"It's okay," I said.

His chin trembled. "Will you . . . will you take me to see Dad?"

"Oh, please, honey." I beckoned, and he ran toward me. I held him tight, as I always had, from when he was very small. I said, "Of course."

Index to the Recipes